TwoKinds

Book Two

D1075917

Thomas Fischbach

TWOKINDS VOL. 2
by Thomas Fischbach

TWOKINDS © and ™ 2022 by Thomas Fischbach

Cover and interior illustrations by Thomas Fischbach.

Published by
Keenspot Entertainment
Los Angeles, CA
E-Mail: keenspot@keenspot.com
Web: www.keenspot.com

Keenspot
CEO & EiC Chris Crosby
PRESIDENT Bobby Crosby

ISBN 978-1-932775-65-5

TWOKINDS VOL. 2 Manga Edition
Second Keenspot Printing, April 2022
PRINTED IN CANADA

Dedicated to the fans

who made this book possible

and to my family

who encouraged me to try.

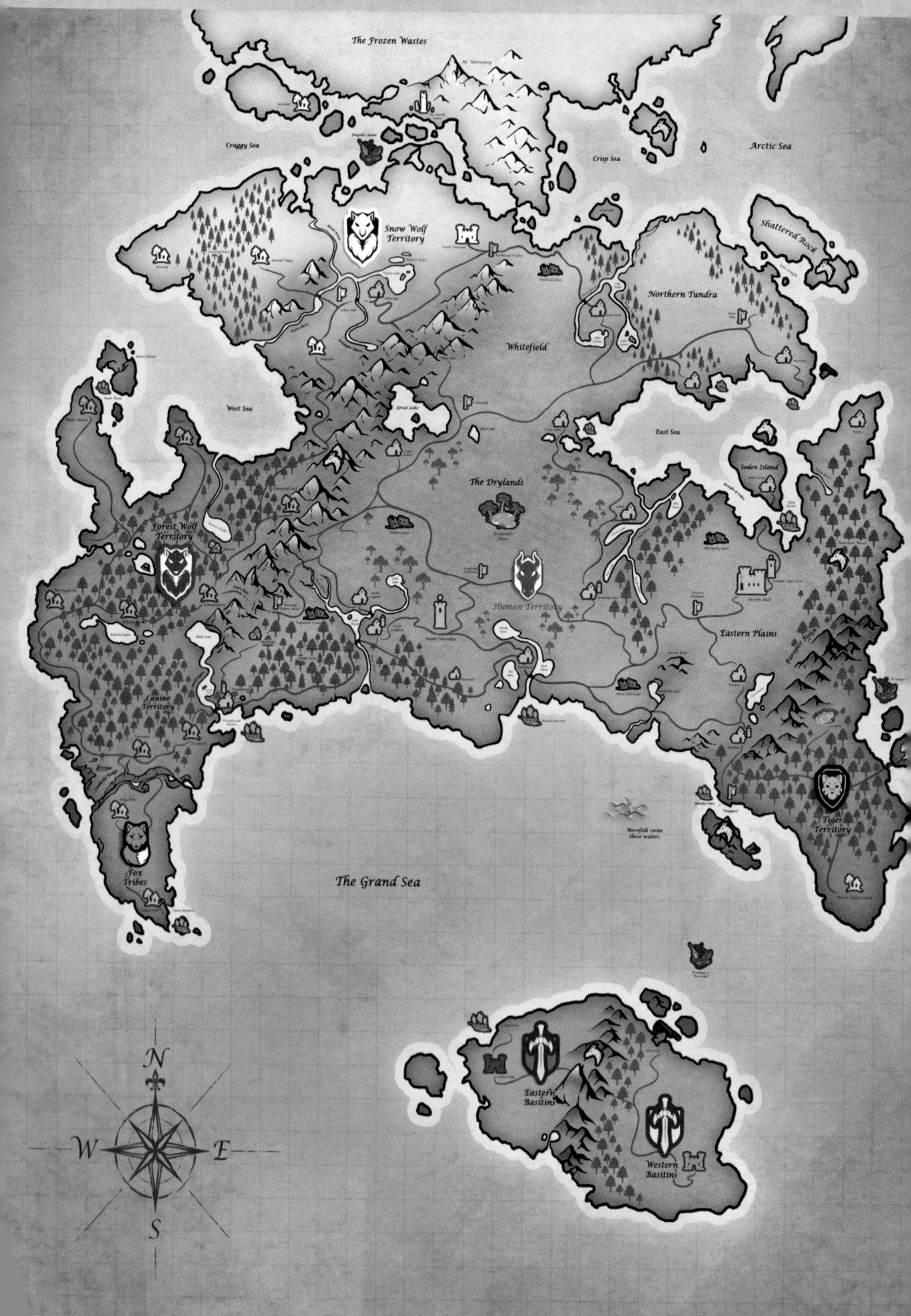
The Frozen Wastes
Craggy Sea
Crisp Sea
Arctic Sea
Snow Wolf Territory
Shattered Rock
Northern Tundra
Whitefield
West Sea
Great Lake
East Sea
Soden Island
The Drylands
Forest Wolf Territory
Human Territory
Eastern Plains
Canine Territory
Merefolk swim these waters
Tiger Territory
Fox Tribes
The Grand Sea
Eastern Basitins
Western Basitins
N
W
E
S

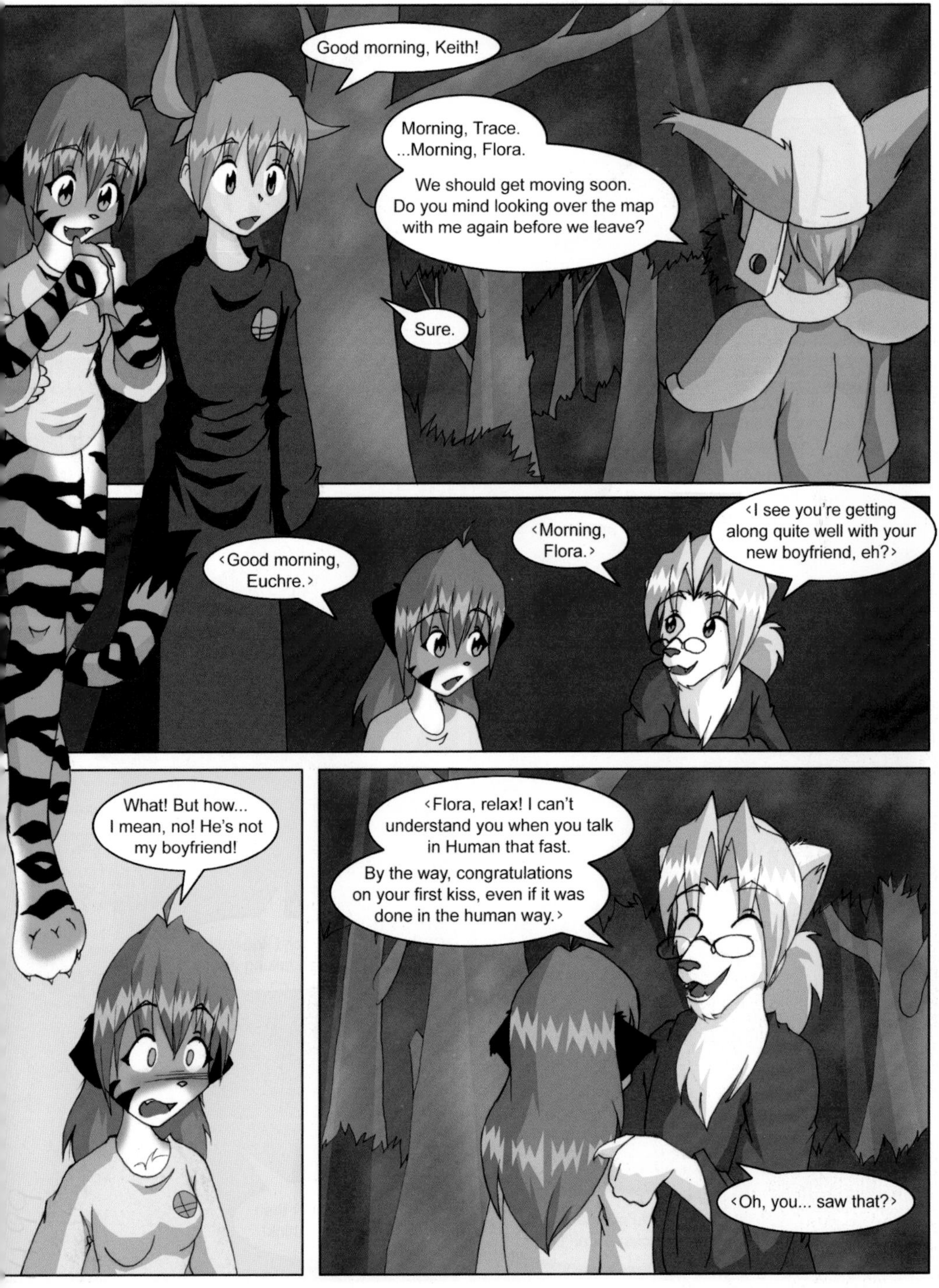

Good morning, Keith!
Morning, Trace. ...Morning, Flora.
We should get moving soon. Do you mind looking over the map with me again before we leave?
Sure.
‹Good morning, Euchre.›
‹Morning, Flora.›
‹I see you're getting along quite well with your new boyfriend, eh?›
What! But how... I mean, no! He's not my boyfriend!
‹Flora, relax! I can't understand you when you talk in Human that fast.
By the way, congratulations on your first kiss, even if it was done in the human way.›
‹Oh, you... saw that?›

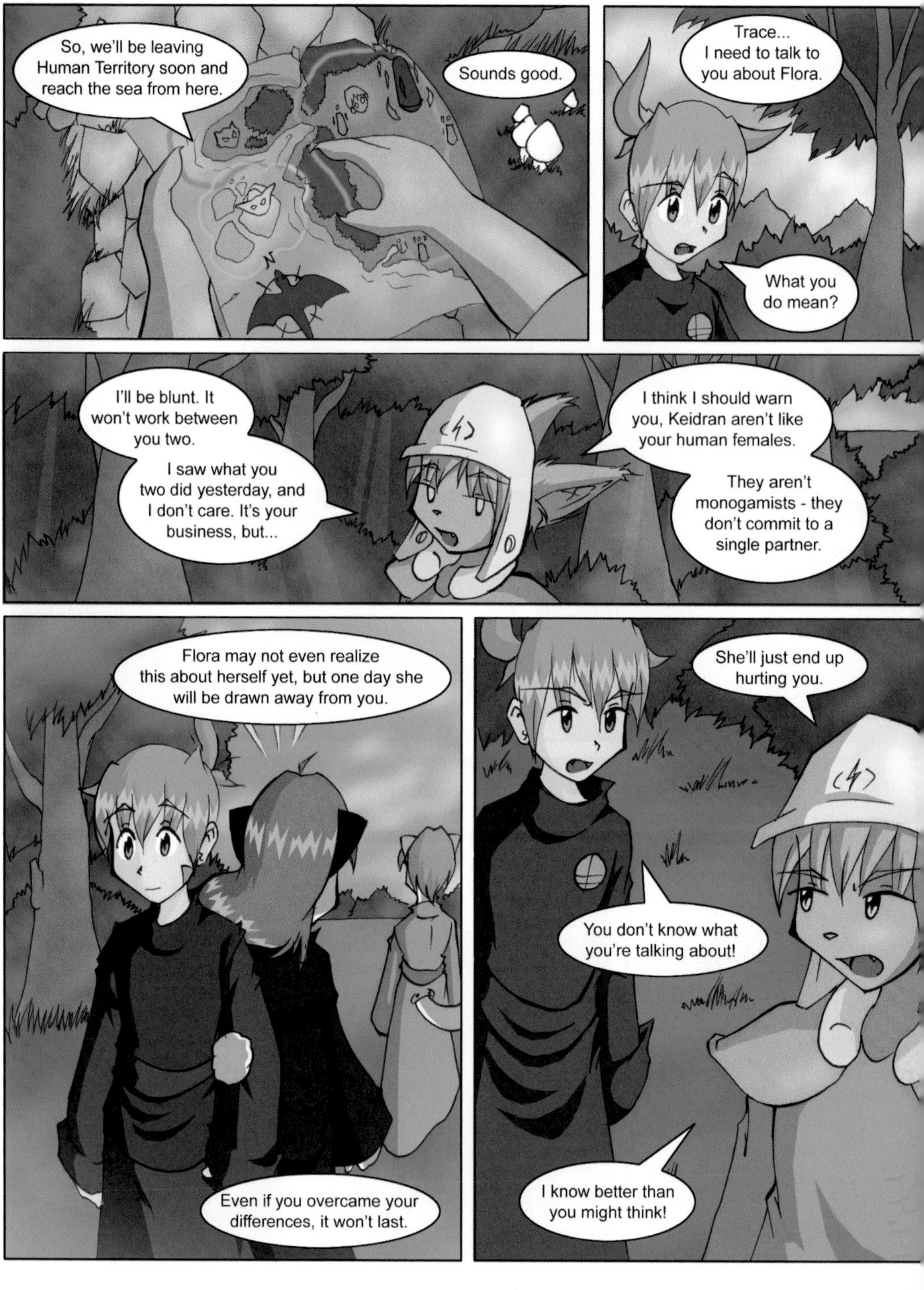

So, we'll be leaving Human Territory soon and reach the sea from here.
Sounds good.
Trace... I need to talk to you about Flora.
What you do mean?
I'll be blunt. It won't work between you two.
I saw what you two did yesterday, and I don't care. It's your business, but...
I think I should warn you, Keidran aren't like your human females.
They aren't monogamists - they don't commit to a single partner.
Flora may not even realize this about herself yet, but one day she will be drawn away from you.
Even if you overcame your differences, it won't last.
She'll just end up hurting you.
You don't know what you're talking about!
I know better than you might think!

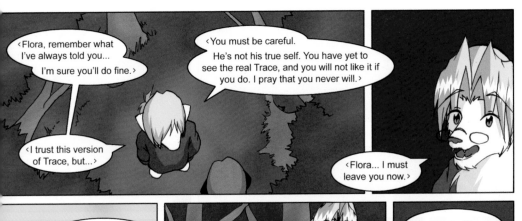

‹Flora, remember what I've always told you... I'm sure you'll do fine.›

‹I trust this version of Trace, but...›

‹You must be careful. He's not his true self. You have yet to see the real Trace, and you will not like it if you do. I pray that you never will.›

‹Flora... I must leave you now.›

‹Leave?! Why? I thought you were coming with me!›

‹I'm afraid not.›
‹Now that I am free, I have some business that I must take care of.›

‹I am sorry, Flora.›

‹Nooo! Please, don't leave me! You can't!›

Flora, are you... eh?

Trace-o-Vision

Euchre, you're one sexy beast.

I am, aren't I?

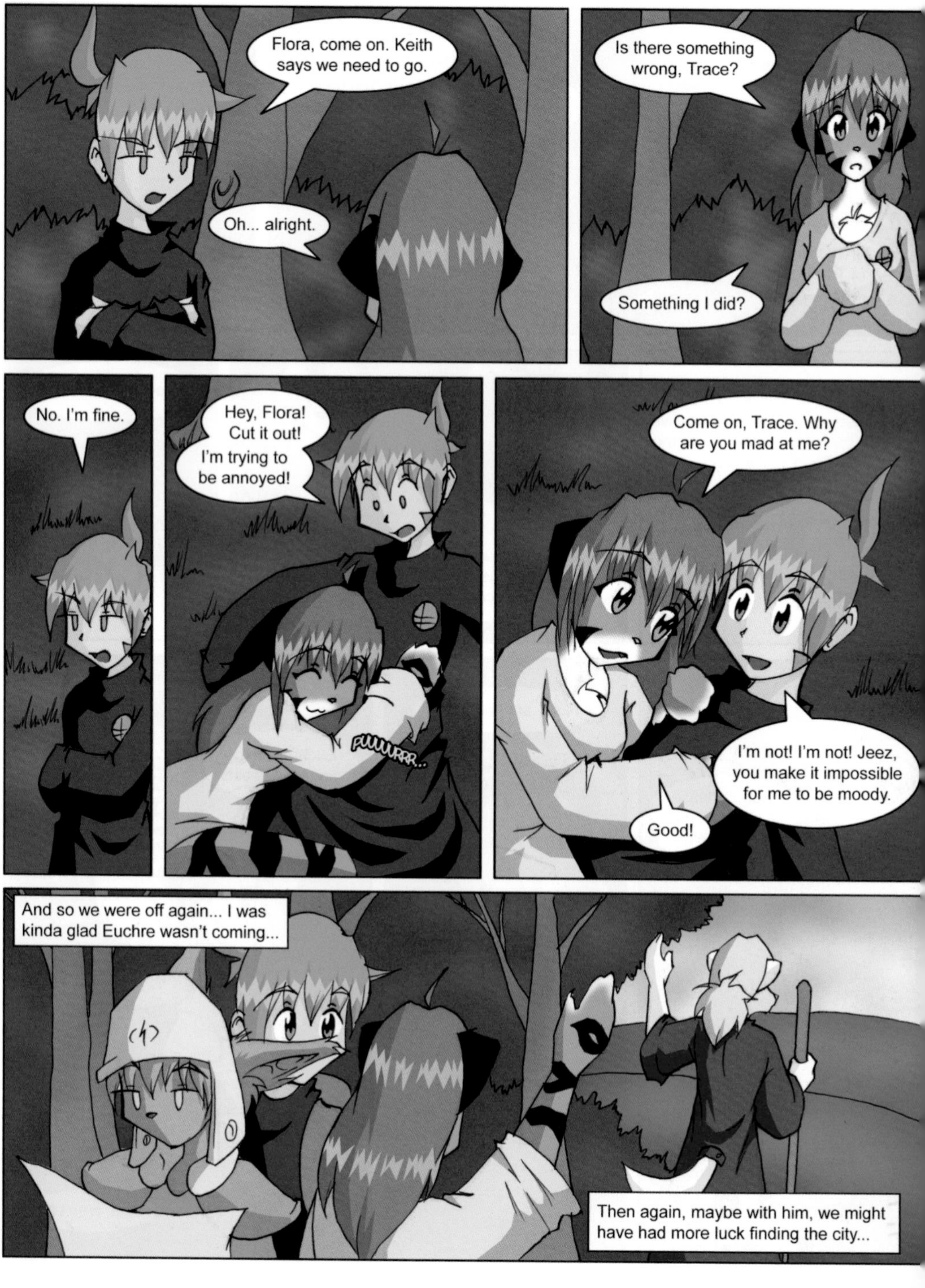

Flora, come on. Keith says we need to go.
Oh... alright.
Is there something wrong, Trace?
Something I did?
No. I'm fine.
Hey, Flora! Cut it out!
I'm trying to be annoyed!
PUUUURRR...
Come on, Trace. Why are you mad at me?
I'm not! I'm not! Jeez, you make it impossible for me to be moody.
Good!
And so we were off again... I was kinda glad Euchre wasn't coming...
Then again, maybe with him, we might have had more luck finding the city...

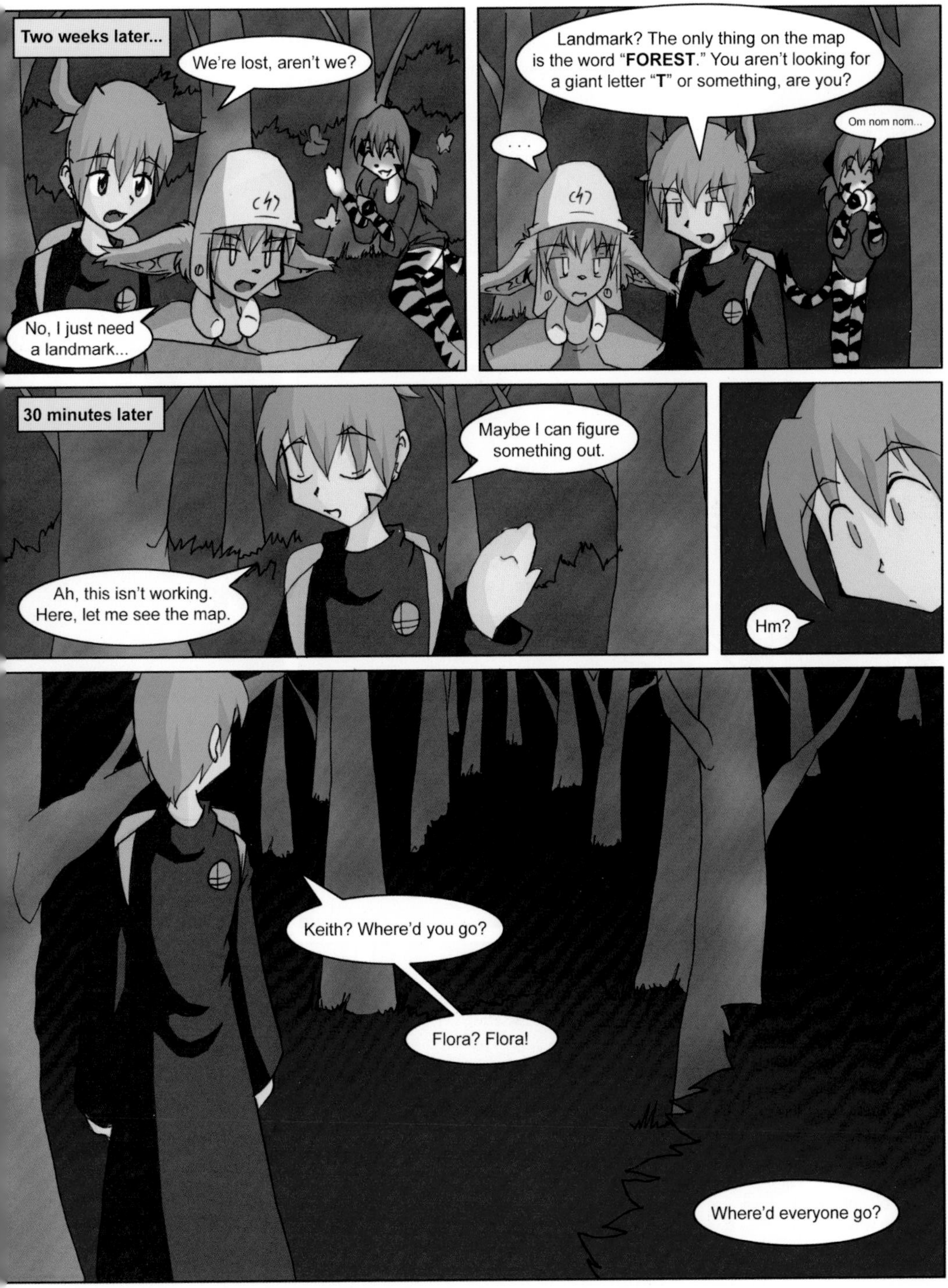

Two weeks later...
We're lost, aren't we?
No, I just need a landmark...
. . .
Landmark? The only thing on the map is the word "**FOREST**." You aren't looking for a giant letter "**T**" or something, are you?
Om nom nom...
30 minutes later
Maybe I can figure something out.
Ah, this isn't working. Here, let me see the map.
Hm?
Keith? Where'd you go?
Flora? Flora!
Where'd everyone go?

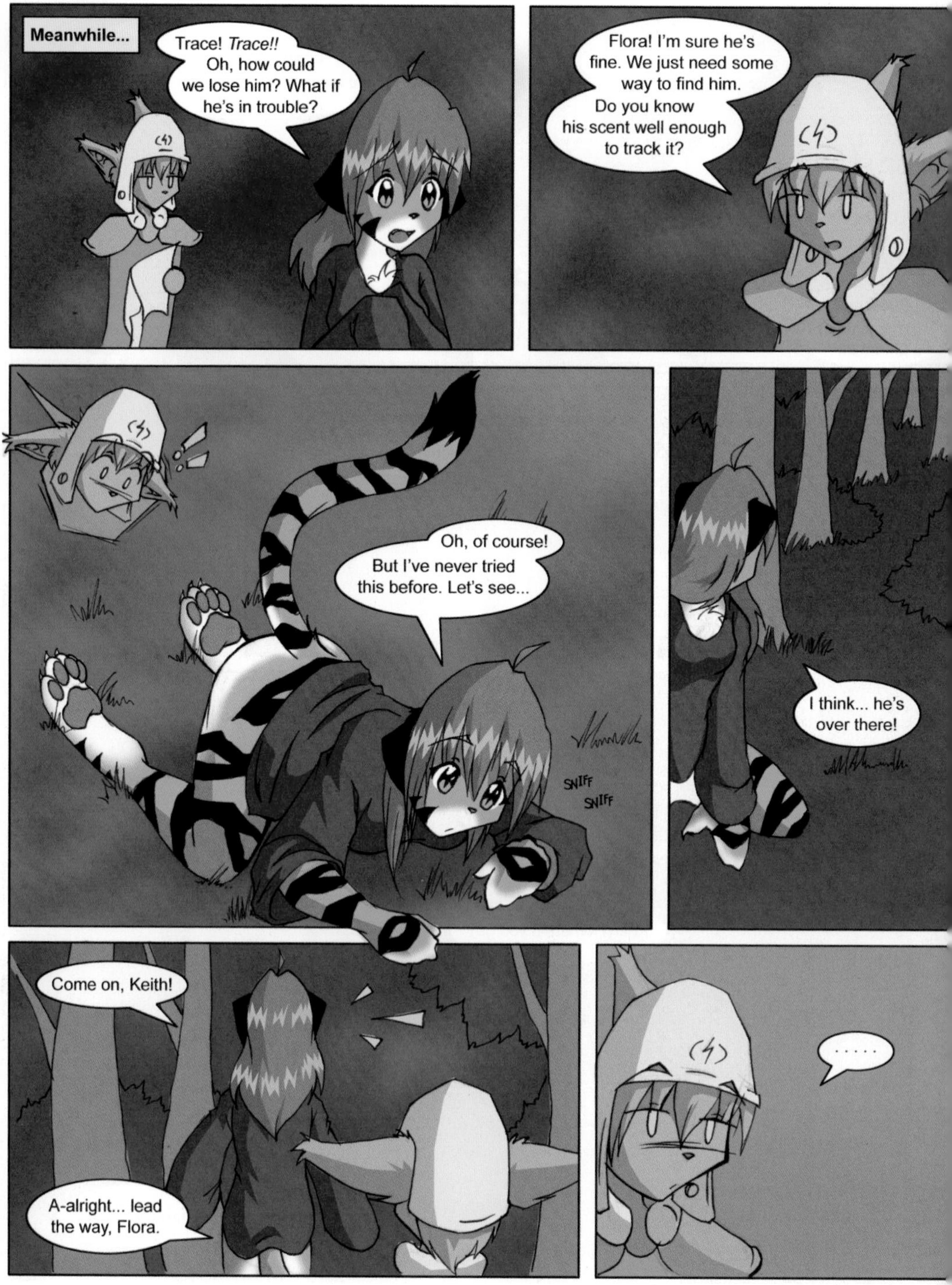
Meanwhile...
Trace! *Trace!!* Oh, how could we lose him? What if he's in trouble?
Flora! I'm sure he's fine. We just need some way to find him. Do you know his scent well enough to track it?
Oh, of course! But I've never tried this before. Let's see...
SNIFF SNIFF
I think... he's over there!
Come on, Keith!
A-alright... lead the way, Flora.
. . . . .

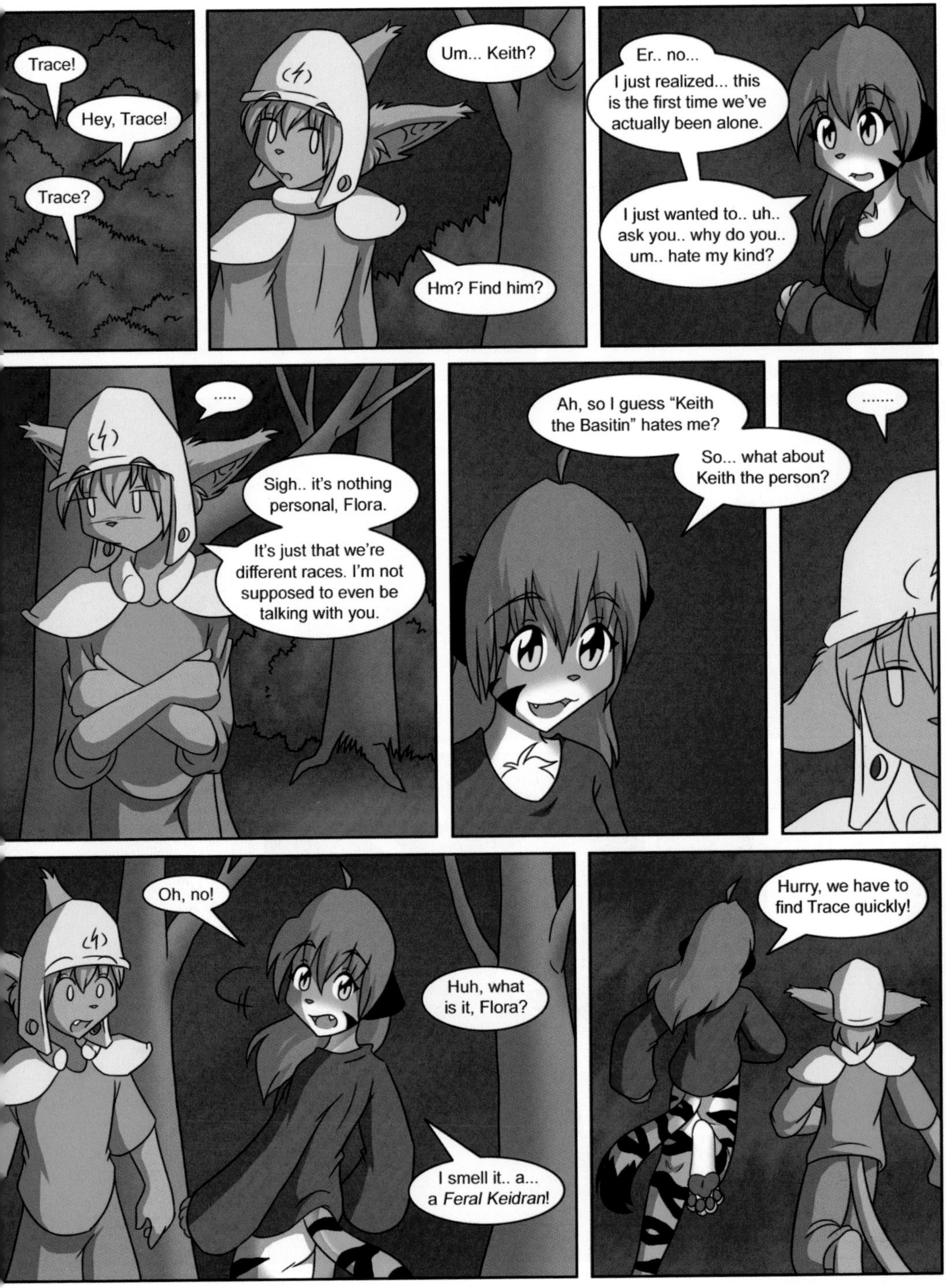

Trace!
Hey, Trace!
Trace?
Um... Keith?
Hm? Find him?
Er.. no...
I just realized... this is the first time we've actually been alone.
I just wanted to.. uh.. ask you.. why do you.. um.. hate my kind?
.....
Sigh.. it's nothing personal, Flora.
It's just that we're different races. I'm not supposed to even be talking with you.
Ah, so I guess "Keith the Basitin" hates me?
So... what about Keith the person?
....
Oh, no!
Huh, what is it, Flora?
I smell it.. a... a *Feral Keidran*!
Hurry, we have to find Trace quickly!

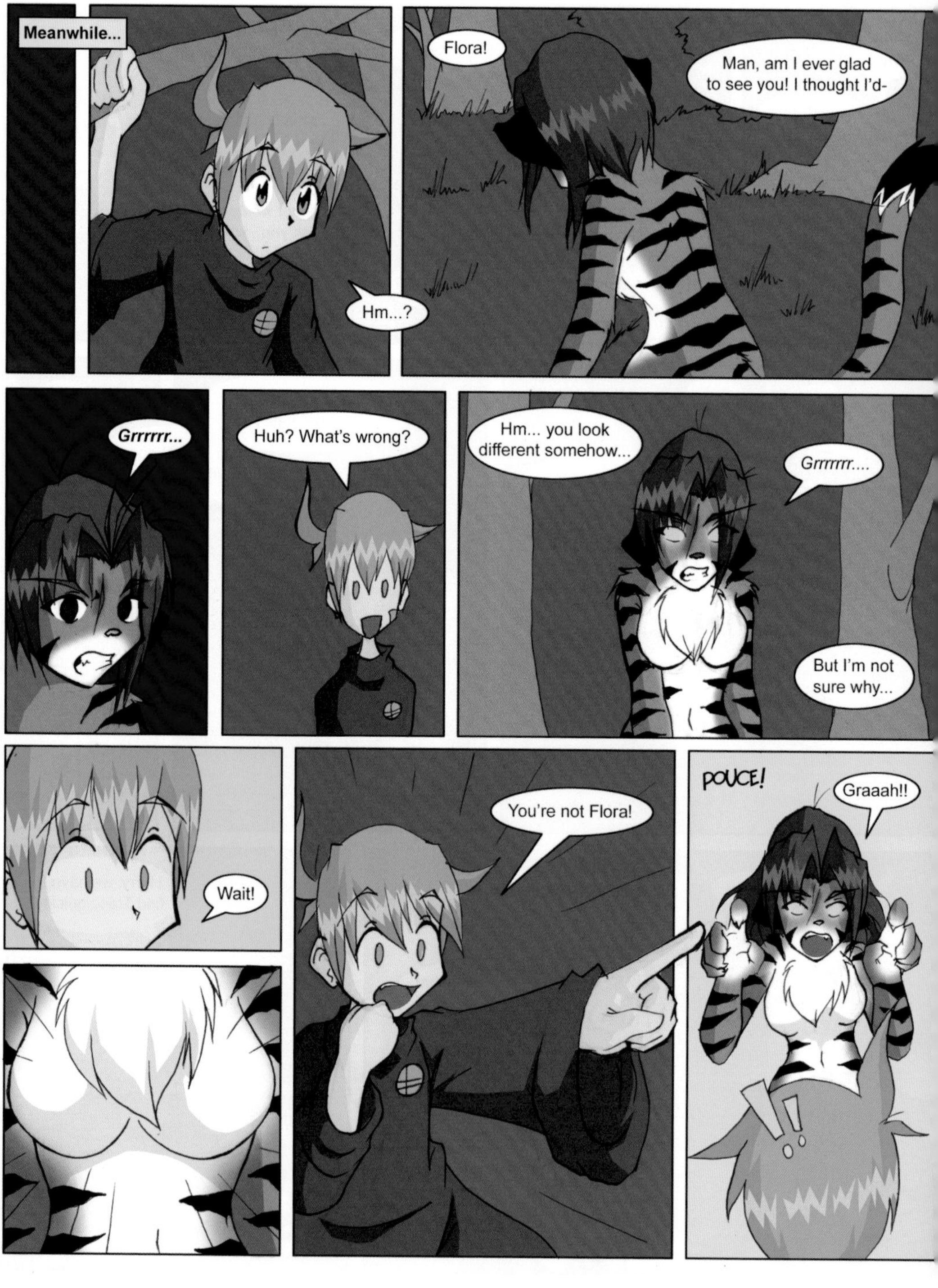
Meanwhile...
Hm...?
Flora!
Man, am I ever glad to see you! I thought I'd-
Grrrrrr...
Huh? What's wrong?
Hm... you look different somehow...
Grrrrrr....
But I'm not sure why...
Wait!
You're not Flora!
POUCE!
Graaah!!

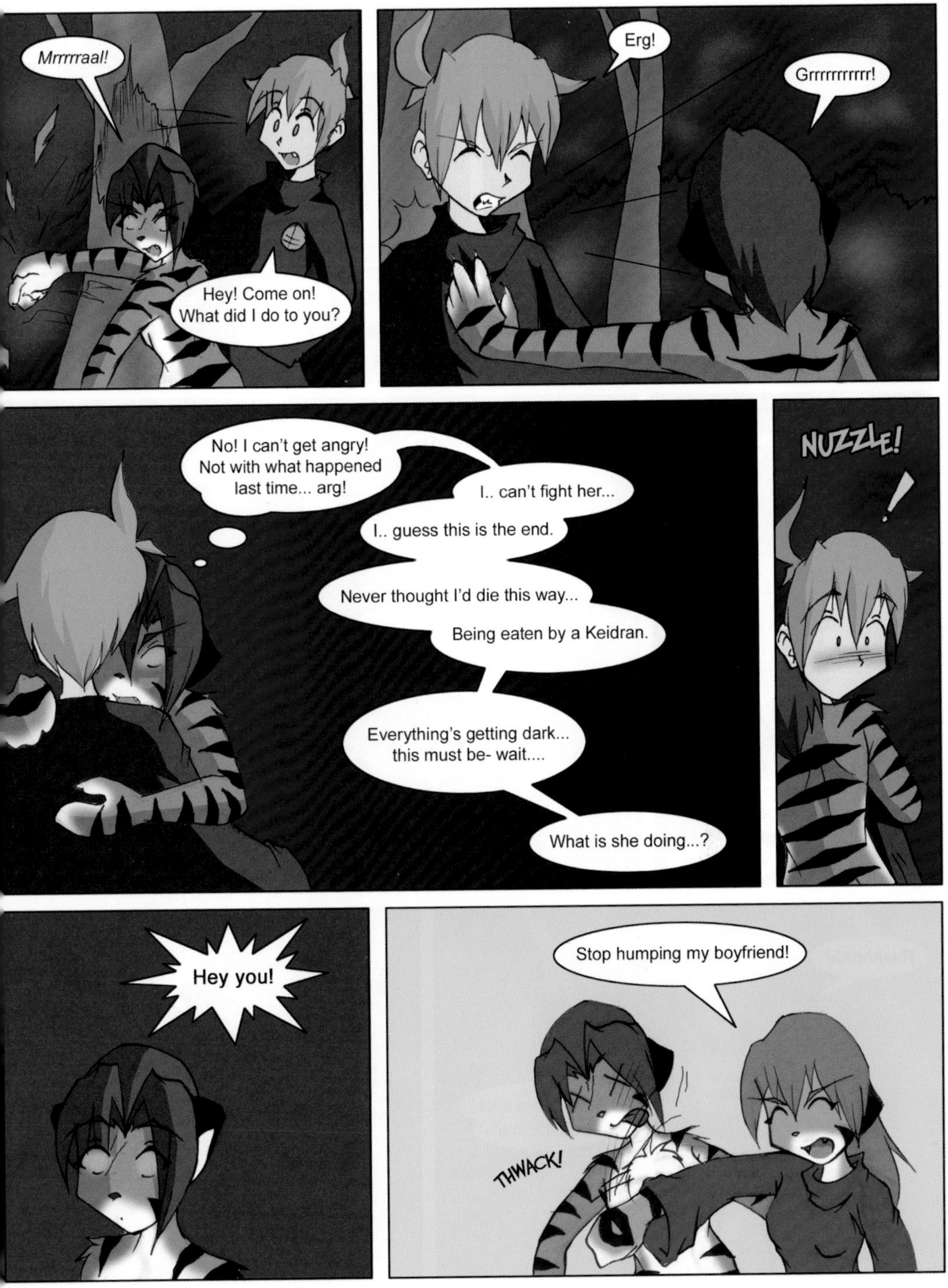
Mrrrrraal!
Hey! Come on! What did I do to you?
Erg!
Grrrrrrrrrrr!
No! I can't get angry! Not with what happened last time... arg!
I.. can't fight her...
I.. guess this is the end.
Never thought I'd die this way...
Being eaten by a Keidran.
Everything's getting dark... this must be- wait....
What is she doing...?
NUZZLE!
!
Hey you!
Stop humping my boyfriend!
THWACK!

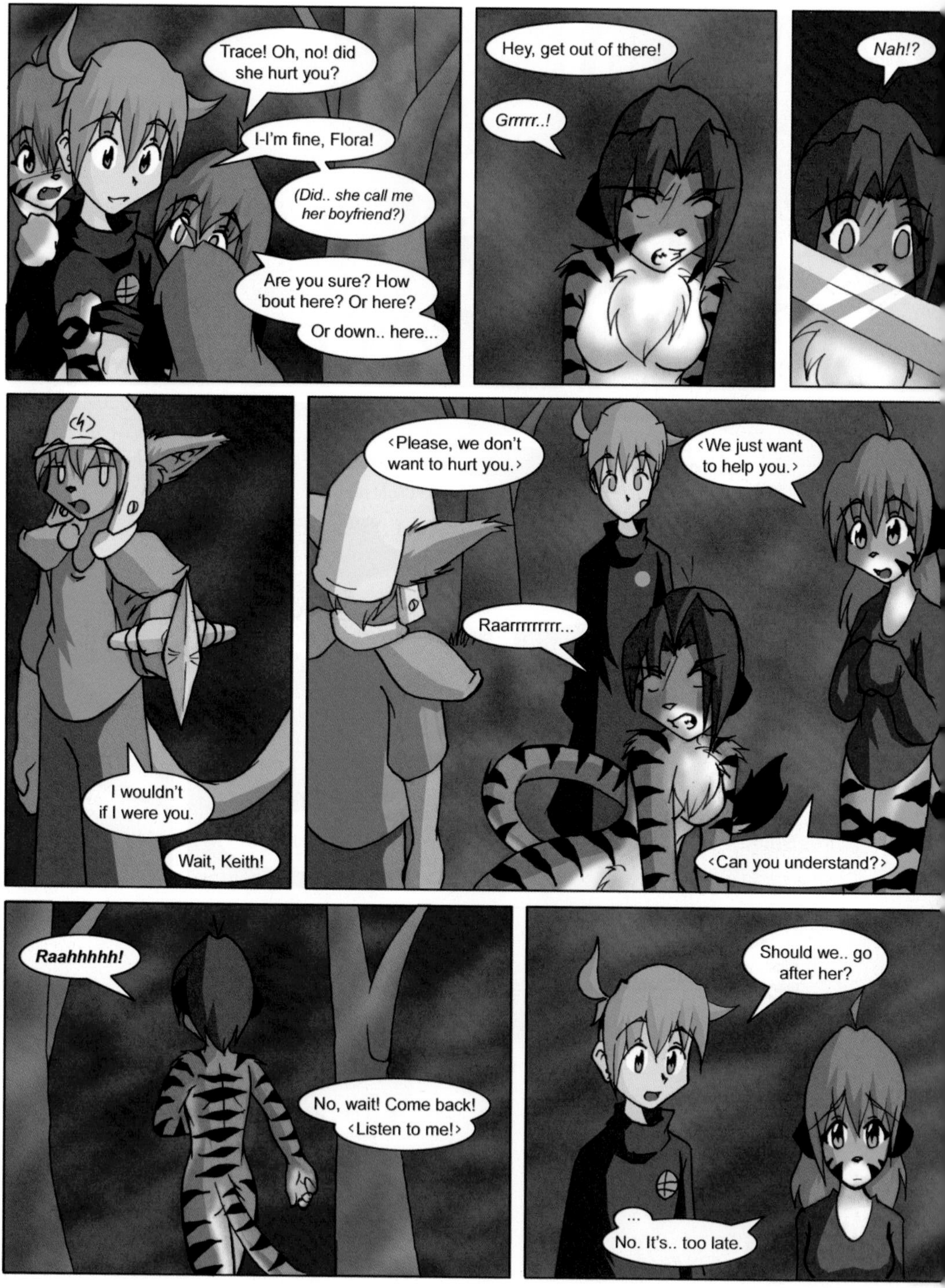
Trace! Oh, no! did she hurt you?
I-I'm fine, Flora!
(Did.. she call me her boyfriend?)
Are you sure? How 'bout here? Or here?
Or down.. here...
Hey, get out of there!
Grrrrr..!
Nah!?
I wouldn't if I were you.
Wait, Keith!
<Please, we don't want to hurt you.>
<We just want to help you.>
Raarrrrrrrrr...
<Can you understand?>
Raahhhhh!
No, wait! Come back! <Listen to me!>
Should we.. go after her?
...
No. It's.. too late.

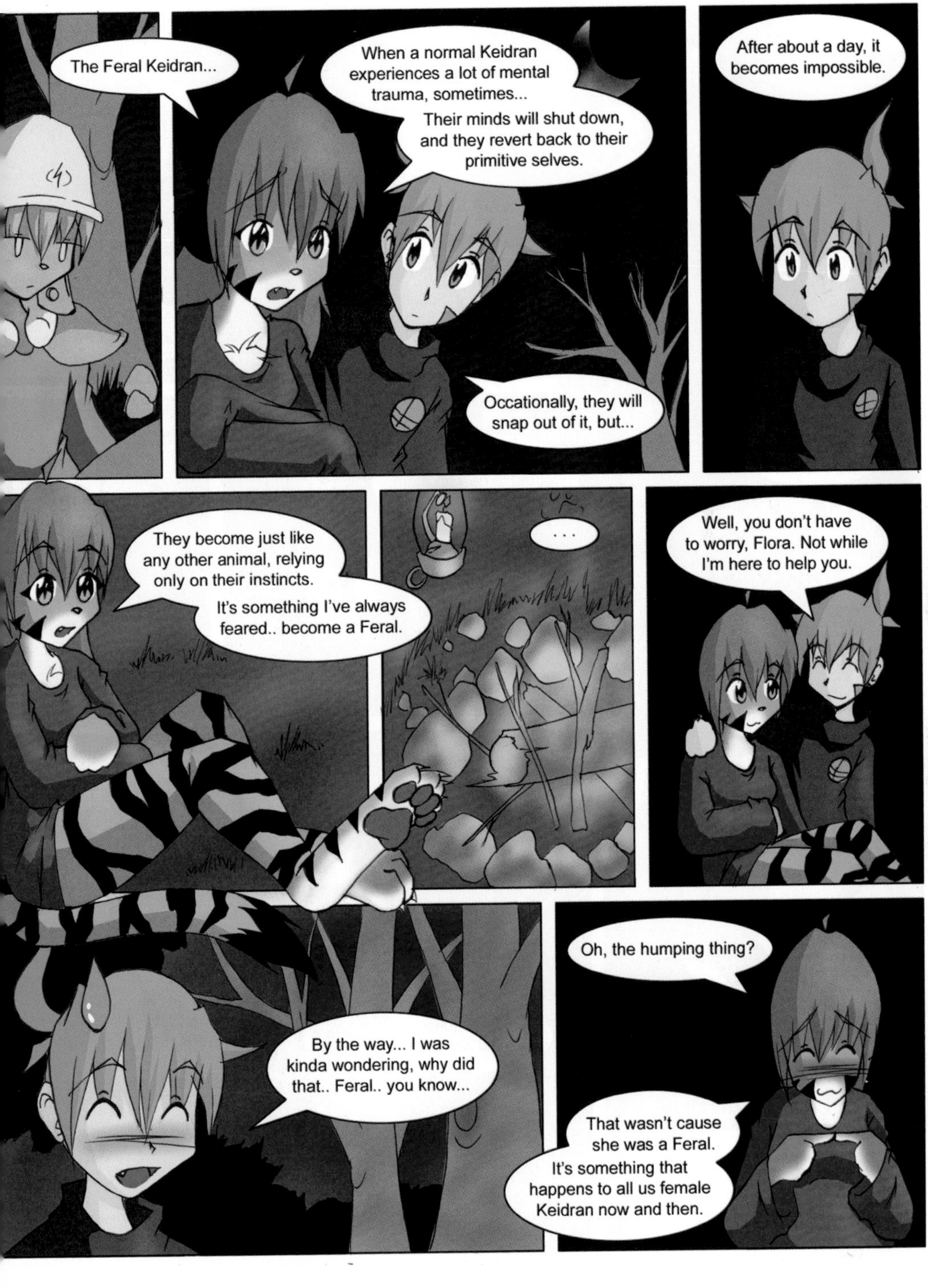

The Feral Keidran...
When a normal Keidran experiences a lot of mental trauma, sometimes...
Their minds will shut down, and they revert back to their primitive selves.
Occationally, they will snap out of it, but...
After about a day, it becomes impossible.
They become just like any other animal, relying only on their instincts.
It's something I've always feared.. become a Feral.
. . .
Well, you don't have to worry, Flora. Not while I'm here to help you.
By the way... I was kinda wondering, why did that.. Feral.. you know...
Oh, the humping thing?
That wasn't cause she was a Feral.
It's something that happens to all us female Keidran now and then.

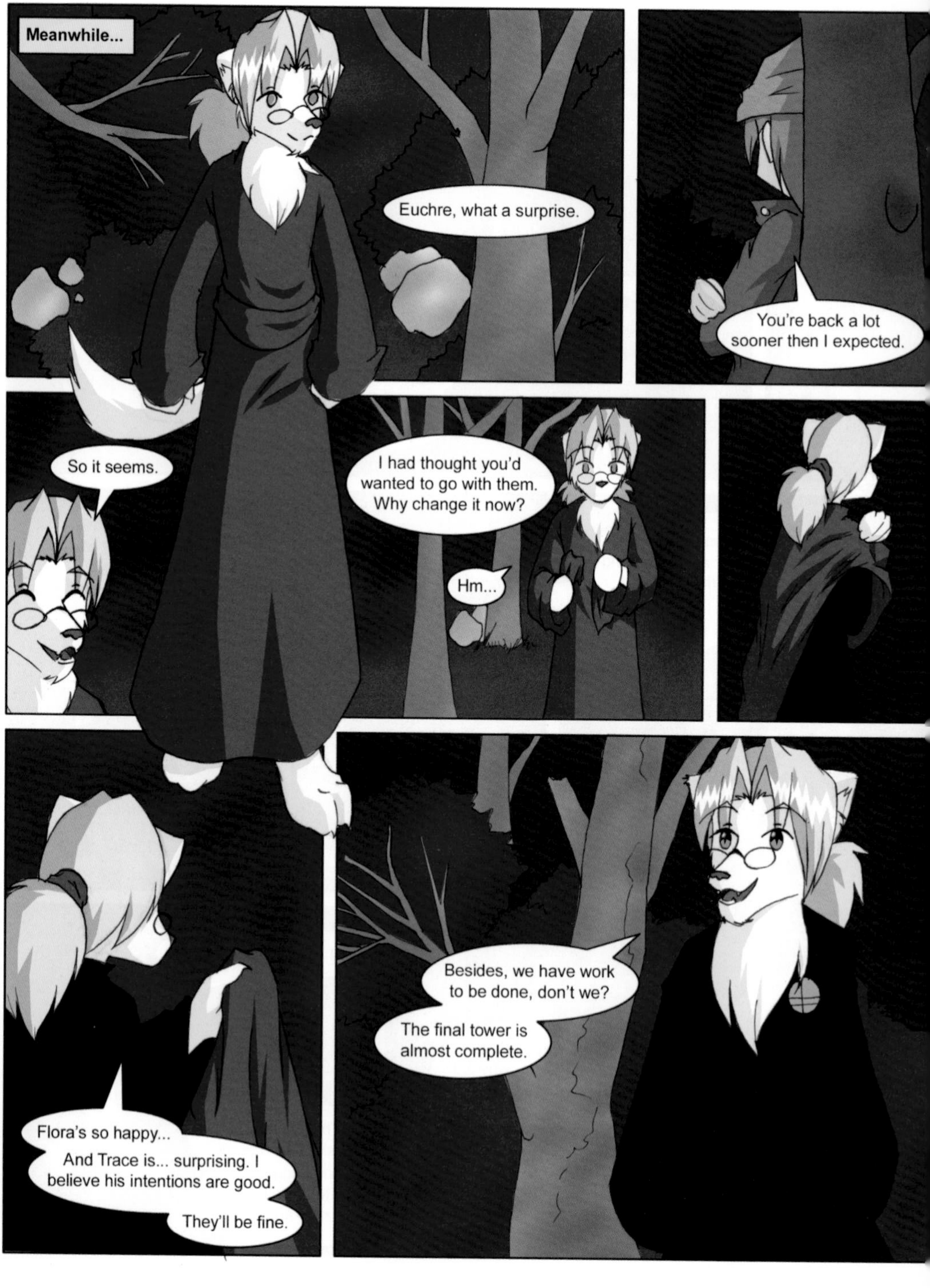
Meanwhile...
Euchre, what a surprise.
You're back a lot sooner then I expected.
So it seems.
I had thought you'd wanted to go with them. Why change it now?
Hm...
Flora's so happy...
And Trace is... surprising. I believe his intentions are good.
They'll be fine.
Besides, we have work to be done, don't we?
The final tower is almost complete.

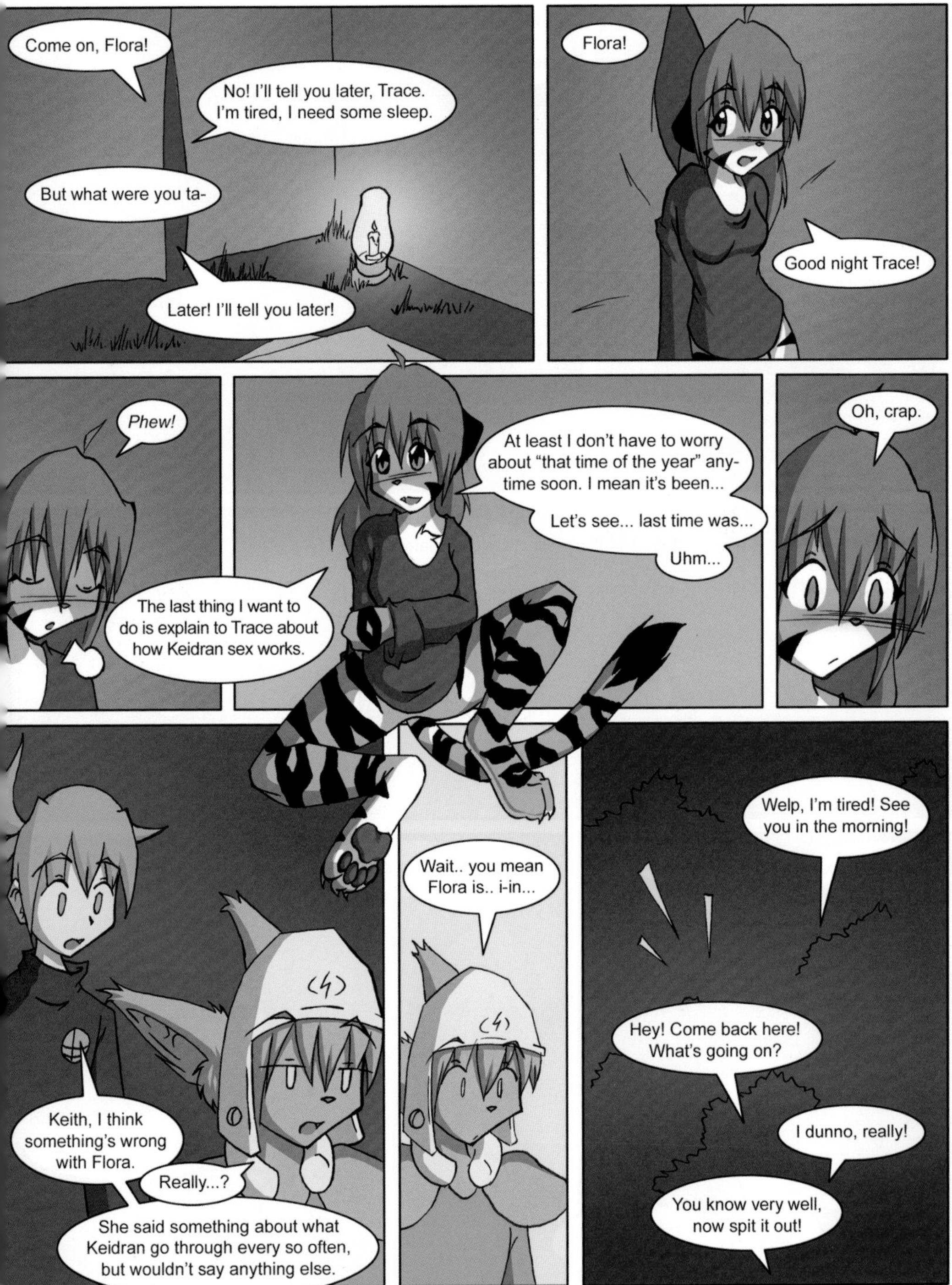
Come on, Flora!
No! I'll tell you later, Trace. I'm tired, I need some sleep.
But what were you ta-
Later! I'll tell you later!
Flora!
Good night Trace!
Phew!
The last thing I want to do is explain to Trace about how Keidran sex works.
At least I don't have to worry about "that time of the year" anytime soon. I mean it's been...
Let's see... last time was...
Uhm...
Oh, crap.
Keith, I think something's wrong with Flora.
Really...?
She said something about what Keidran go through every so often, but wouldn't say anything else.
Wait.. you mean Flora is.. i-in...
Welp, I'm tired! See you in the morning!
Hey! Come back here! What's going on?
I dunno, really!
You know very well, now spit it out!

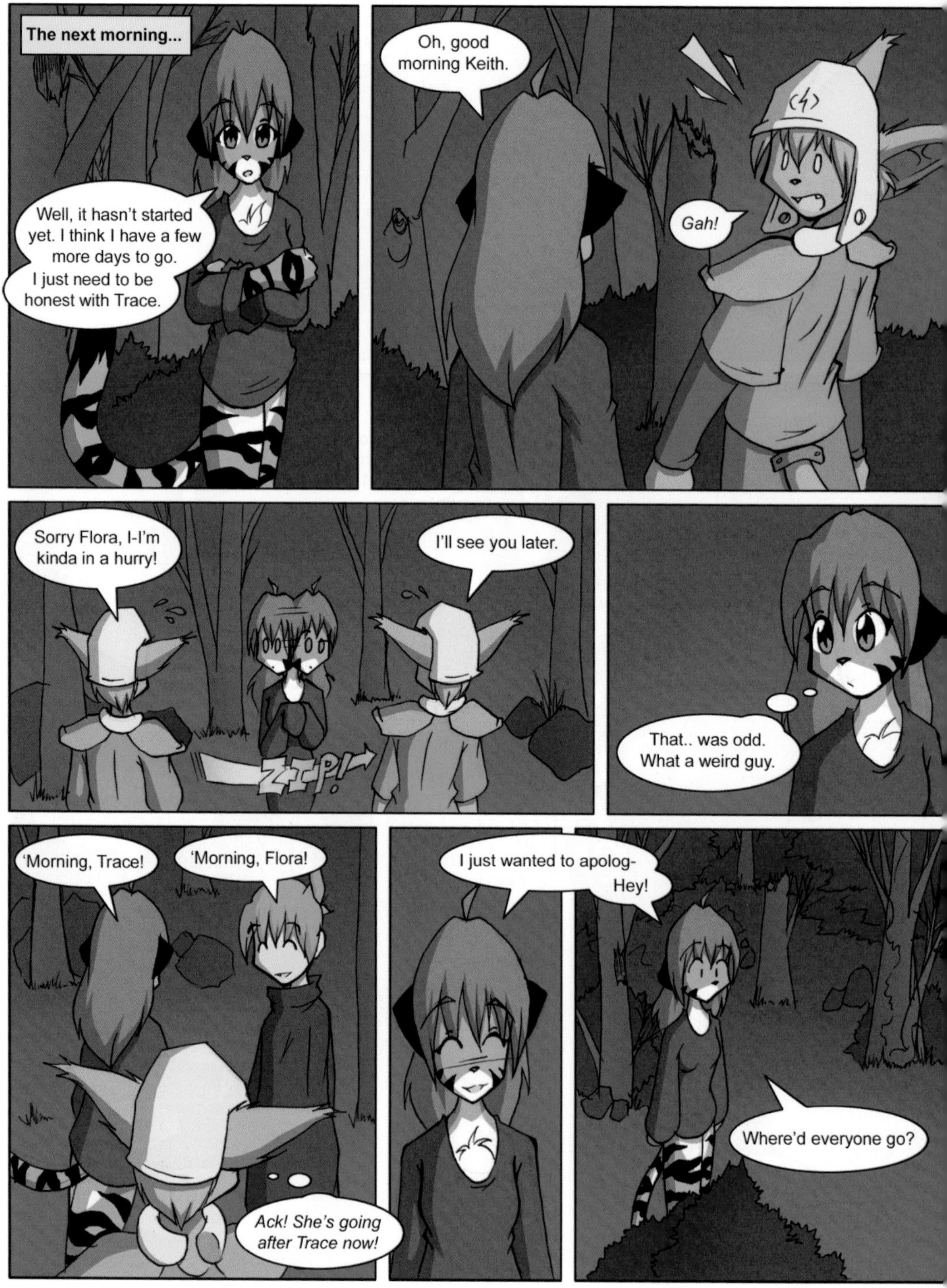

The next morning...
Well, it hasn't started yet. I think I have a few more days to go. I just need to be honest with Trace.
Oh, good morning Keith.
Gah!
Sorry Flora, I-I'm kinda in a hurry!
I'll see you later.
ZIP!
That.. was odd. What a weird guy.
'Morning, Trace!
'Morning, Flora!
Ack! She's going after Trace now!
I just wanted to apolog-
Hey!
Where'd everyone go?

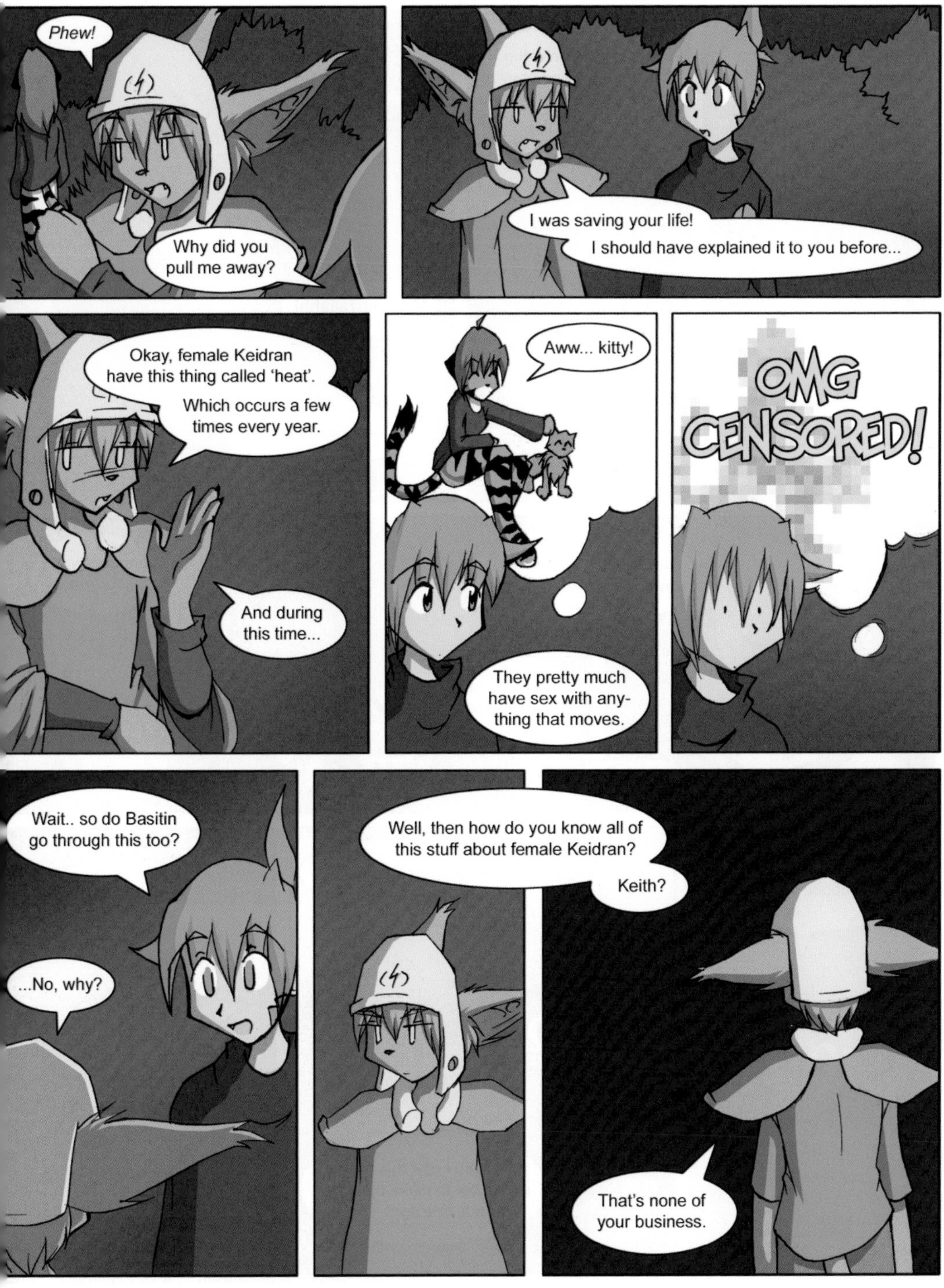
Phew!
Why did you pull me away?
I was saving your life!
I should have explained it to you before...
Okay, female Keidran have this thing called 'heat'.
Which occurs a few times every year.
And during this time...
Aww... kitty!
They pretty much have sex with any-thing that moves.
OMG CENSORED!
Wait.. so do Basitin go through this too?
...No, why?
Well, then how do you know all of this stuff about female Keidran?
Keith?
That's none of your business.

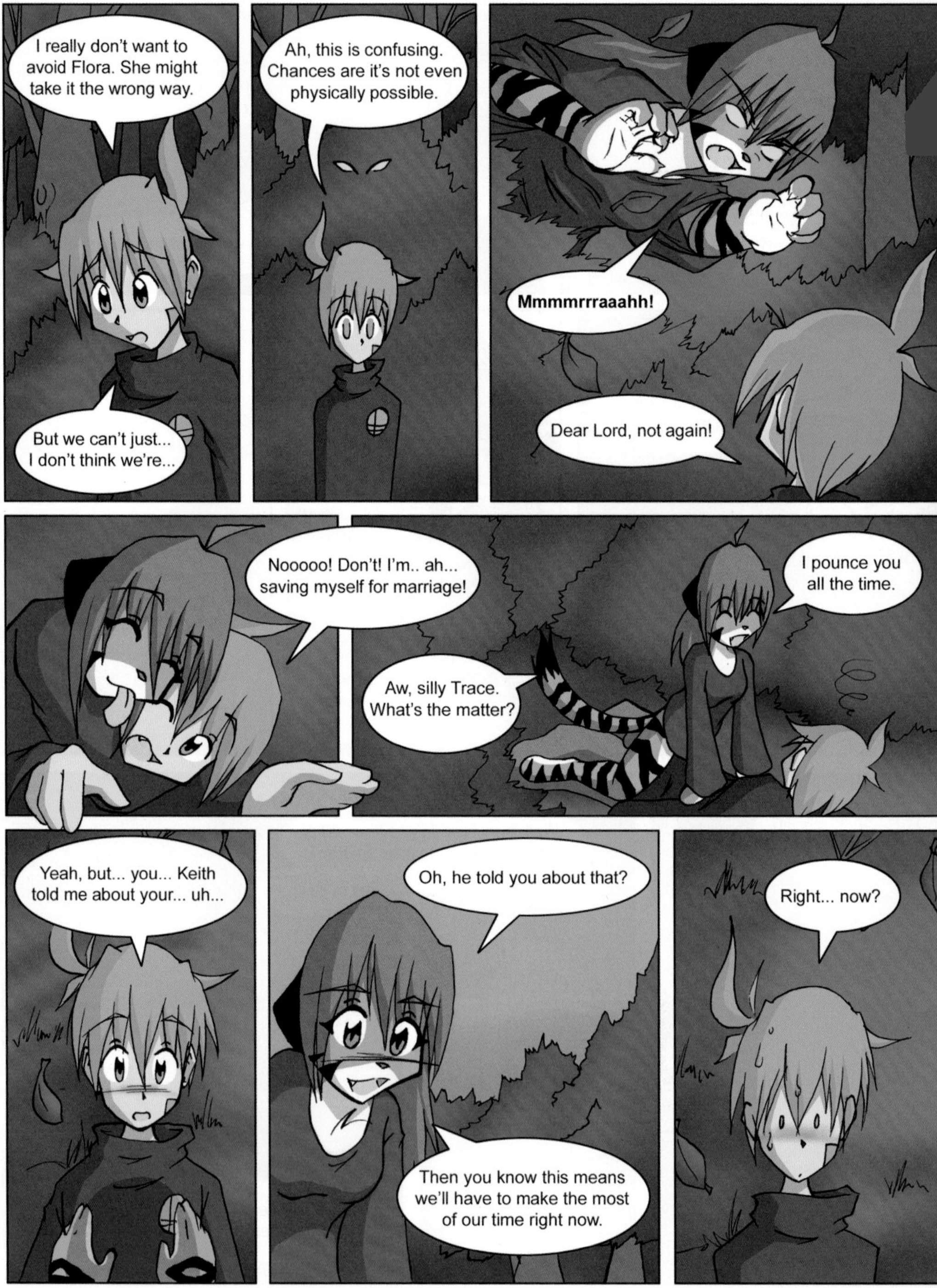
I really don't want to avoid Flora. She might take it the wrong way.
But we can't just... I don't think we're...
Ah, this is confusing. Chances are it's not even physically possible.
Mmmmrrraaahh!
Dear Lord, not again!
Nooooo! Don't! I'm.. ah... saving myself for marriage!
Aw, silly Trace. What's the matter?
I pounce you all the time.
Yeah, but... you... Keith told me about your... uh...
Oh, he told you about that?
Then you know this means we'll have to make the most of our time right now.
Right... now?

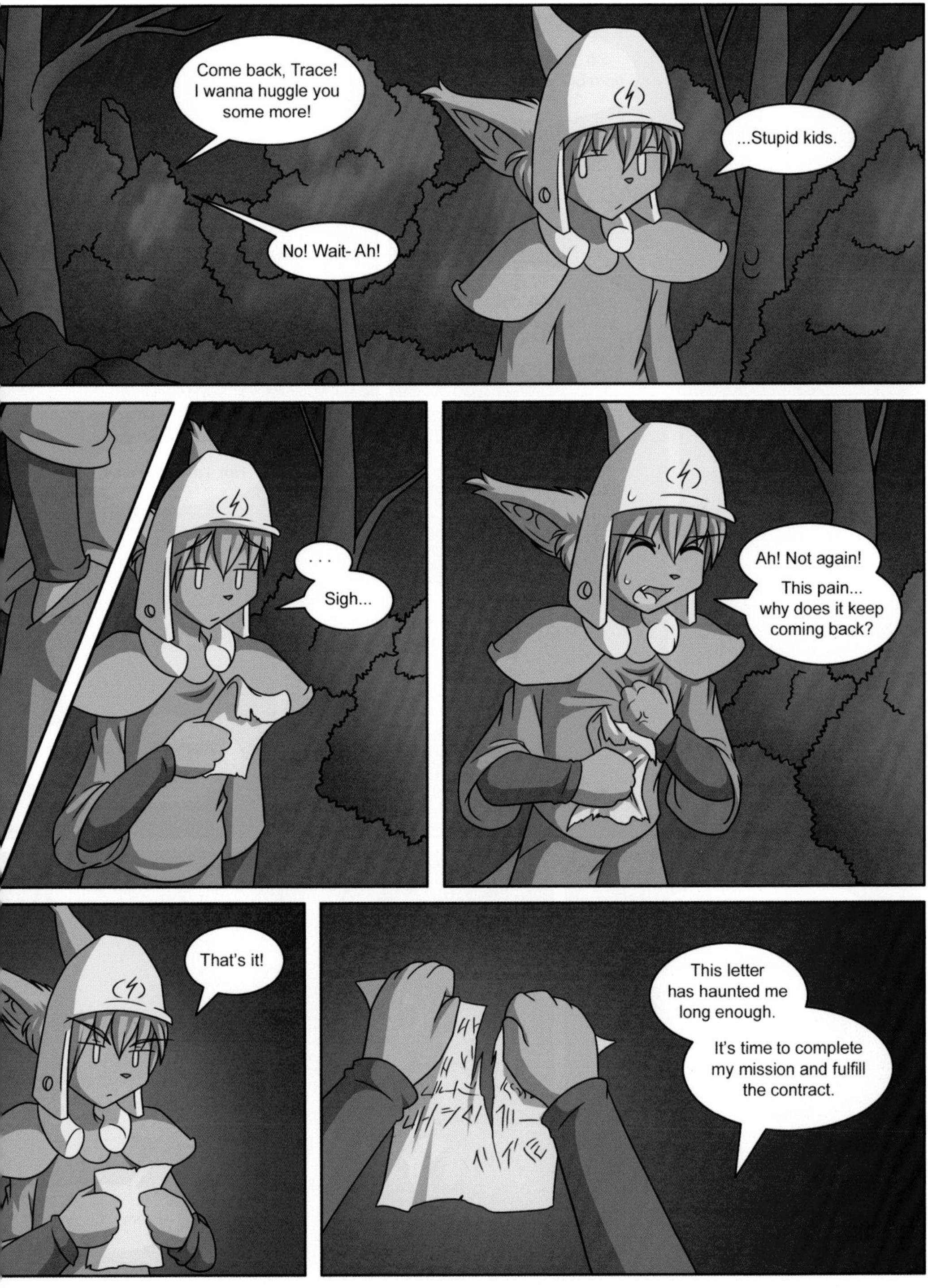
Come back, Trace! I wanna huggle you some more!
No! Wait- Ah!
...Stupid kids.
. . .
Sigh...
Ah! Not again!
This pain... why does it keep coming back?
That's it!
This letter has haunted me long enough.
It's time to complete my mission and fulfill the contract.

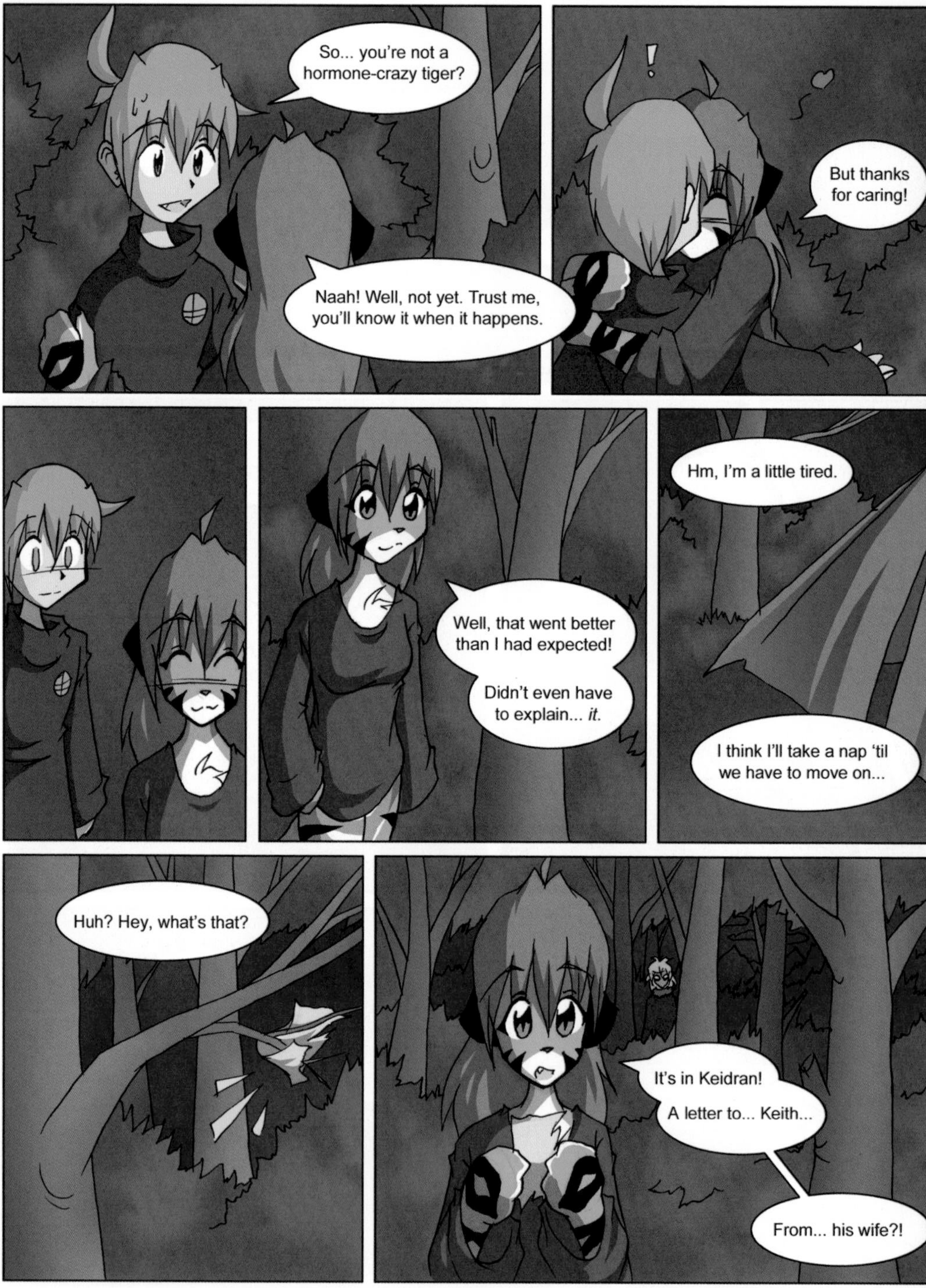

So... you're not a hormone-crazy tiger?
Naah! Well, not yet. Trust me, you'll know it when it happens.
!
But thanks for caring!
Well, that went better than I had expected!
Didn't even have to explain... *it*.
Hm, I'm a little tired.
I think I'll take a nap 'til we have to move on...
Huh? Hey, what's that?
It's in Keidran!
A letter to... Keith...
From... his wife?!

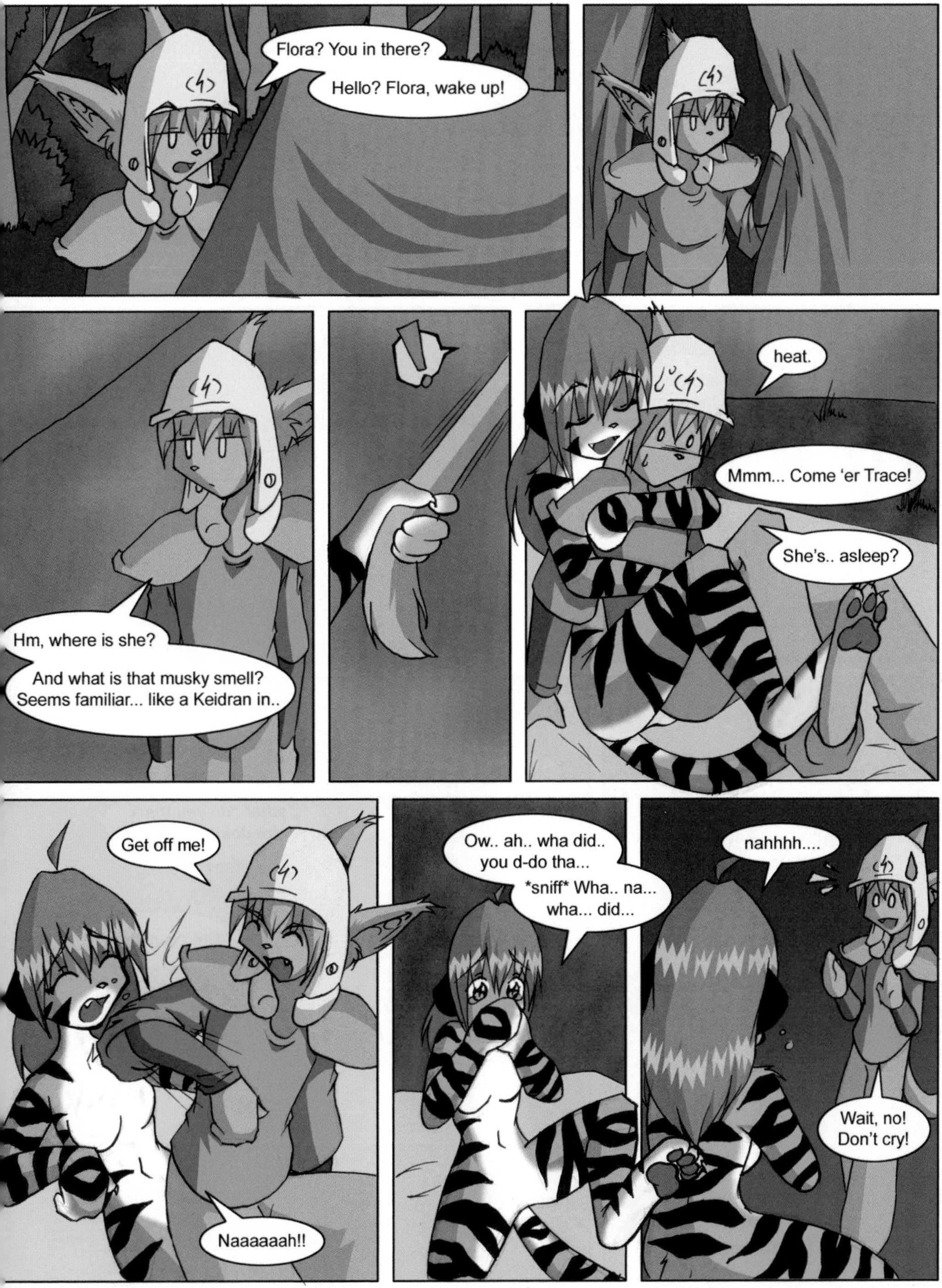
Flora? You in there?
Hello? Flora, wake up!
Hm, where is she?
And what is that musky smell? Seems familiar... like a Keidran in..
!
heat.
Mmm... Come 'er Trace!
She's.. asleep?
Get off me!
Naaaaaah!!
Ow.. ah.. wha did.. you d-do tha...
sniff Wha.. na... wha... did...
nahhhh....
Wait, no! Don't cry!

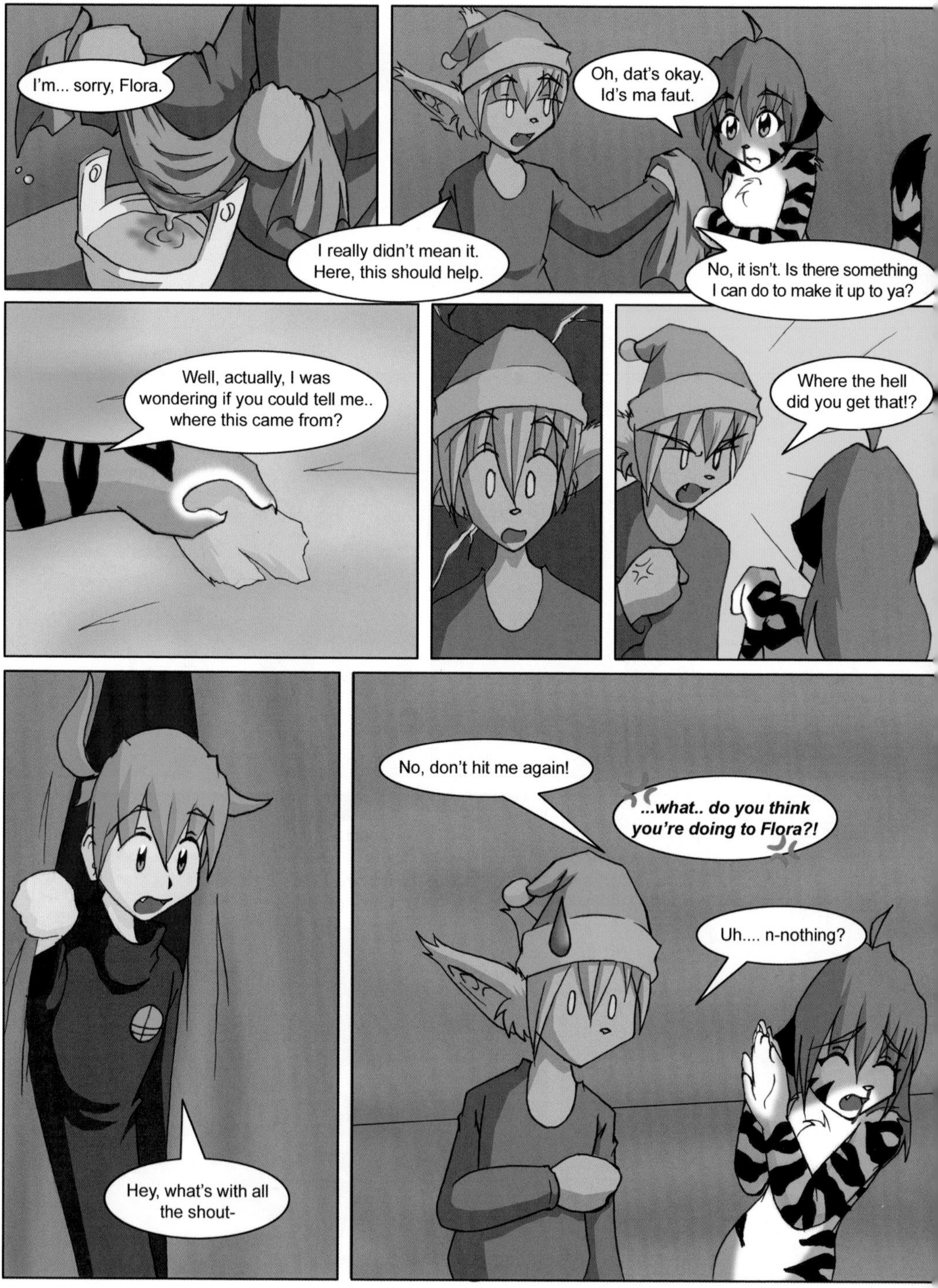
I'm... sorry, Flora.
Oh, dat's okay. Id's ma faut.
I really didn't mean it. Here, this should help.
No, it isn't. Is there something I can do to make it up to ya?
Well, actually, I was wondering if you could tell me.. where this came from?
Where the hell did you get that!?
Hey, what's with all the shout-
No, don't hit me again!
...what.. do you think you're doing to Flora?!
Uh.... n-nothing?

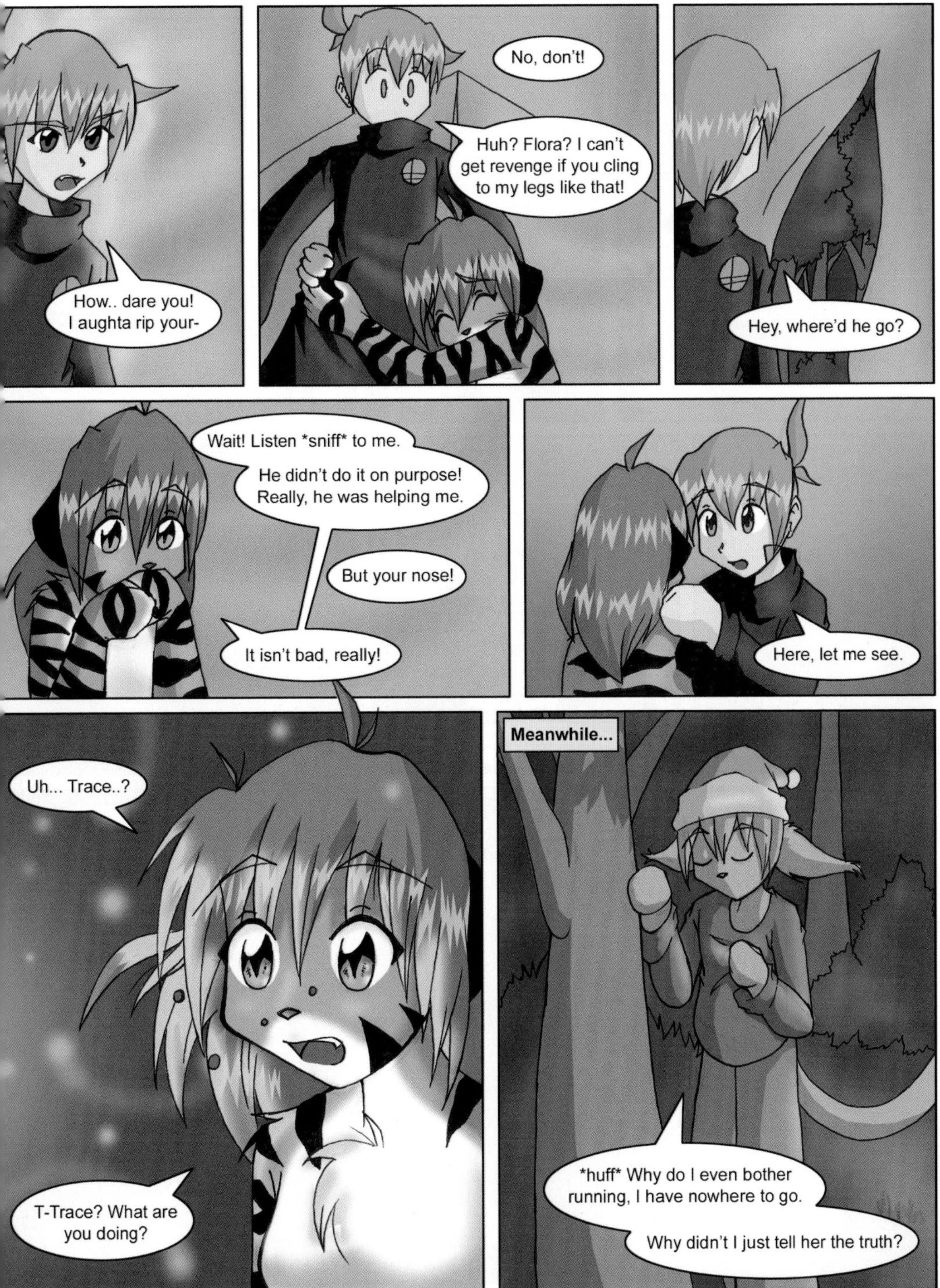
How.. dare you!
I aughta rip your-
No, don't!
Huh? Flora? I can't get revenge if you cling to my legs like that!
Hey, where'd he go?
Wait! Listen *sniff* to me.
He didn't do it on purpose! Really, he was helping me.
But your nose!
It isn't bad, really!
Here, let me see.
Uh... Trace..?
T-Trace? What are you doing?
Meanwhile...
huff Why do I even bother running, I have nowhere to go.
Why didn't I just tell her the truth?

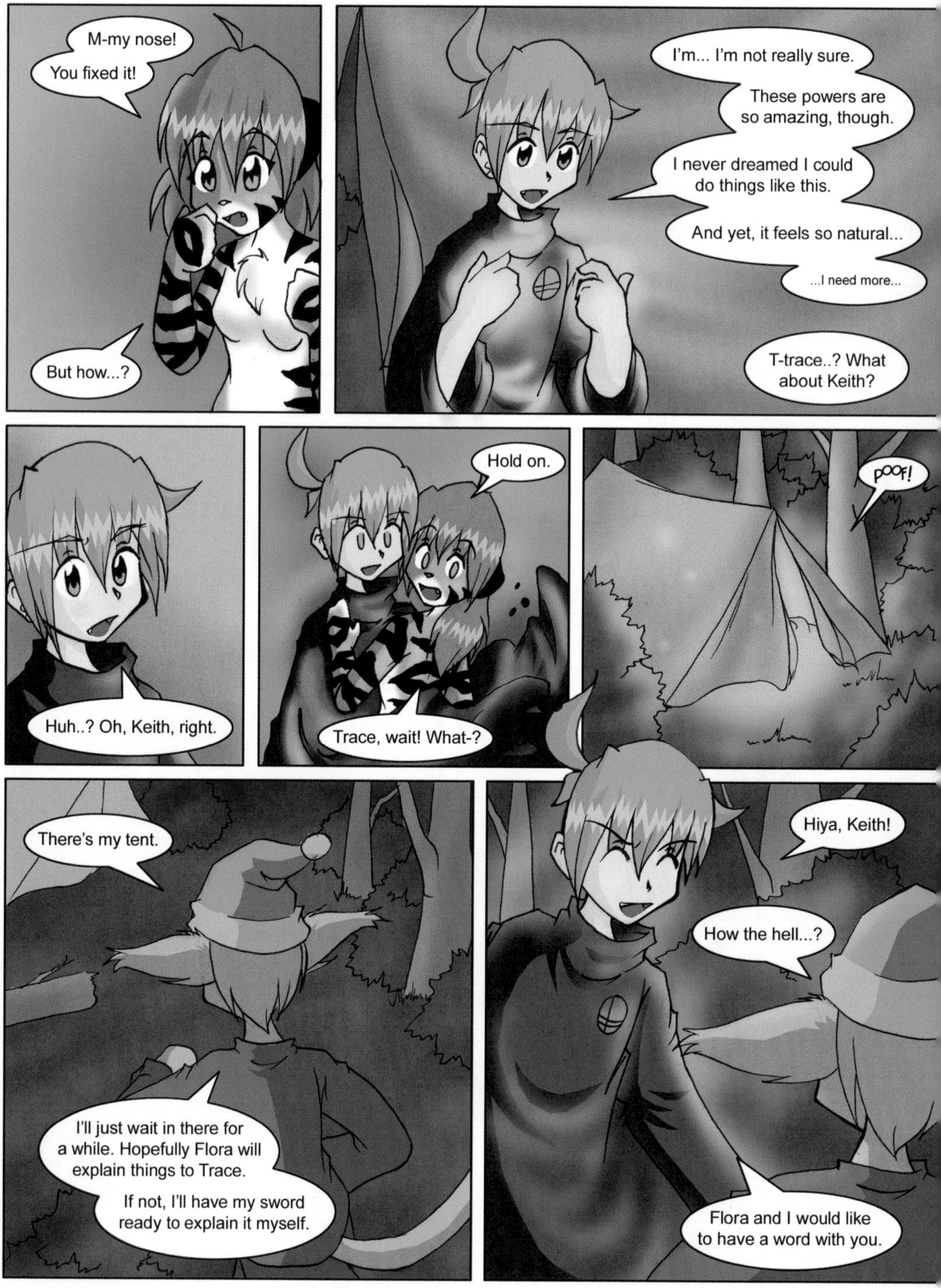
M-my nose!
You fixed it!
But how...?
I'm... I'm not really sure.
These powers are so amazing, though.
I never dreamed I could do things like this.
And yet, it feels so natural...
...I need more...
T-trace..? What about Keith?
Huh..? Oh, Keith, right.
Hold on.
Trace, wait! What-?
pOOF!
There's my tent.
I'll just wait in there for a while. Hopefully Flora will explain things to Trace.
If not, I'll have my sword ready to explain it myself.
Hiya, Keith!
How the hell...?
Flora and I would like to have a word with you.

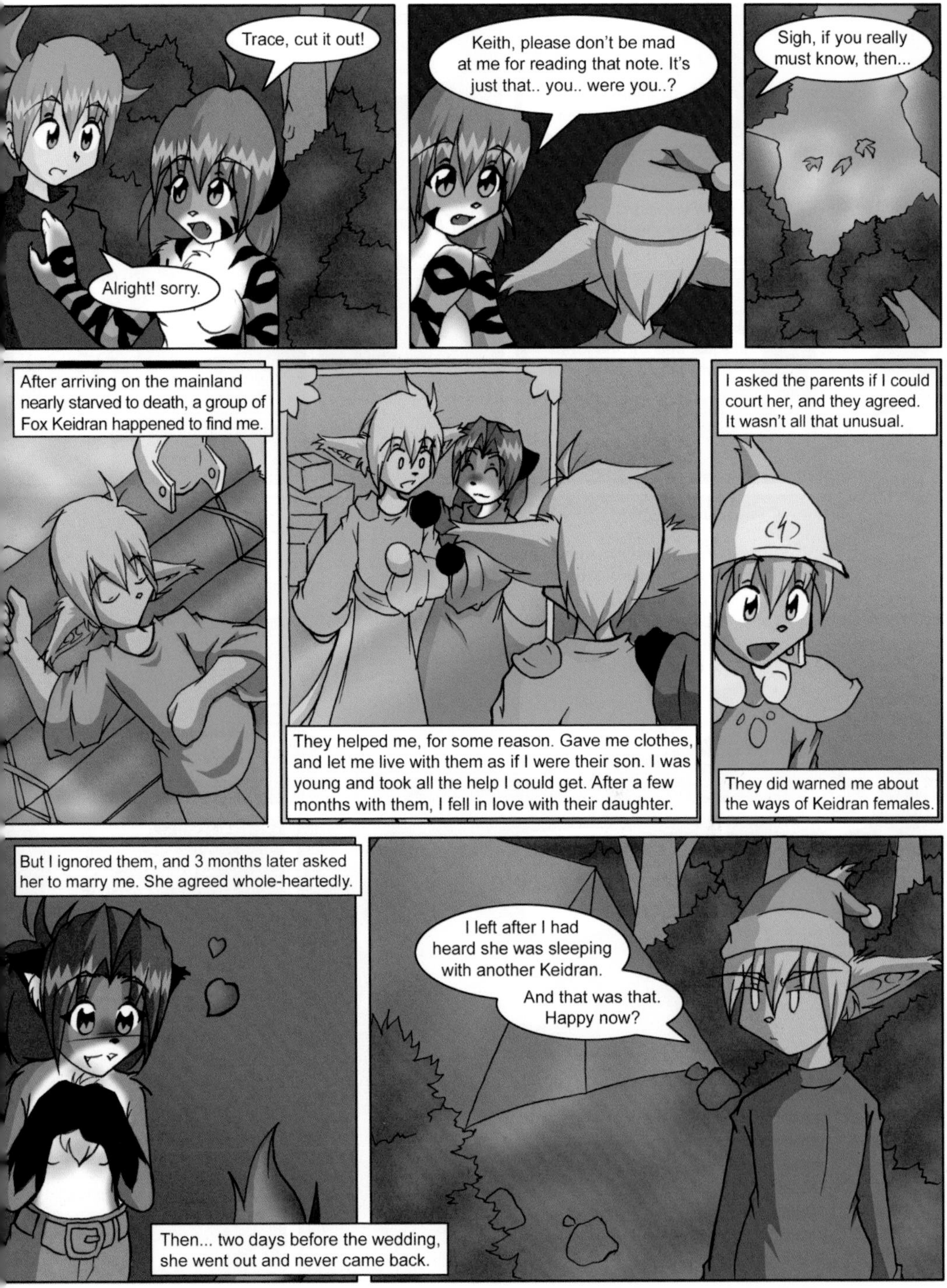

Trace, cut it out!
Alright! sorry.
Keith, please don't be mad at me for reading that note. It's just that.. you.. were you..?
Sigh, if you really must know, then...
After arriving on the mainland nearly starved to death, a group of Fox Keidran happened to find me.
They helped me, for some reason. Gave me clothes, and let me live with them as if I were their son. I was young and took all the help I could get. After a few months with them, I fell in love with their daughter.
I asked the parents if I could court her, and they agreed. It wasn't all that unusual.
They did warned me about the ways of Keidran females.
But I ignored them, and 3 months later asked her to marry me. She agreed whole-heartedly.
Then... two days before the wedding, she went out and never came back.
I left after I had heard she was sleeping with another Keidran.
And that was that. Happy now?

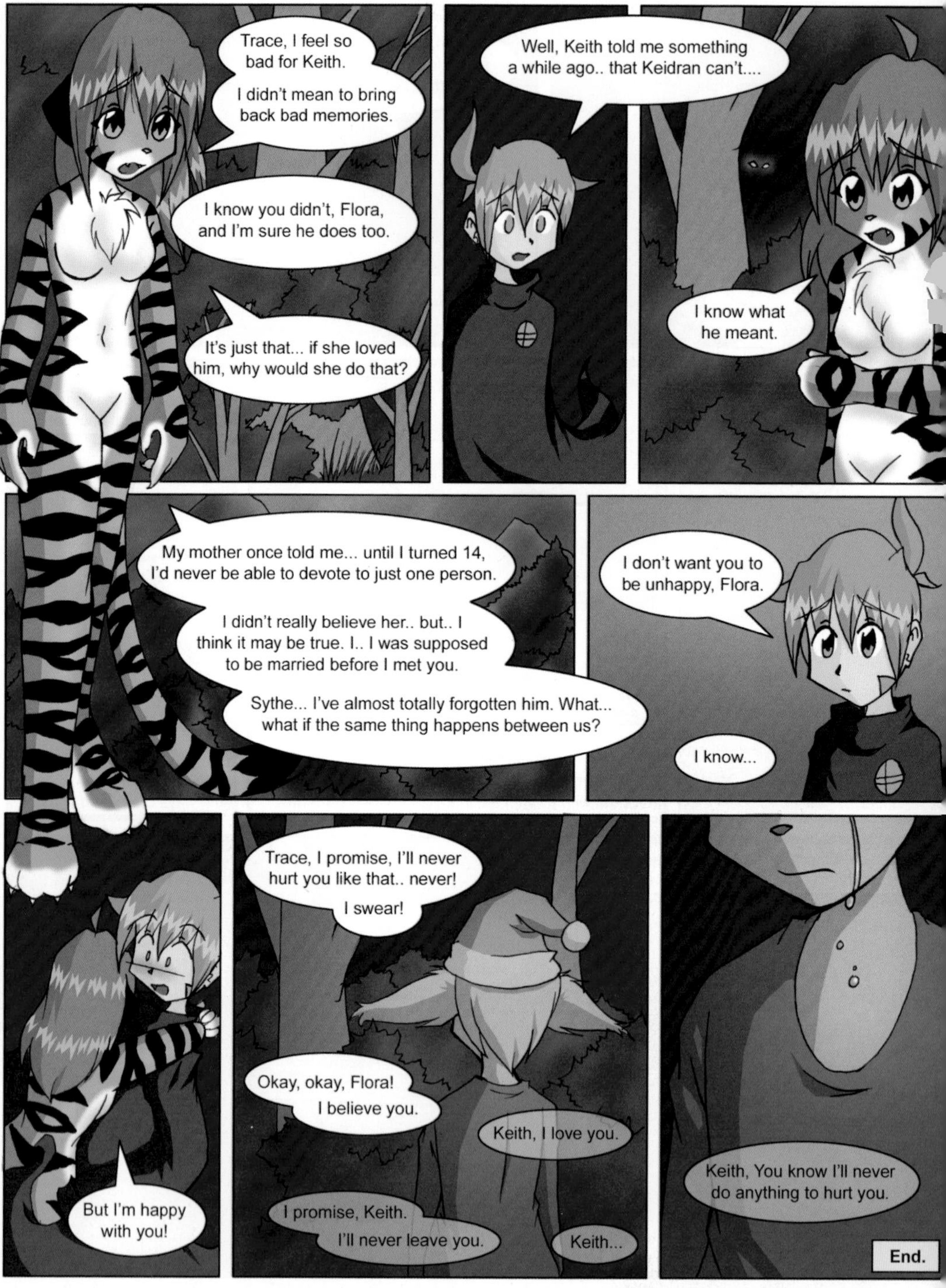

Trace, I feel so bad for Keith.
I didn't mean to bring back bad memories.
I know you didn't, Flora, and I'm sure he does too.
It's just that... if she loved him, why would she do that?
Well, Keith told me something a while ago.. that Keidran can't....
I know what he meant.
My mother once told me... until I turned 14, I'd never be able to devote to just one person.
I didn't really believe her.. but.. I think it may be true. I.. I was supposed to be married before I met you.
Sythe... I've almost totally forgotten him. What... what if the same thing happens between us?
I don't want you to be unhappy, Flora.
I know...
But I'm happy with you!
Trace, I promise, I'll never hurt you like that.. never!
I swear!
Okay, okay, Flora!
I believe you.
Keith, I love you.
I promise, Keith.
I'll never leave you.
Keith...
Keith, You know I'll never do anything to hurt you.
End.

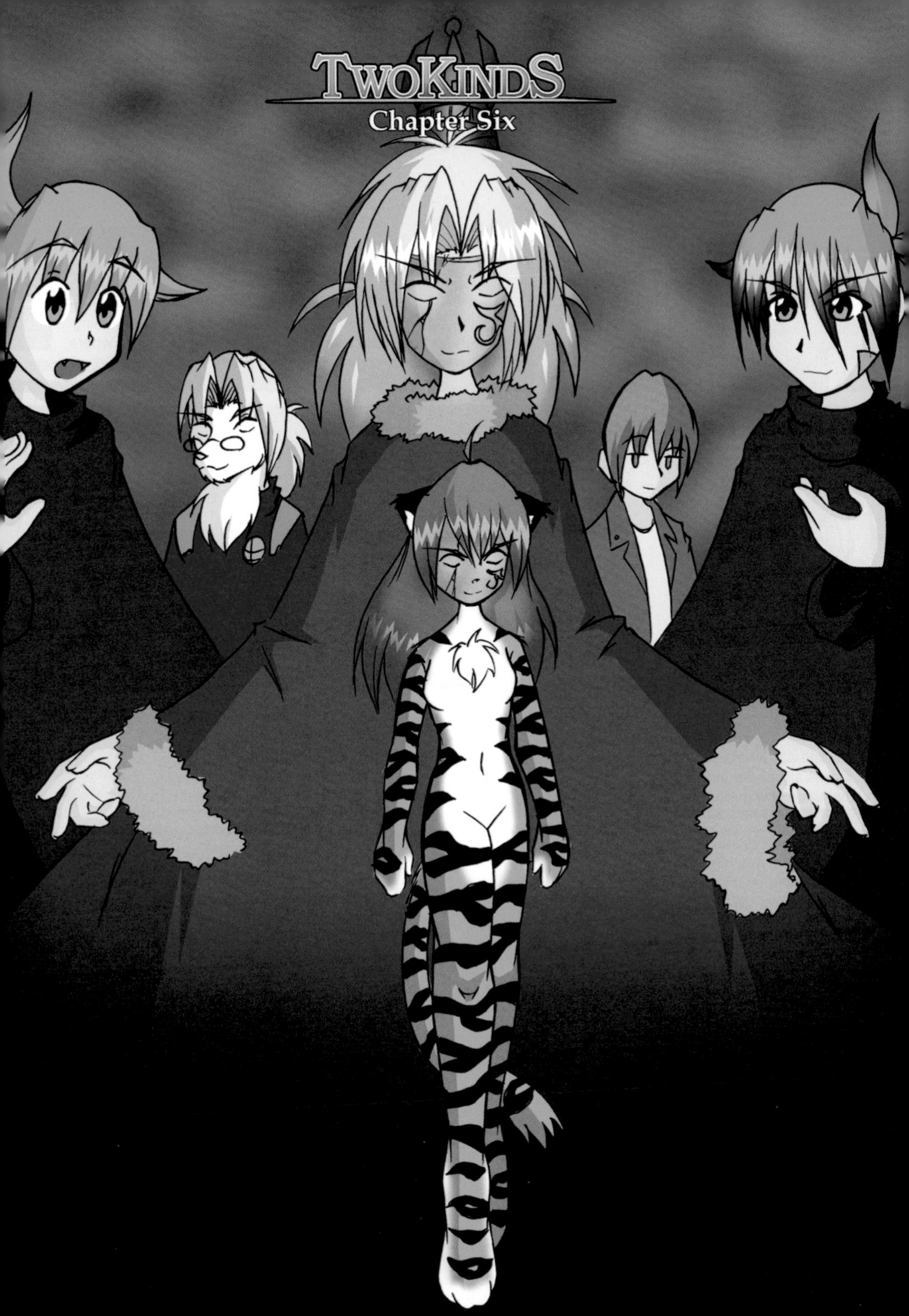
TwoKindS
Chapter Six

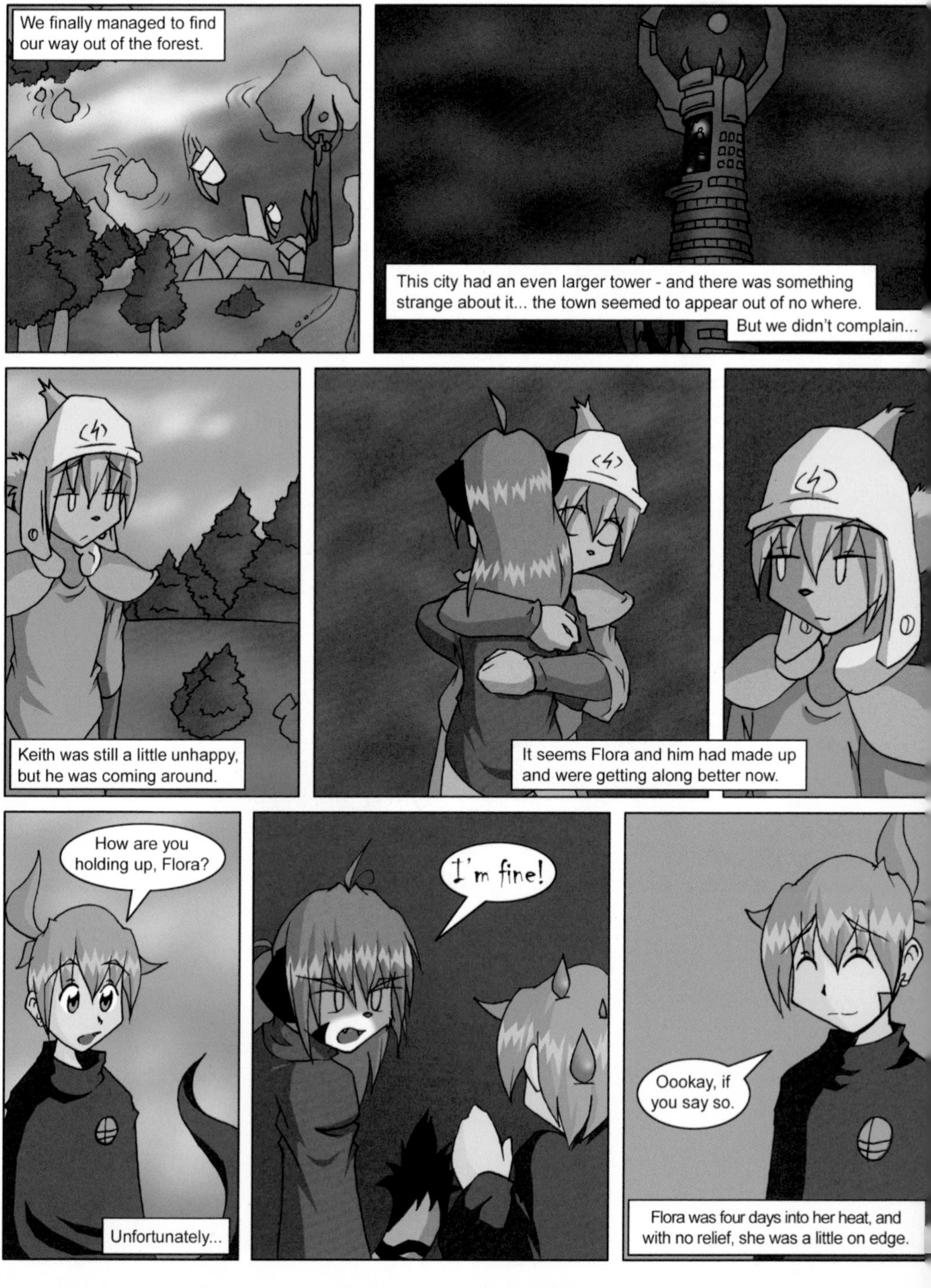

We finally managed to find our way out of the forest.
This city had an even larger tower - and there was something strange about it... the town seemed to appear out of no where.
But we didn't complain...
Keith was still a little unhappy, but he was coming around.
It seems Flora and him had made up and were getting along better now.
How are you holding up, Flora?
Unfortunately...
I'm fine!
Oookay, if you say so.
Flora was four days into her heat, and with no relief, she was a little on edge.

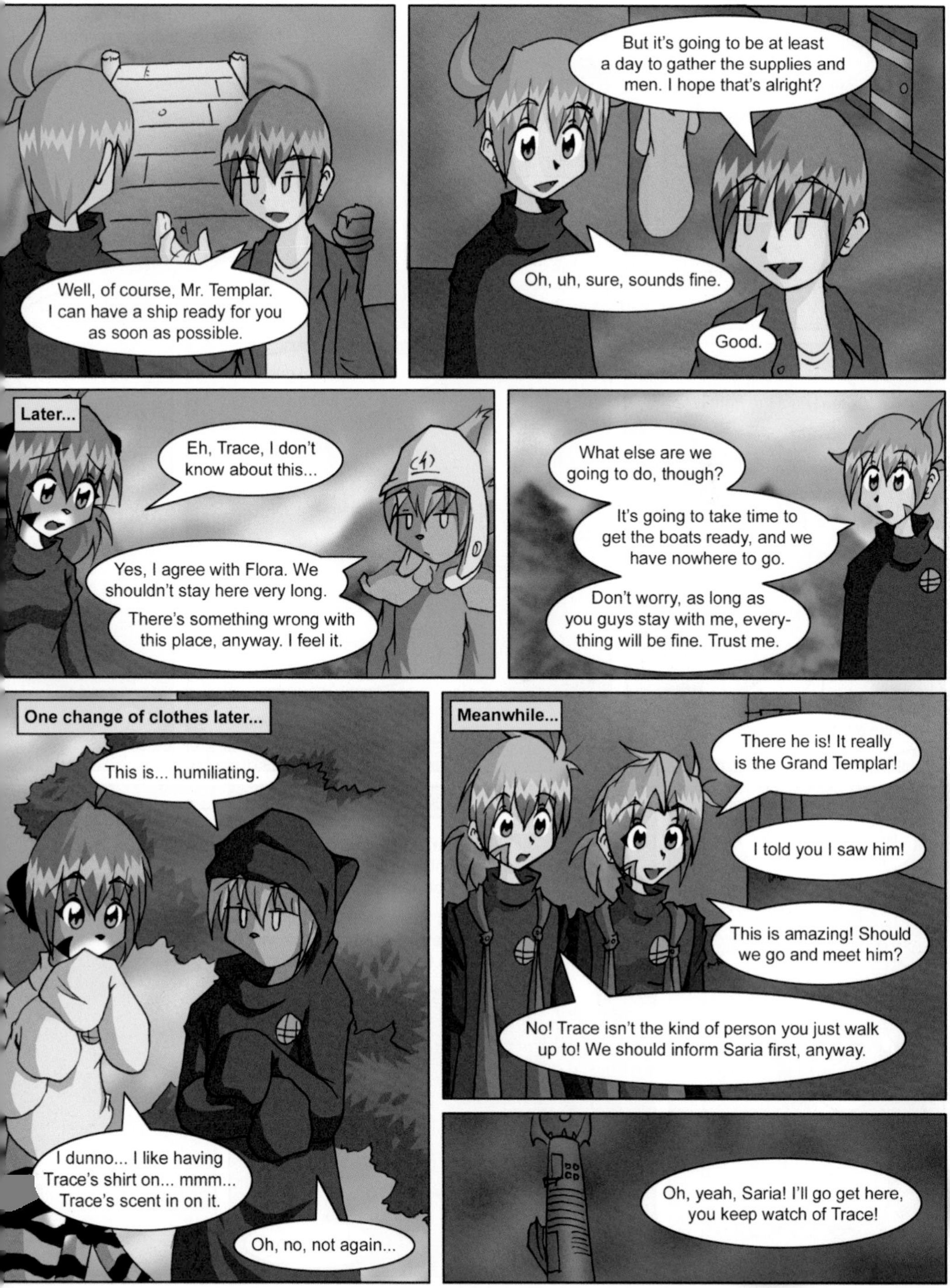
Well, of course, Mr. Templar. I can have a ship ready for you as soon as possible.
But it's going to be at least a day to gather the supplies and men. I hope that's alright?
Oh, uh, sure, sounds fine.
Good.
Later...
Eh, Trace, I don't know about this...
Yes, I agree with Flora. We shouldn't stay here very long.
There's something wrong with this place, anyway. I feel it.
What else are we going to do, though?
It's going to take time to get the boats ready, and we have nowhere to go.
Don't worry, as long as you guys stay with me, every-thing will be fine. Trust me.
One change of clothes later...
This is... humiliating.
I dunno... I like having Trace's shirt on... mmm... Trace's scent in on it.
Oh, no, not again...
Meanwhile...
There he is! It really is the Grand Templar!
I told you I saw him!
This is amazing! Should we go and meet him?
No! Trace isn't the kind of person you just walk up to! We should inform Saria first, anyway.
Oh, yeah, Saria! I'll go get here, you keep watch of Trace!

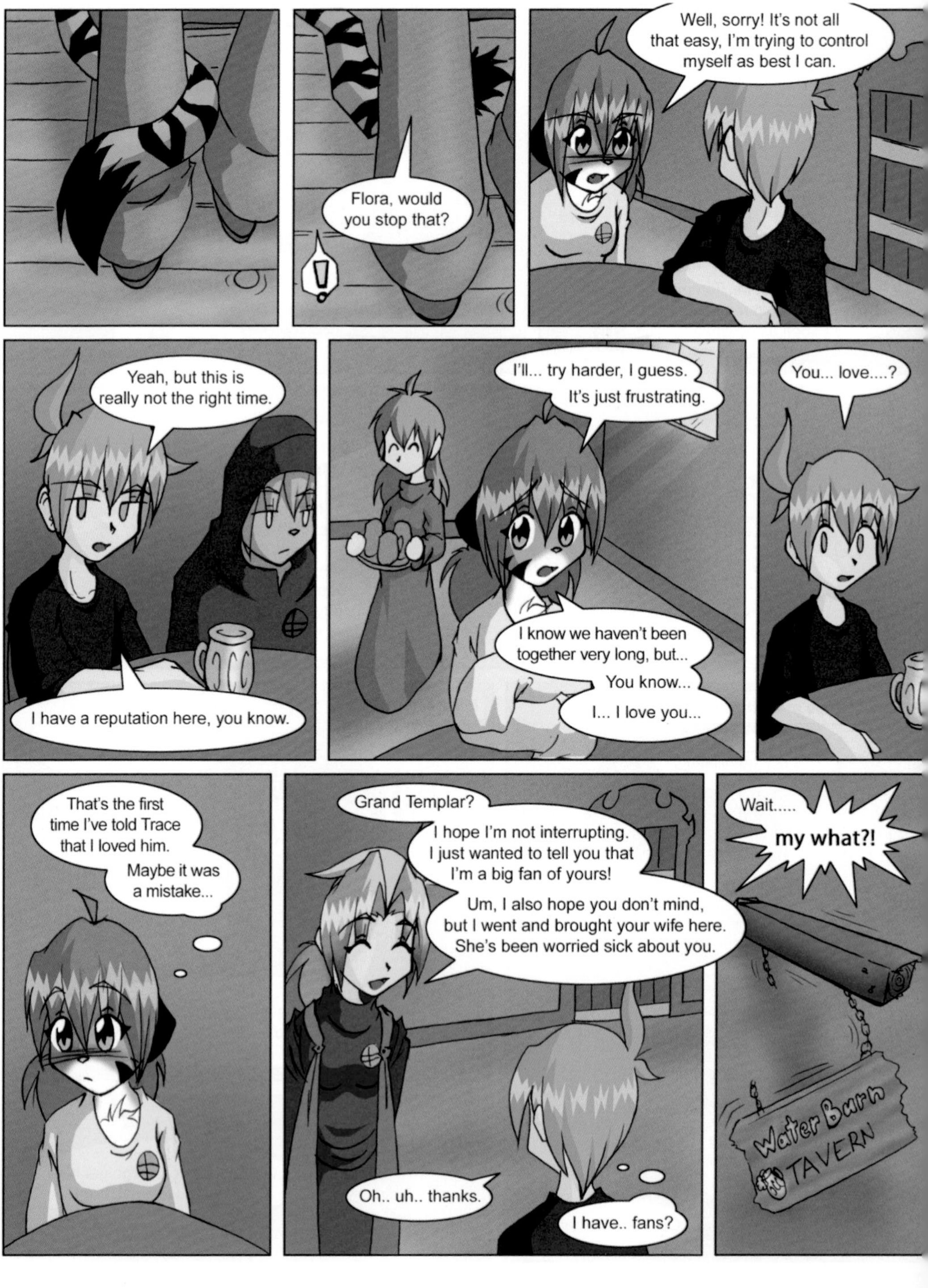
Flora, would you stop that?
!
Well, sorry! It's not all that easy, I'm trying to control myself as best I can.
Yeah, but this is really not the right time.
I have a reputation here, you know.
I'll... try harder, I guess.
It's just frustrating.
I know we haven't been together very long, but...
You know...
I... I love you...
You... love....?
That's the first time I've told Trace that I loved him.
Maybe it was a mistake...
Grand Templar?
I hope I'm not interrupting. I just wanted to tell you that I'm a big fan of yours!
Um, I also hope you don't mind, but I went and brought your wife here. She's been worried sick about you.
Oh.. uh.. thanks.
I have.. fans?
Wait.....
my what?!
Water Burn TAVERN

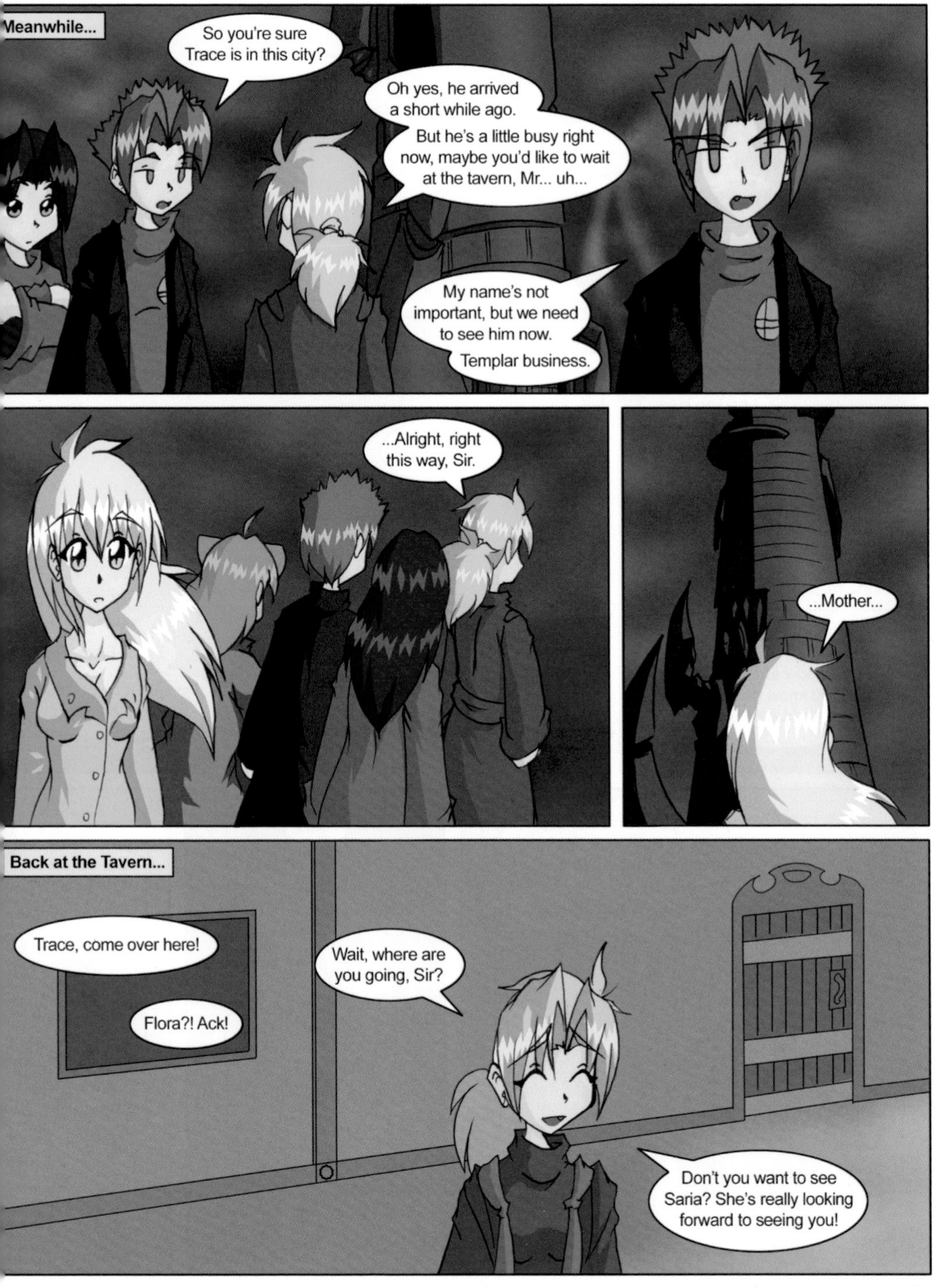
Meanwhile...
So you're sure Trace is in this city?
Oh yes, he arrived a short while ago.
But he's a little busy right now, maybe you'd like to wait at the tavern, Mr... uh...
My name's not important, but we need to see him now.
Templar business.
...Alright, right this way, Sir.
...Mother...
Back at the Tavern...
Trace, come over here!
Flora?! Ack!
Wait, where are you going, Sir?
Don't you want to see Saria? She's really looking forward to seeing you!

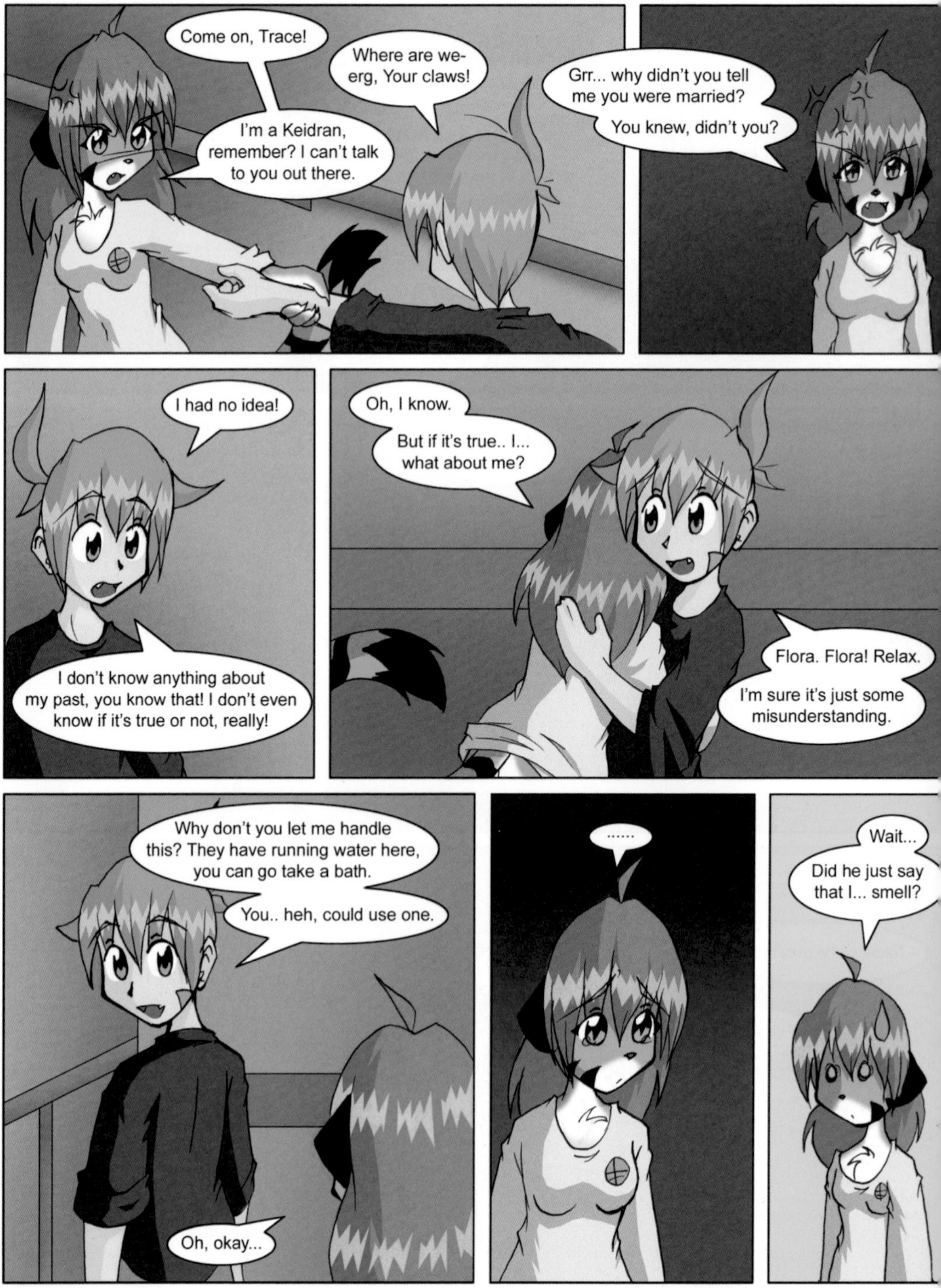

Come on, Trace!
Where are we-
erg, Your claws!
I'm a Keidran, remember? I can't talk to you out there.
Grr... why didn't you tell me you were married?
You knew, didn't you?
I had no idea!
I don't know anything about my past, you know that! I don't even know if it's true or not, really!
Oh, I know.
But if it's true.. I... what about me?
Flora. Flora! Relax.
I'm sure it's just some misunderstanding.
Why don't you let me handle this? They have running water here, you can go take a bath.
You.. heh, could use one.
Oh, okay...
......
Wait...
Did he just say that I... smell?

Darn that Trace.

I should have clawed his eyes out like I wanted to.

The jerk.

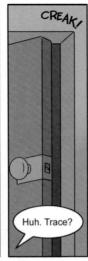

CREAK!

Huh. Trace?

Oh, hey, I didn't expect a Keidran in the public baths.

Ah! A human...

Can you talk? What's your name?

F-Flora...

Oh, mind if I join you, Flora?

I'm not here to hurt you.

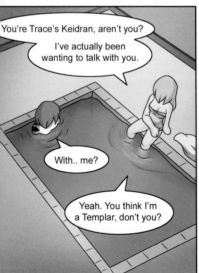

You're Trace's Keidran, aren't you?

I've actually been wanting to talk with you.

With.. me?

Yeah. You think I'm a Templar, don't you?

Truth is, I am. But I'm also a member of the **Resistance**.

I can help you if you want. I can get you out of here.

I can take you home!

Go... home..?

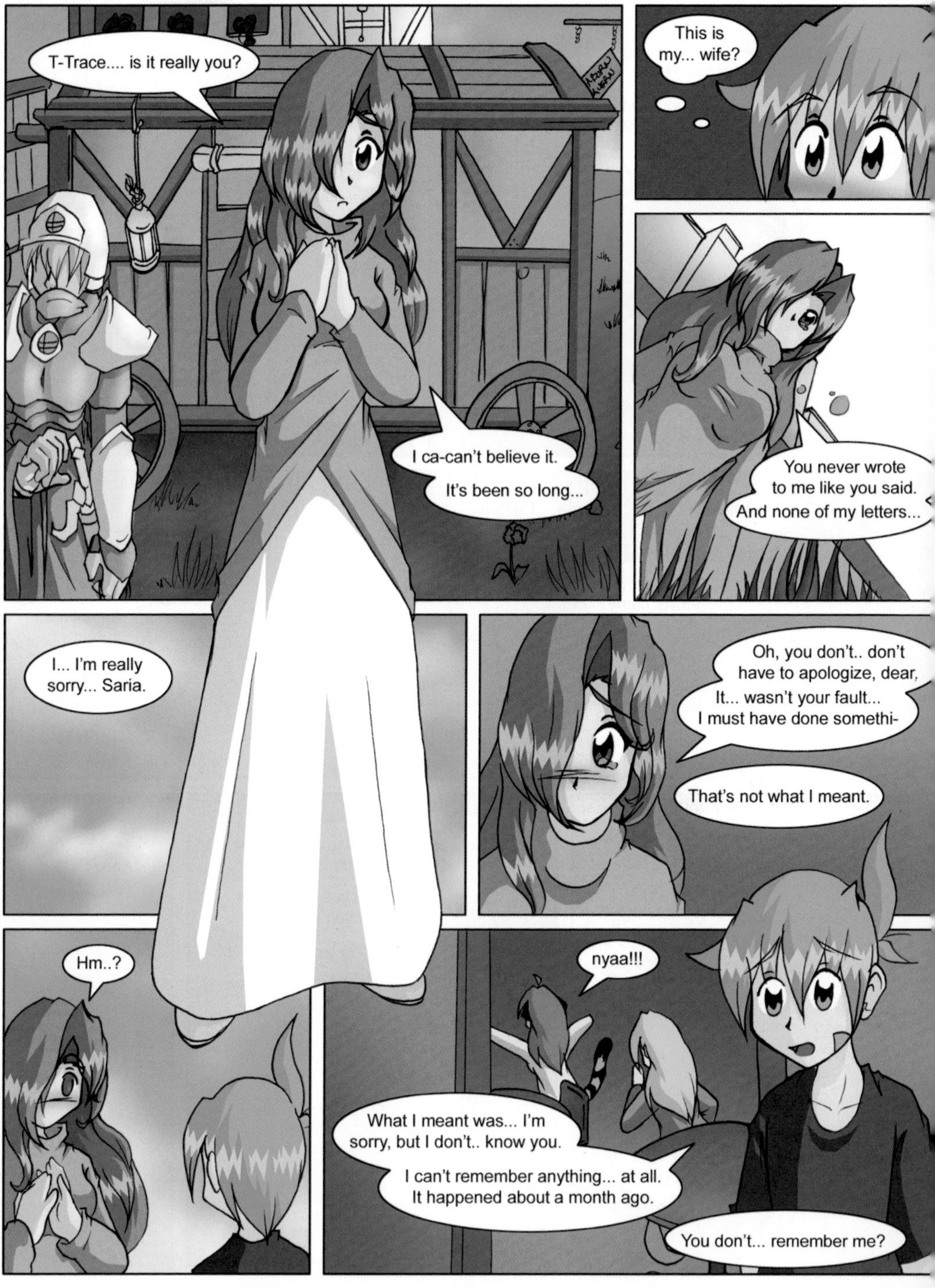

T-Trace.... is it really you?
I ca-can't believe it.
It's been so long...
This is my... wife?
You never wrote to me like you said. And none of my letters...
I... I'm really sorry... Saria.
Oh, you don't.. don't have to apologize, dear, It... wasn't your fault... I must have done somethi-
That's not what I meant.
Hm..?
nyaa!!!
What I meant was... I'm sorry, but I don't.. know you.
I can't remember anything... at all. It happened about a month ago.
You don't... remember me?

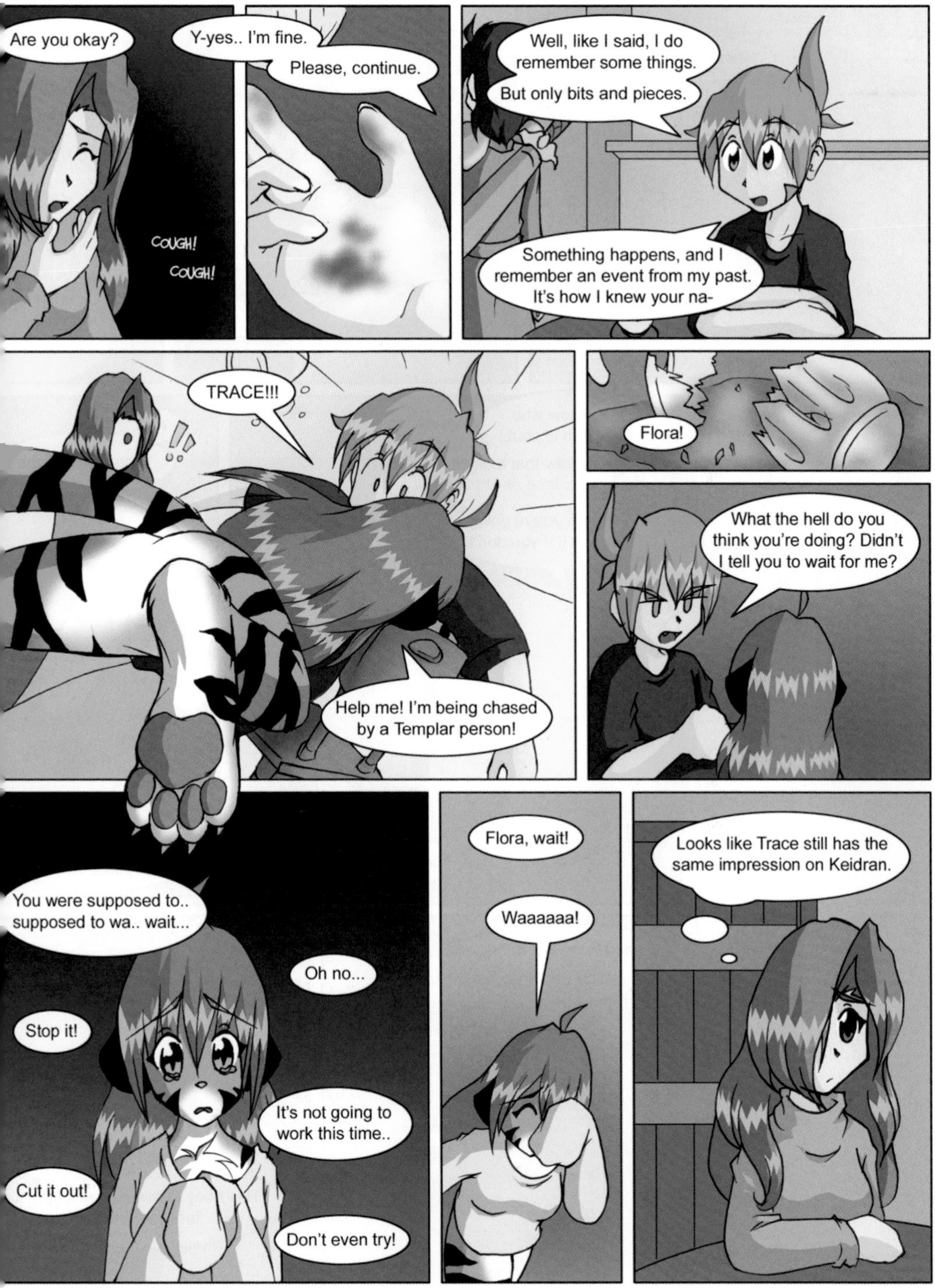
Are you okay?
COUGH!
COUGH!
Y-yes.. I'm fine.
Please, continue.
Well, like I said, I do remember some things.
But only bits and pieces.
Something happens, and I remember an event from my past. It's how I knew your na-
TRACE!!!
Help me! I'm being chased by a Templar person!
Flora!
What the hell do you think you're doing? Didn't I tell you to wait for me?
You were supposed to.. supposed to wa.. wait...
Oh no...
Stop it!
It's not going to work this time..
Cut it out!
Don't even try!
Flora, wait!
Waaaaaa!
Looks like Trace still has the same impression on Keidran.

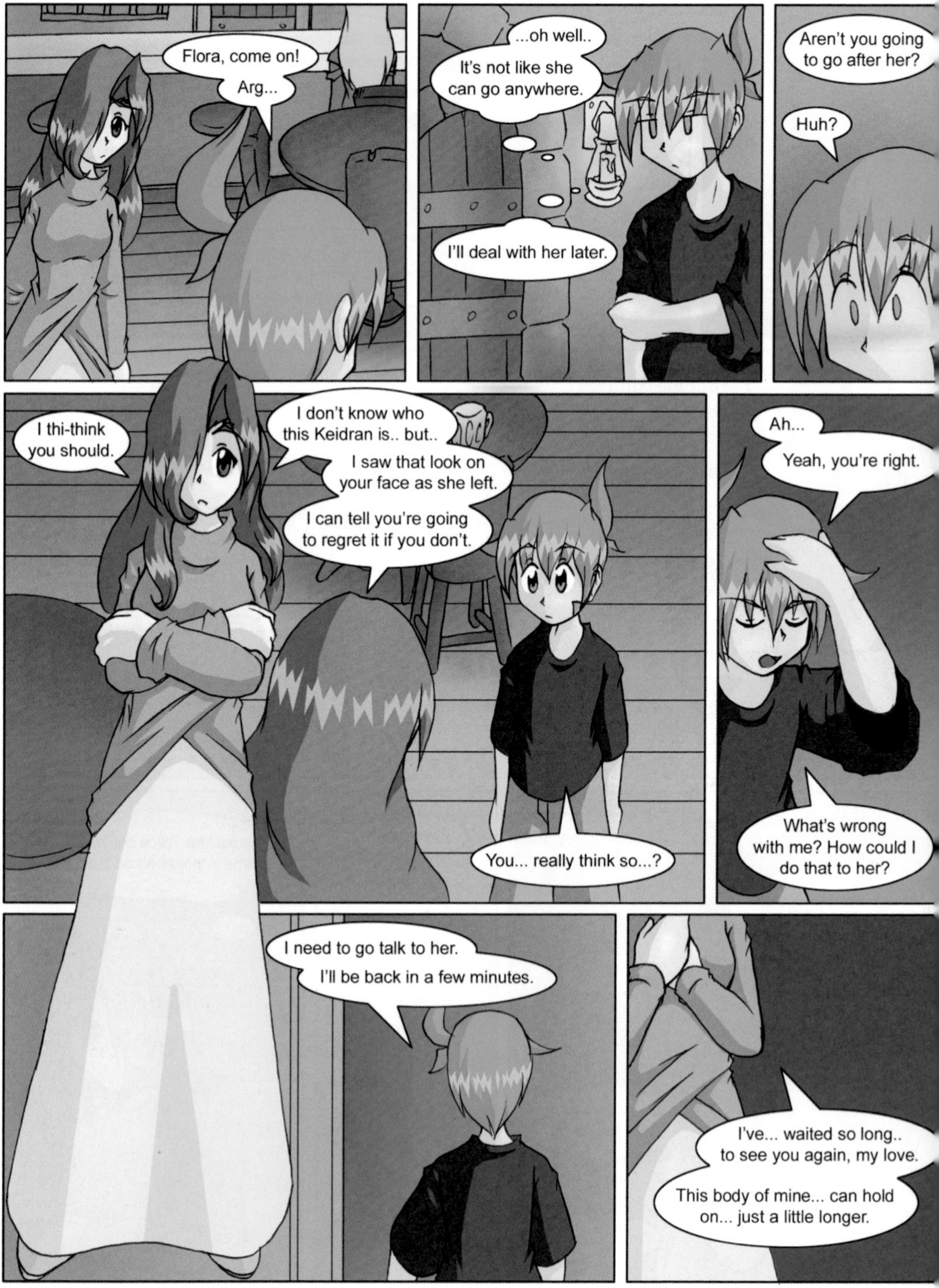
Flora, come on!
Arg...
...oh well..
It's not like she can go anywhere.
I'll deal with her later.
Aren't you going to go after her?
Huh?
I thi-think you should.
I don't know who this Keidran is.. but..
I saw that look on your face as she left.
I can tell you're going to regret it if you don't.
You... really think so...?
Ah...
Yeah, you're right.
What's wrong with me? How could I do that to her?
I need to go talk to her.
I'll be back in a few minutes.
I've... waited so long.. to see you again, my love.
This body of mine... can hold on... just a little longer.

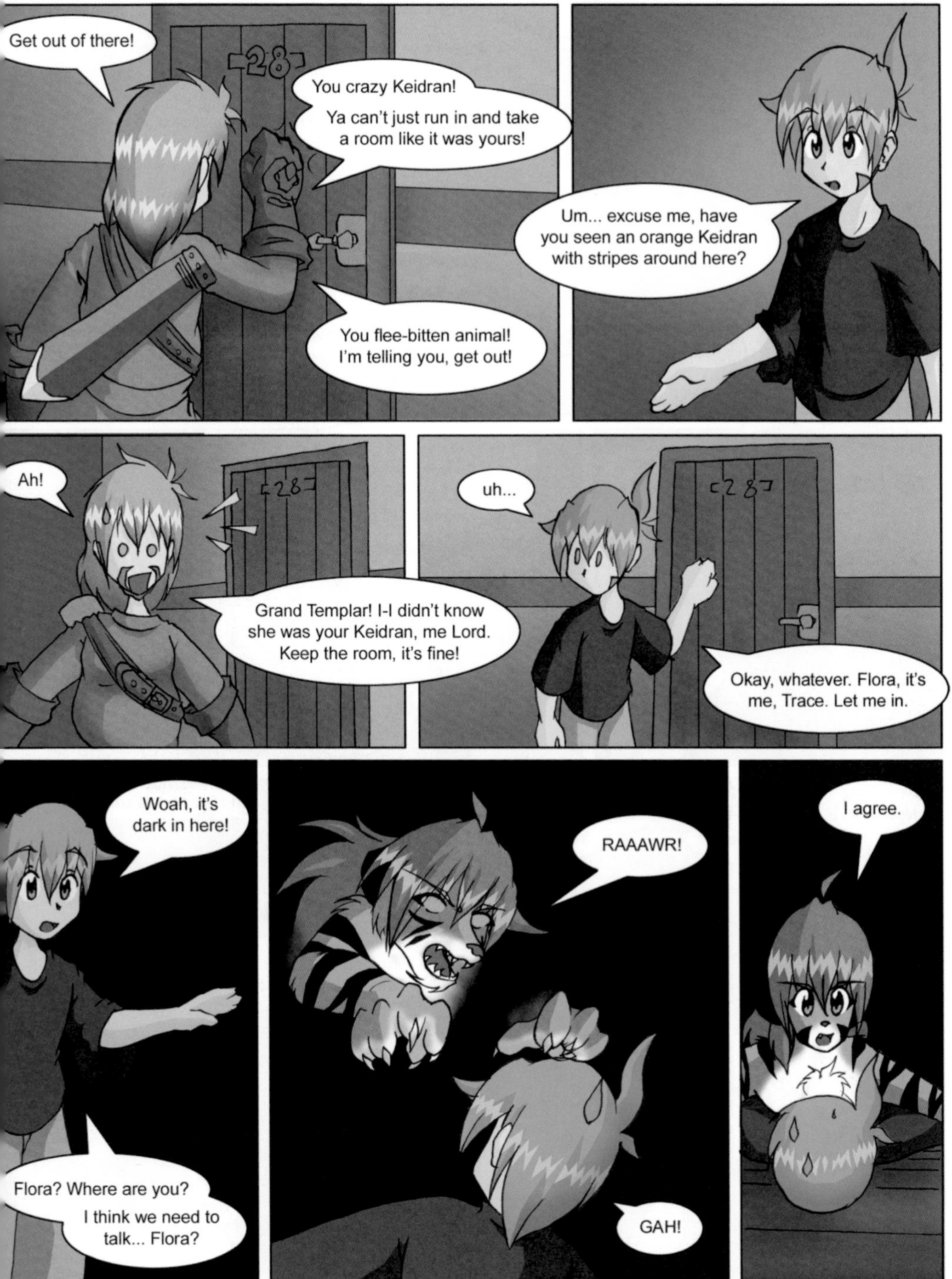
Get out of there!
You crazy Keidran!
Ya can't just run in and take a room like it was yours!
You flee-bitten animal! I'm telling you, get out!
Um... excuse me, have you seen an orange Keidran with stripes around here?
Ah!
Grand Templar! I-I didn't know she was your Keidran, me Lord. Keep the room, it's fine!
uh...
Okay, whatever. Flora, it's me, Trace. Let me in.
Woah, it's dark in here!
Flora? Where are you?
I think we need to talk... Flora?
RAAAWR!
GAH!
I agree.

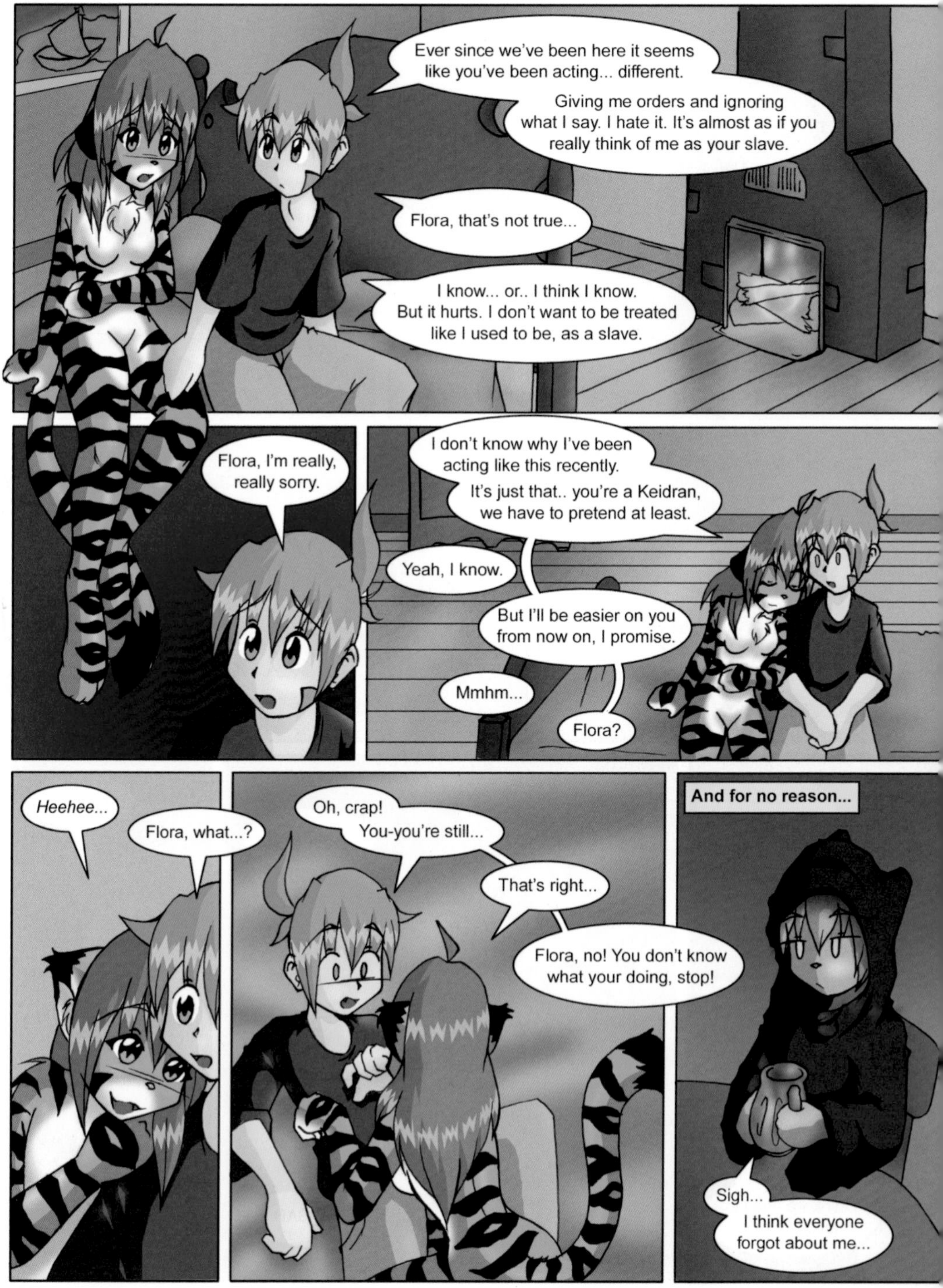

Ever since we've been here it seems like you've been acting... different.
Giving me orders and ignoring what I say. I hate it. It's almost as if you really think of me as your slave.
Flora, that's not true...
I know... or.. I think I know. But it hurts. I don't want to be treated like I used to be, as a slave.
Flora, I'm really, really sorry.
I don't know why I've been acting like this recently.
It's just that.. you're a Keidran, we have to pretend at least.
Yeah, I know.
But I'll be easier on you from now on, I promise.
Mmhm...
Flora?
Heehee...
Flora, what...?
Oh, crap!
You-you're still...
That's right...
Flora, no! You don't know what your doing, stop!
And for no reason...
Sigh...
I think everyone forgot about me...

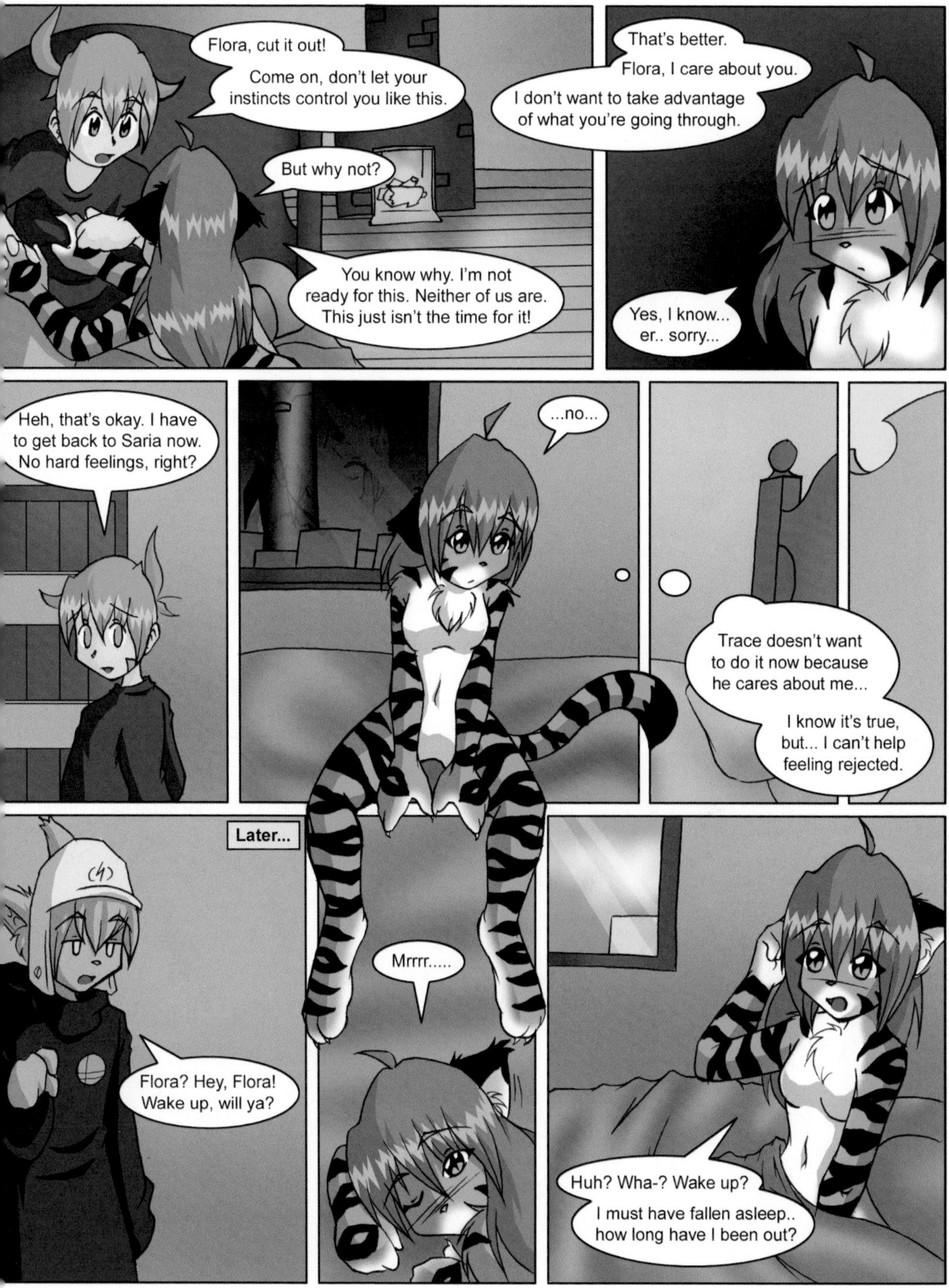
Flora, cut it out!
Come on, don't let your instincts control you like this.
But why not?
You know why. I'm not ready for this. Neither of us are. This just isn't the time for it!
That's better.
Flora, I care about you.
I don't want to take advantage of what you're going through.
Yes, I know... er.. sorry...
Heh, that's okay. I have to get back to Saria now. No hard feelings, right?
...no...
Trace doesn't want to do it now because he cares about me...
I know it's true, but... I can't help feeling rejected.
Later...
Flora? Hey, Flora! Wake up, will ya?
Mrrrr.....
Huh? Wha-? Wake up?
I must have fallen asleep.. how long have I been out?

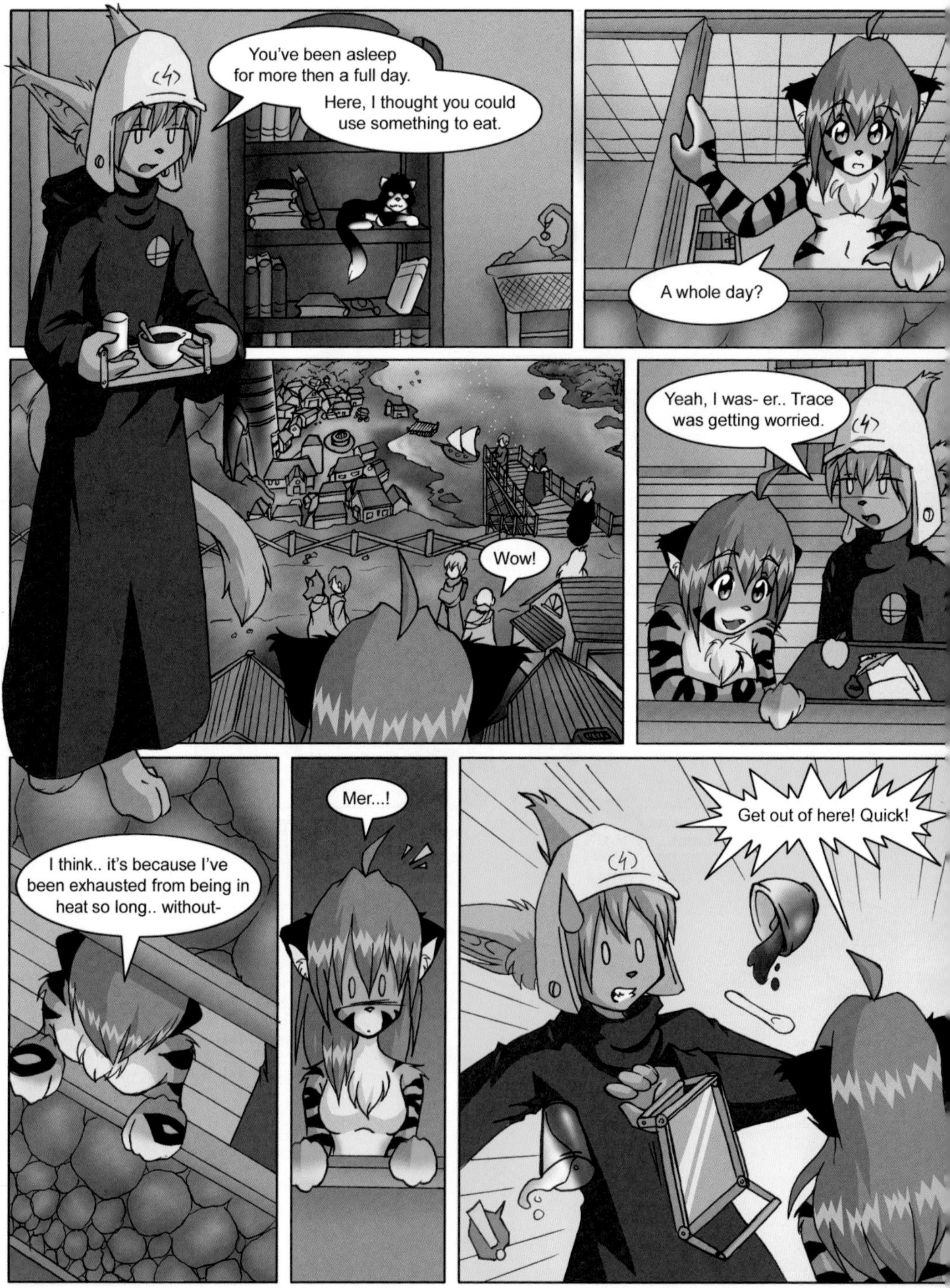
You've been asleep for more then a full day.
Here, I thought you could use something to eat.
A whole day?
Wow!
Yeah, I was- er.. Trace was getting worried.
I think.. it's because I've been exhausted from being in heat so long.. without-
Mer...!
Get out of here! Quick!

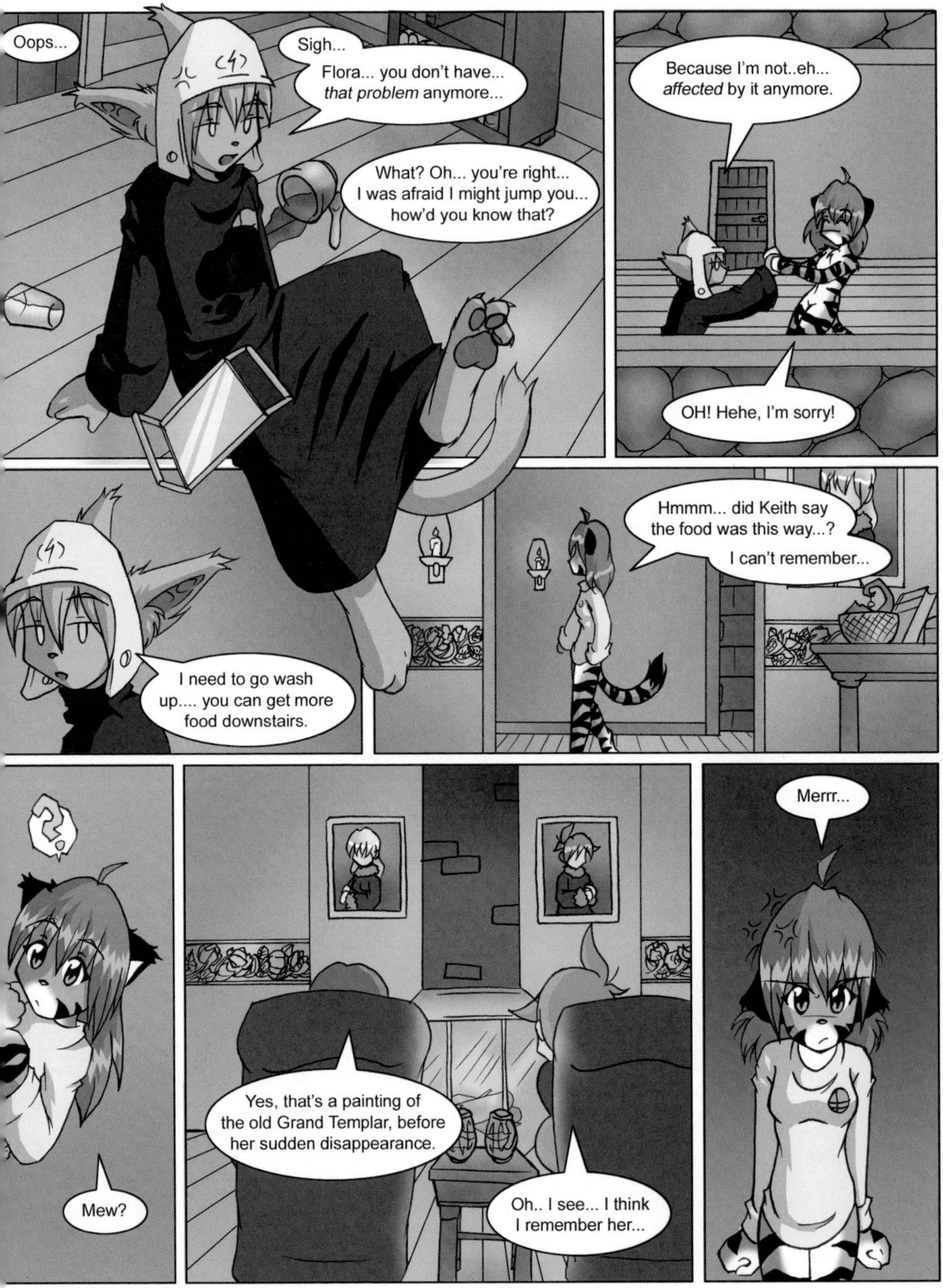
Oops...
Sigh...
Flora... you don't have... *that problem* anymore...
What? Oh... you're right... I was afraid I might jump you... how'd you know that?
Because I'm not..eh... *affected* by it anymore.
OH! Hehe, I'm sorry!
I need to go wash up.... you can get more food downstairs.
Hmmm... did Keith say the food was this way...?
I can't remember...
Mew?
Yes, that's a painting of the old Grand Templar, before her sudden disappearance.
Oh.. I see... I think I remember her...
Merrr...

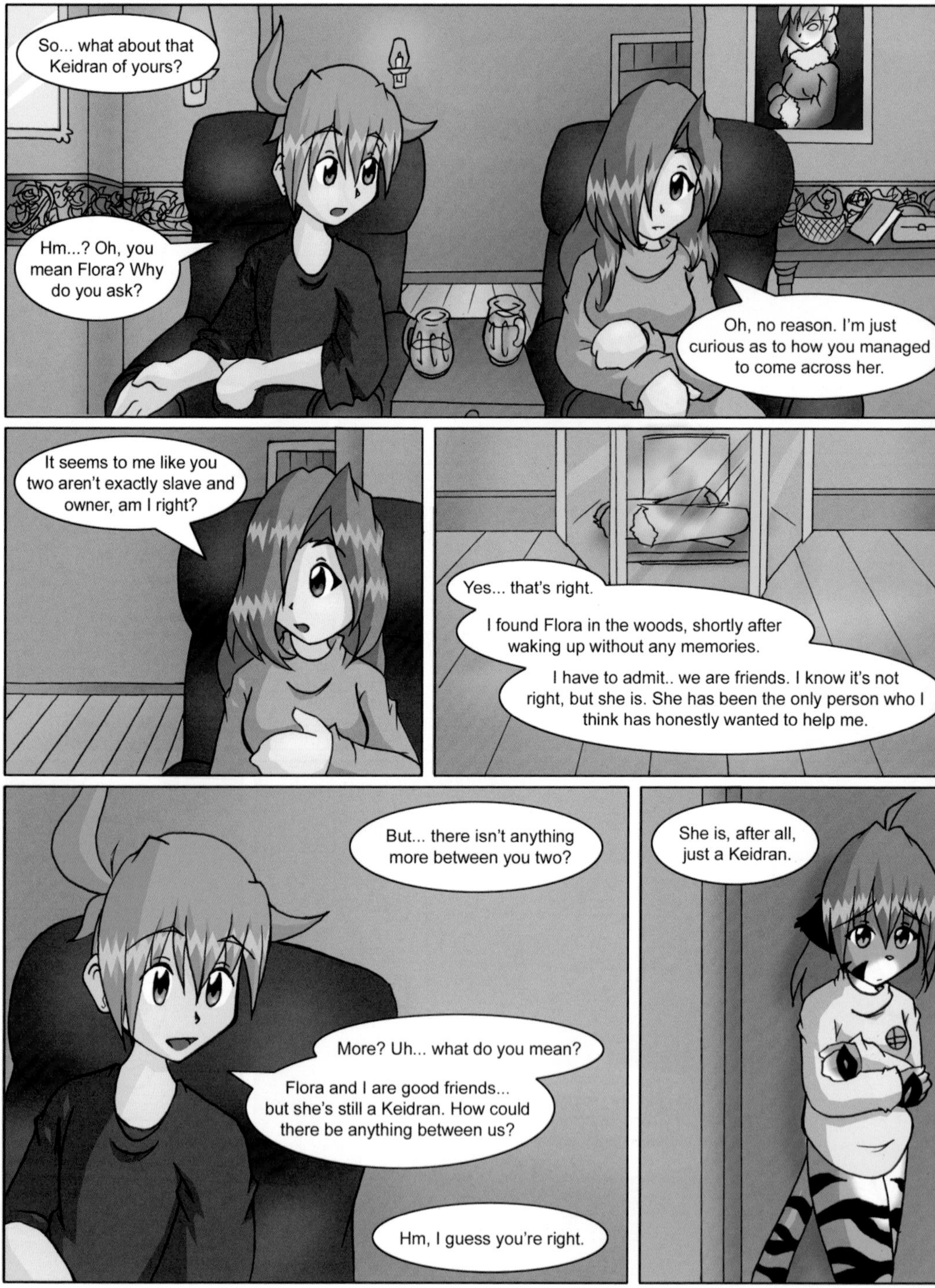
So... what about that Keidran of yours?
Hm...? Oh, you mean Flora? Why do you ask?
Oh, no reason. I'm just curious as to how you managed to come across her.
It seems to me like you two aren't exactly slave and owner, am I right?
Yes... that's right.
I found Flora in the woods, shortly after waking up without any memories.
I have to admit.. we are friends. I know it's not right, but she is. She has been the only person who I think has honestly wanted to help me.
But... there isn't anything more between you two?
More? Uh... what do you mean?
Flora and I are good friends... but she's still a Keidran. How could there be anything between us?
Hm, I guess you're right.
She is, after all, just a Keidran.

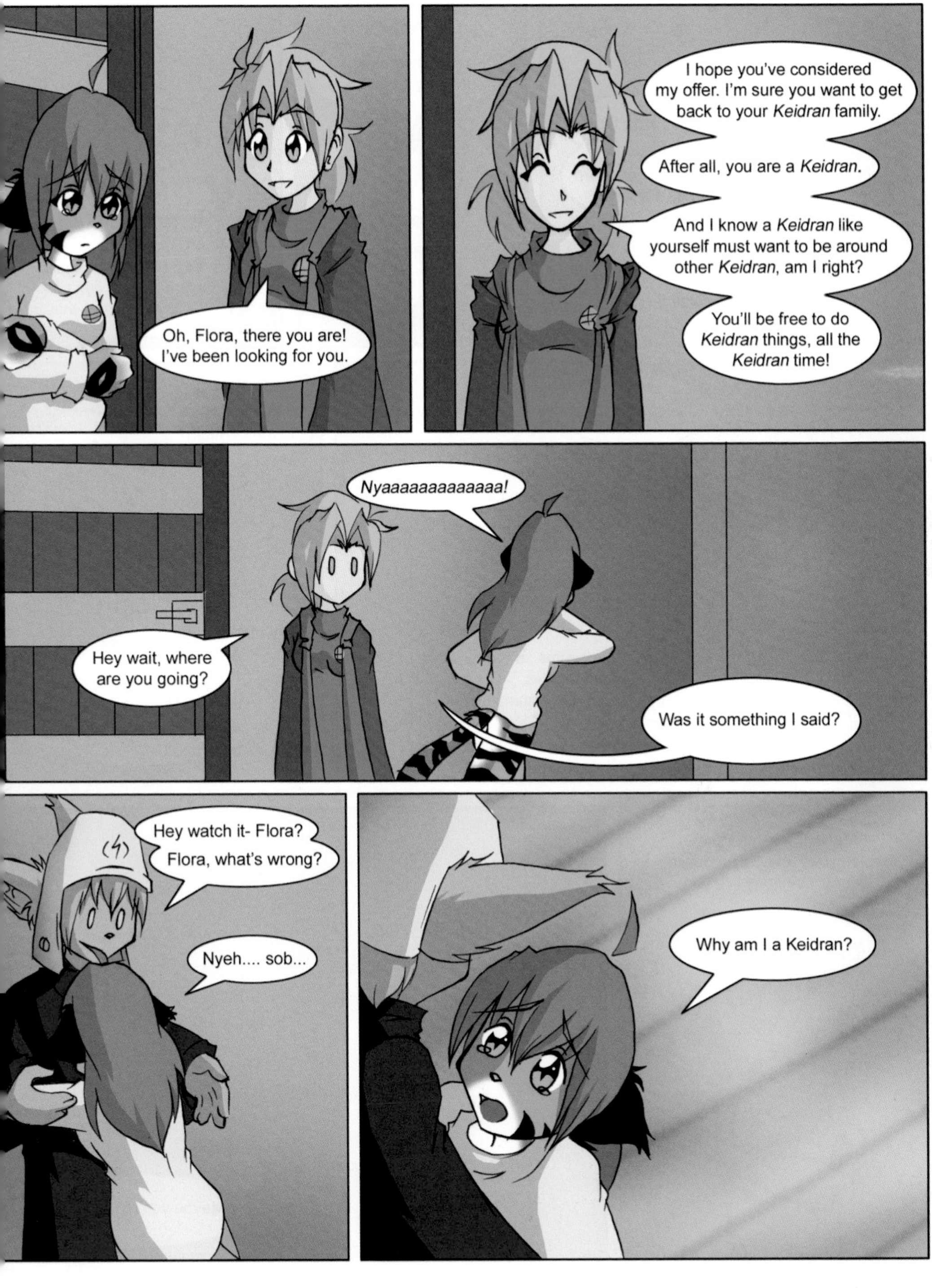
Oh, Flora, there you are!
I've been looking for you.
I hope you've considered my offer. I'm sure you want to get back to your *Keidran* family.
After all, you are a *Keidran*.
And I know a *Keidran* like yourself must want to be around other *Keidran*, am I right?
You'll be free to do *Keidran* things, all the *Keidran* time!
Nyaaaaaaaaaaaaa!
Hey wait, where are you going?
Was it something I said?
Hey watch it- Flora?
Flora, what's wrong?
Nyeh.... sob...
Why am I a Keidran?

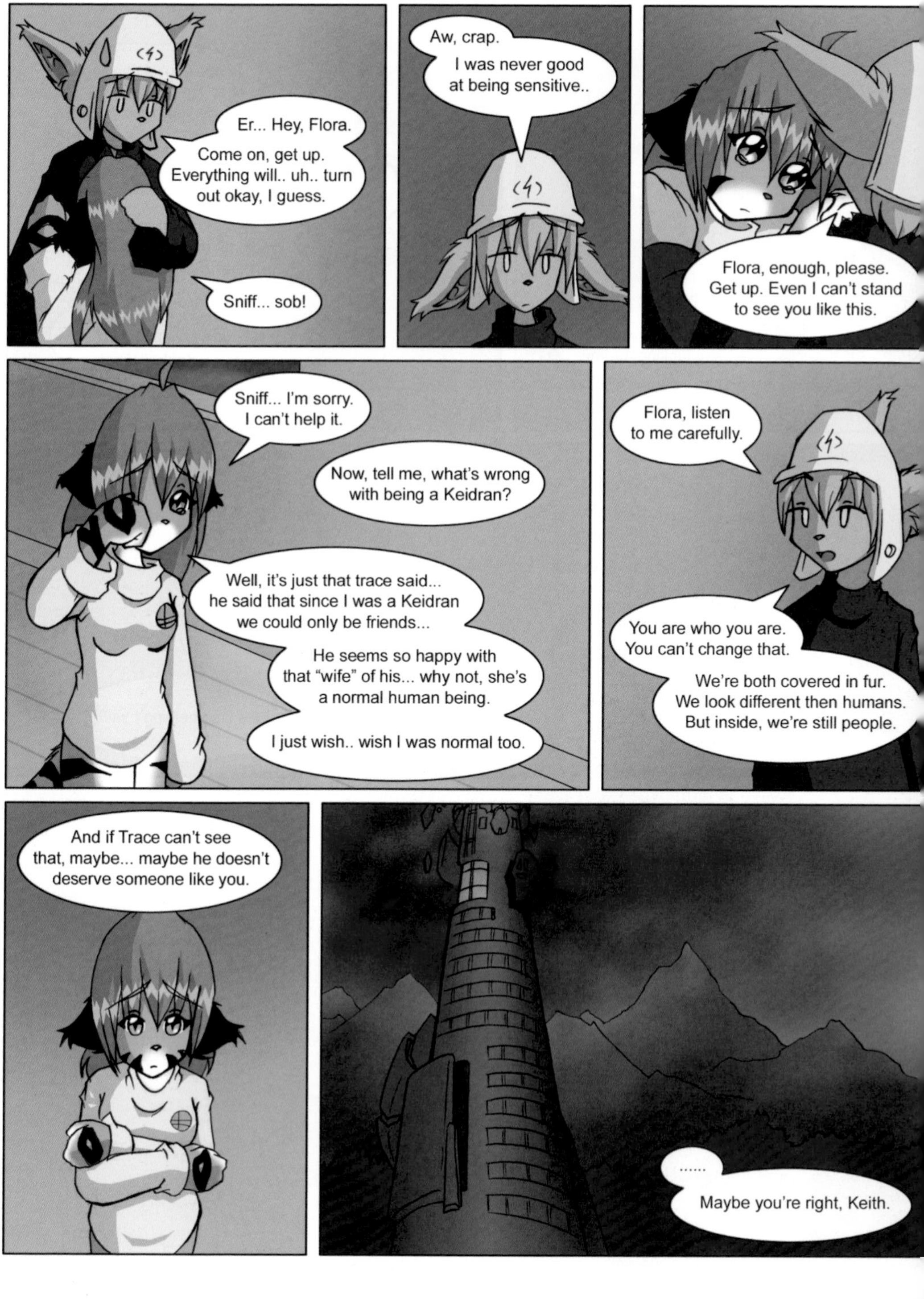

Er... Hey, Flora.
Come on, get up. Everything will.. uh.. turn out okay, I guess.
Sniff... sob!
Aw, crap.
I was never good at being sensitive..
Flora, enough, please. Get up. Even I can't stand to see you like this.
Sniff... I'm sorry. I can't help it.
Now, tell me, what's wrong with being a Keidran?
Well, it's just that trace said... he said that since I was a Keidran we could only be friends...
He seems so happy with that "wife" of his... why not, she's a normal human being.
I just wish.. wish I was normal too.
Flora, listen to me carefully.
You are who you are. You can't change that.
We're both covered in fur. We look different then humans. But inside, we're still people.
And if Trace can't see that, maybe... maybe he doesn't deserve someone like you.
......
Maybe you're right, Keith.

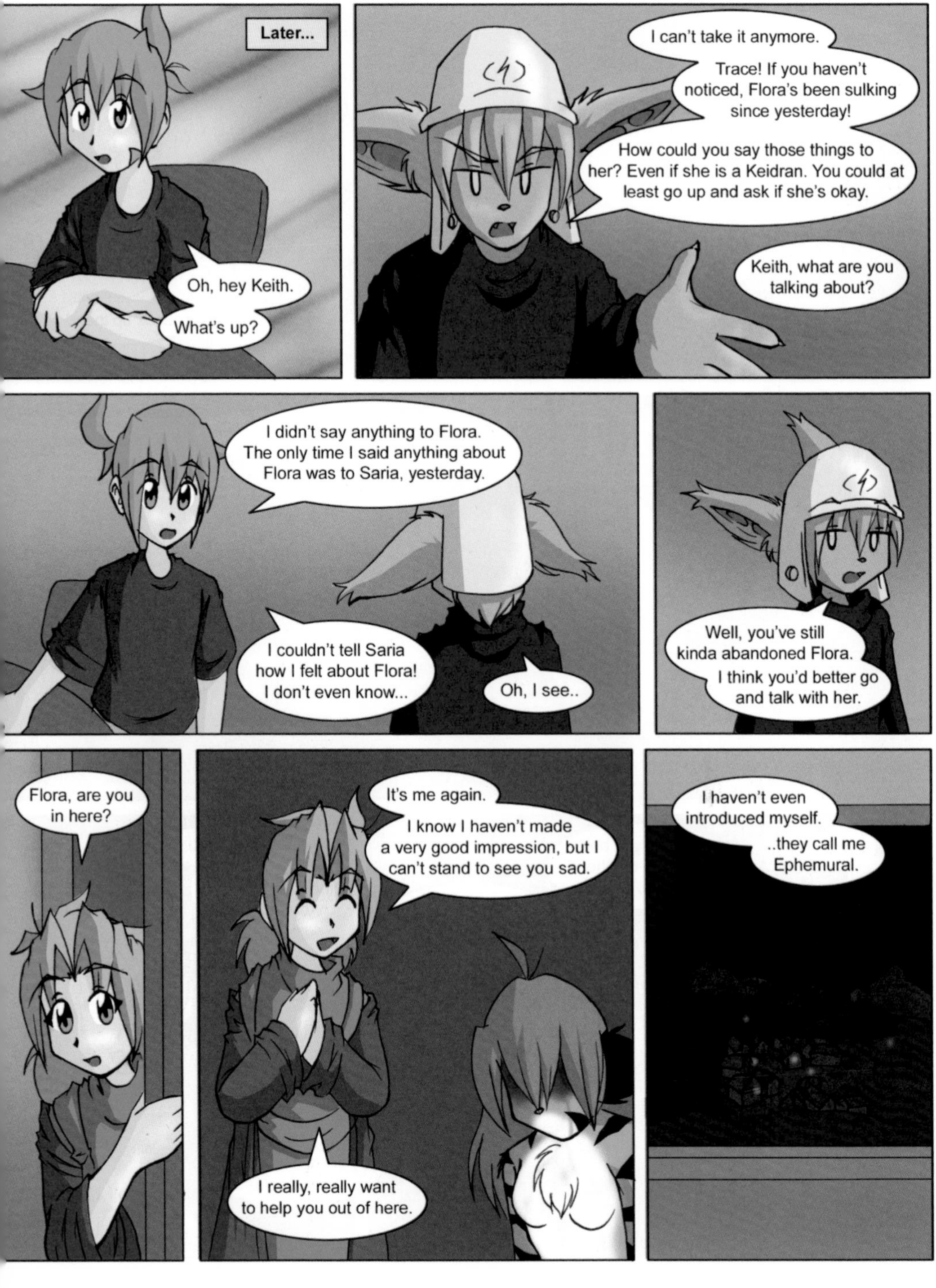
Later...
Oh, hey Keith.
What's up?
I can't take it anymore.
Trace! If you haven't noticed, Flora's been sulking since yesterday!
How could you say those things to her? Even if she is a Keidran. You could at least go up and ask if she's okay.
Keith, what are you talking about?
I didn't say anything to Flora. The only time I said anything about Flora was to Saria, yesterday.
I couldn't tell Saria how I felt about Flora! I don't even know...
Oh, I see..
Well, you've still kinda abandoned Flora.
I think you'd better go and talk with her.
Flora, are you in here?
It's me again.
I know I haven't made a very good impression, but I can't stand to see you sad.
I really, really want to help you out of here.
I haven't even introduced myself.
..they call me Ephemural.

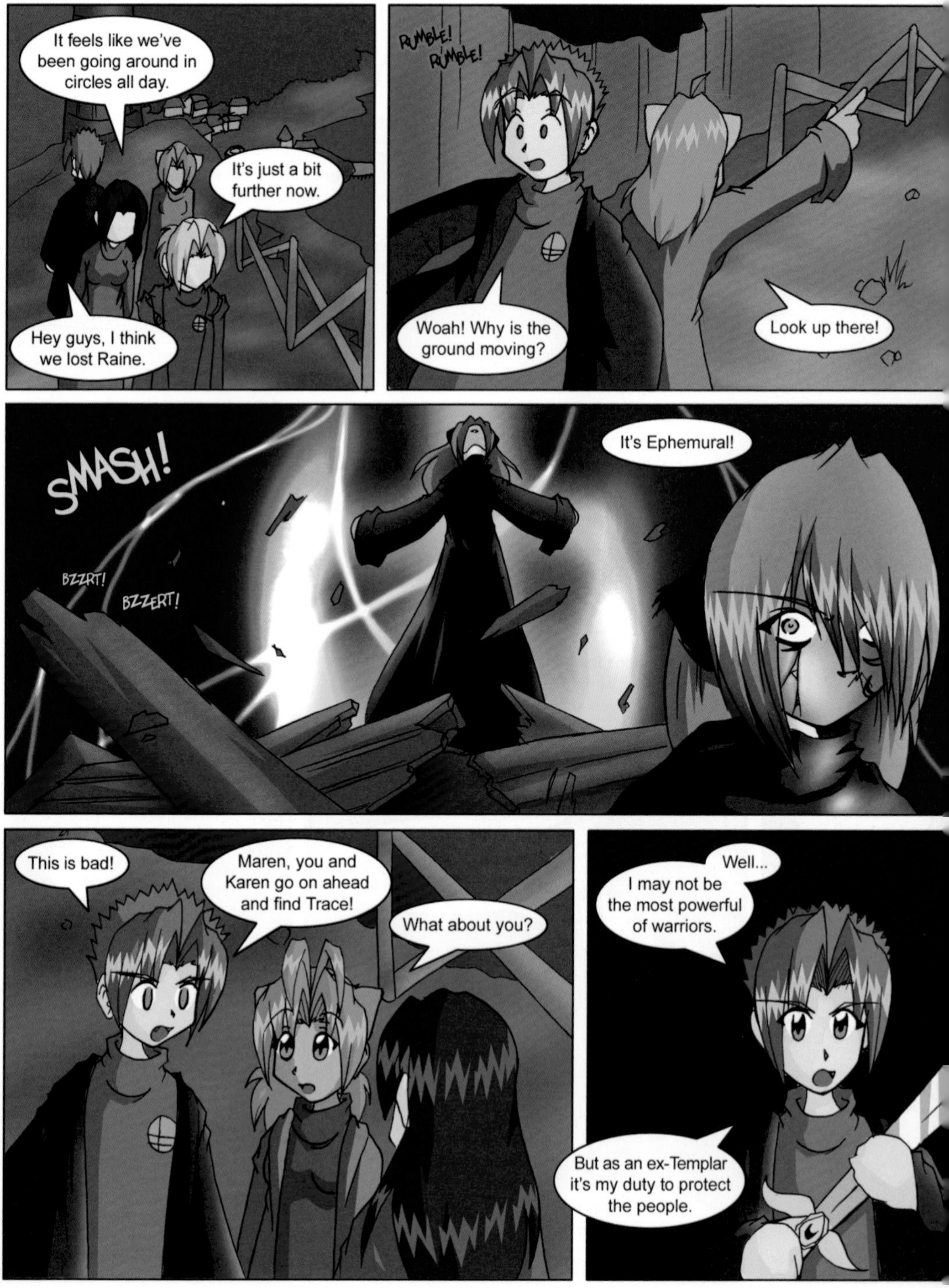

It feels like we've been going around in circles all day.
It's just a bit further now.
Hey guys, I think we lost Raine.
RUMBLE! RUMBLE!
Woah! Why is the ground moving?
Look up there!
SMASH!
BZZRT!
BZZERT!
It's Ephemural!
This is bad!
Maren, you and Karen go on ahead and find Trace!
What about you?
Well...
I may not be the most powerful of warriors.
But as an ex-Templar it's my duty to protect the people.

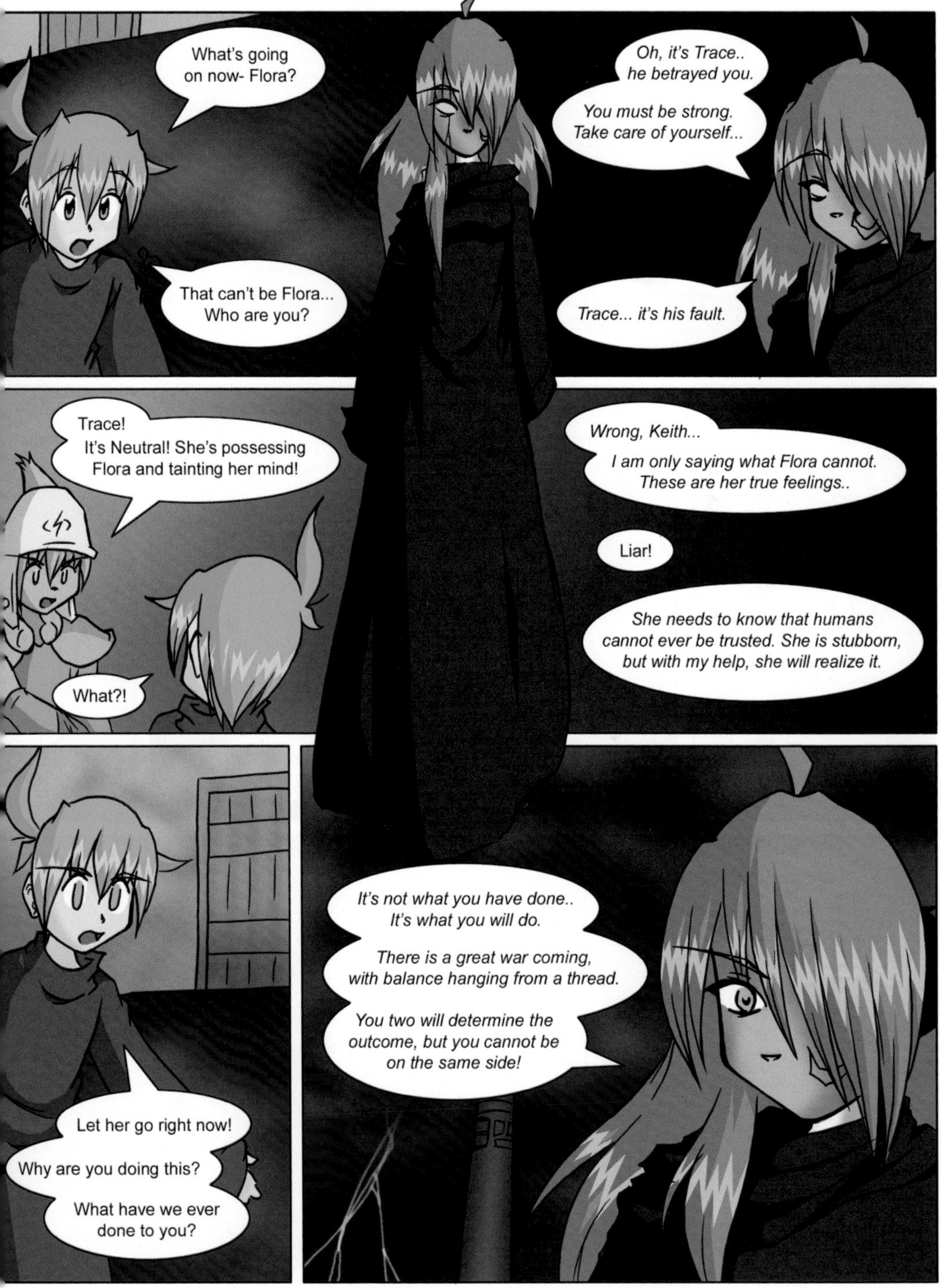

What's going on now- Flora?
That can't be Flora... Who are you?
Oh, it's Trace.. he betrayed you.
You must be strong. Take care of yourself...
Trace... it's his fault.
Trace! It's Neutral! She's possessing Flora and tainting her mind!
What?!
Wrong, Keith... I am only saying what Flora cannot. These are her true feelings..
Liar!
She needs to know that humans cannot ever be trusted. She is stubborn, but with my help, she will realize it.
Let her go right now!
Why are you doing this?
What have we ever done to you?
It's not what you have done.. It's what you will do.
There is a great war coming, with balance hanging from a thread.
You two will determine the outcome, but you cannot be on the same side!

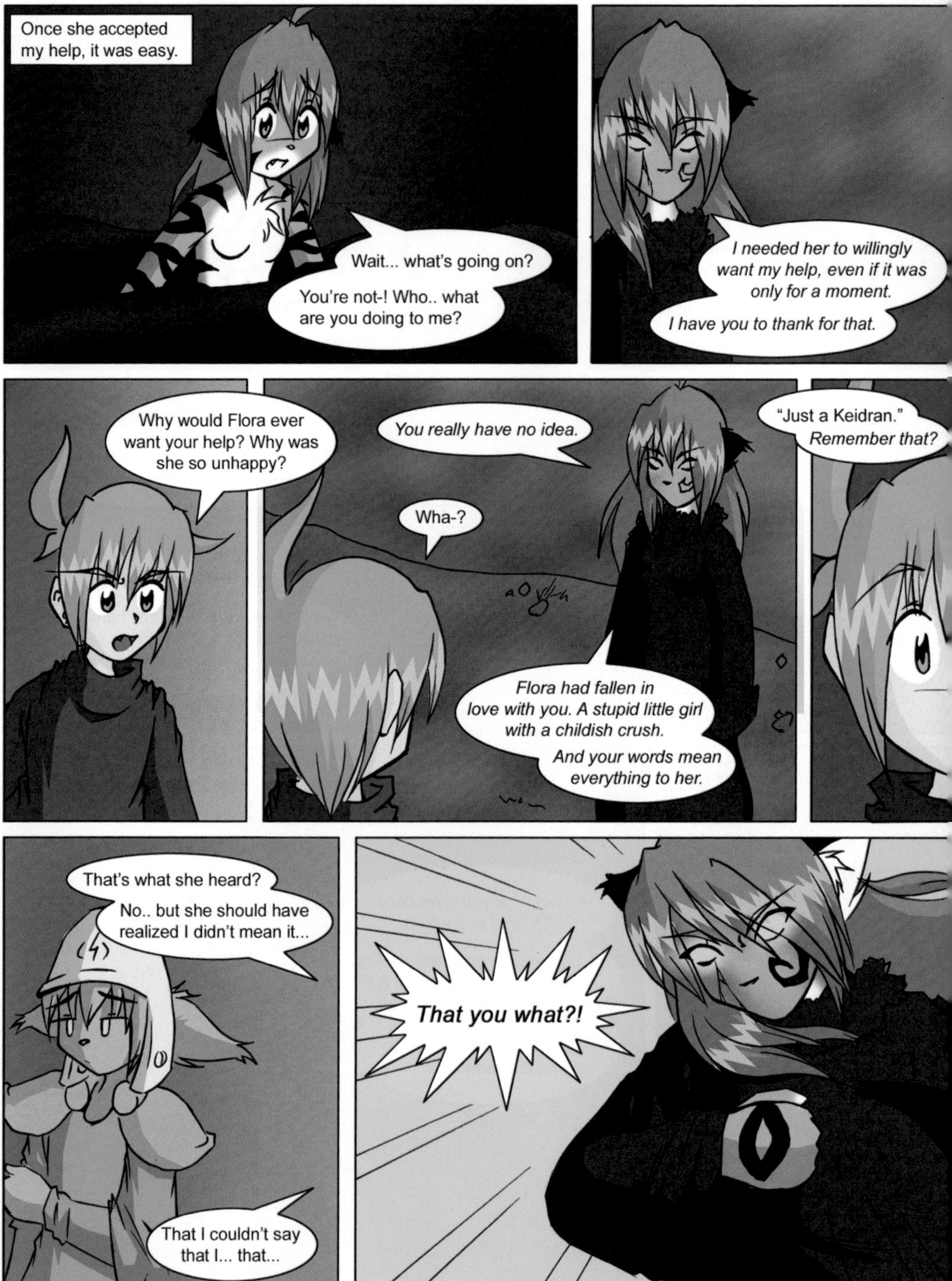
Once she accepted my help, it was easy.
Wait... what's going on?
You're not-! Who.. what are you doing to me?
I needed her to willingly want my help, even if it was only for a moment.
I have you to thank for that.
Why would Flora ever want your help? Why was she so unhappy?
You really have no idea.
Wha-?
Flora had fallen in love with you. A stupid little girl with a childish crush.
And your words mean everything to her.
"Just a Keidran."
Remember that?
That's what she heard?
No.. but she should have realized I didn't mean it...
That I couldn't say that I... that...
That you what?!

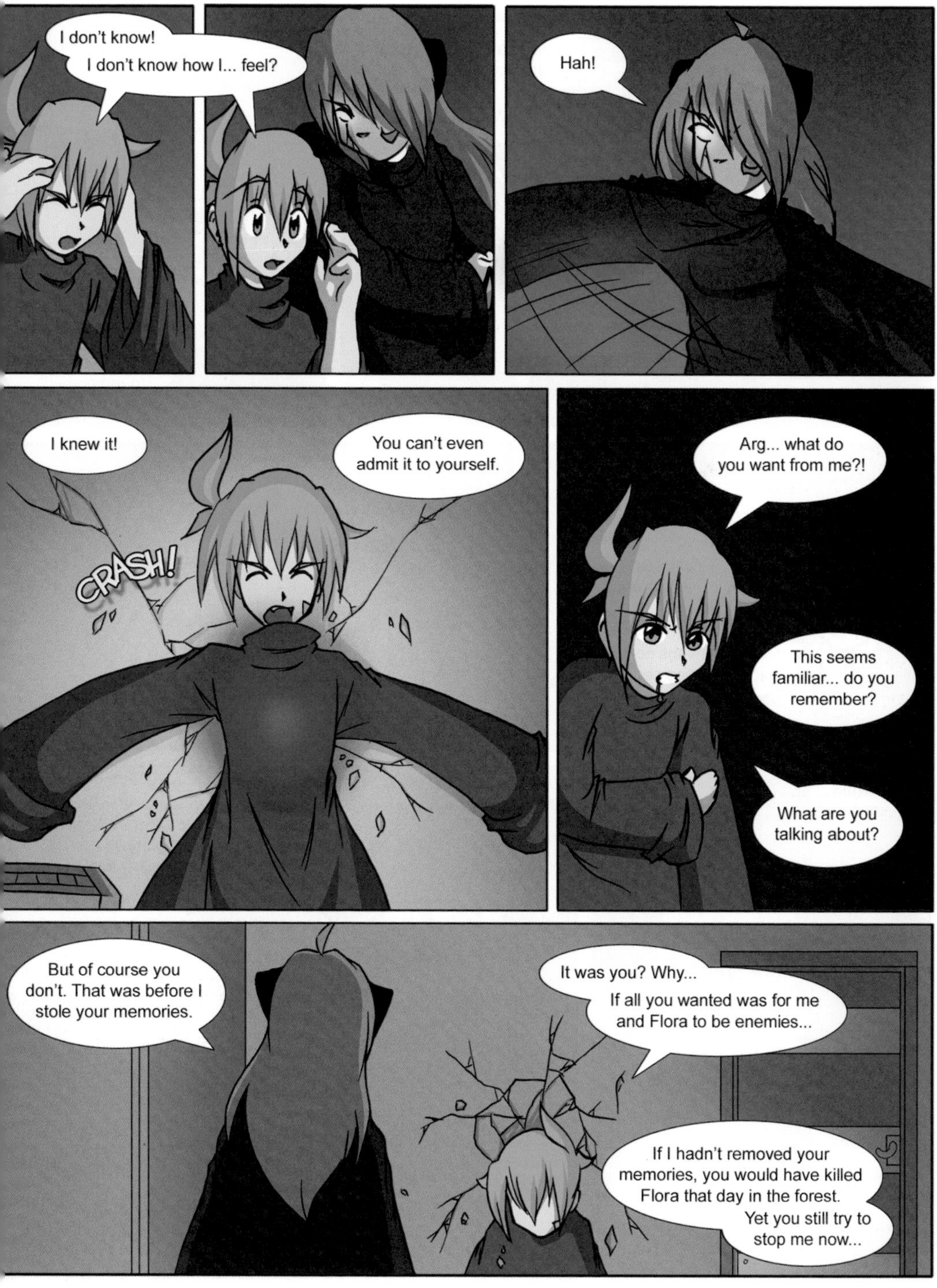
I don't know!
I don't know how I... feel?
Hah!
I knew it!
You can't even admit it to yourself.
CRASH!
Arg... what do you want from me?!
This seems familiar... do you remember?
What are you talking about?
But of course you don't. That was before I stole your memories.
It was you? Why...
If all you wanted was for me and Flora to be enemies...
If I hadn't removed your memories, you would have killed Flora that day in the forest.
Yet you still try to stop me now...

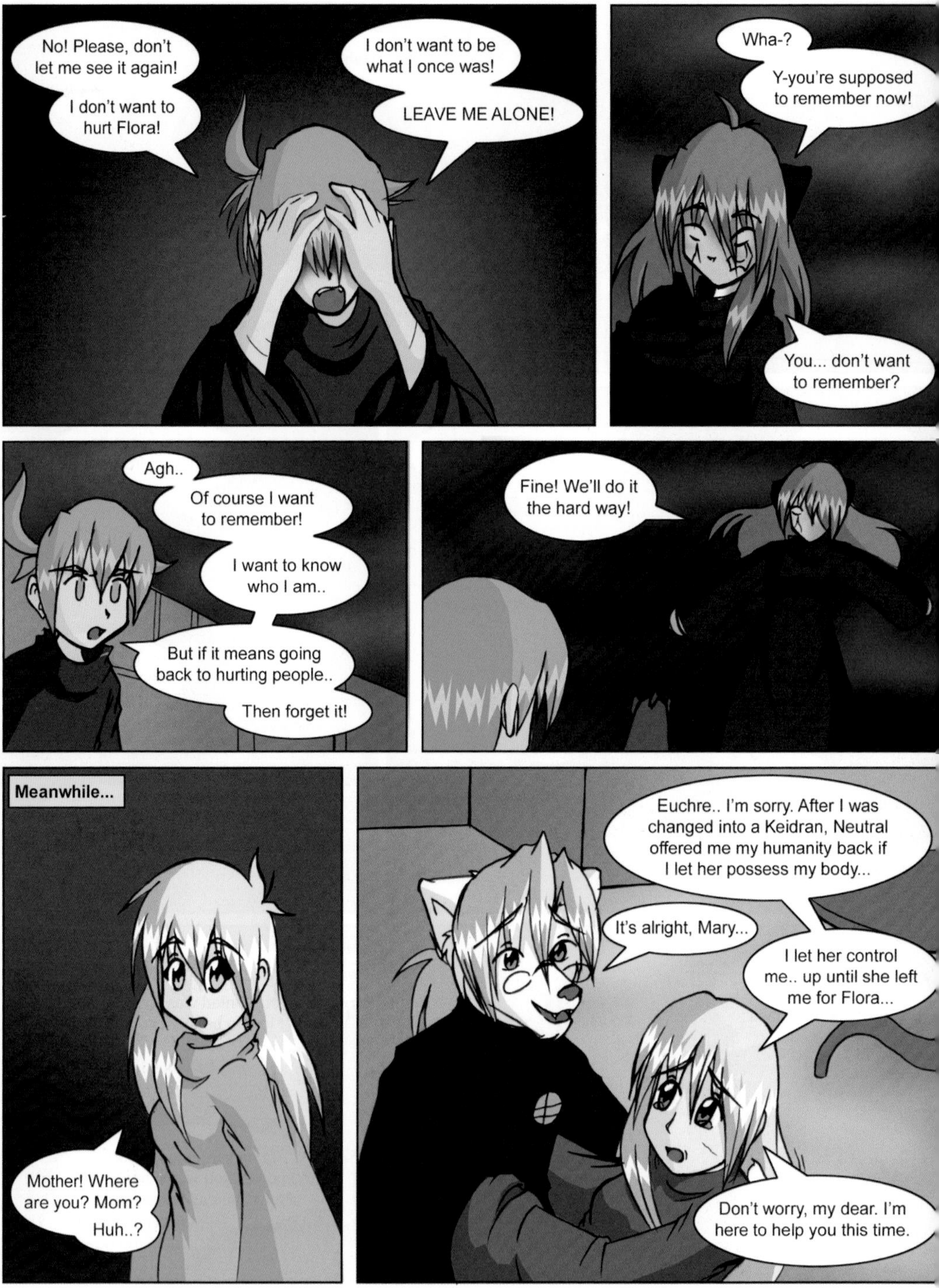
No! Please, don't let me see it again!
I don't want to hurt Flora!
I don't want to be what I once was!
LEAVE ME ALONE!
Wha-?
Y-you're supposed to remember now!
You... don't want to remember?
Agh..
Of course I want to remember!
I want to know who I am..
But if it means going back to hurting people..
Then forget it!
Fine! We'll do it the hard way!
Meanwhile...
Mother! Where are you? Mom?
Huh..?
Euchre.. I'm sorry. After I was changed into a Keidran, Neutral offered me my humanity back if I let her possess my body...
It's alright, Mary...
I let her control me.. up until she left me for Flora...
Don't worry, my dear. I'm here to help you this time.

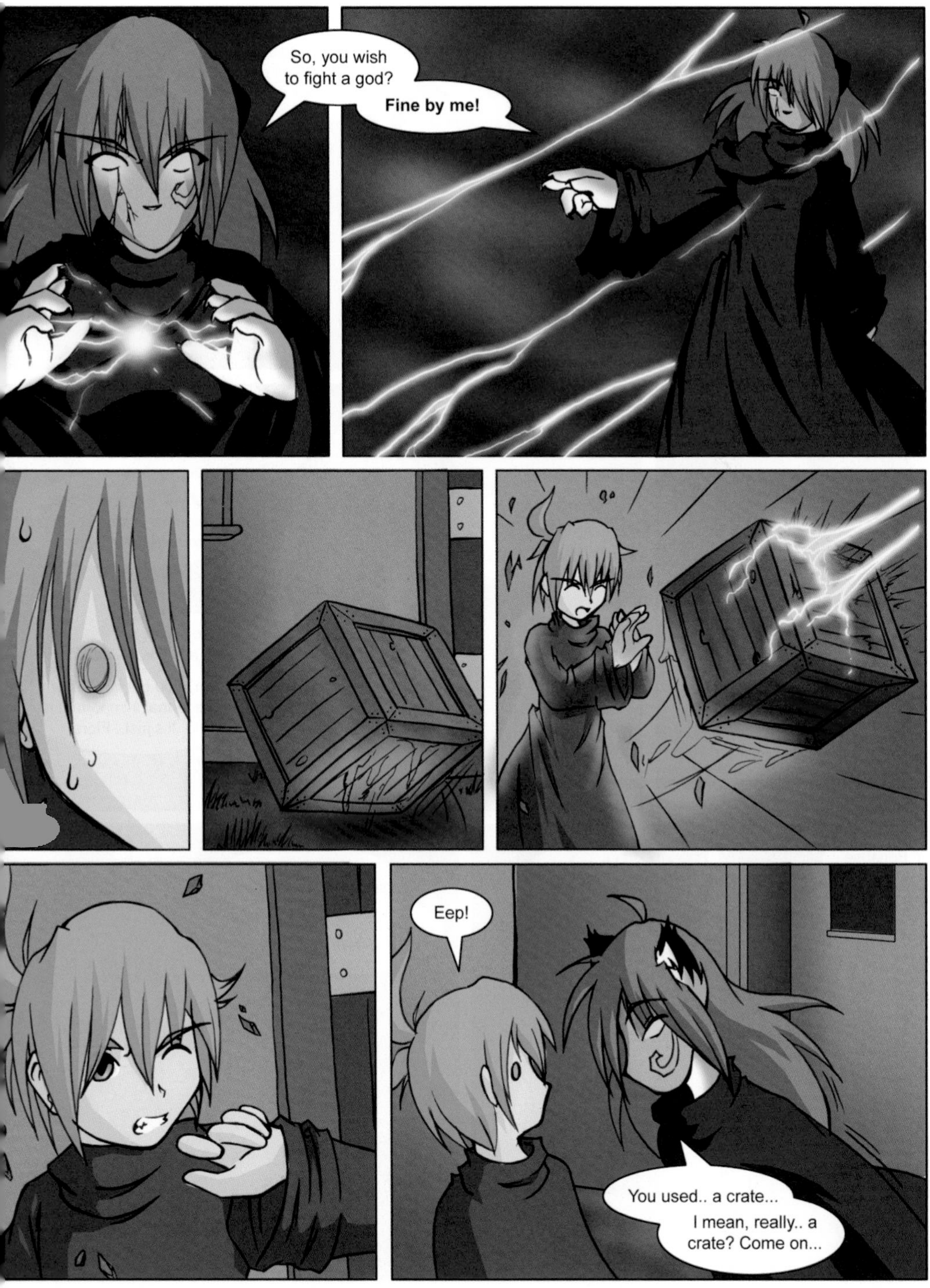
So, you wish to fight a god?
Fine by me!
Eep!
You used.. a crate...
I mean, really.. a crate? Come on...

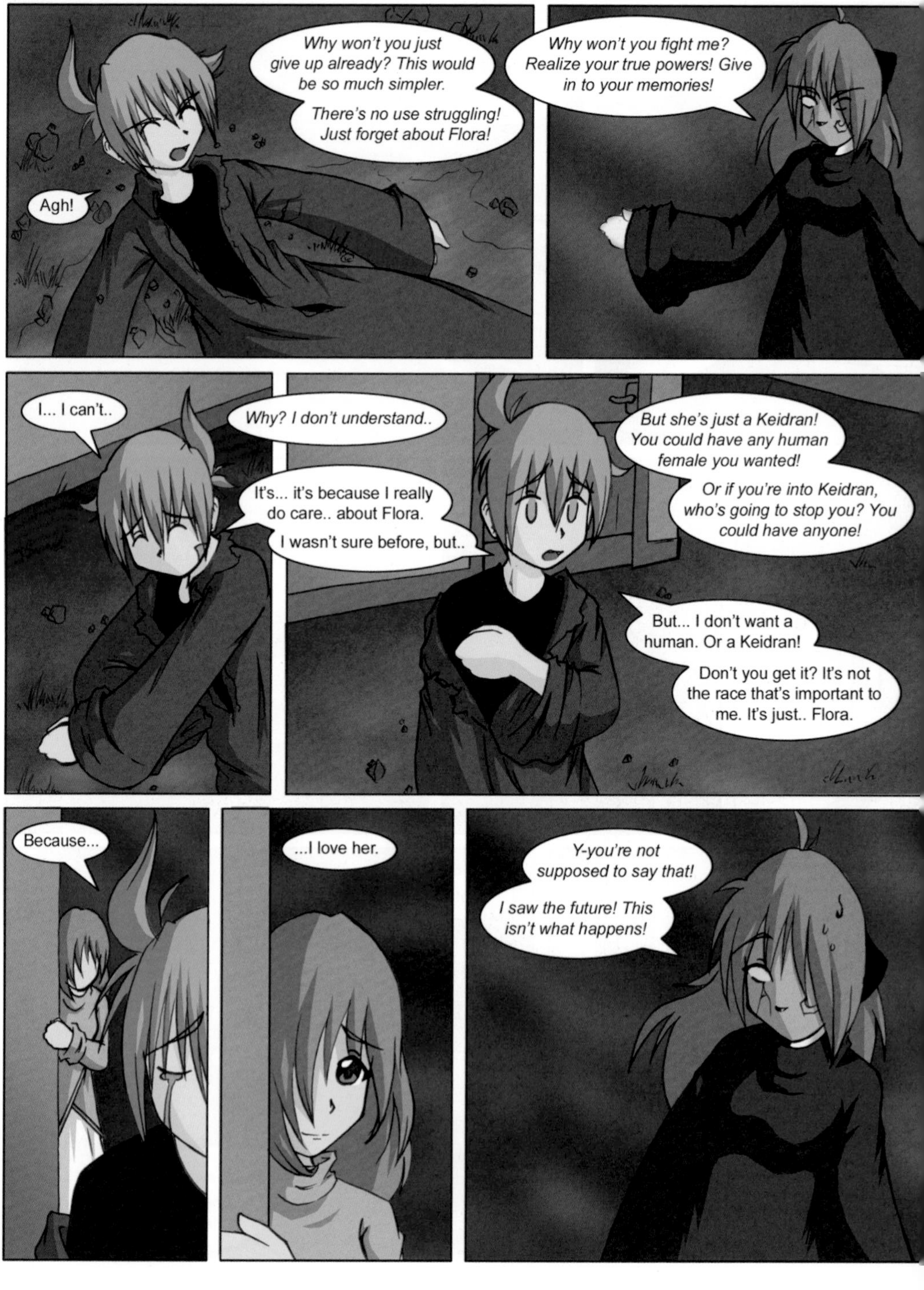

Why won't you just give up already? This would be so much simpler.
There's no use struggling! Just forget about Flora!
Agh!
Why won't you fight me? Realize your true powers! Give in to your memories!
I... I can't..
Why? I don't understand..
It's... it's because I really do care.. about Flora.
I wasn't sure before, but..
But she's just a Keidran! You could have any human female you wanted!
Or if you're into Keidran, who's going to stop you? You could have anyone!
But... I don't want a human. Or a Keidran!
Don't you get it? It's not the race that's important to me. It's just.. Flora.
Because...
...I love her.
Y-you're not supposed to say that!
I saw the future! This isn't what happens!

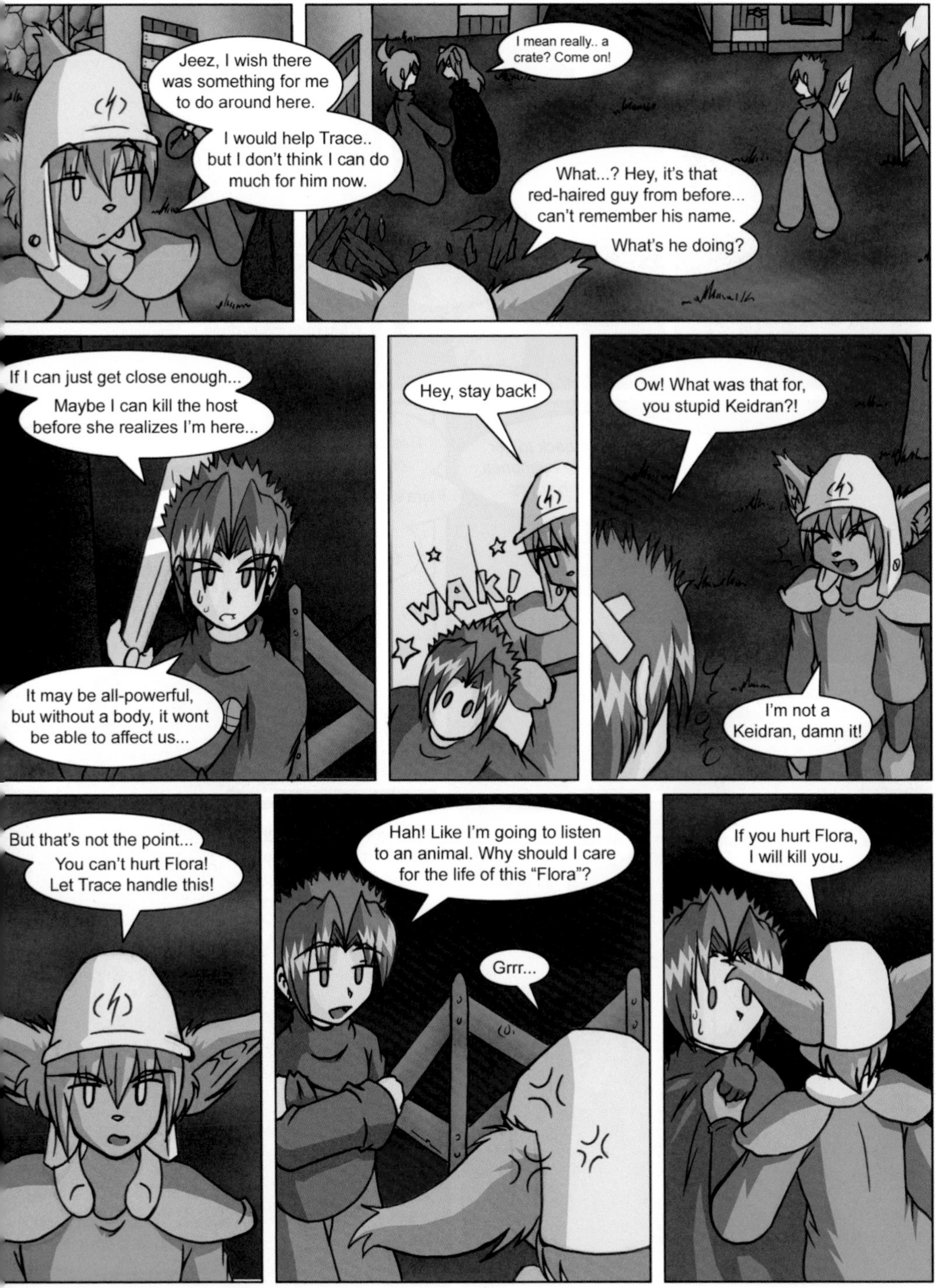
Jeez, I wish there was something for me to do around here.
I would help Trace.. but I don't think I can do much for him now.
I mean really.. a crate? Come on!
What...? Hey, it's that red-haired guy from before... can't remember his name.
What's he doing?
If I can just get close enough...
Maybe I can kill the host before she realizes I'm here...
It may be all-powerful, but without a body, it wont be able to affect us...
Hey, stay back!
WAK!
Ow! What was that for, you stupid Keidran?!
I'm not a Keidran, damn it!
But that's not the point...
You can't hurt Flora! Let Trace handle this!
Hah! Like I'm going to listen to an animal. Why should I care for the life of this "Flora"?
Grrr...
If you hurt Flora, I will kill you.

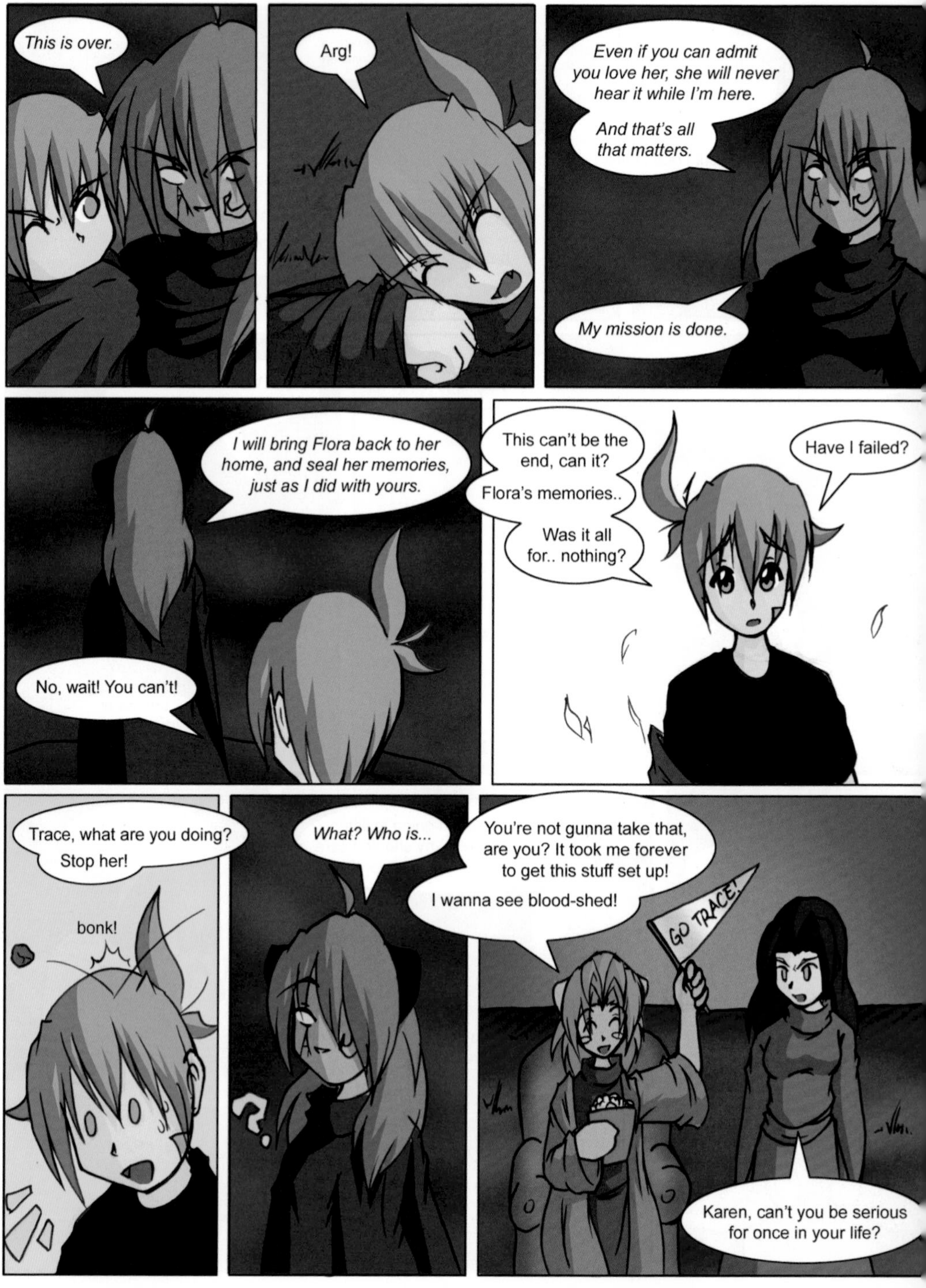

This is over.
Arg!
Even if you can admit you love her, she will never hear it while I'm here.
And that's all that matters.
My mission is done.
I will bring Flora back to her home, and seal her memories, just as I did with yours.
No, wait! You can't!
This can't be the end, can it?
Flora's memories..
Was it all for.. nothing?
Have I failed?
Trace, what are you doing?
Stop her!
bonk!
What? Who is...
You're not gunna take that, are you? It took me forever to get this stuff set up!
I wanna see blood-shed!
GO TRACE!
Karen, can't you be serious for once in your life?

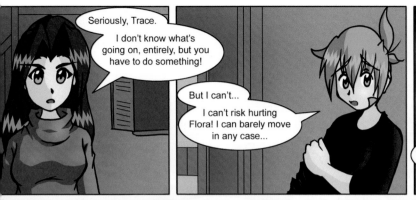

Seriously, Trace.

I don't know what's going on, entirely, but you have to do something!

But I can't...

I can't risk hurting Flora! I can barely move in any case...

Maybe you just need a little help?

It's you! Uh.. Euchre?

I'm honored you remember me.

I must say, I have to agree with this human.

What?!

But... what about Flora?

You're practically her brother!

Are you saying you would fight her too?

Me? Heck, no! I'd be killed!

Listen Trace, it's true that the masks know everything.

Past, present, and future.

But there's one thing that they cannot predict...

Who is this Keidran?

How does he know so much about us?

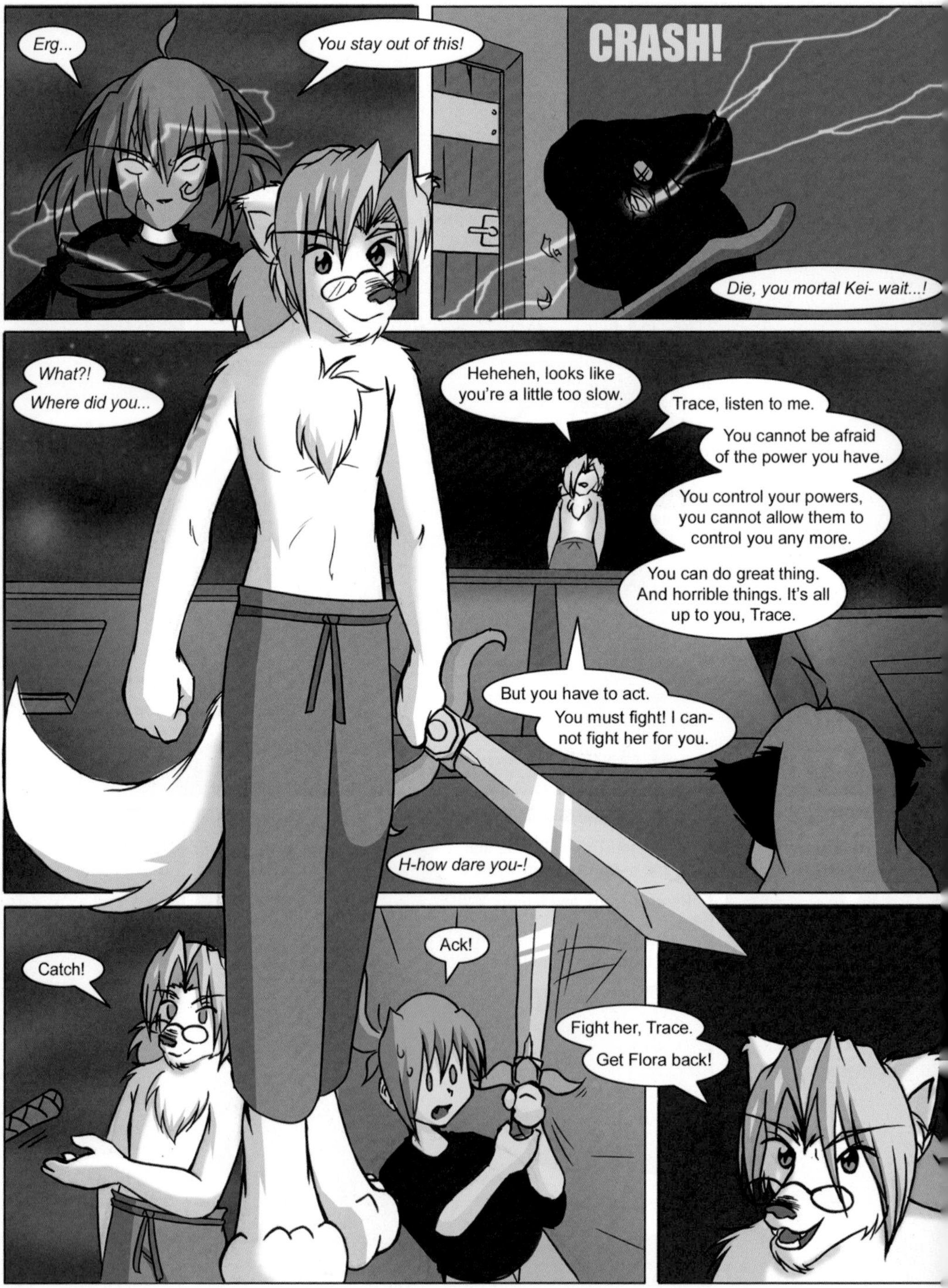
Erg...
You stay out of this!
CRASH!
Die, you mortal Kei- wait...!
What?! Where did you...
Heheheh, looks like you're a little too slow.
Trace, listen to me.
You cannot be afraid of the power you have.
You control your powers, you cannot allow them to control you any more.
You can do great thing. And horrible things. It's all up to you, Trace.
But you have to act.
You must fight! I can-not fight her for you.
H-how dare you-!
Catch!
Ack!
Fight her, Trace.
Get Flora back!

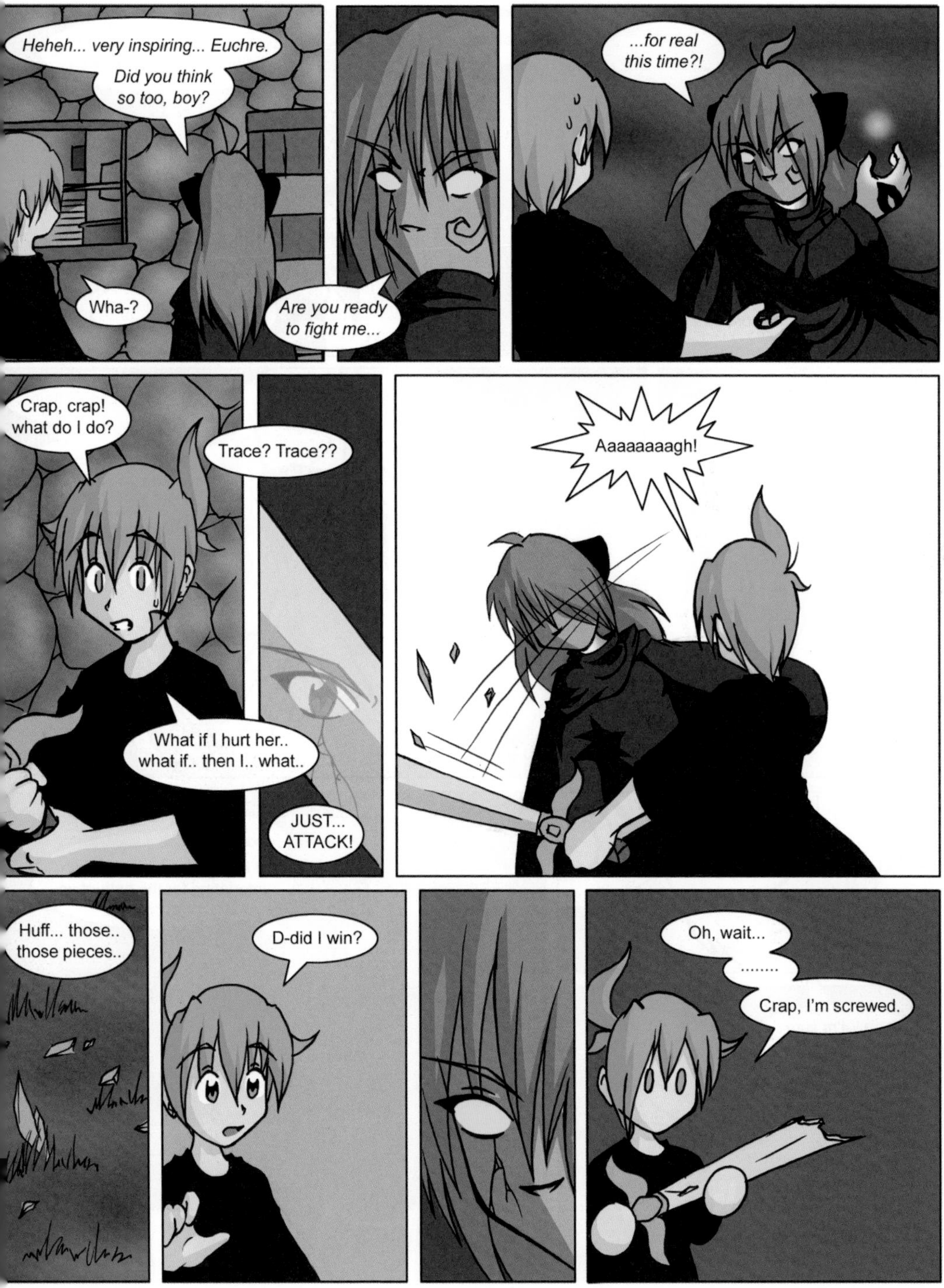

Heheh... very inspiring... Euchre.
Did you think so too, boy?
Wha-?
Are you ready to fight me...
...for real this time?!
Crap, crap! what do I do?
Trace? Trace??
What if I hurt her.. what if.. then I.. what..
JUST... ATTACK!
Aaaaaaaagh!
Huff... those.. those pieces..
D-did I win?
Oh, wait...
....
Crap, I'm screwed.

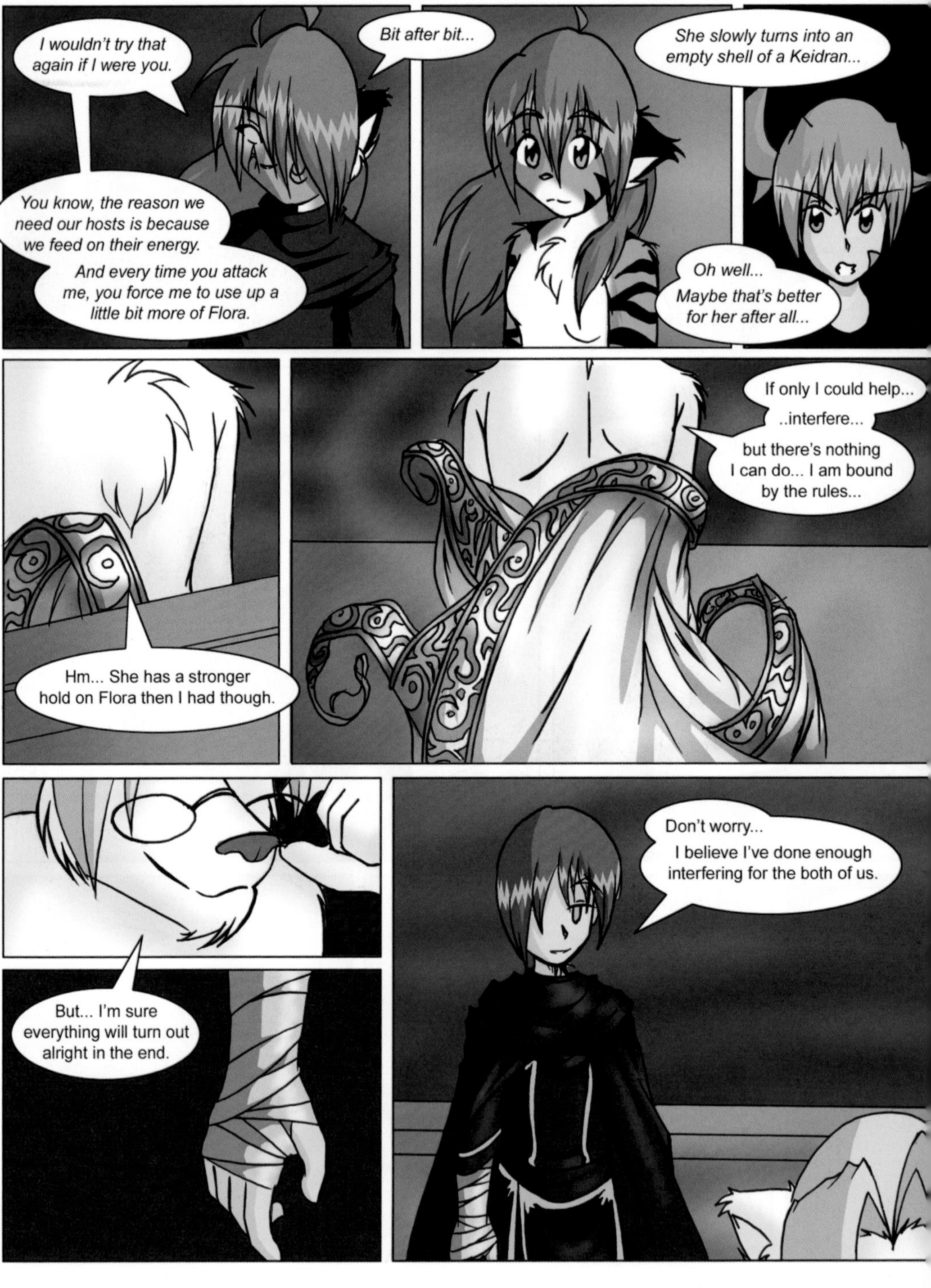
I wouldn't try that again if I were you.
You know, the reason we need our hosts is because we feed on their energy.
And every time you attack me, you force me to use up a little bit more of Flora.
Bit after bit...
She slowly turns into an empty shell of a Keidran...
Oh well... Maybe that's better for her after all...
Hm... She has a stronger hold on Flora then I had though.
If only I could help...
..interfere...
but there's nothing I can do... I am bound by the rules...
But... I'm sure everything will turn out alright in the end.
Don't worry...
I believe I've done enough interfering for the both of us.

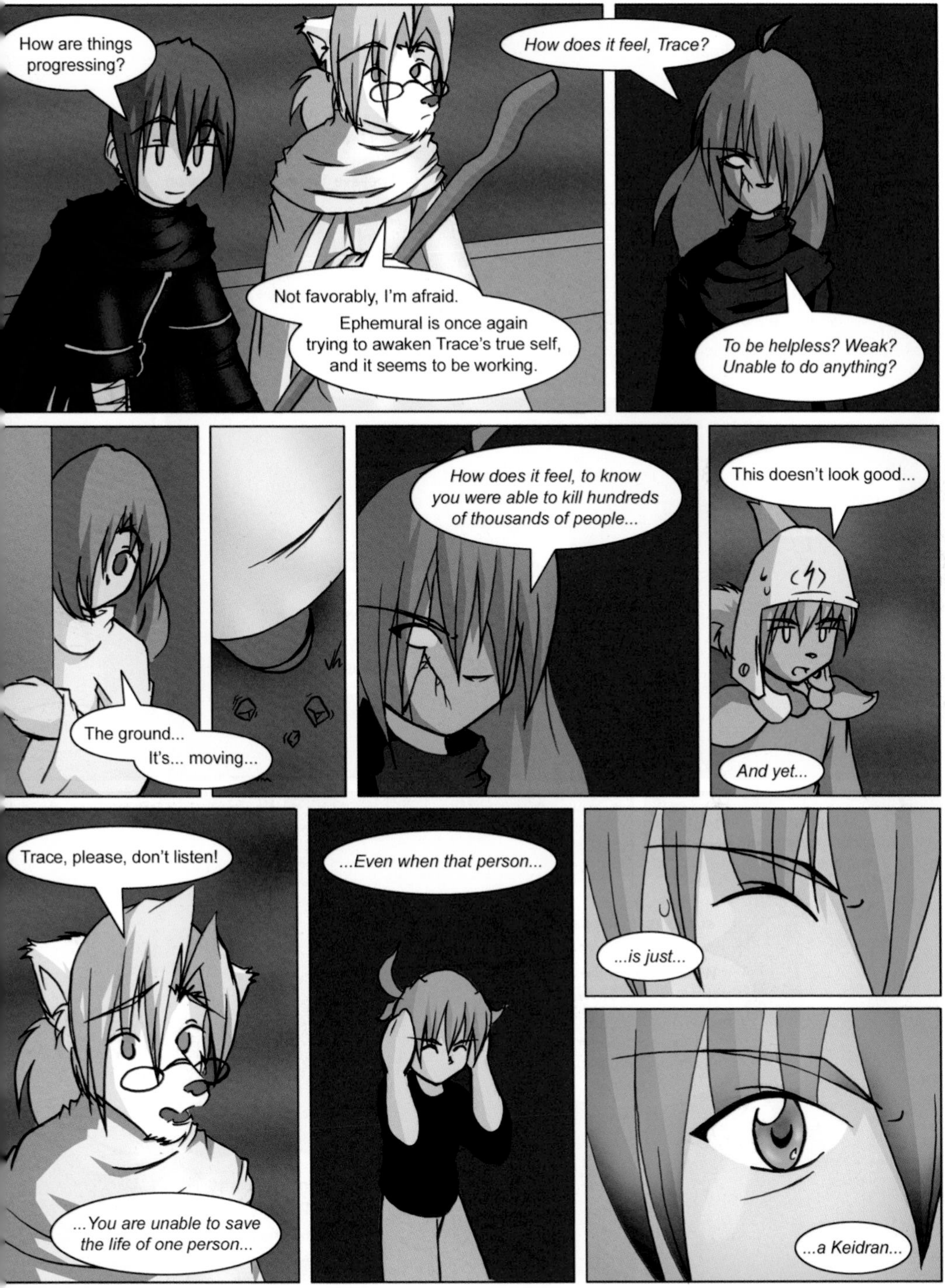
How are things progressing?
Not favorably, I'm afraid.
Ephemural is once again trying to awaken Trace's true self, and it seems to be working.
How does it feel, Trace?
To be helpless? Weak? Unable to do anything?
The ground... It's... moving...
How does it feel, to know you were able to kill hundreds of thousands of people...
This doesn't look good...
And yet...
Trace, please, don't listen!
...You are unable to save the life of one person...
...Even when that person...
...is just...
...a Keidran...

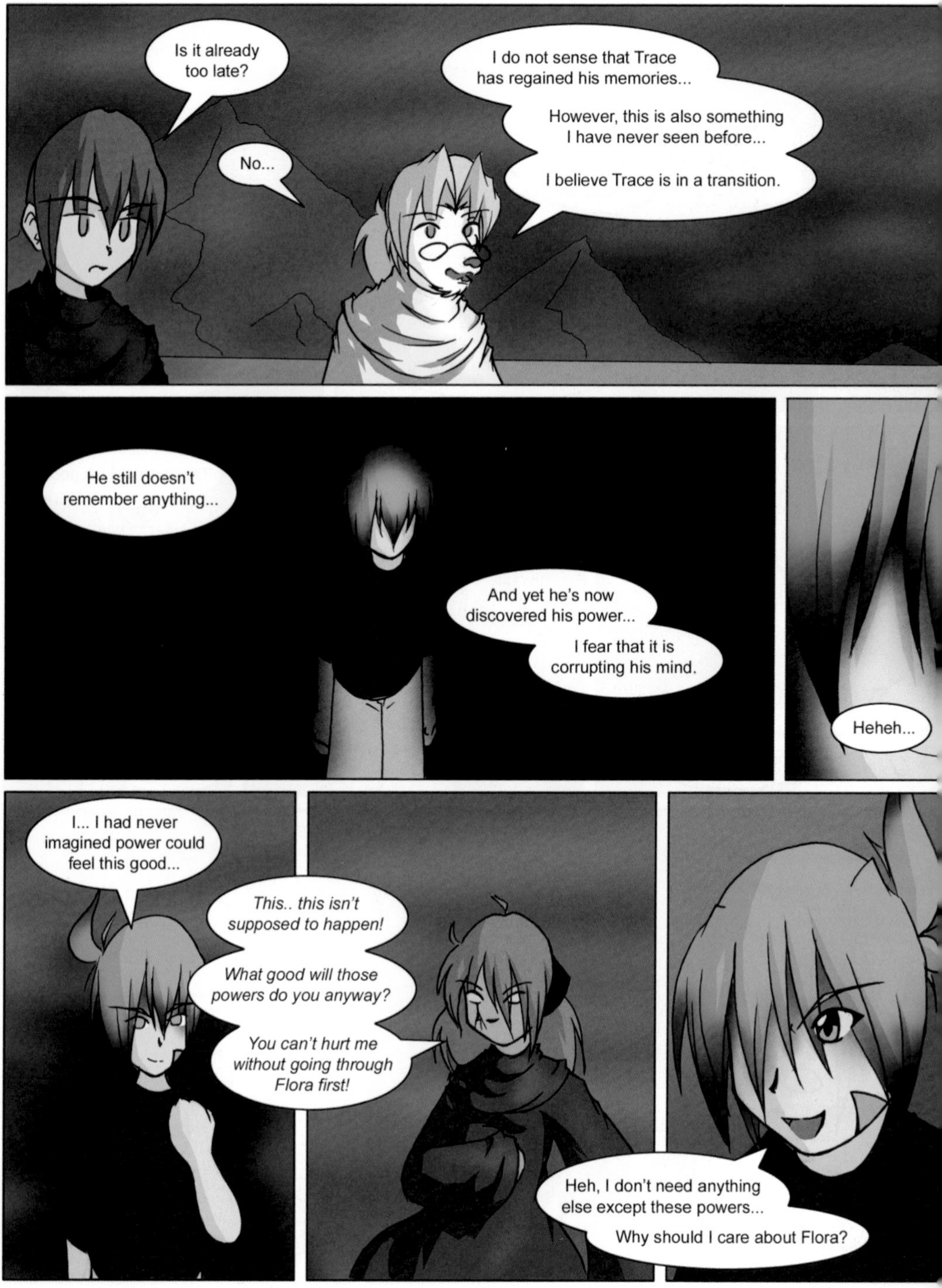
Is it already too late?
I do not sense that Trace has regained his memories...
However, this is also something I have never seen before...
I believe Trace is in a transition.
No...
He still doesn't remember anything...
And yet he's now discovered his power...
I fear that it is corrupting his mind.
Heheh...
I... I had never imagined power could feel this good...
This.. this isn't supposed to happen!
What good will those powers do you anyway?
You can't hurt me without going through Flora first!
Heh, I don't need anything else except these powers...
Why should I care about Flora?

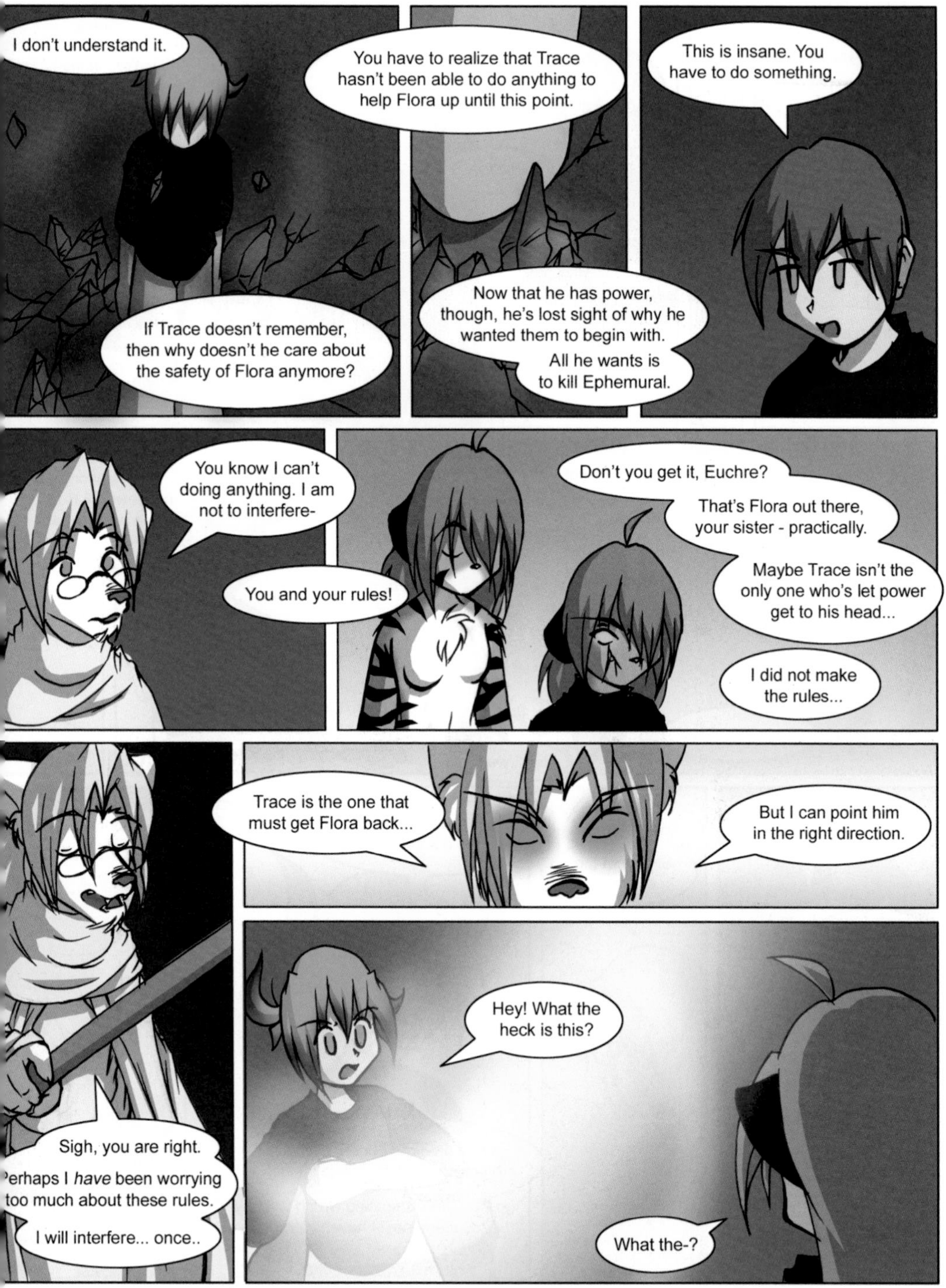
I don't understand it.
If Trace doesn't remember, then why doesn't he care about the safety of Flora anymore?
You have to realize that Trace hasn't been able to do anything to help Flora up until this point.
Now that he has power, though, he's lost sight of why he wanted them to begin with.
All he wants is to kill Ephemural.
This is insane. You have to do something.
You know I can't doing anything. I am not to interfere-
You and your rules!
Don't you get it, Euchre?
That's Flora out there, your sister - practically.
Maybe Trace isn't the only one who's let power get to his head...
I did not make the rules...
Trace is the one that must get Flora back...
But I can point him in the right direction.
Sigh, you are right.
erhaps I *have* been worrying too much about these rules.
I will interfere... once..
Hey! What the heck is this?
What the-?

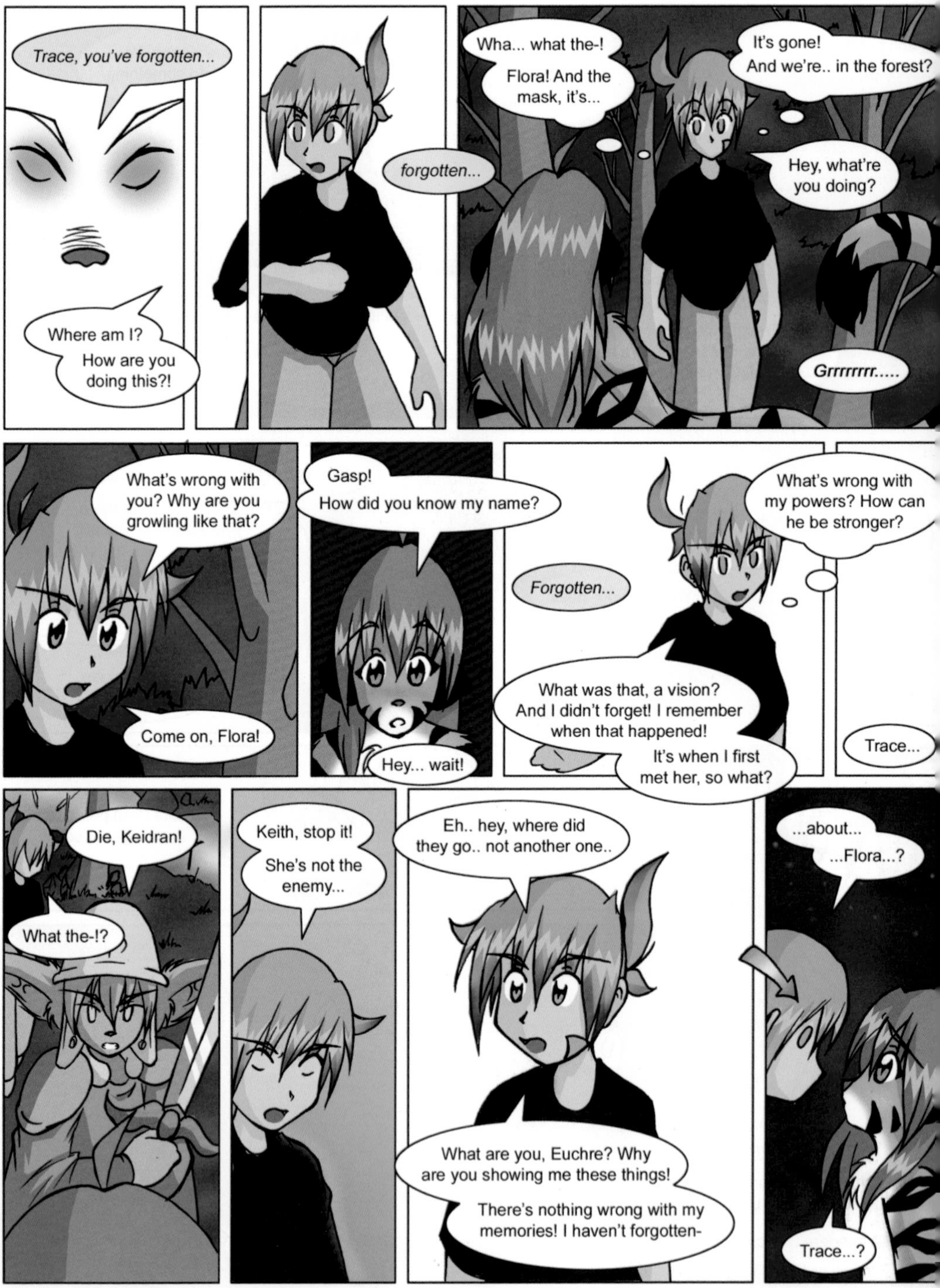

Trace, you've forgotten...
Where am I? How are you doing this?!
forgotten...
Wha... what the-! Flora! And the mask, it's...
It's gone! And we're.. in the forest?
Hey, what're you doing?
Grrrrrrrr.....
What's wrong with you? Why are you growling like that?
Come on, Flora!
Gasp! How did you know my name?
Hey... wait!
Forgotten...
What's wrong with my powers? How can he be stronger?
What was that, a vision? And I didn't forget! I remember when that happened!
It's when I first met her, so what?
Trace...
Die, Keidran!
What the-!?
Keith, stop it! She's not the enemy...
Eh.. hey, where did they go.. not another one..
What are you, Euchre? Why are you showing me these things!
There's nothing wrong with my memories! I haven't forgotten-
...about... ...Flora...?
Trace...?

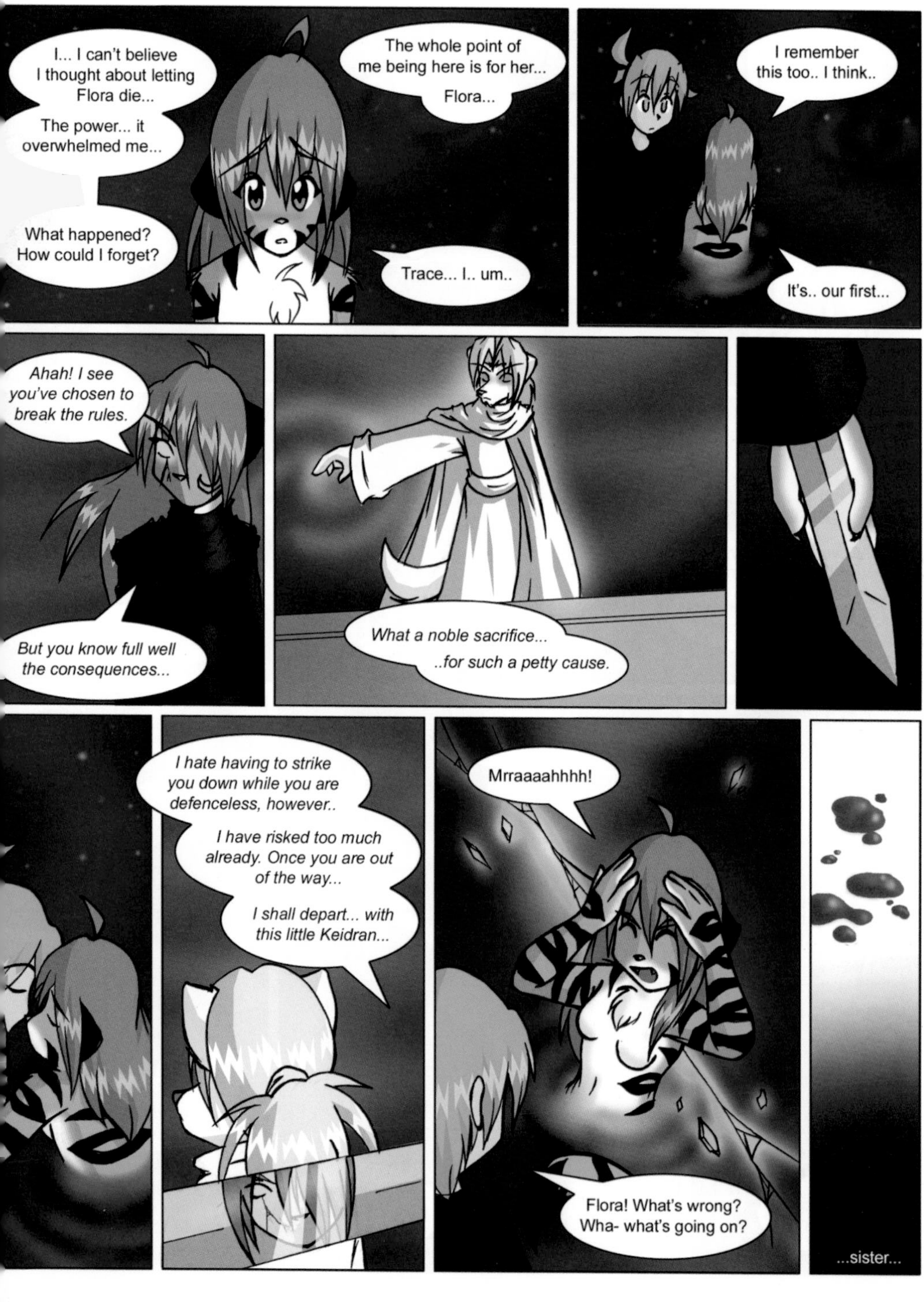

I... I can't believe I thought about letting Flora die...
The power... it overwhelmed me...
What happened? How could I forget?
The whole point of me being here is for her...
Flora...
Trace... I.. um..
I remember this too.. I think..
It's.. our first...
Ahah! I see you've chosen to break the rules.
But you know full well the consequences...
What a noble sacrifice...
..for such a petty cause.
I hate having to strike you down while you are defenceless, however..
I have risked too much already. Once you are out of the way...
I shall depart... with this little Keidran...
Mrraaaahhhh!
Flora! What's wrong? Wha- what's going on?
...sister...

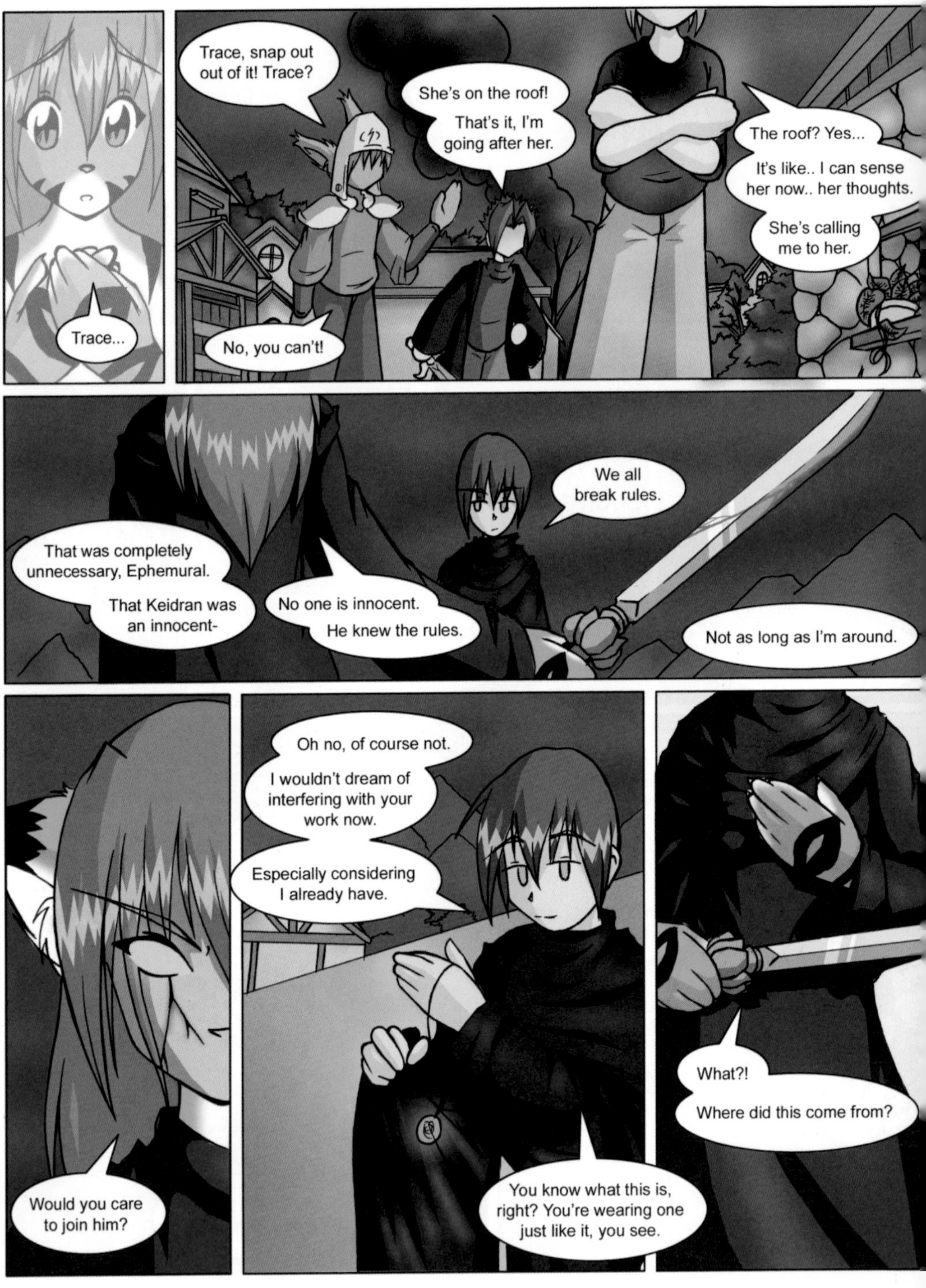
Trace...
Trace, snap out out of it! Trace?
No, you can't!
She's on the roof!
That's it, I'm going after her.
The roof? Yes...
It's like.. I can sense her now.. her thoughts.
She's calling me to her.
That was completely unnecessary, Ephemural.
That Keidran was an innocent-
No one is innocent.
He knew the rules.
We all break rules.
Not as long as I'm around.
Would you care to join him?
Oh no, of course not.
I wouldn't dream of interfering with your work now.
Especially considering I already have.
You know what this is, right? You're wearing one just like it, you see.
What?!
Where did this come from?

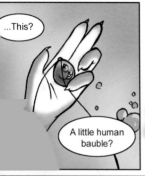

...This?

A little human bauble?

Yes, but one of my own designs.

Hmph...

I don't see what you though you could accomplish with this little thing.

Flora... Flora, can you hear me?

Please, tell me your still there.

Flora?

Grr.. What is that human muttering about?

He should know by now that Flora isn't-

eh...

Mew...?

...e, when I first met you in the wood I wasn't
...tions were. But as we continued in our tra...
...a human of all people. It wasn't until later t...
...ly love you. Its so st... ...ms like it...
...ickly. I mis... ...ck. I...
...e don... ...of fig... ...wee...
...et... ...hat's n...nal. I have never h...
... together before. Trace, I...
...eel the same way? I hop...
...hen you said those me...
...hurts. I don't want to b...
...Keidran, but I can't...
...s just who I am. B...
...t that I still love y...
...being a Keidra...
...t you to worry...
...lot. Sometimes...
...was tougher. I can't help it.
...don't mind. I love Trace! I ca...
...n't care who knows it! W...
...a little. but it's not...
...e you afraid of...
...d of me?

No, get away!

What's going on? This is impossible!

Agh! What is this?

AAAAAAAHHH!

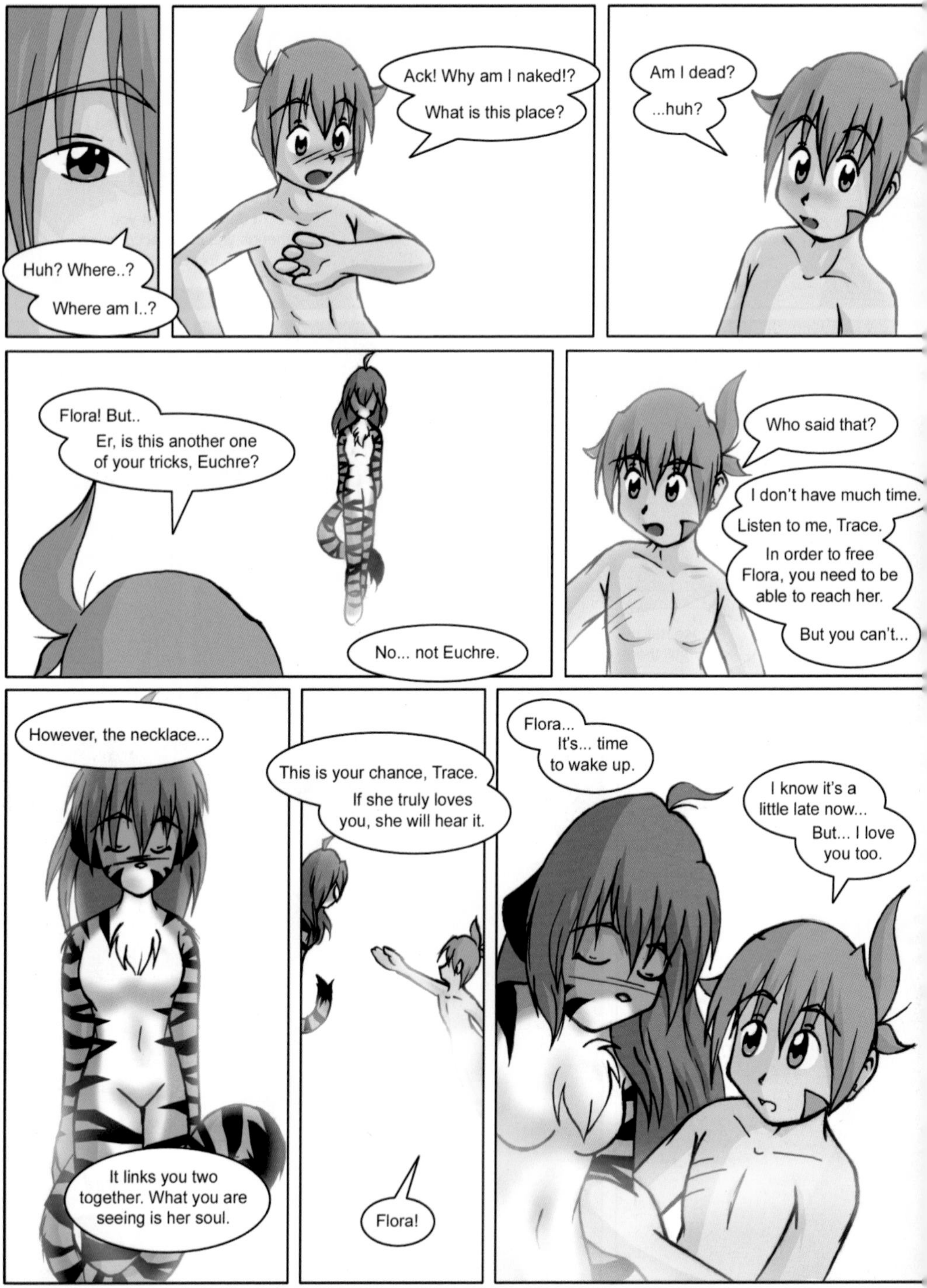
Huh? Where..?
Where am I..?
Ack! Why am I naked!?
What is this place?
Am I dead?
...huh?
Flora! But..
Er, is this another one of your tricks, Euchre?
No... not Euchre.
Who said that?
I don't have much time.
Listen to me, Trace.
In order to free Flora, you need to be able to reach her.
But you can't...
However, the necklace...
It links you two together. What you are seeing is her soul.
This is your chance, Trace.
If she truly loves you, she will hear it.
Flora!
Flora...
It's... time to wake up.
I know it's a little late now...
But... I love you too.

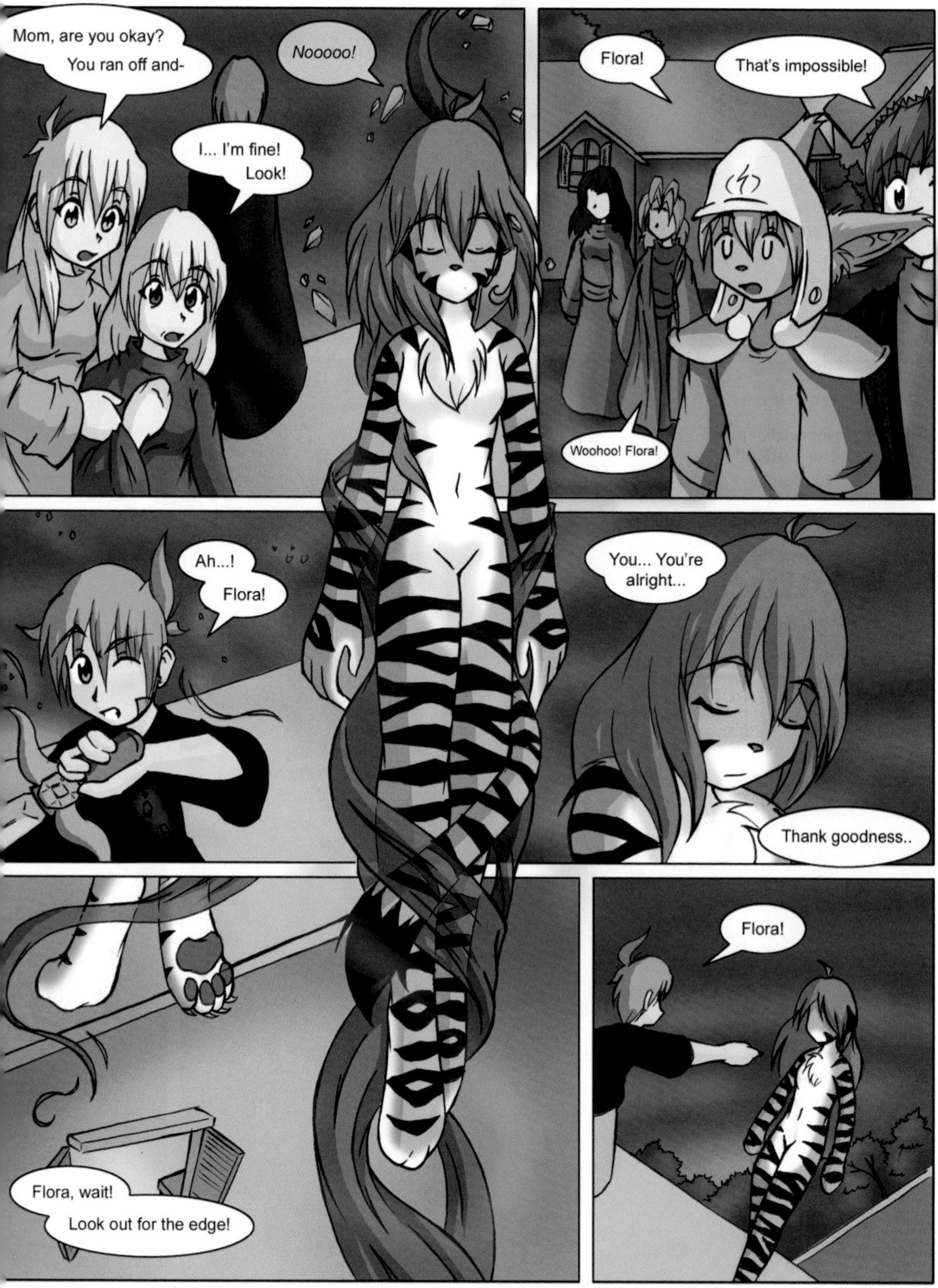
Mom, are you okay? You ran off and-
Nooooo!
I... I'm fine! Look!
Flora!
That's impossible!
Woohoo! Flora!
Ah...! Flora!
You... You're alright...
Thank goodness..
Flora, wait! Look out for the edge!
Flora!

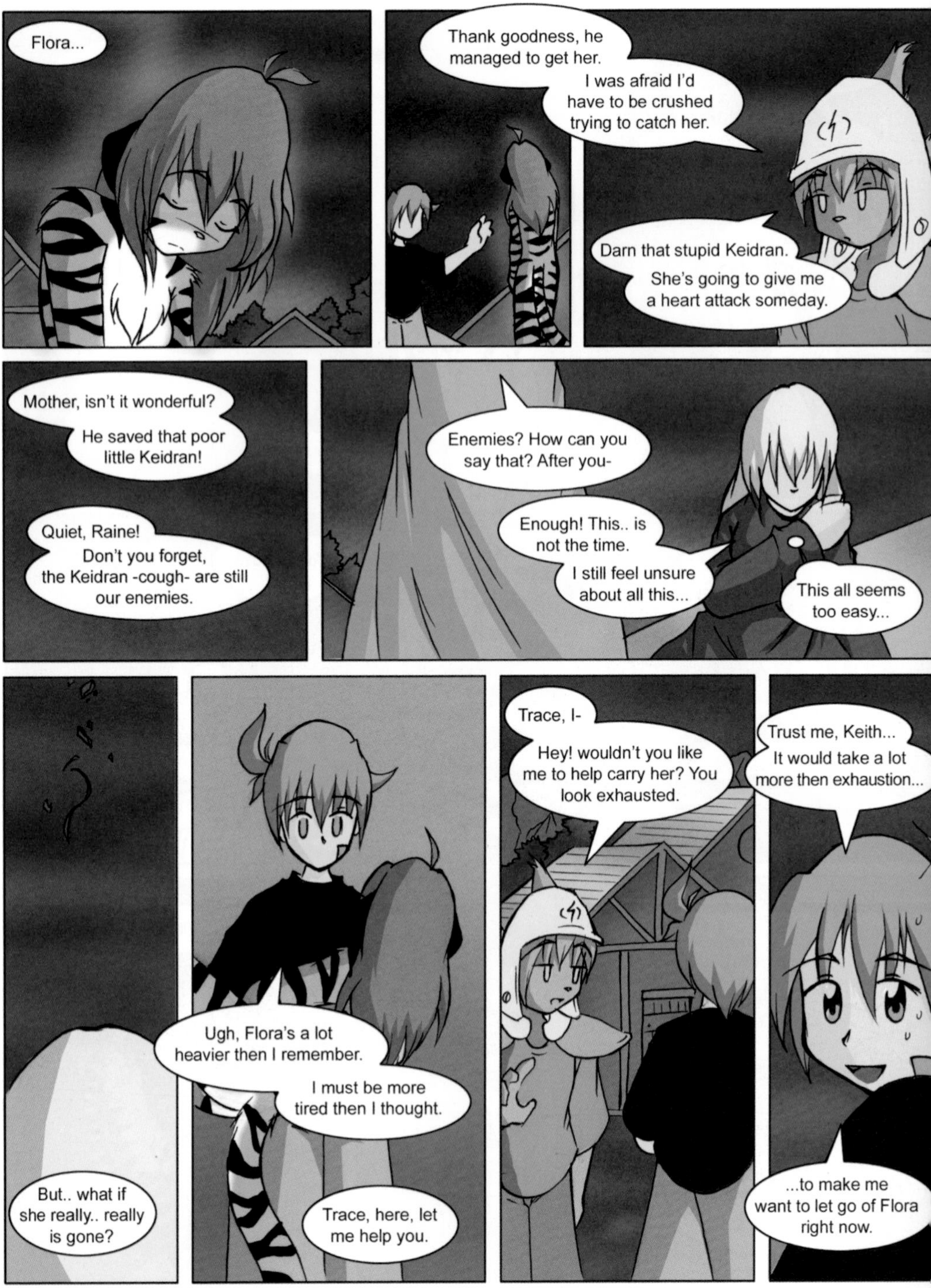
Flora...
Thank goodness, he managed to get her.
I was afraid I'd have to be crushed trying to catch her.
Darn that stupid Keidran.
She's going to give me a heart attack someday.
Mother, isn't it wonderful?
He saved that poor little Keidran!
Quiet, Raine!
Don't you forget, the Keidran -cough- are still our enemies.
Enemies? How can you say that? After you-
Enough! This.. is not the time.
I still feel unsure about all this...
This all seems too easy...
But.. what if she really.. really is gone?
Ugh, Flora's a lot heavier then I remember.
I must be more tired then I thought.
Trace, here, let me help you.
Trace, I-
Hey! wouldn't you like me to help carry her? You look exhausted.
Trust me, Keith...
It would take a lot more then exhaustion...
...to make me want to let go of Flora right now.

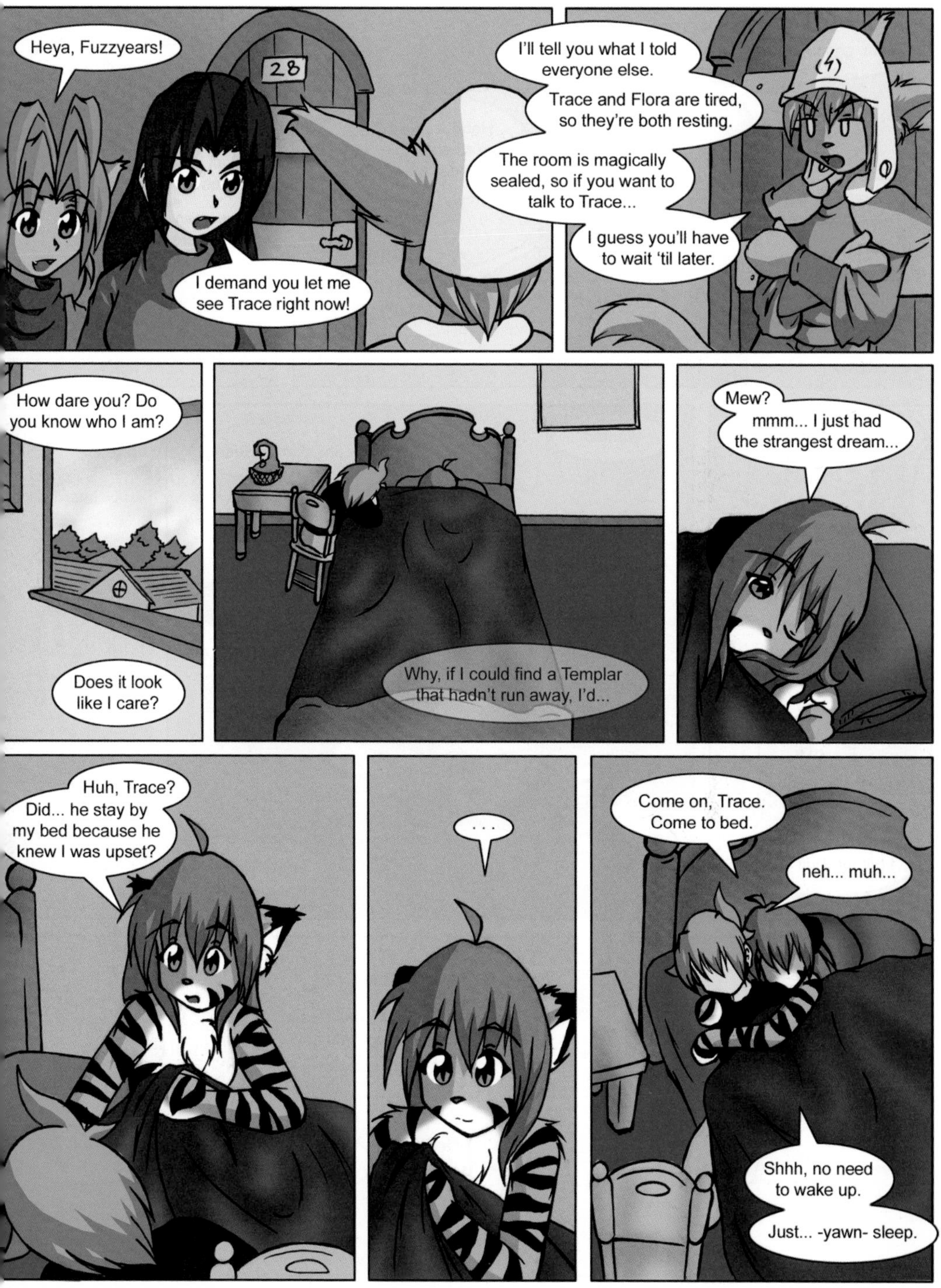
Heya, Fuzzyears!
I demand you let me see Trace right now!
I'll tell you what I told everyone else.
Trace and Flora are tired, so they're both resting.
The room is magically sealed, so if you want to talk to Trace...
I guess you'll have to wait 'til later.
How dare you? Do you know who I am?
Does it look like I care?
Why, if I could find a Templar that hadn't run away, I'd...
Mew? mmm... I just had the strangest dream...
Huh, Trace? Did... he stay by my bed because he knew I was upset?
. . .
Come on, Trace. Come to bed.
neh... muh...
Shhh, no need to wake up.
Just... -yawn- sleep.

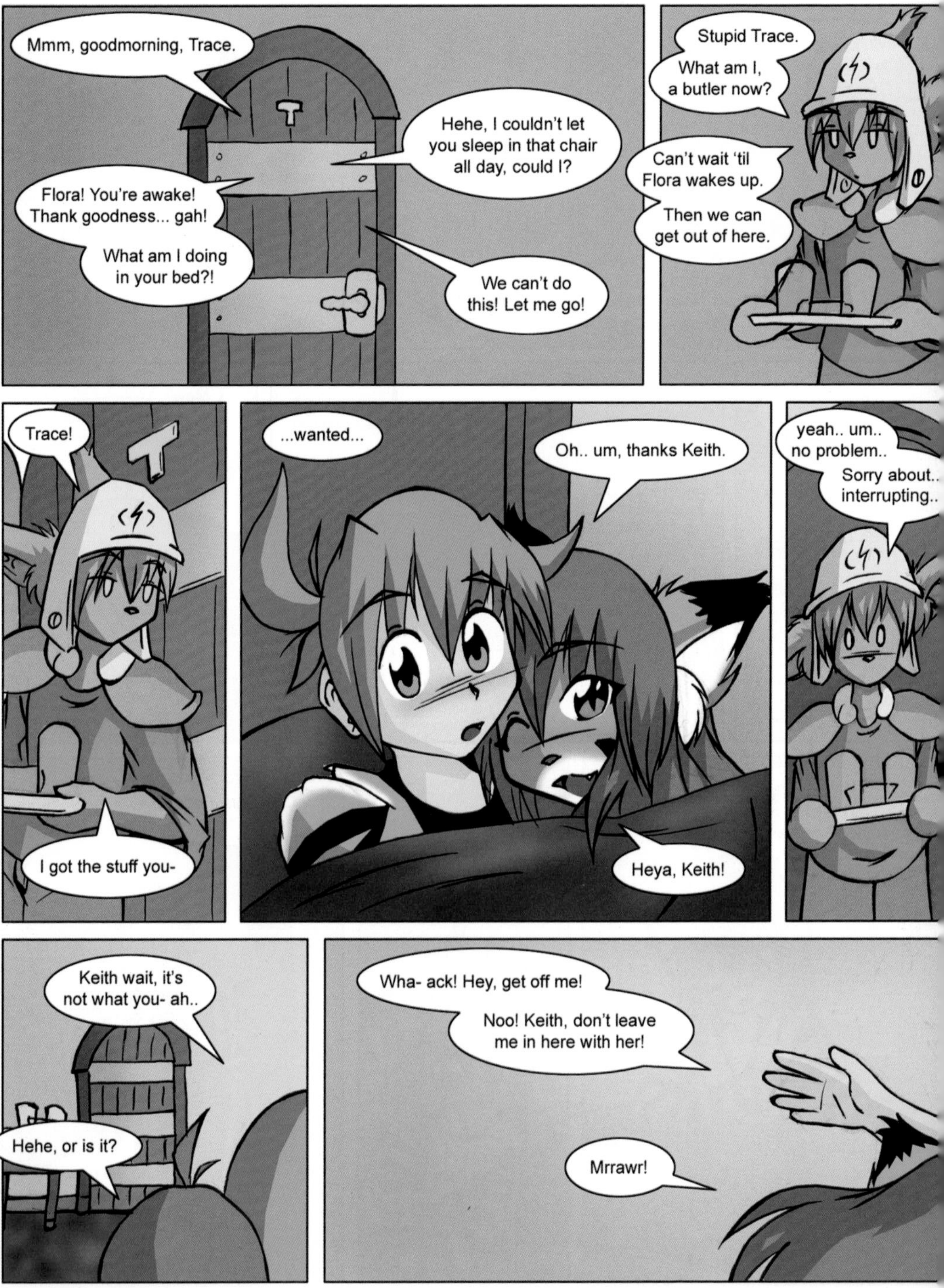
Mmm, goodmorning, Trace.
Flora! You're awake! Thank goodness... gah!
What am I doing in your bed?!
Hehe, I couldn't let you sleep in that chair all day, could I?
We can't do this! Let me go!
Stupid Trace.
What am I, a butler now?
Can't wait 'til Flora wakes up.
Then we can get out of here.
Trace!
I got the stuff you-
...wanted...
Oh.. um, thanks Keith.
Heya, Keith!
yeah.. um.. no problem..
Sorry about.. interrupting..
Keith wait, it's not what you- ah..
Hehe, or is it?
Wha- ack! Hey, get off me!
Noo! Keith, don't leave me in here with her!
Mrrawr!

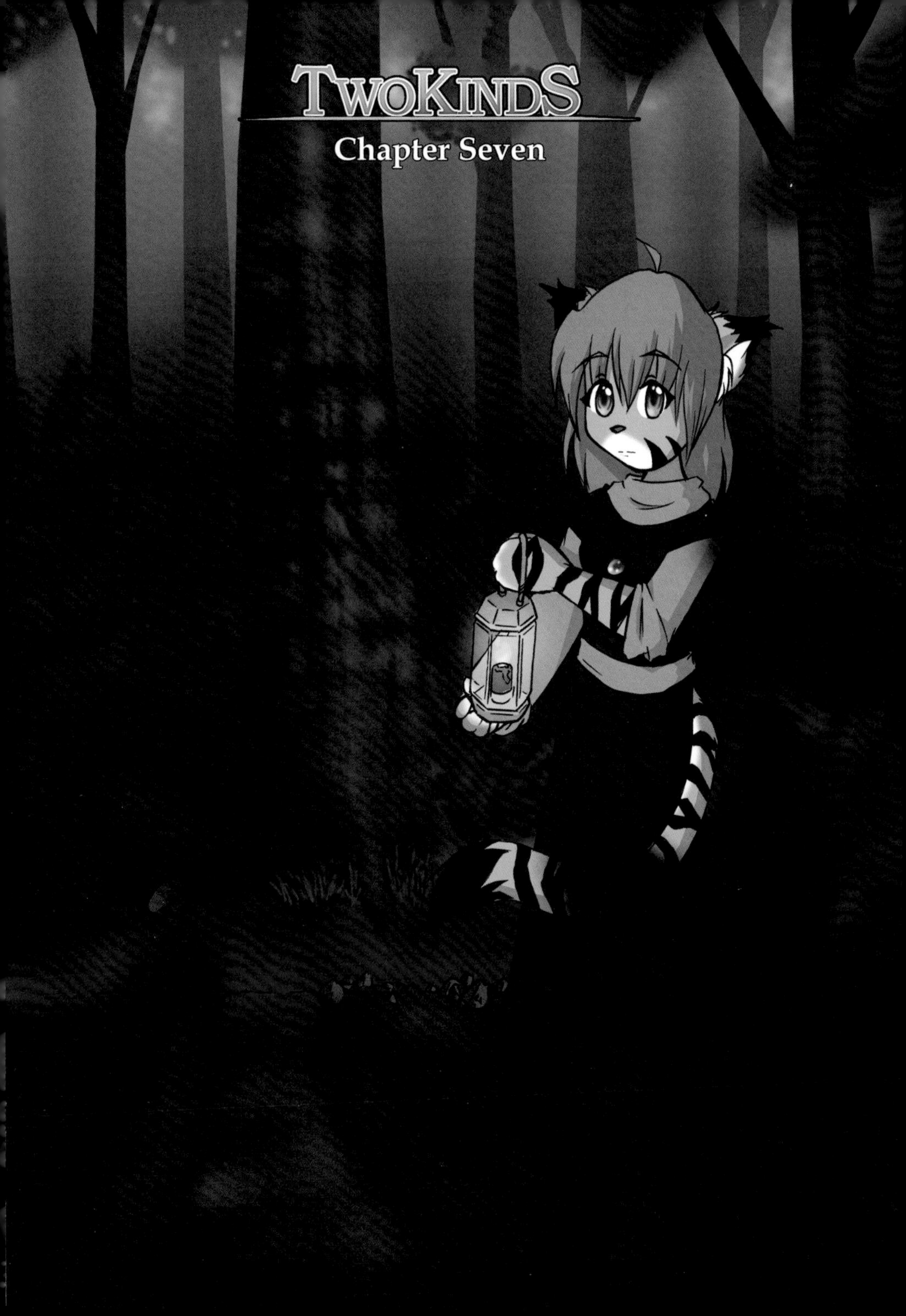
TwoKinds
Chapter Seven

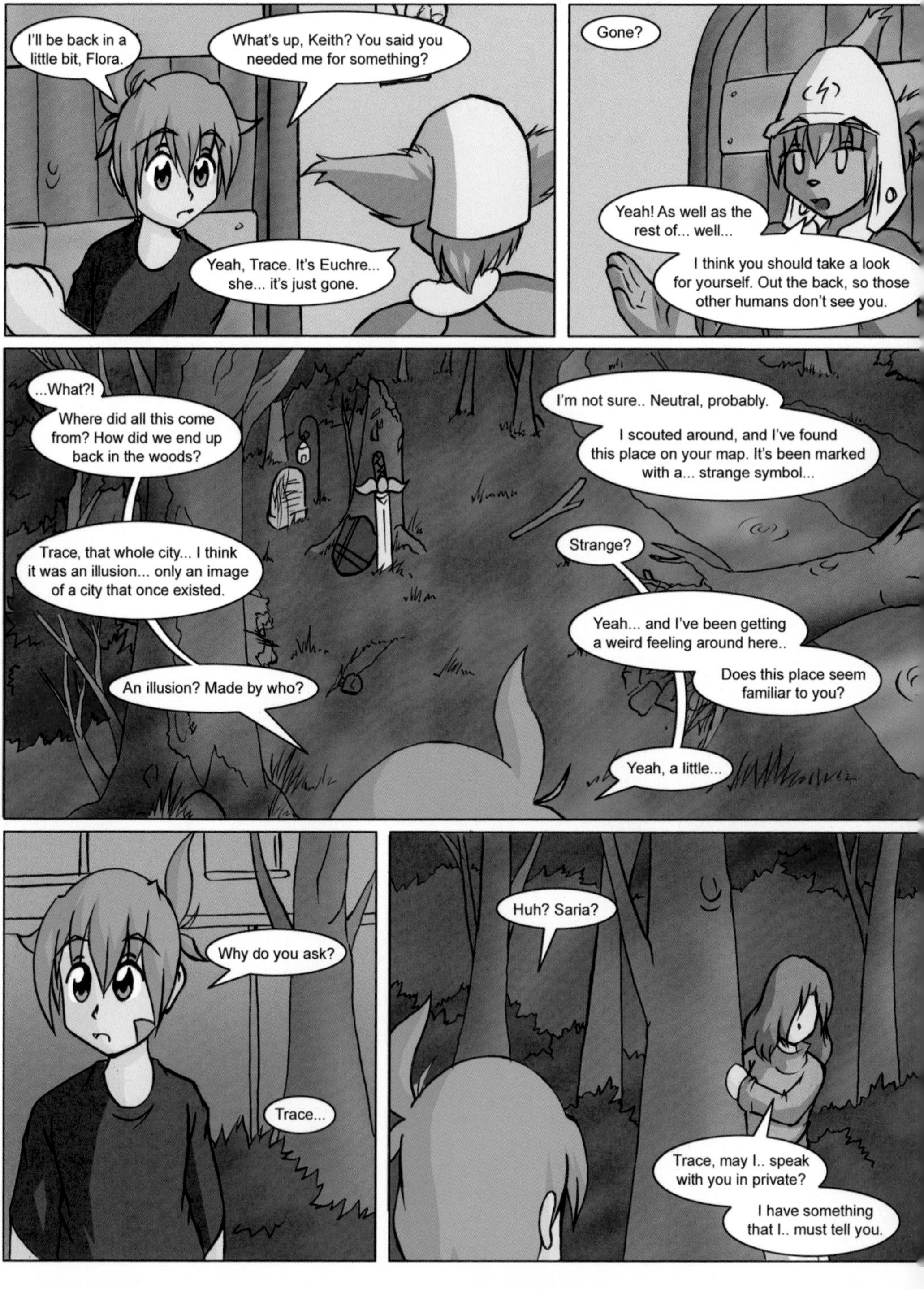
I'll be back in a little bit, Flora.
What's up, Keith? You said you needed me for something?
Yeah, Trace. It's Euchre... she... it's just gone.
Gone?
Yeah! As well as the rest of... well...
I think you should take a look for yourself. Out the back, so those other humans don't see you.
...What?!
Where did all this come from? How did we end up back in the woods?
Trace, that whole city... I think it was an illusion... only an image of a city that once existed.
An illusion? Made by who?
I'm not sure.. Neutral, probably.
I scouted around, and I've found this place on your map. It's been marked with a... strange symbol...
Strange?
Yeah... and I've been getting a weird feeling around here..
Does this place seem familiar to you?
Yeah, a little...
Why do you ask?
Trace...
Huh? Saria?
Trace, may I.. speak with you in private?
I have something that I.. must tell you.

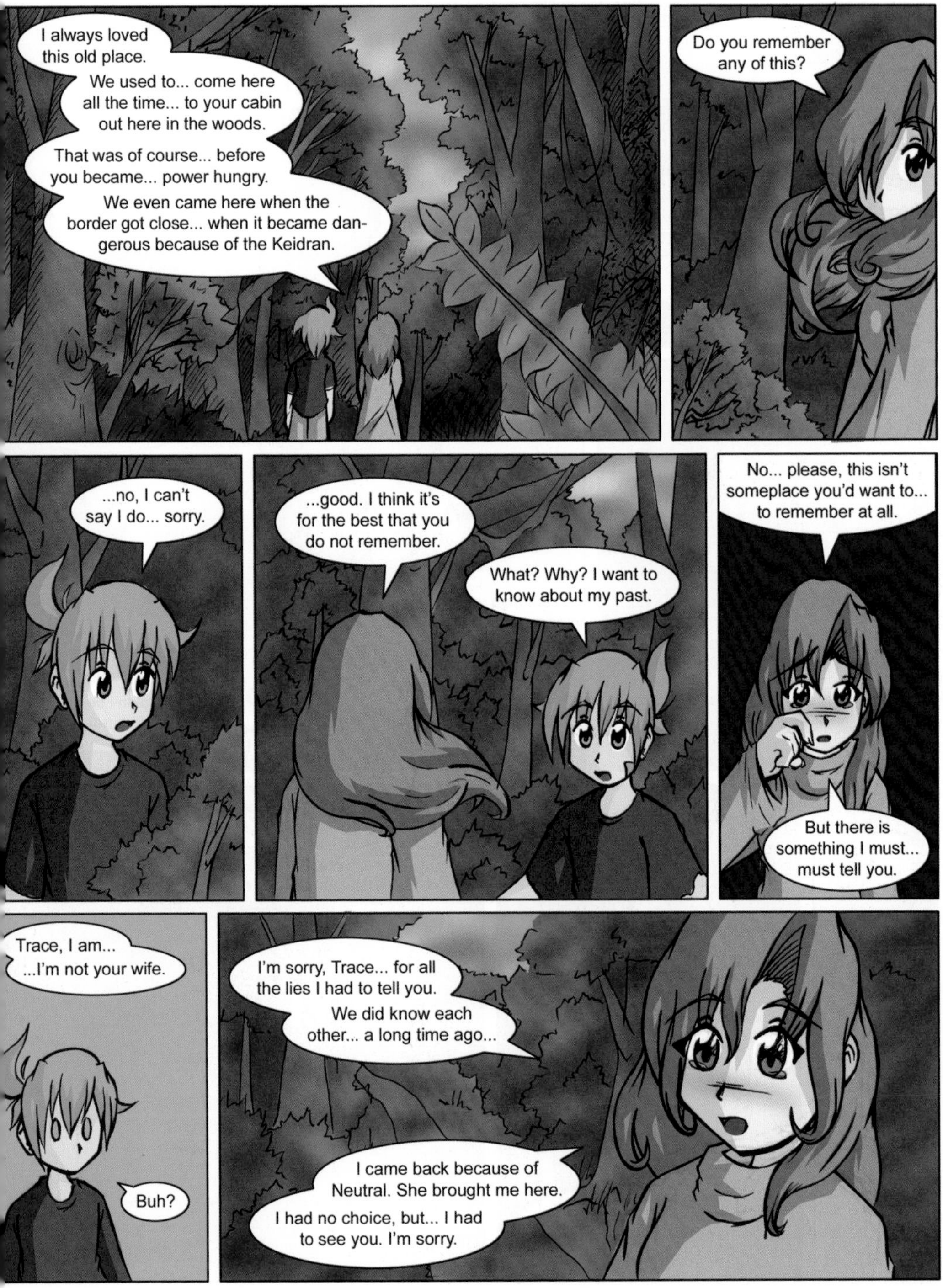
I always loved this old place.
We used to... come here all the time... to your cabin out here in the woods.
That was of course... before you became... power hungry.
We even came here when the border got close... when it became dangerous because of the Keidran.
Do you remember any of this?
...no, I can't say I do... sorry.
...good. I think it's for the best that you do not remember.
What? Why? I want to know about my past.
No... please, this isn't someplace you'd want to... to remember at all.
But there is something I must... must tell you.
Trace, I am...
...I'm not your wife.
Buh?
I'm sorry, Trace... for all the lies I had to tell you.
We did know each other... a long time ago...
I came back because of Neutral. She brought me here.
I had no choice, but... I had to see you. I'm sorry.

Trace, seeing you in this brief moment in time...

...has brought me greater happiness then I fear you will ever understand.

For a while.. I'd thought you'd never be happy again.

But seeing you with that girl...

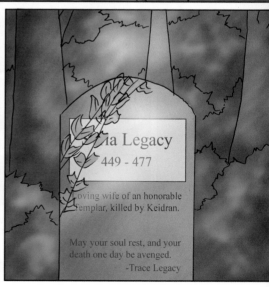

I hope you will forgive me someday, Trace.

...I am glad you've found someone that can make you smile once more.

Even if she is... a Keidran.

I just.. couldn't bear... couldn't bear to burden you...

With the memory of my passing...

...ia Legacy

449 - 477

...oving wife of an honorable ...emplar, killed by Keidran.

May your soul rest, and your death one day be avenged.

-Trace Legacy

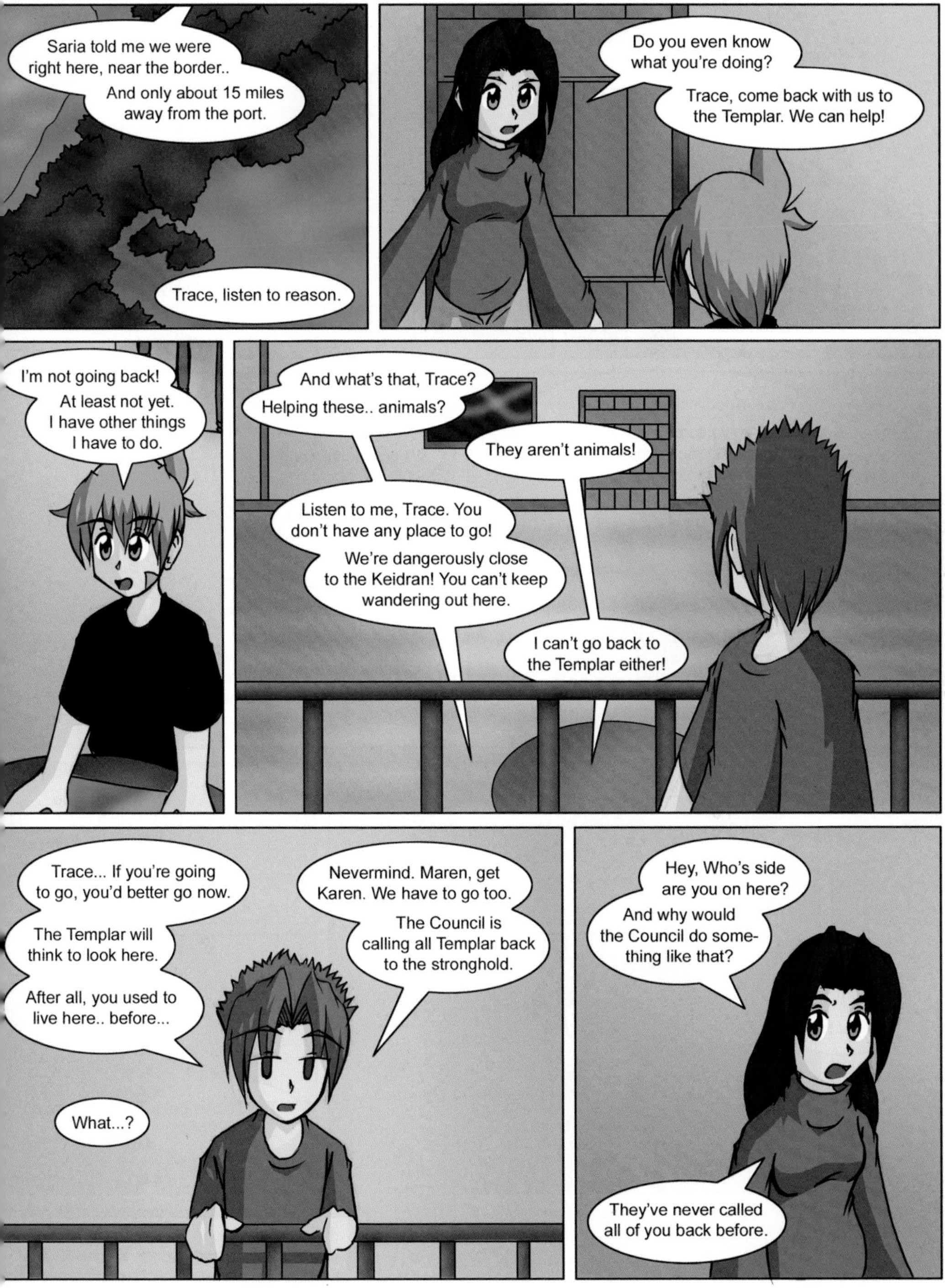
Saria told me we were right here, near the border..
And only about 15 miles away from the port.
Trace, listen to reason.
Do you even know what you're doing?
Trace, come back with us to the Templar. We can help!
I'm not going back!
At least not yet. I have other things I have to do.
And what's that, Trace?
Helping these.. animals?
They aren't animals!
Listen to me, Trace. You don't have any place to go!
We're dangerously close to the Keidran! You can't keep wandering out here.
I can't go back to the Templar either!
Trace... If you're going to go, you'd better go now.
The Templar will think to look here.
After all, you used to live here.. before...
What...?
Nevermind. Maren, get Karen. We have to go too.
The Council is calling all Templar back to the stronghold.
Hey, Who's side are you on here?
And why would the Council do something like that?
They've never called all of you back before.

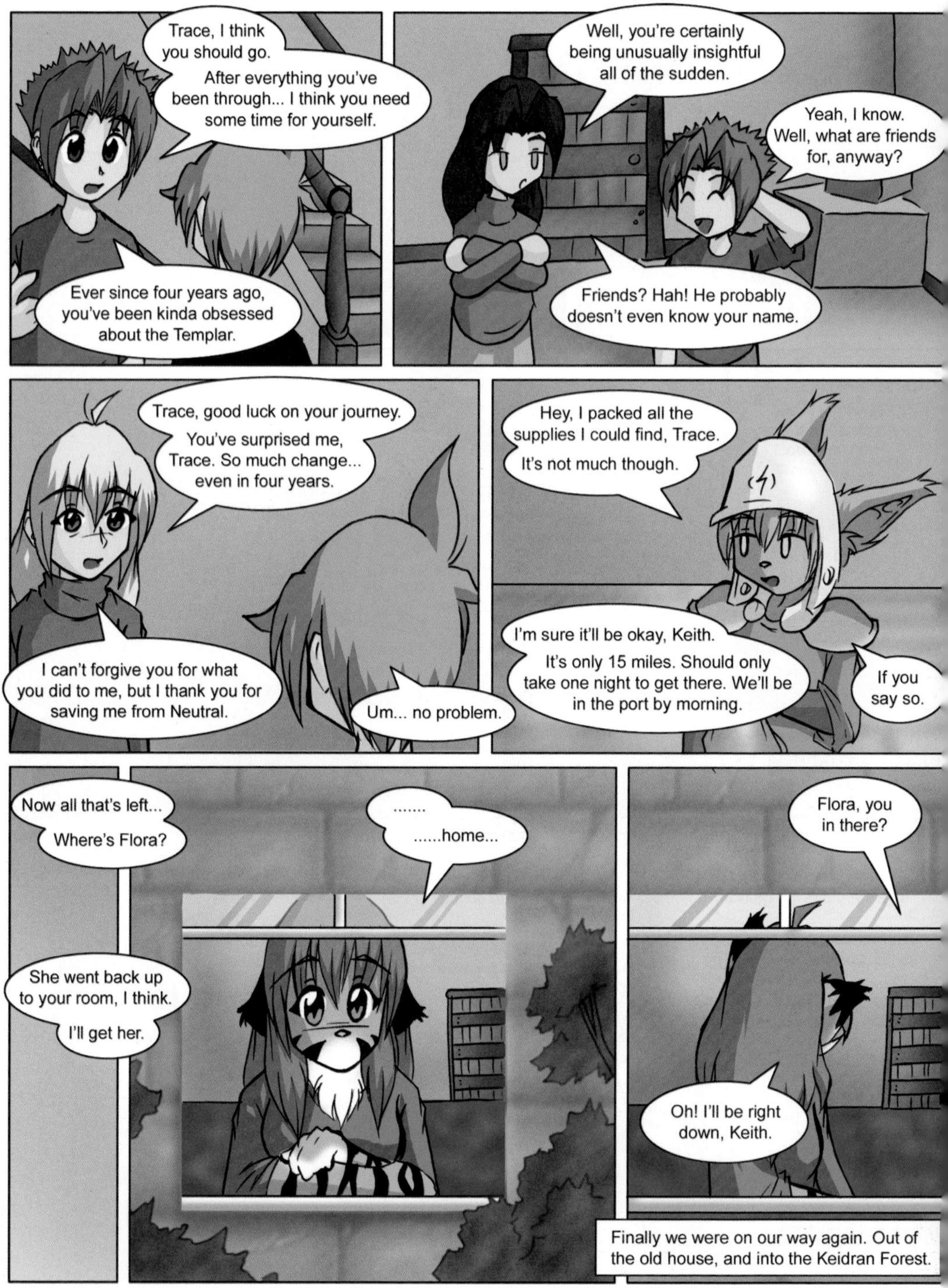
Trace, I think you should go.
After everything you've been through... I think you need some time for yourself.
Ever since four years ago, you've been kinda obsessed about the Templar.
Well, you're certainly being unusually insightful all of the sudden.
Yeah, I know. Well, what are friends for, anyway?
Friends? Hah! He probably doesn't even know your name.
Trace, good luck on your journey.
You've surprised me, Trace. So much change... even in four years.
I can't forgive you for what you did to me, but I thank you for saving me from Neutral.
Um... no problem.
Hey, I packed all the supplies I could find, Trace.
It's not much though.
I'm sure it'll be okay, Keith.
It's only 15 miles. Should only take one night to get there. We'll be in the port by morning.
If you say so.
Now all that's left...
Where's Flora?
She went back up to your room, I think.
I'll get her.
....
......home...
Flora, you in there?
Oh! I'll be right down, Keith.
Finally we were on our way again. Out of the old house, and into the Keidran Forest.

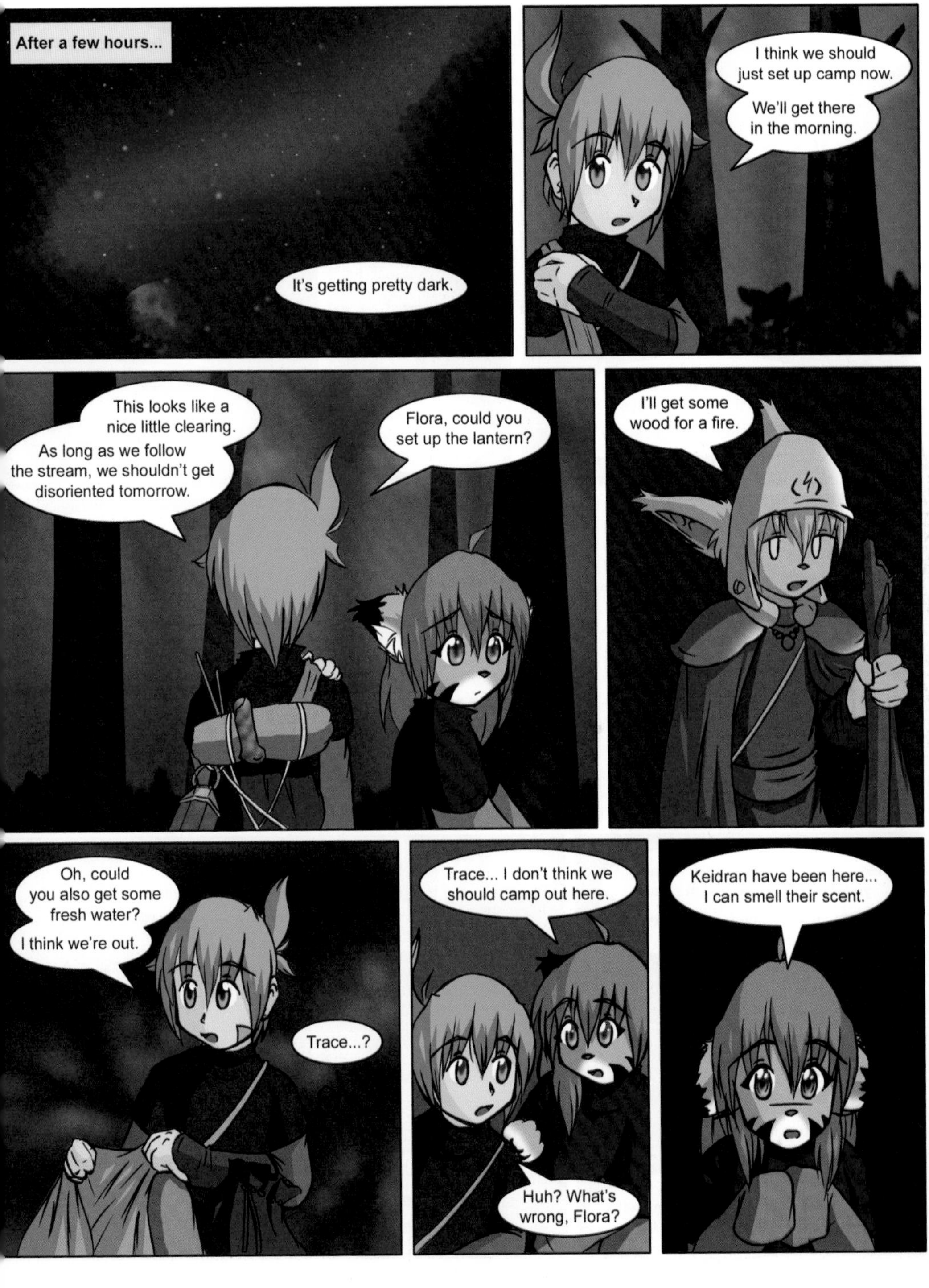
After a few hours...
It's getting pretty dark.
I think we should just set up camp now.
We'll get there in the morning.
This looks like a nice little clearing.
As long as we follow the stream, we shouldn't get disoriented tomorrow.
Flora, could you set up the lantern?
I'll get some wood for a fire.
Oh, could you also get some fresh water?
I think we're out.
Trace...?
Trace... I don't think we should camp out here.
Huh? What's wrong, Flora?
Keidran have been here... I can smell their scent.

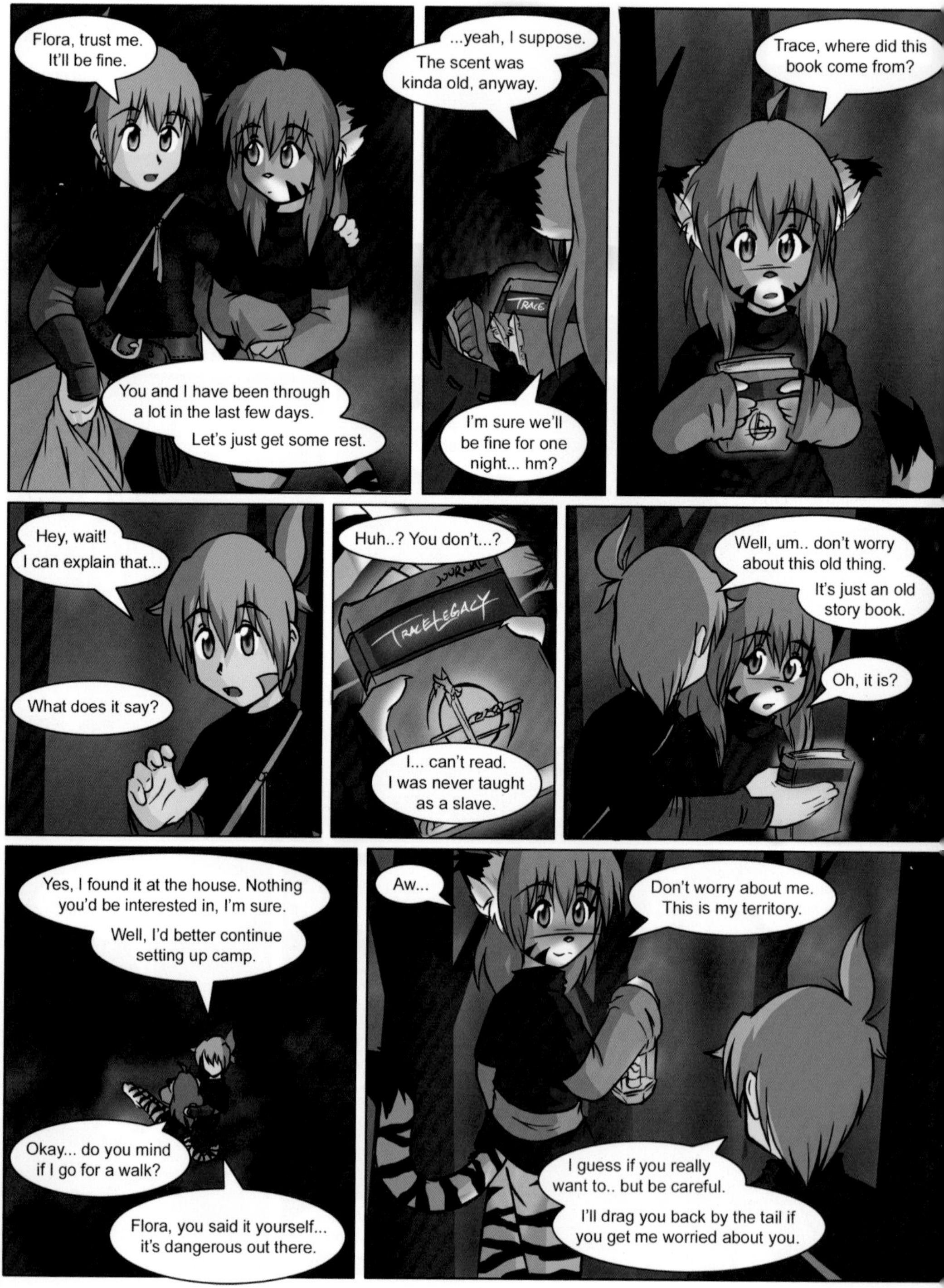

Flora, trust me. It'll be fine.
You and I have been through a lot in the last few days.
Let's just get some rest.
...yeah, I suppose.
The scent was kinda old, anyway.
TRACE
I'm sure we'll be fine for one night... hm?
Trace, where did this book come from?
Hey, wait! I can explain that...
What does it say?
Huh..? You don't...?
JOURNAL
TRACELEGACY
I... can't read. I was never taught as a slave.
Well, um.. don't worry about this old thing.
It's just an old story book.
Oh, it is?
Yes, I found it at the house. Nothing you'd be interested in, I'm sure.
Well, I'd better continue setting up camp.
Okay... do you mind if I go for a walk?
Flora, you said it yourself... it's dangerous out there.
Aw...
Don't worry about me. This is my territory.
I guess if you really want to.. but be careful.
I'll drag you back by the tail if you get me worried about you.

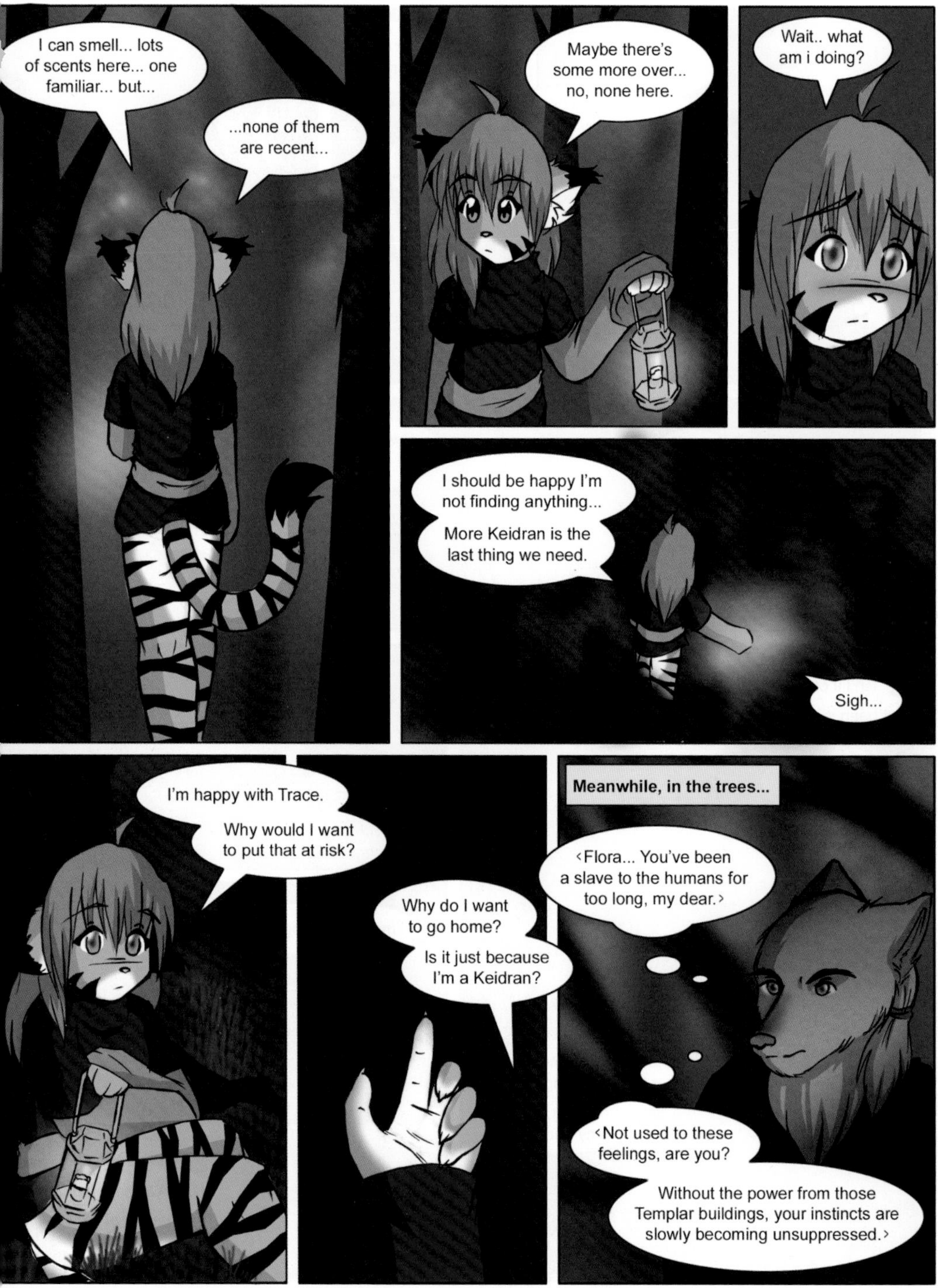
I can smell... lots of scents here... one familiar... but...
...none of them are recent...
Maybe there's some more over... no, none here.
Wait.. what am i doing?
I should be happy I'm not finding anything...
More Keidran is the last thing we need.
Sigh...
I'm happy with Trace.
Why would I want to put that at risk?
Why do I want to go home?
Is it just because I'm a Keidran?
Meanwhile, in the trees...
‹Flora... You've been a slave to the humans for too long, my dear.›
‹Not used to these feelings, are you?
Without the power from those Templar buildings, your instincts are slowly becoming unsuppressed.›

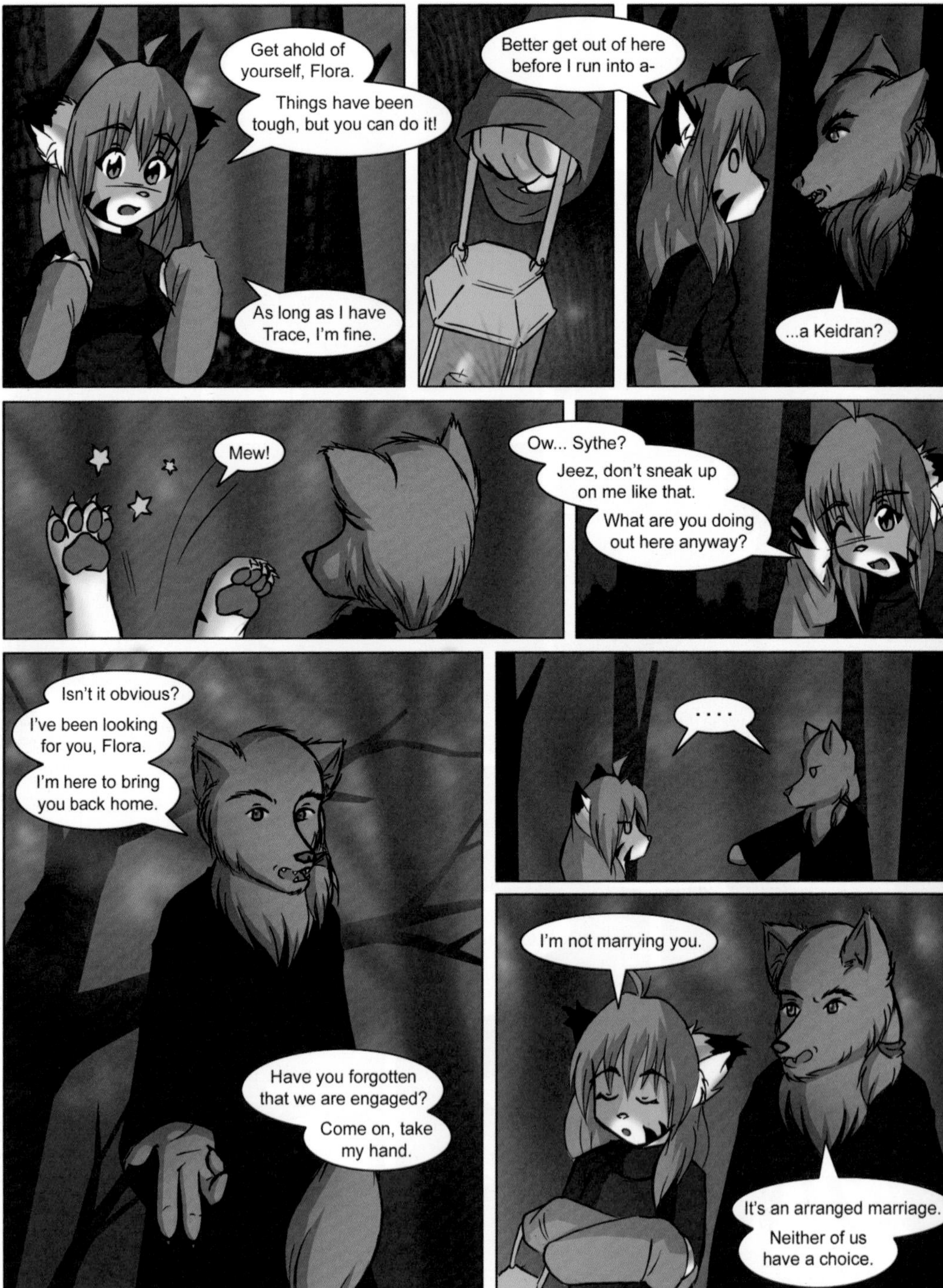
Get ahold of yourself, Flora.
Things have been tough, but you can do it!
As long as I have Trace, I'm fine.
Better get out of here before I run into a-
...a Keidran?
Mew!
Ow... Sythe?
Jeez, don't sneak up on me like that.
What are you doing out here anyway?
Isn't it obvious?
I've been looking for you, Flora.
I'm here to bring you back home.
Have you forgotten that we are engaged?
Come on, take my hand.
....
I'm not marrying you.
It's an arranged marriage.
Neither of us have a choice.

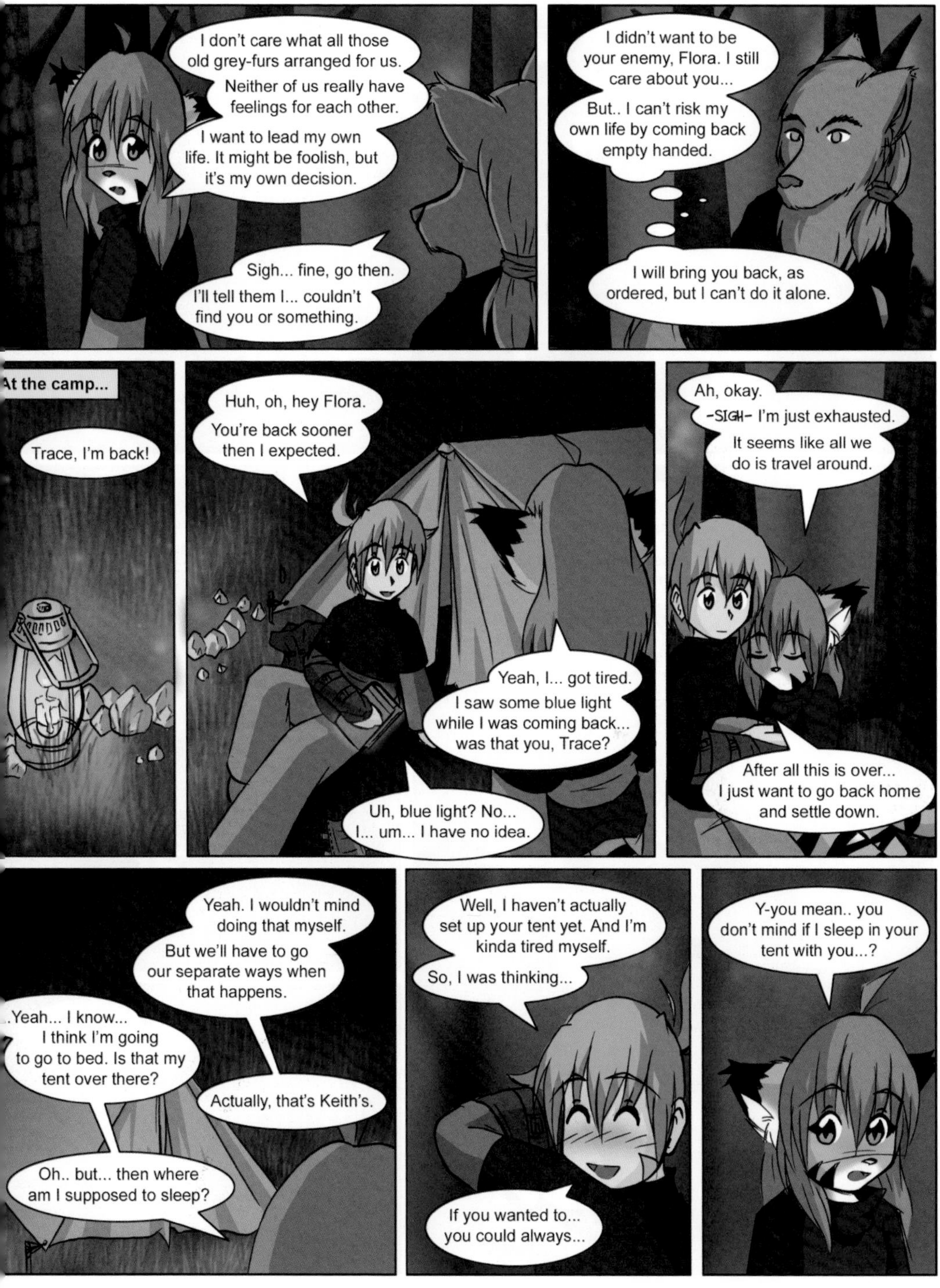
I don't care what all those old grey-furs arranged for us.
Neither of us really have feelings for each other.
I want to lead my own life. It might be foolish, but it's my own decision.
Sigh... fine, go then.
I'll tell them I... couldn't find you or something.
I didn't want to be your enemy, Flora. I still care about you...
But.. I can't risk my own life by coming back empty handed.
I will bring you back, as ordered, but I can't do it alone.
At the camp...
Trace, I'm back!
Huh, oh, hey Flora.
You're back sooner then I expected.
Yeah, I... got tired.
I saw some blue light while I was coming back... was that you, Trace?
Uh, blue light? No... I... um... I have no idea.
Ah, okay.
-SIGH- I'm just exhausted.
It seems like all we do is travel around.
After all this is over... I just want to go back home and settle down.
Yeah. I wouldn't mind doing that myself.
But we'll have to go our separate ways when that happens.
..Yeah... I know... I think I'm going to go to bed. Is that my tent over there?
Actually, that's Keith's.
Oh.. but... then where am I supposed to sleep?
Well, I haven't actually set up your tent yet. And I'm kinda tired myself.
So, I was thinking...
If you wanted to... you could always...
Y-you mean.. you don't mind if I sleep in your tent with you...?

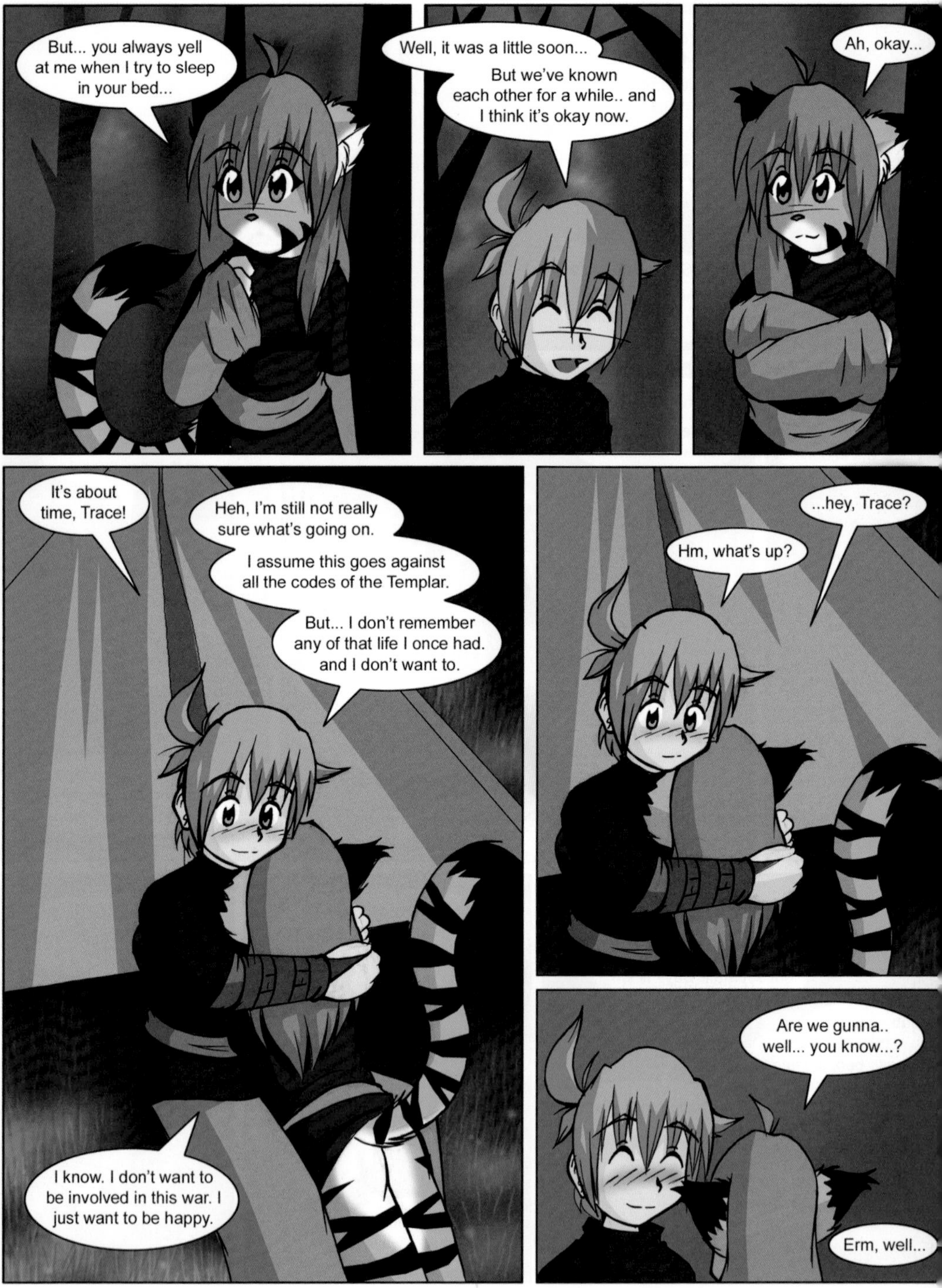
But... you always yell at me when I try to sleep in your bed...
Well, it was a little soon...
But we've known each other for a while.. and I think it's okay now.
Ah, okay...
It's about time, Trace!
Heh, I'm still not really sure what's going on.
I assume this goes against all the codes of the Templar.
But... I don't remember any of that life I once had. and I don't want to.
I know. I don't want to be involved in this war. I just want to be happy.
...hey, Trace?
Hm, what's up?
Are we gunna.. well... you know...?
Erm, well...

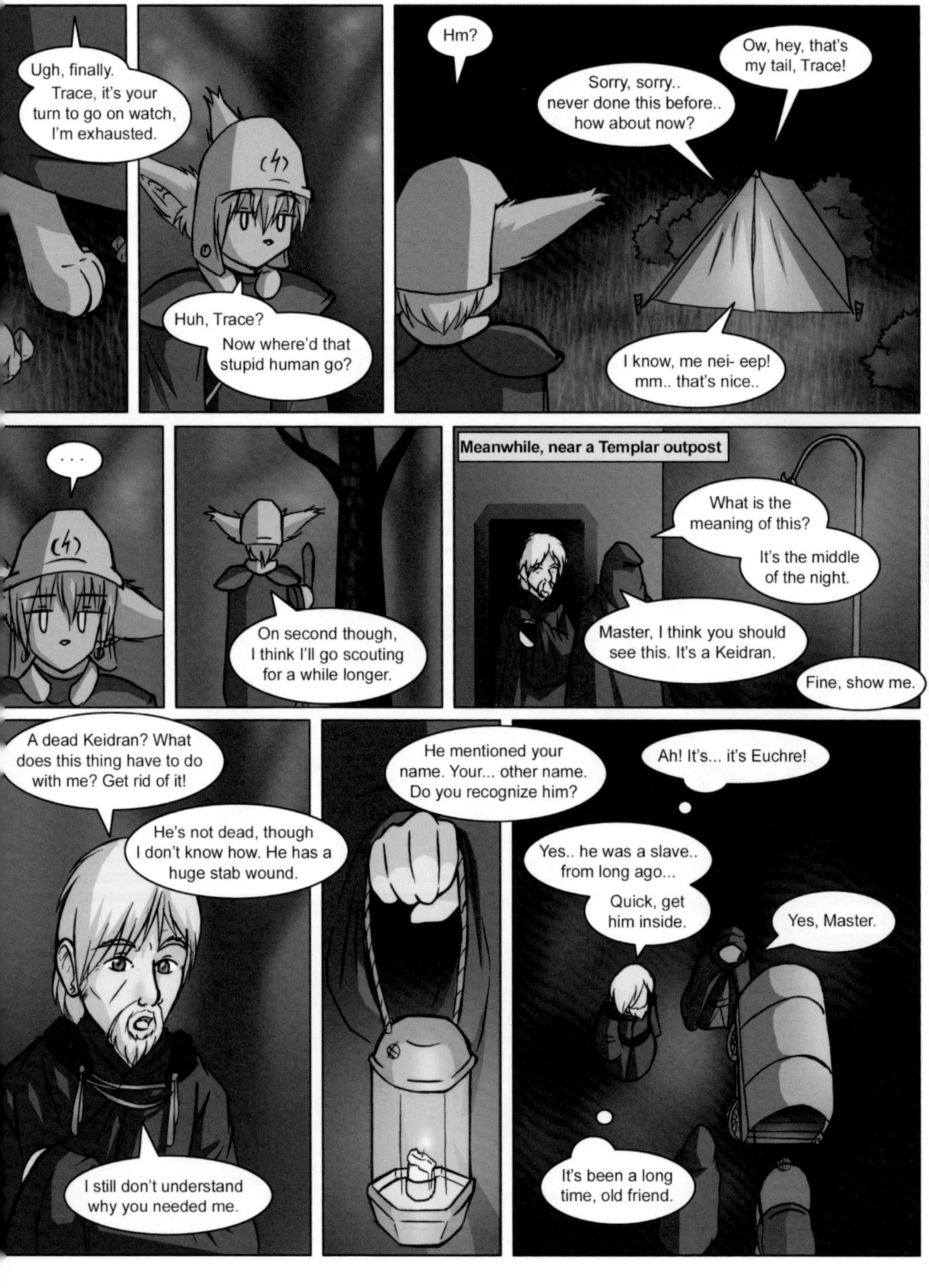

Ugh, finally. Trace, it's your turn to go on watch, I'm exhausted.
Huh, Trace? Now where'd that stupid human go?
Hm?
Ow, hey, that's my tail, Trace!
Sorry, sorry.. never done this before.. how about now?
I know, me nei- eep! mm.. that's nice..
. . .
On second though, I think I'll go scouting for a while longer.
Meanwhile, near a Templar outpost
What is the meaning of this? It's the middle of the night.
Master, I think you should see this. It's a Keidran.
Fine, show me.
A dead Keidran? What does this thing have to do with me? Get rid of it!
He's not dead, though I don't know how. He has a huge stab wound.
I still don't understand why you needed me.
He mentioned your name. Your... other name. Do you recognize him?
Ah! It's... it's Euchre!
Yes.. he was a slave.. from long ago...
Quick, get him inside.
Yes, Master.
It's been a long time, old friend.

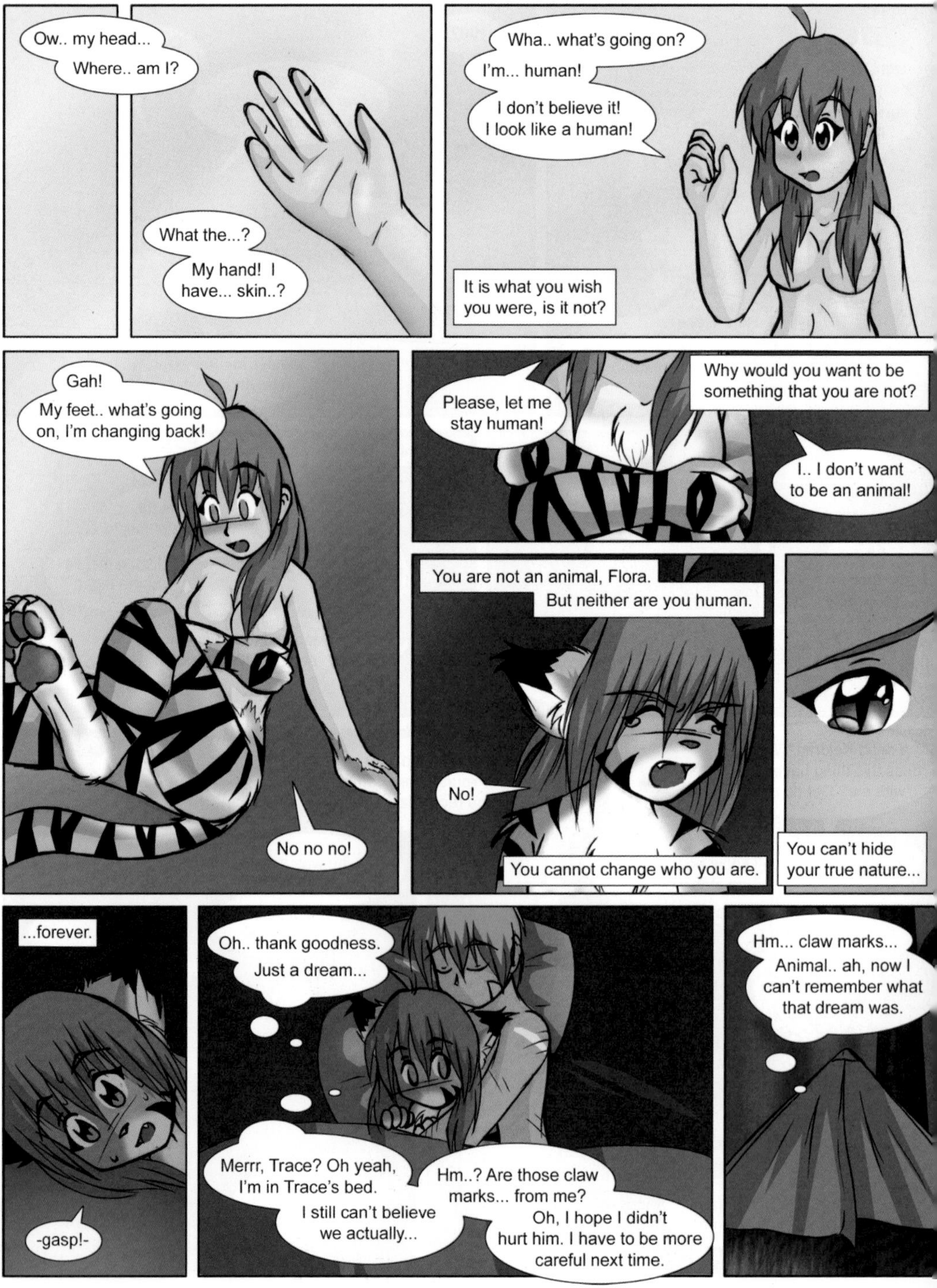
Ow.. my head...
Where.. am I?
What the...?
My hand! I have... skin..?
Wha.. what's going on?
I'm... human!
I don't believe it! I look like a human!
It is what you wish you were, is it not?
Gah! My feet.. what's going on, I'm changing back!
No no no!
Please, let me stay human!
Why would you want to be something that you are not?
I.. I don't want to be an animal!
You are not an animal, Flora.
But neither are you human.
No!
You cannot change who you are.
You can't hide your true nature...
...forever.
-gasp!-
Oh.. thank goodness. Just a dream...
Merrr, Trace? Oh yeah, I'm in Trace's bed.
I still can't believe we actually...
Hm..? Are those claw marks... from me?
Oh, I hope I didn't hurt him. I have to be more careful next time.
Hm... claw marks...
Animal.. ah, now I can't remember what that dream was.

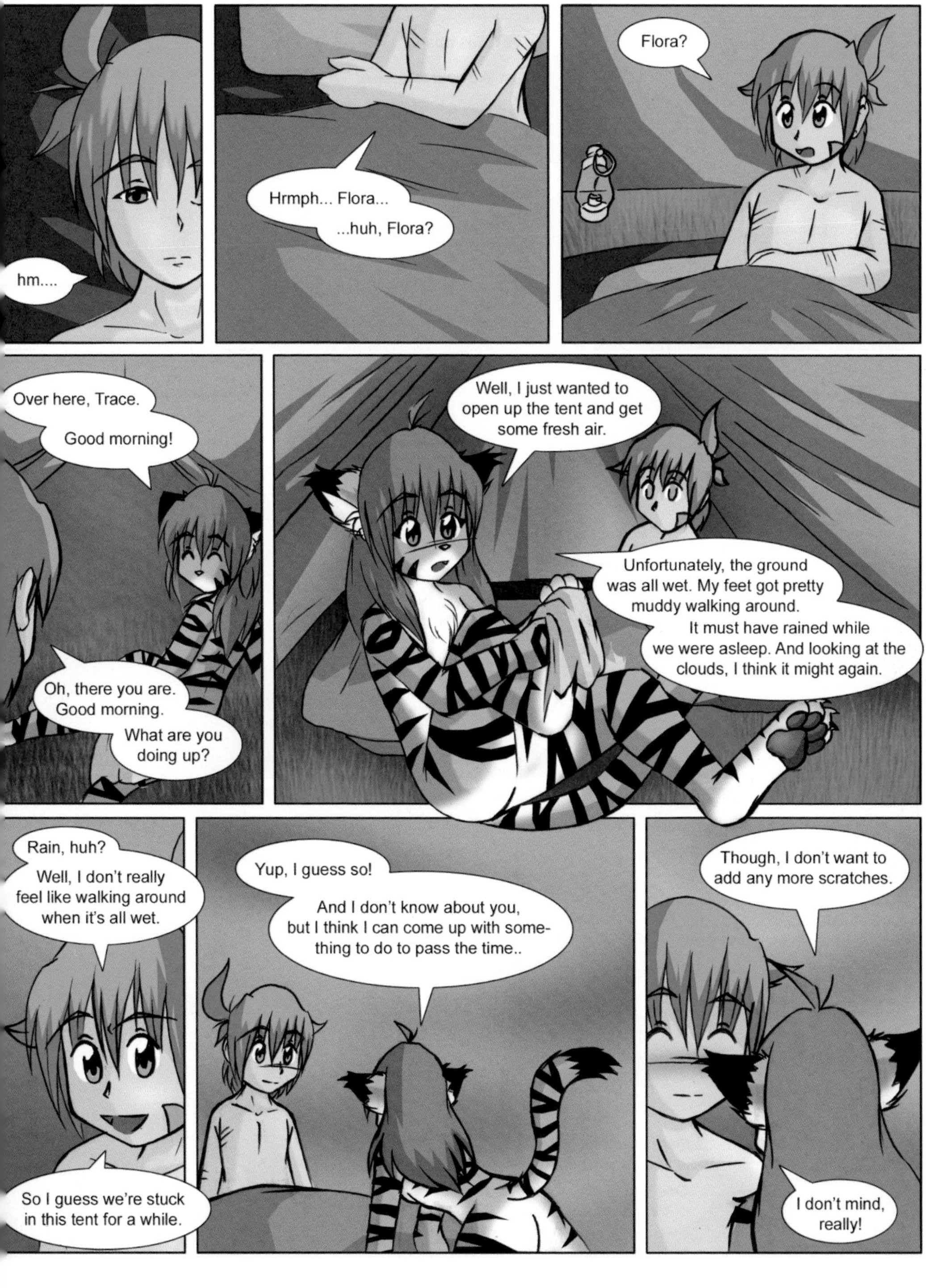
hm....
Hrmph... Flora...
...huh, Flora?
Flora?
Over here, Trace.
Good morning!
Oh, there you are. Good morning.
What are you doing up?
Well, I just wanted to open up the tent and get some fresh air.
Unfortunately, the ground was all wet. My feet got pretty muddy walking around.
It must have rained while we were asleep. And looking at the clouds, I think it might again.
Rain, huh?
Well, I don't really feel like walking around when it's all wet.
So I guess we're stuck in this tent for a while.
Yup, I guess so!
And I don't know about you, but I think I can come up with some-thing to do to pass the time..
Though, I don't want to add any more scratches.
I don't mind, really!

Welcome back, Ephemural.

It's been a while since you've come to this realm.

You've fallen apart.

Just like your little race.

It was a bold move, altering the mind of my warrior.

You knew if you killed him, more would just take his place.

Instead you had him fall for the enemy. Now that's clever.

Unfortunately, that little Keidran fell in love as well.

When the time came, you couldn't split them up.

Now, without Flora, the Tiger and Wolf Clans have no alliance.

Already, the wolves have chosen not to join the others, so sure that they can defend themselves.

One by one, the clans will fall.

Until only my race shall rule this earth.

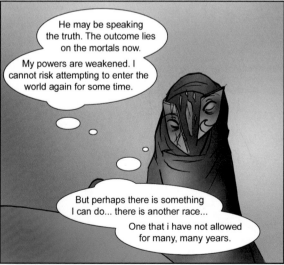

He may be speaking the truth. The outcome lies on the mortals now.

My powers are weakened. I cannot risk attempting to enter the world again for some time.

But perhaps there is something I can do... there is another race...

One that i have not allowed for many, many years.

I have no choice. I must ensure at least some Keidran blood survives.

From this point forth...

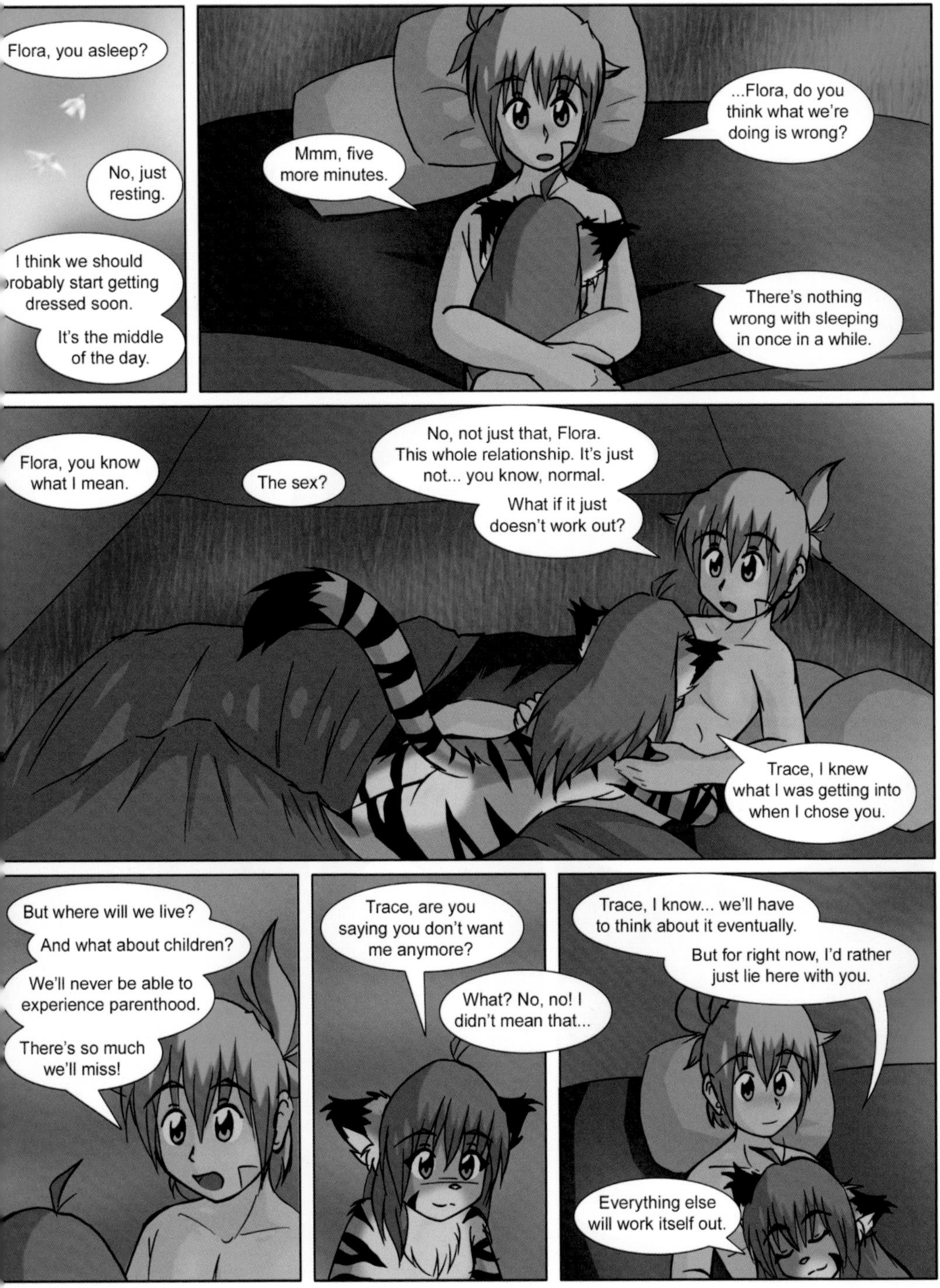
Flora, you asleep?
Mmm, five more minutes.
No, just resting.
I think we should probably start getting dressed soon.
It's the middle of the day.
There's nothing wrong with sleeping in once in a while.
...Flora, do you think what we're doing is wrong?
Flora, you know what I mean.
The sex?
No, not just that, Flora. This whole relationship. It's just not... you know, normal.
What if it just doesn't work out?
Trace, I knew what I was getting into when I chose you.
But where will we live?
And what about children?
We'll never be able to experience parenthood.
There's so much we'll miss!
Trace, are you saying you don't want me anymore?
What? No, no! I didn't mean that...
Trace, I know... we'll have to think about it eventually.
But for right now, I'd rather just lie here with you.
Everything else will work itself out.

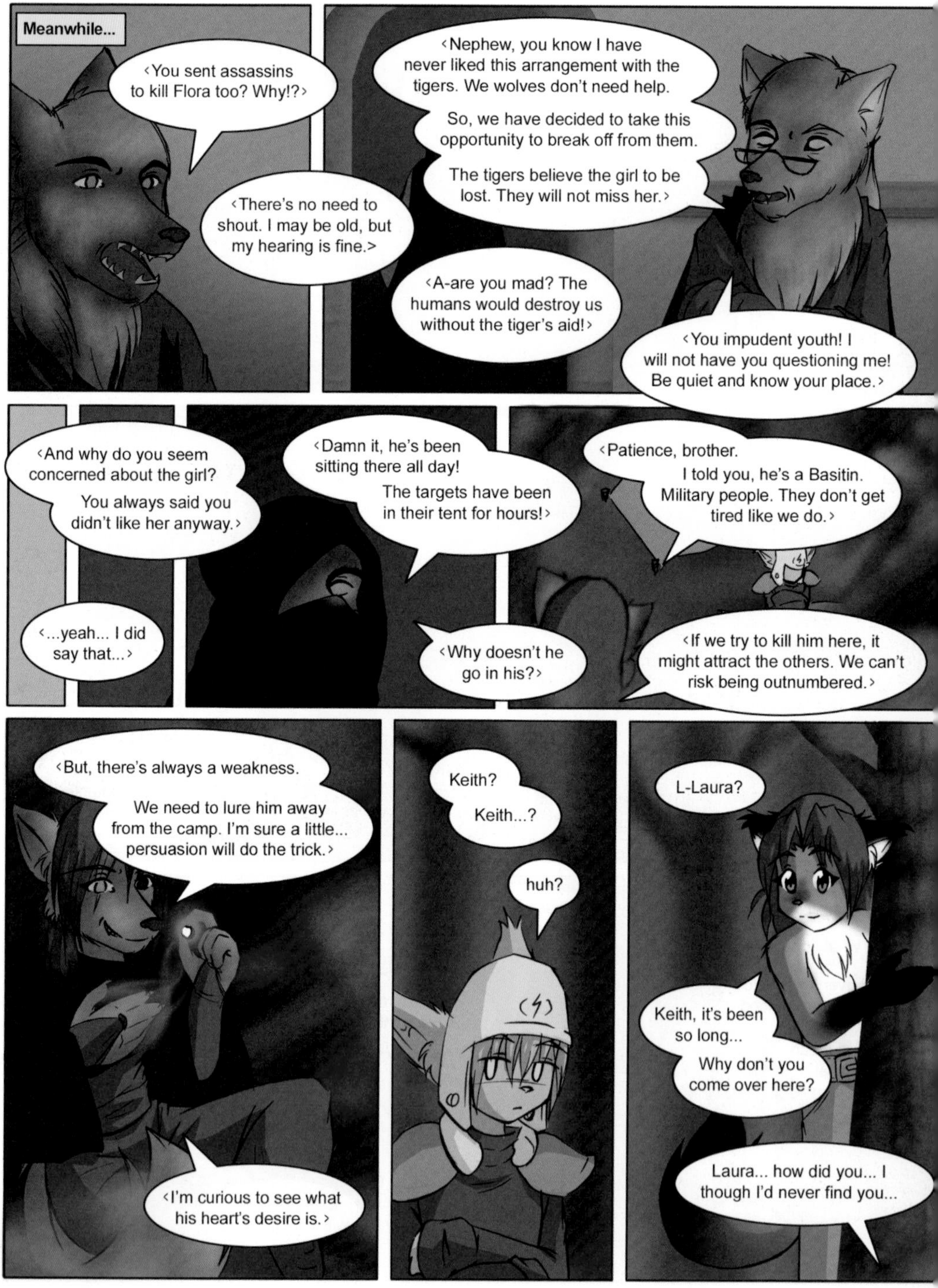
Meanwhile...
<You sent assassins to kill Flora too? Why!?>
<There's no need to shout. I may be old, but my hearing is fine.>
<Nephew, you know I have never liked this arrangement with the tigers. We wolves don't need help.
So, we have decided to take this opportunity to break off from them.
The tigers believe the girl to be lost. They will not miss her.>
<A-are you mad? The humans would destroy us without the tiger's aid!>
<You impudent youth! I will not have you questioning me! Be quiet and know your place.>
<And why do you seem concerned about the girl?
You always said you didn't like her anyway.>
<...yeah... I did say that...>
<Damn it, he's been sitting there all day!
The targets have been in their tent for hours!>
<Why doesn't he go in his?>
<Patience, brother.
I told you, he's a Basitin. Military people. They don't get tired like we do.>
<If we try to kill him here, it might attract the others. We can't risk being outnumbered.>
<But, there's always a weakness.
We need to lure him away from the camp. I'm sure a little... persuasion will do the trick.>
<I'm curious to see what his heart's desire is.>
Keith?
Keith...?
huh?
L-Laura?
Keith, it's been so long...
Why don't you come over here?
Laura... how did you... I though I'd never find you...

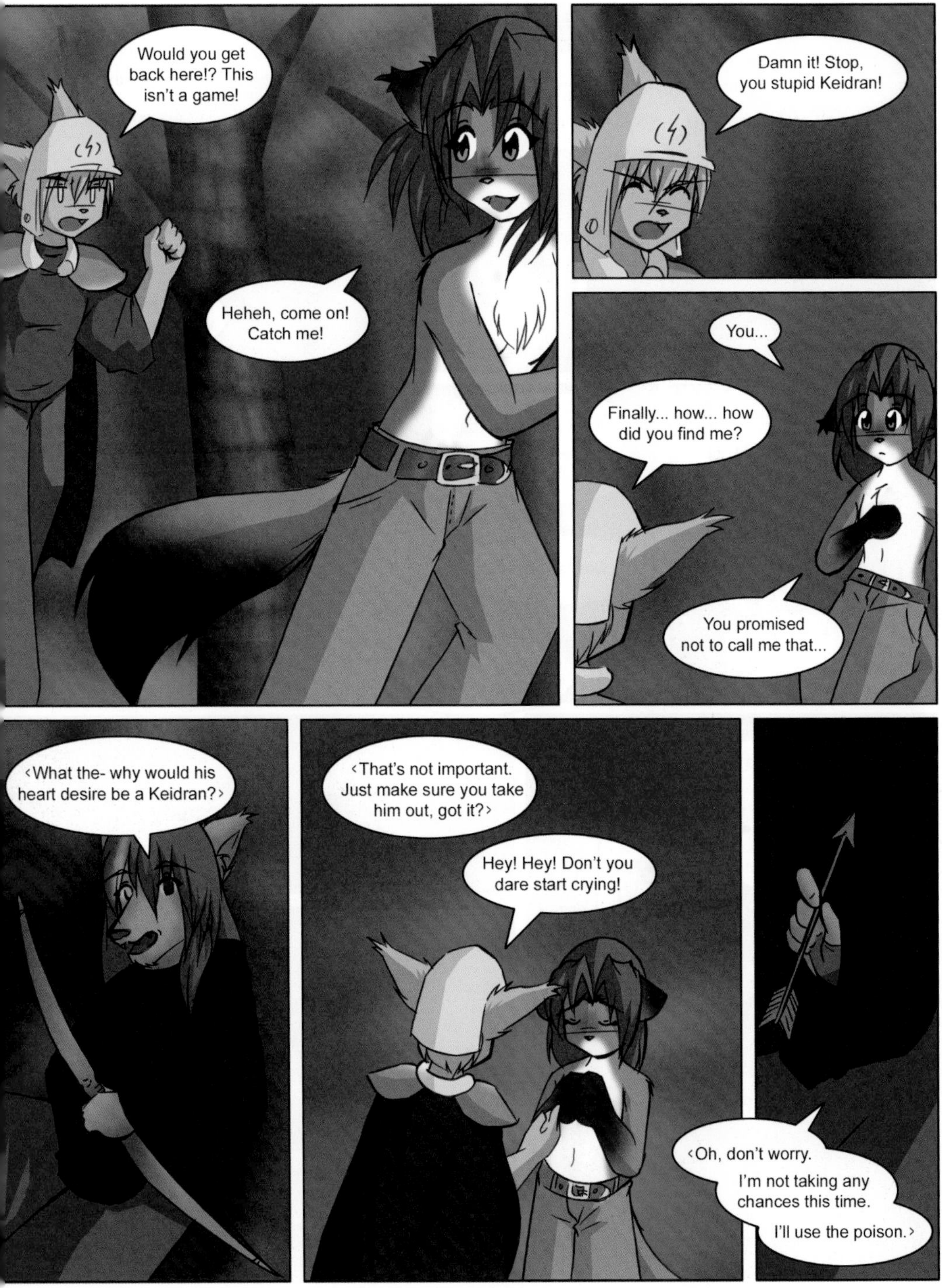

Would you get back here!? This isn't a game!
Heheh, come on! Catch me!
Damn it! Stop, you stupid Keidran!
You...
Finally... how... how did you find me?
You promised not to call me that...
‹What the- why would his heart desire be a Keidran?›
‹That's not important. Just make sure you take him out, got it?›
Hey! Hey! Don't you dare start crying!
‹Oh, don't worry.
I'm not taking any chances this time.
I'll use the poison.›

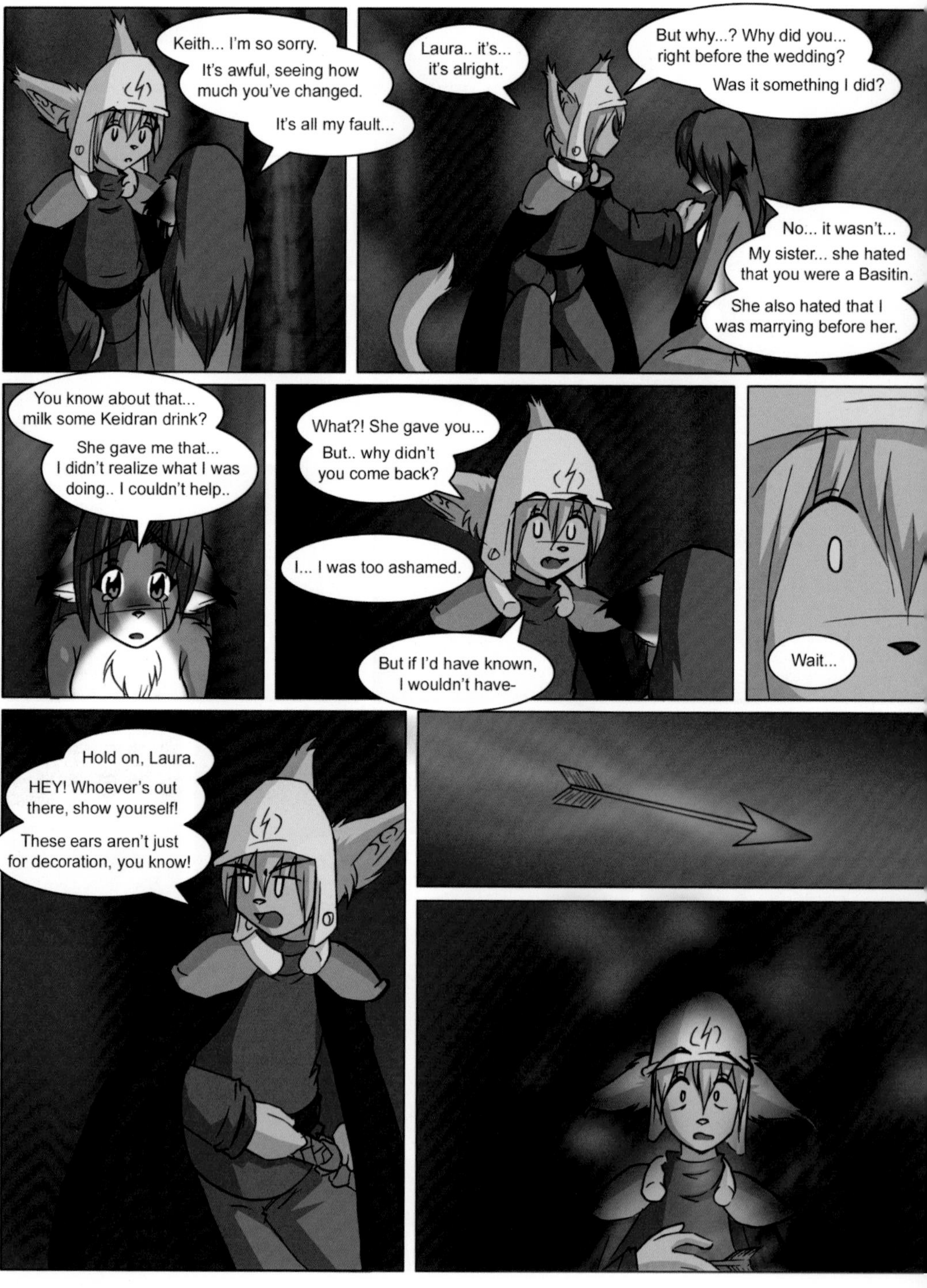
Keith... I'm so sorry.
It's awful, seeing how much you've changed.
It's all my fault...
Laura.. it's... it's alright.
But why...? Why did you... right before the wedding?
Was it something I did?
No... it wasn't...
My sister... she hated that you were a Basitin.
She also hated that I was marrying before her.
You know about that... milk some Keidran drink?
She gave me that... I didn't realize what I was doing.. I couldn't help..
What?! She gave you...
But.. why didn't you come back?
I... I was too ashamed.
But if I'd have known, I wouldn't have-
Wait...
Hold on, Laura.
HEY! Whoever's out there, show yourself!
These ears aren't just for decoration, you know!

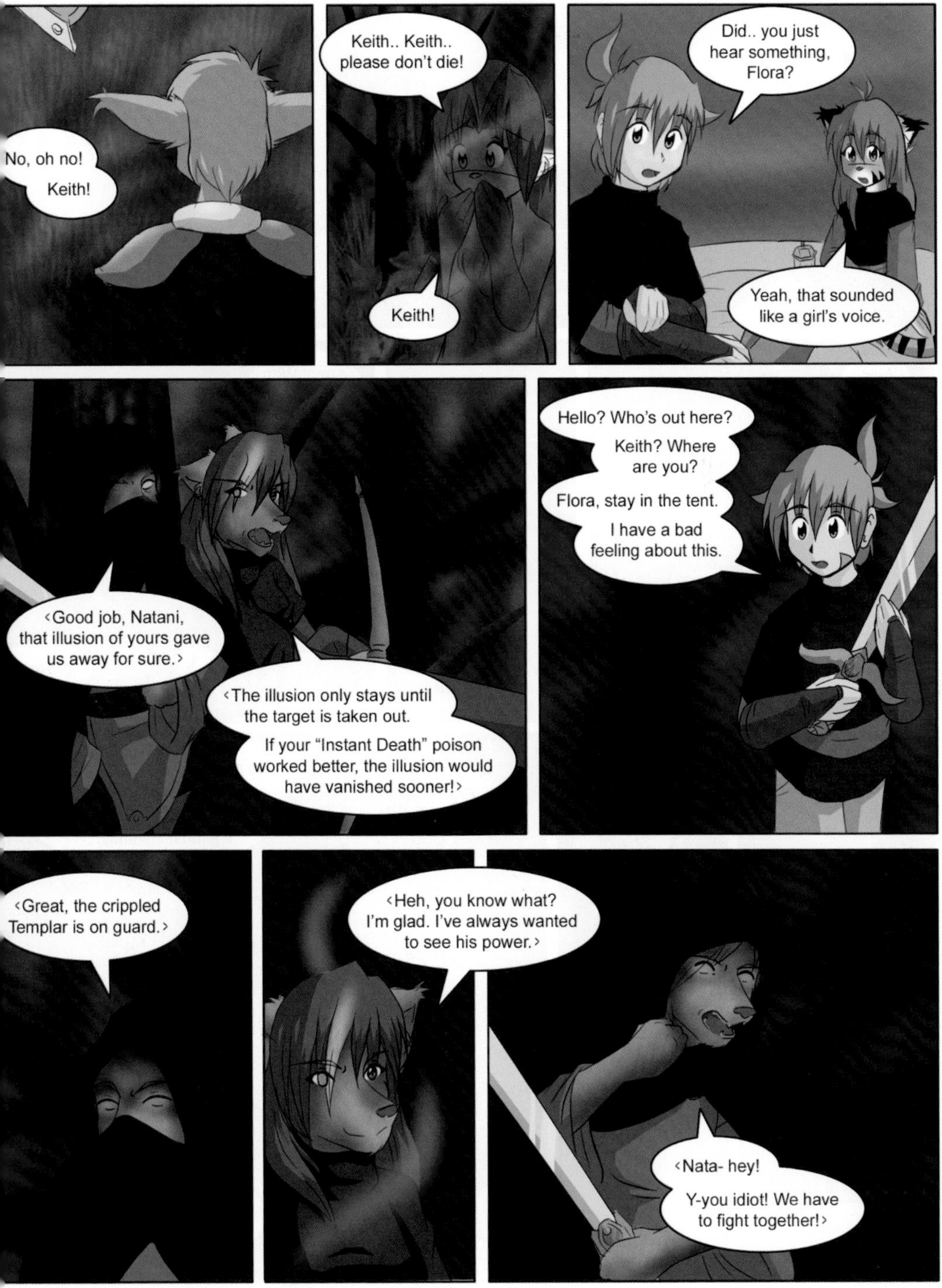
No, oh no!
Keith!
Keith.. Keith.. please don't die!
Keith!
Did.. you just hear something, Flora?
Yeah, that sounded like a girl's voice.
‹Good job, Natani, that illusion of yours gave us away for sure.›
‹The illusion only stays until the target is taken out.
If your "Instant Death" poison worked better, the illusion would have vanished sooner!›
Hello? Who's out here?
Keith? Where are you?
Flora, stay in the tent.
I have a bad feeling about this.
‹Great, the crippled Templar is on guard.›
‹Heh, you know what? I'm glad. I've always wanted to see his power.›
‹Nata- hey!
Y-you idiot! We have to fight together!›

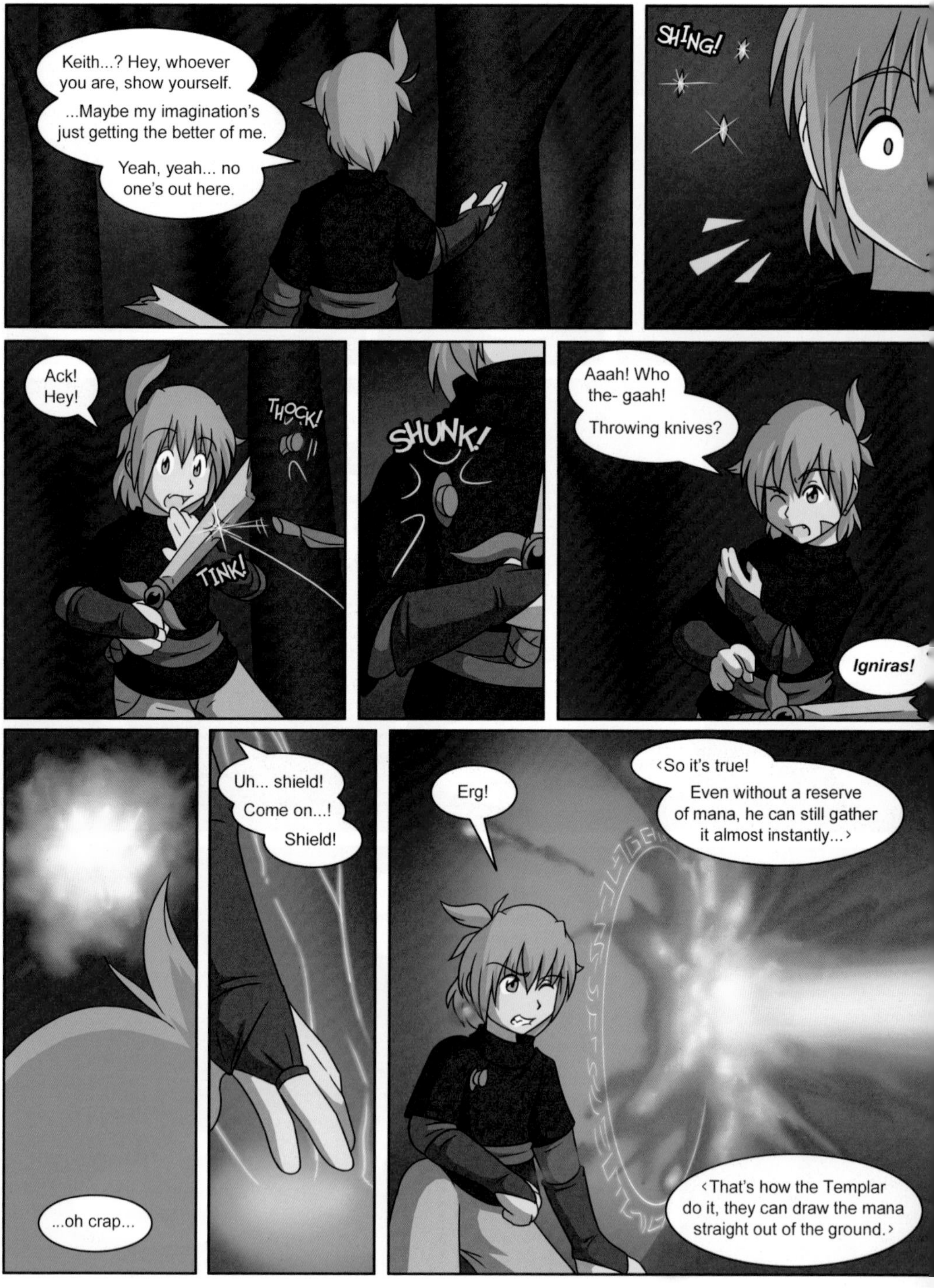
Keith...? Hey, whoever you are, show yourself.
...Maybe my imagination's just getting the better of me.
Yeah, yeah... no one's out here.
SHING!
Ack! Hey!
THOCK!
TINK!
SHUNK!
Aaah! Who the- gaah!
Throwing knives?
Igniras!
...oh crap...
Uh... shield!
Come on...!
Shield!
Erg!
‹So it's true!
Even without a reserve of mana, he can still gather it almost instantly...›
‹That's how the Templar do it, they can draw the mana straight out of the ground.›

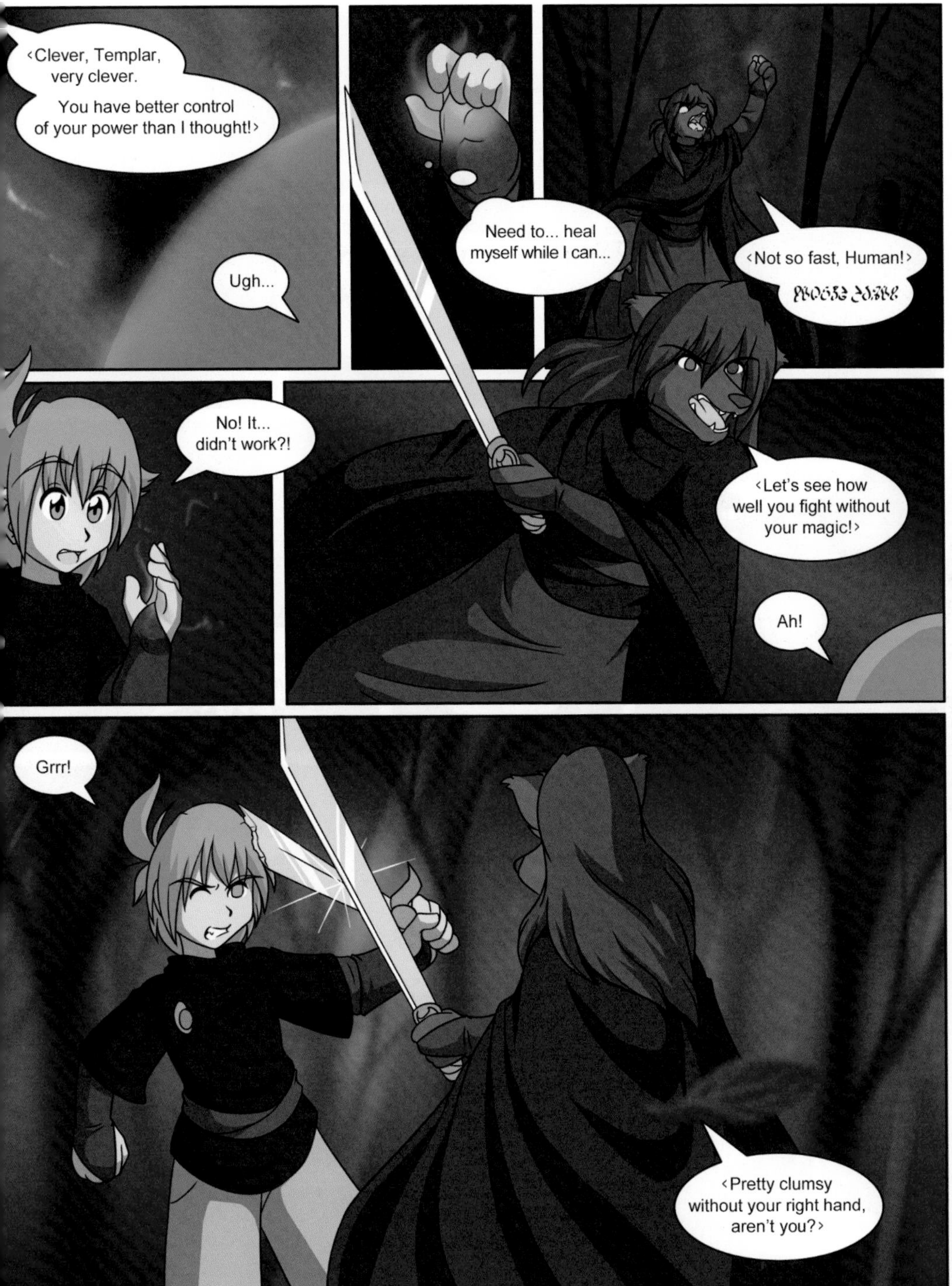
‹Clever, Templar, very clever.
You have better control of your power than I thought!›
Ugh...
Need to... heal myself while I can...
‹Not so fast, Human!›
No! It... didn't work?!
‹Let's see how well you fight without your magic!›
Ah!
Grrr!
‹Pretty clumsy without your right hand, aren't you?›

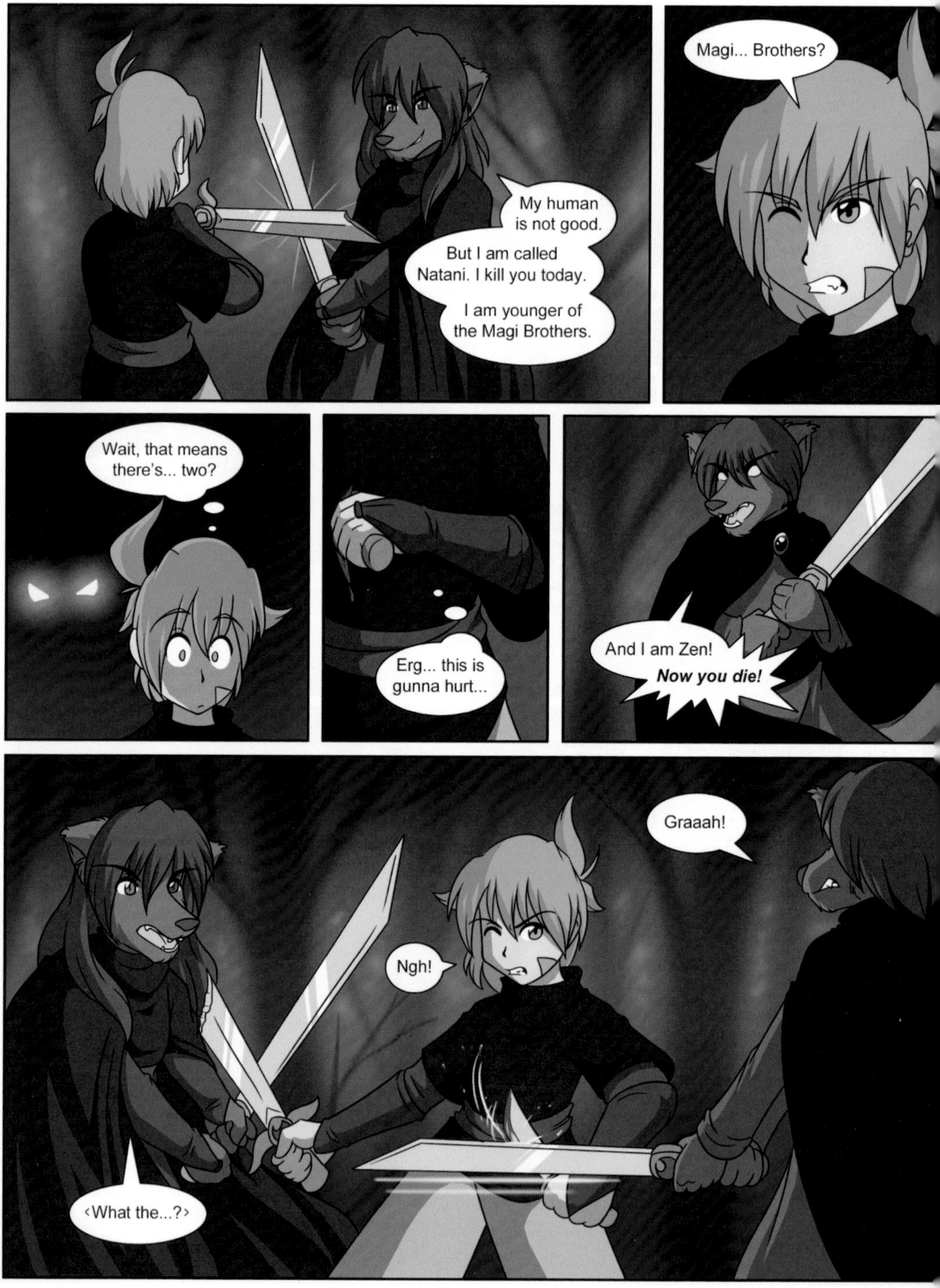
My human is not good.
But I am called Natani. I kill you today.
I am younger of the Magi Brothers.
Magi... Brothers?
Wait, that means there's... two?
Erg... this is gunna hurt...
And I am Zen!
Now you die!
Graaah!
Ngh!
‹What the...?›

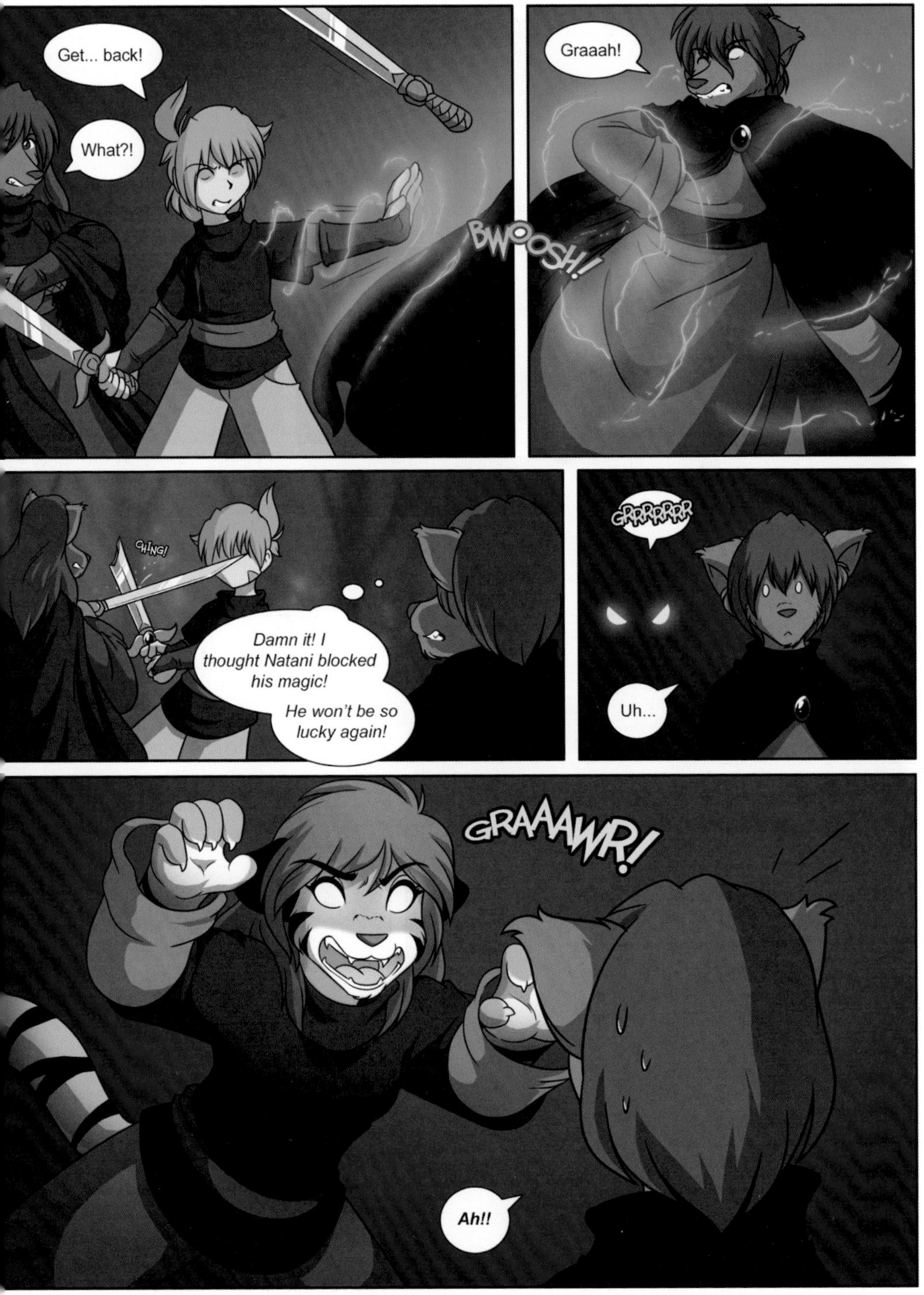
Get... back!
What?!
Graaah!
BWOOSH!
CHING!
Damn it! I thought Natani blocked his magic!
He won't be so lucky again!
GRRRRRRR
Uh...
GRAAAWR!
Ah!!

‹That wound is weakening him.›

‹He must be losing a lot of blood.›

Aaaah!

‹Time to finish him off...›

Igniras!

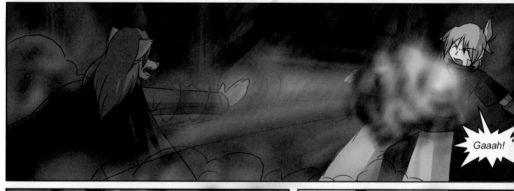

Gaaah!

Agh!

CRACK!

Urgh... t-that hurt...

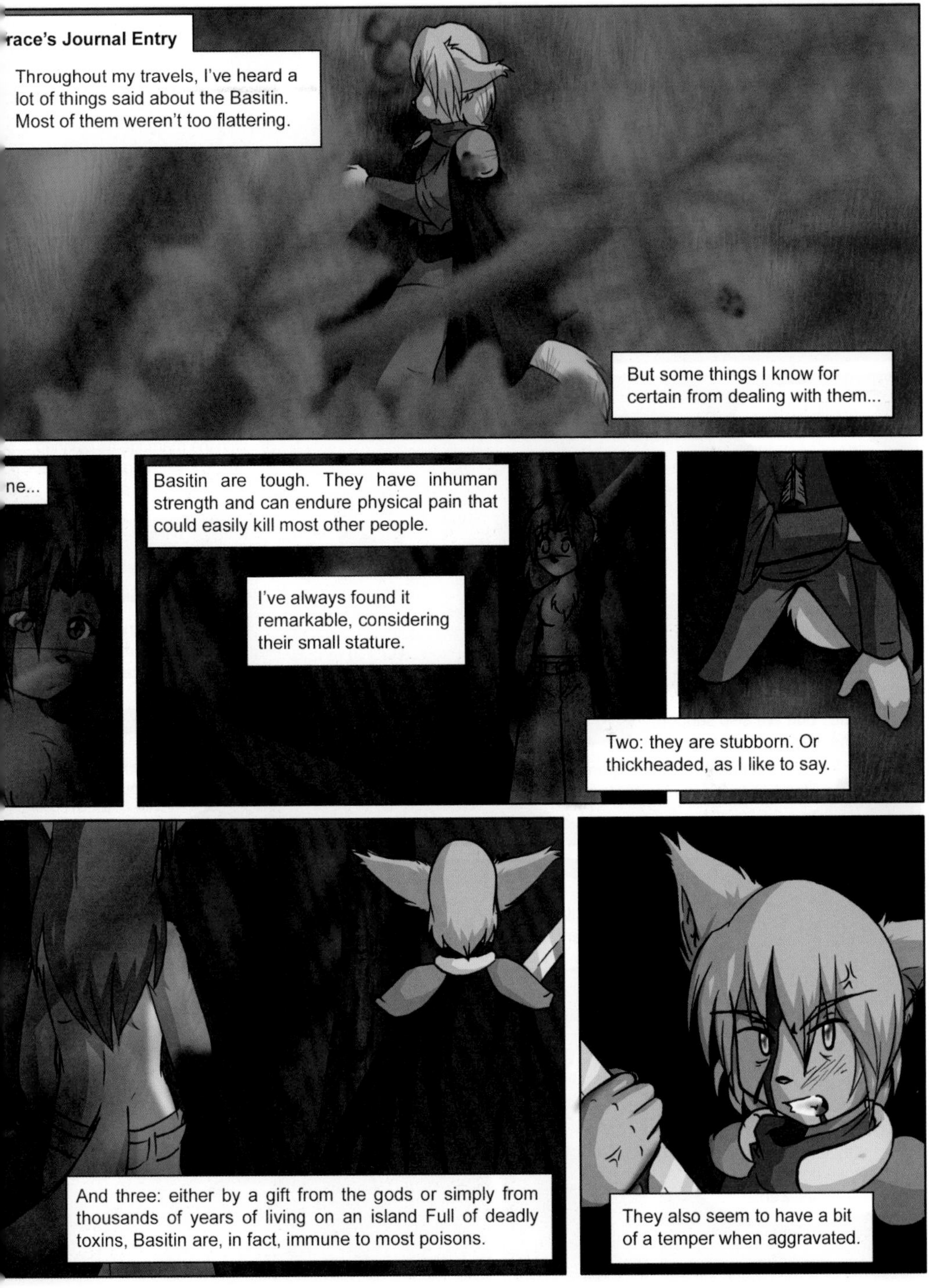
race's Journal Entry
Throughout my travels, I've heard a lot of things said about the Basitin. Most of them weren't too flattering.
But some things I know for certain from dealing with them...
ne...
Basitin are tough. They have inhuman strength and can endure physical pain that could easily kill most other people.
I've always found it remarkable, considering their small stature.
Two: they are stubborn. Or thickheaded, as I like to say.
And three: either by a gift from the gods or simply from thousands of years of living on an island Full of deadly toxins, Basitin are, in fact, immune to most poisons.
They also seem to have a bit of a temper when aggravated.

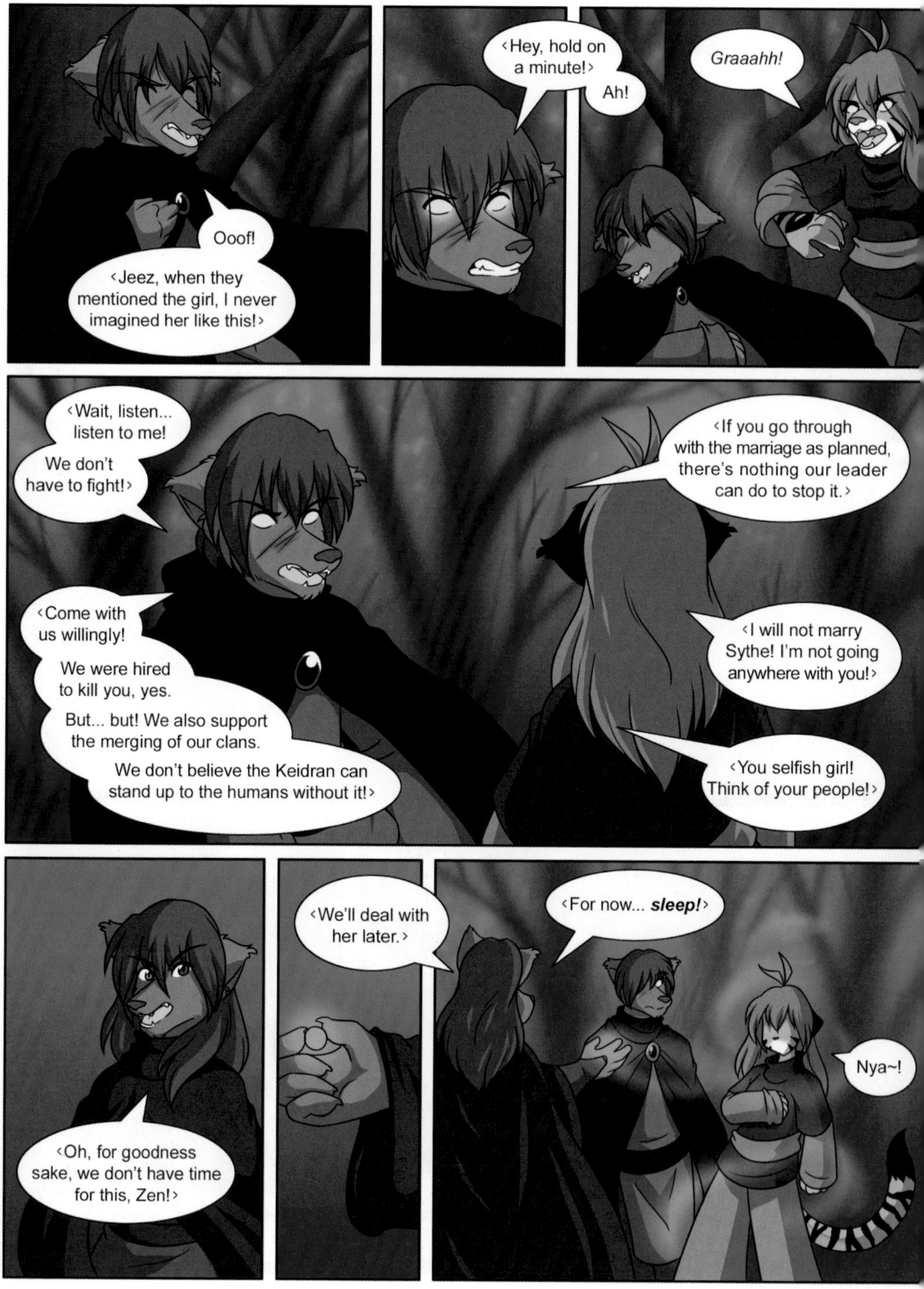
Ooof!
‹Jeez, when they mentioned the girl, I never imagined her like this!›
‹Hey, hold on a minute!›
Ah!
Graaahh!
‹Wait, listen... listen to me!
We don't have to fight!›
‹If you go through with the marriage as planned, there's nothing our leader can do to stop it.›
‹Come with us willingly!
We were hired to kill you, yes.
But... but! We also support the merging of our clans.
We don't believe the Keidran can stand up to the humans without it!›
‹I will not marry Sythe! I'm not going anywhere with you!›
‹You selfish girl! Think of your people!›
‹Oh, for goodness sake, we don't have time for this, Zen!›
‹We'll deal with her later.›
‹For now... sleep!›
Nya~!

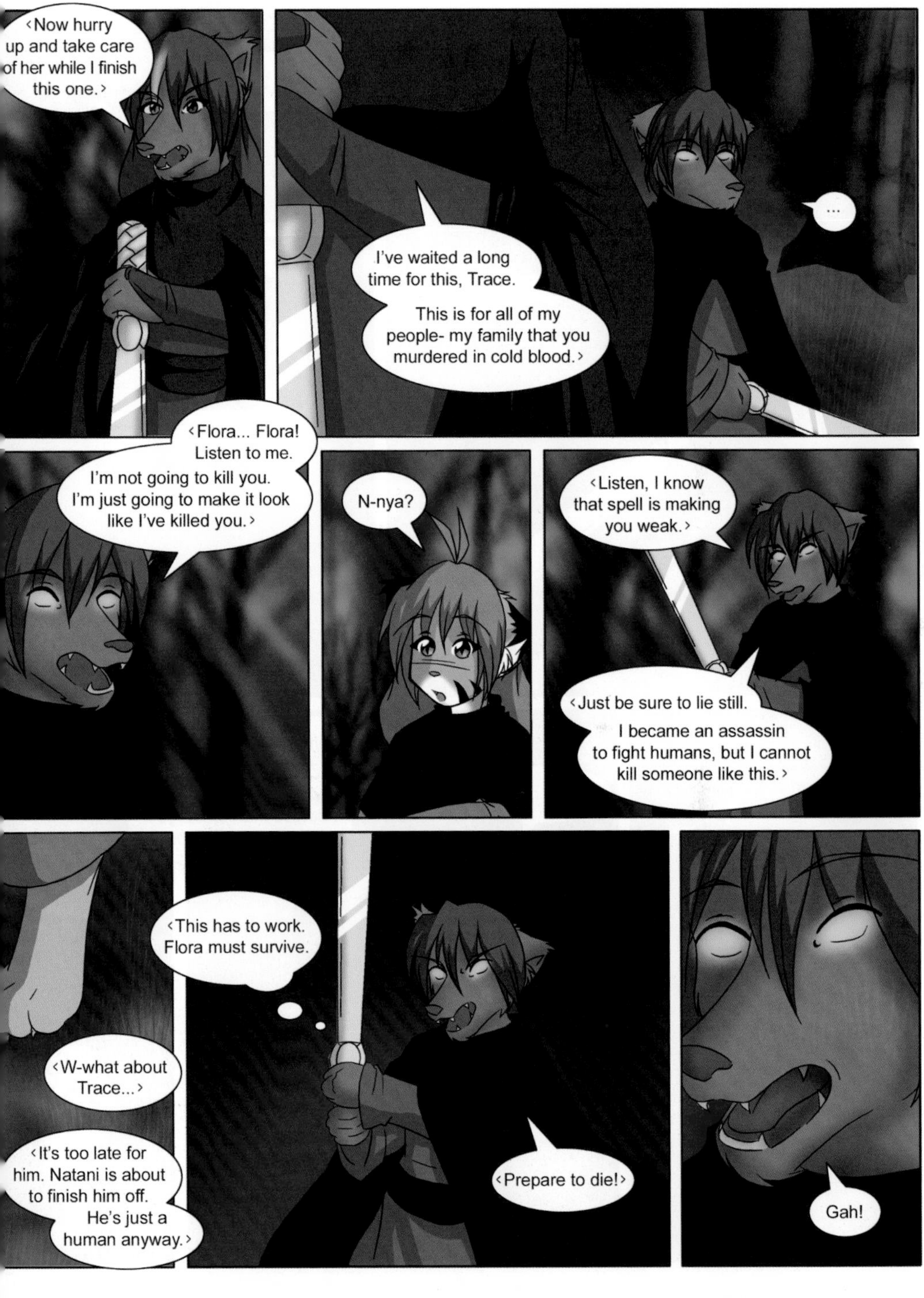
‹Now hurry up and take care of her while I finish this one.›
I've waited a long time for this, Trace.
This is for all of my people- my family that you murdered in cold blood.›
...
‹Flora... Flora! Listen to me.
I'm not going to kill you. I'm just going to make it look like I've killed you.›
N-nya?
‹Listen, I know that spell is making you weak.›
‹Just be sure to lie still.
I became an assassin to fight humans, but I cannot kill someone like this.›
‹This has to work. Flora must survive.
‹W-what about Trace...›
‹It's too late for him. Natani is about to finish him off.
He's just a human anyway.›
‹Prepare to die!›
Gah!

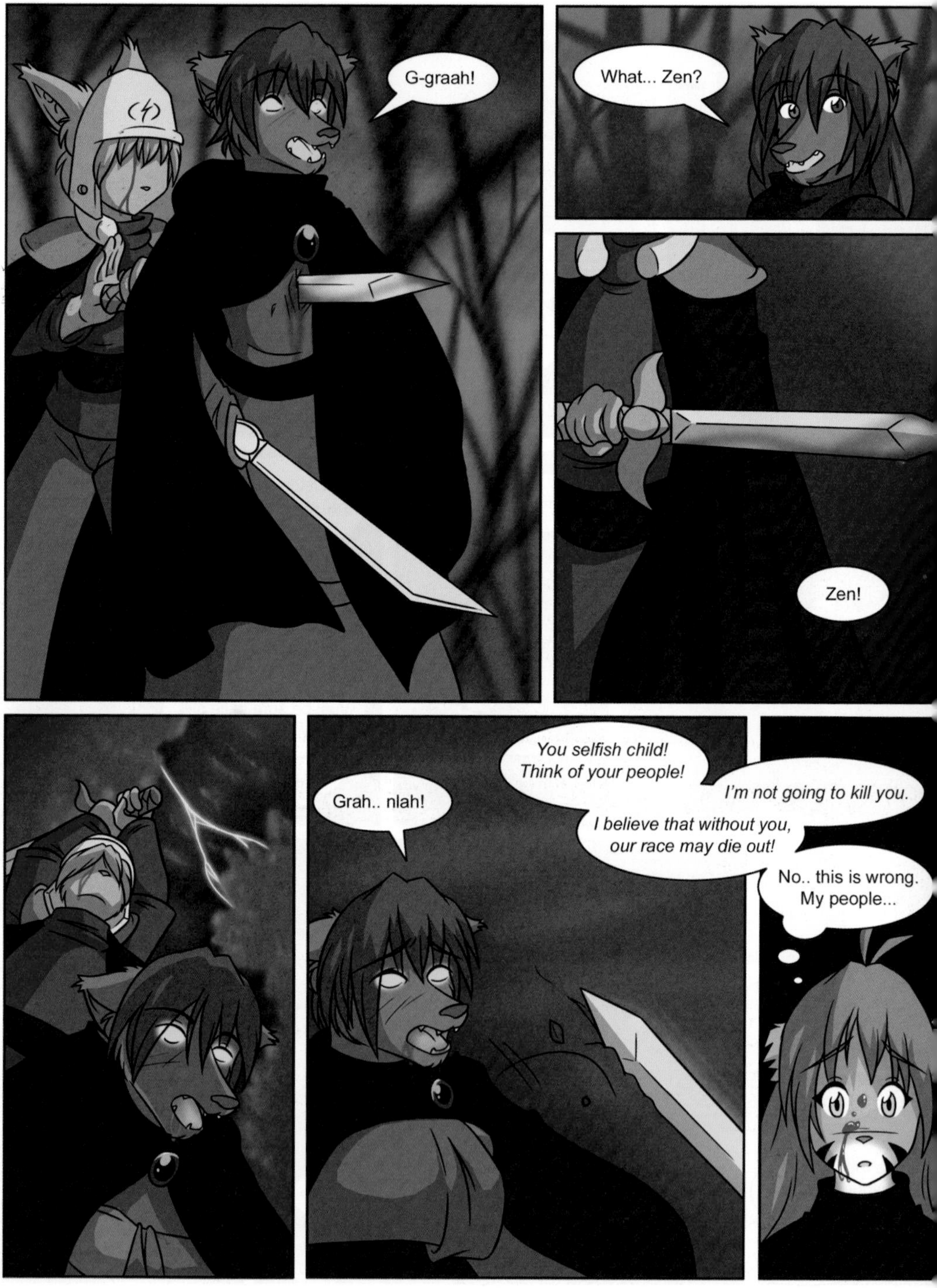

G-graah!
What... Zen?
Zen!
Grah.. nlah!
You selfish child! Think of your people!
I'm not going to kill you.
I believe that without you, our race may die out!
No.. this is wrong. My people...

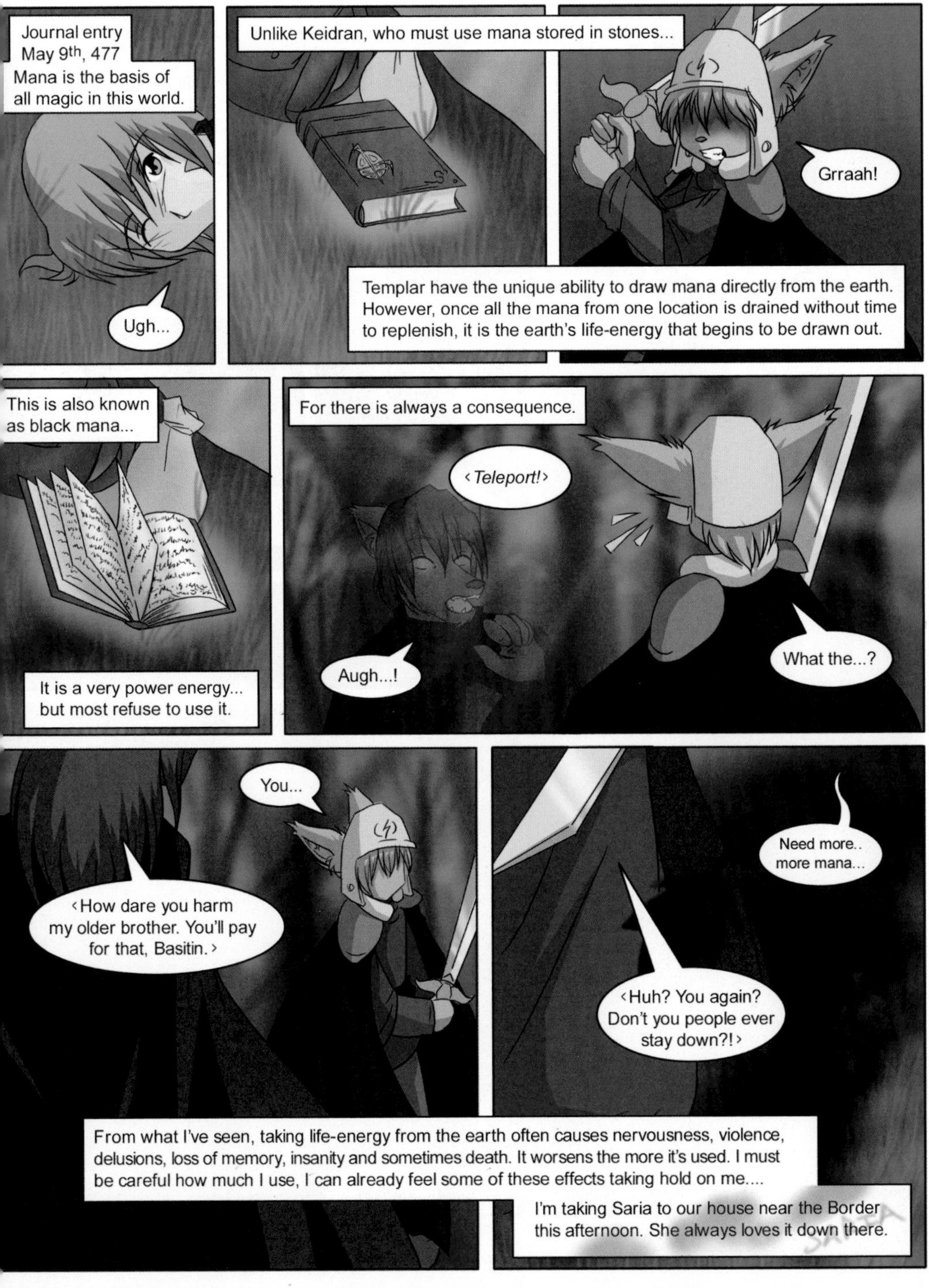

Journal entry
May 9th, 477
Mana is the basis of all magic in this world.
Ugh...
Unlike Keidran, who must use mana stored in stones...
Grraah!
Templar have the unique ability to draw mana directly from the earth. However, once all the mana from one location is drained without time to replenish, it is the earth's life-energy that begins to be drawn out.
This is also known as black mana...
It is a very power energy... but most refuse to use it.
For there is always a consequence.
‹Teleport!›
Augh...!
What the...?
You...
‹How dare you harm my older brother. You'll pay for that, Basitin.›
Need more.. more mana...
‹Huh? You again? Don't you people ever stay down?!›
From what I've seen, taking life-energy from the earth often causes nervousness, violence, delusions, loss of memory, insanity and sometimes death. It worsens the more it's used. I must be careful how much I use, I can already feel some of these effects taking hold on me....
I'm taking Saria to our house near the Border this afternoon. She always loves it down there.

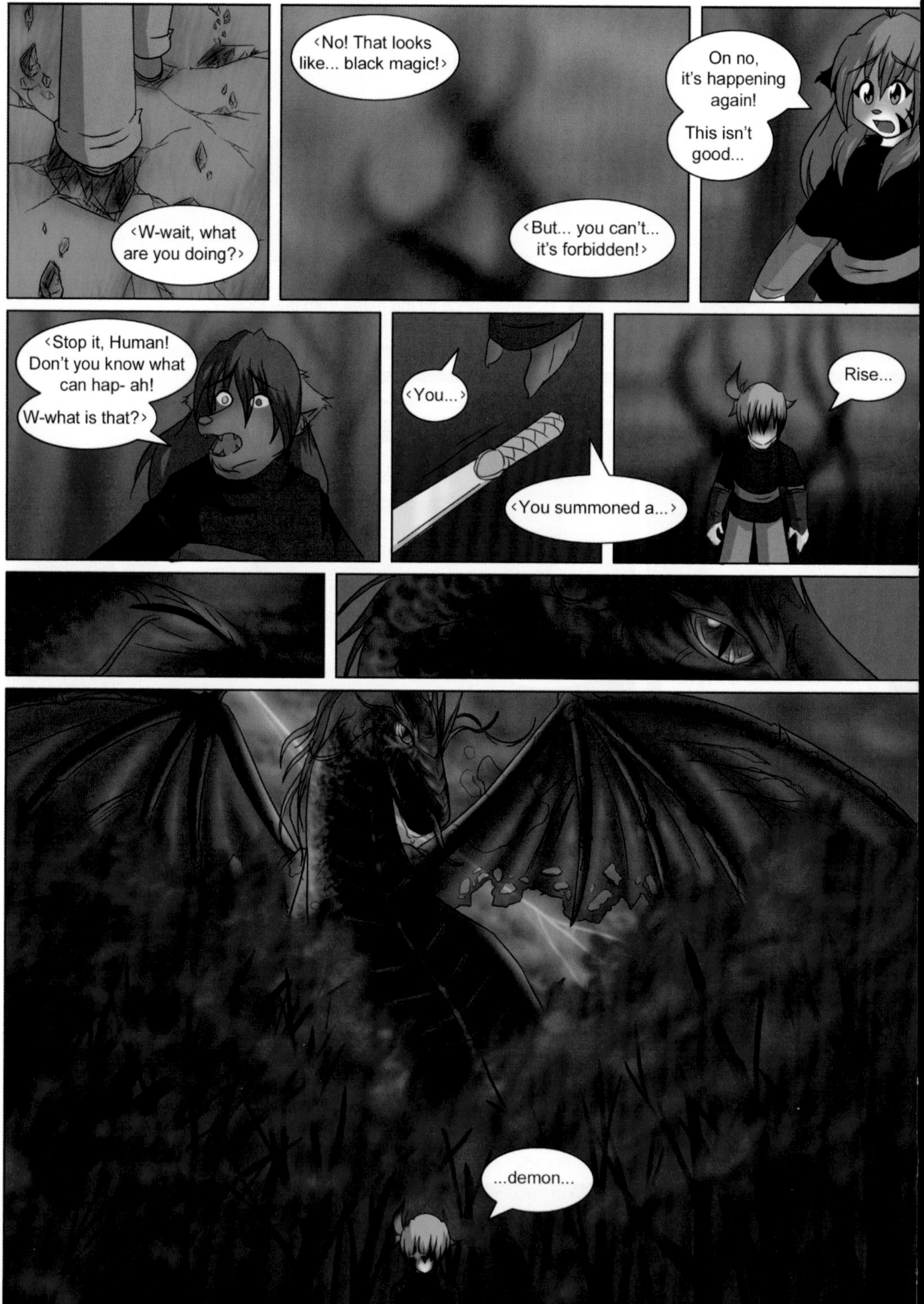

‹W-wait, what are you doing?›
‹No! That looks like... black magic!›
‹But... you can't... it's forbidden!›
On no, it's happening again!
This isn't good...
‹Stop it, Human! Don't you know what can hap- ah!
W-what is that?›
‹You...›
‹You summoned a...›
Rise...
...demon...

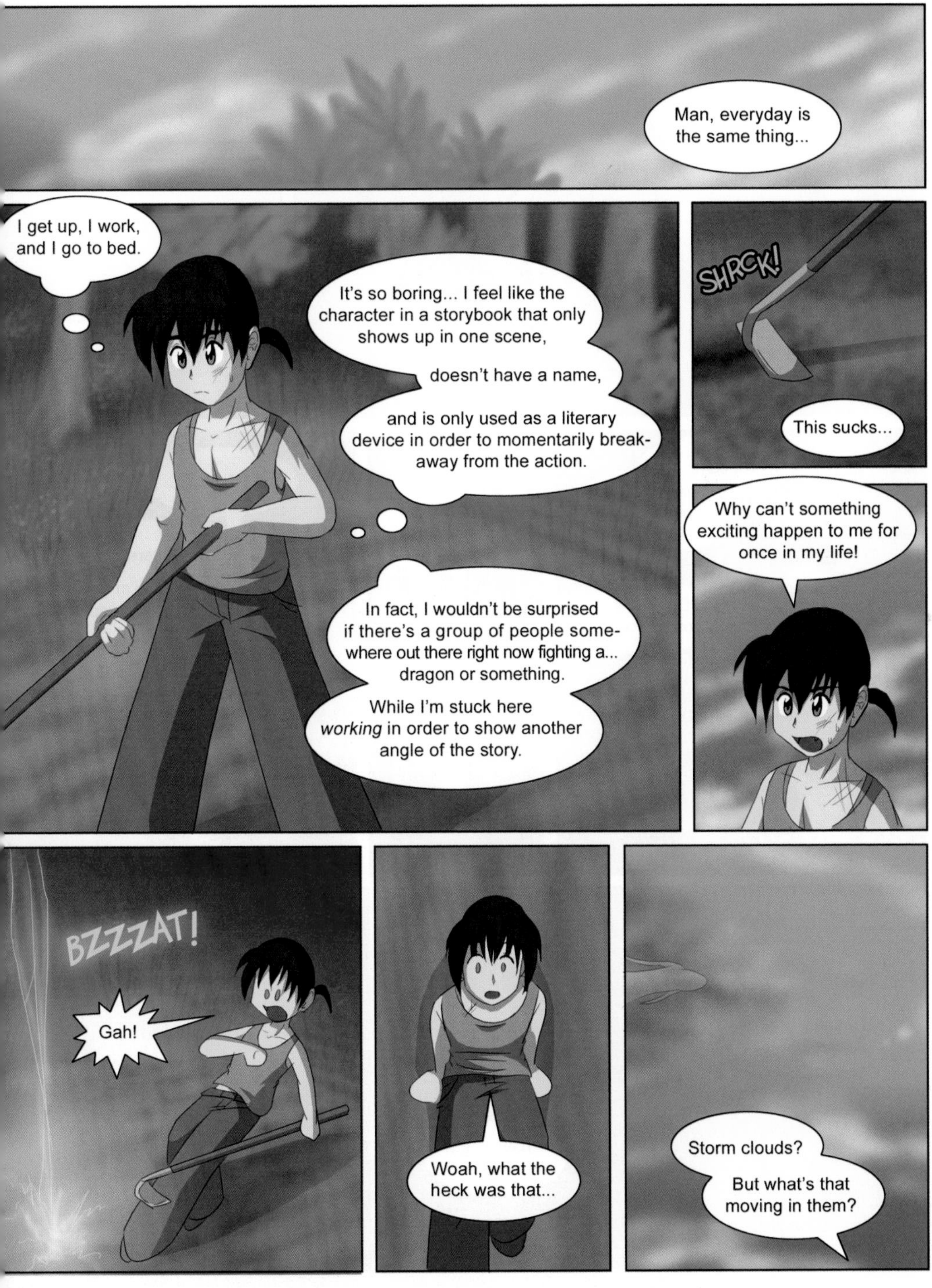
Man, everyday is the same thing...
I get up, I work, and I go to bed.
It's so boring... I feel like the character in a storybook that only shows up in one scene,
doesn't have a name,
and is only used as a literary device in order to momentarily break-away from the action.
In fact, I wouldn't be surprised if there's a group of people some-where out there right now fighting a... dragon or something.
While I'm stuck here *working* in order to show another angle of the story.
SHRCK!
This sucks...
Why can't something exciting happen to me for once in my life!
BZZZAT!
Gah!
Woah, what the heck was that...
Storm clouds?
But what's that moving in them?

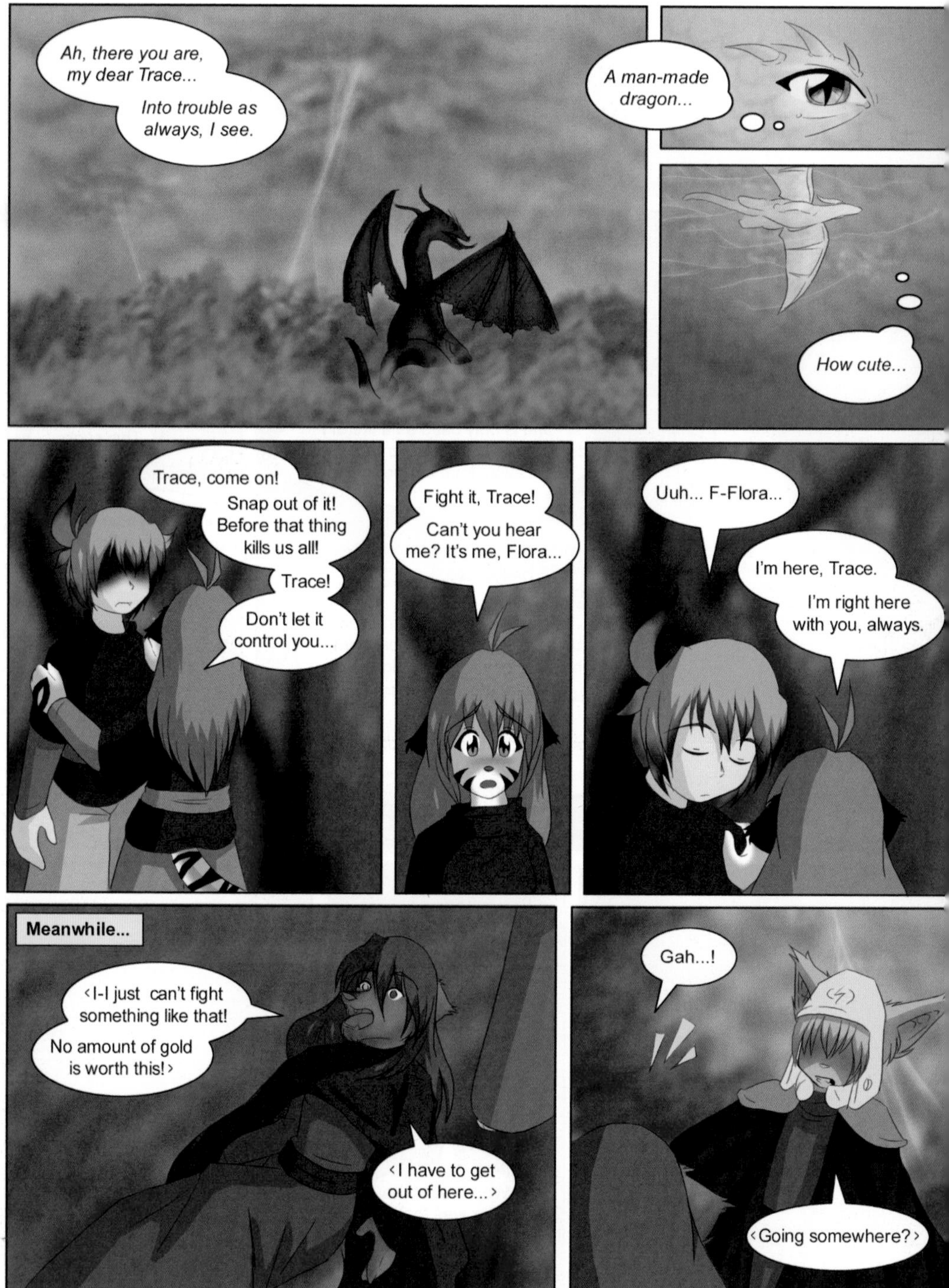
Ah, there you are, my dear Trace...
Into trouble as always, I see.
A man-made dragon...
How cute...
Trace, come on!
Snap out of it! Before that thing kills us all!
Trace!
Don't let it control you...
Fight it, Trace!
Can't you hear me? It's me, Flora...
Uuh... F-Flora...
I'm here, Trace.
I'm right here with you, always.
Meanwhile...
‹I-I just can't fight something like that!
No amount of gold is worth this!›
‹I have to get out of here...›
Gah...!
‹Going somewhere?›

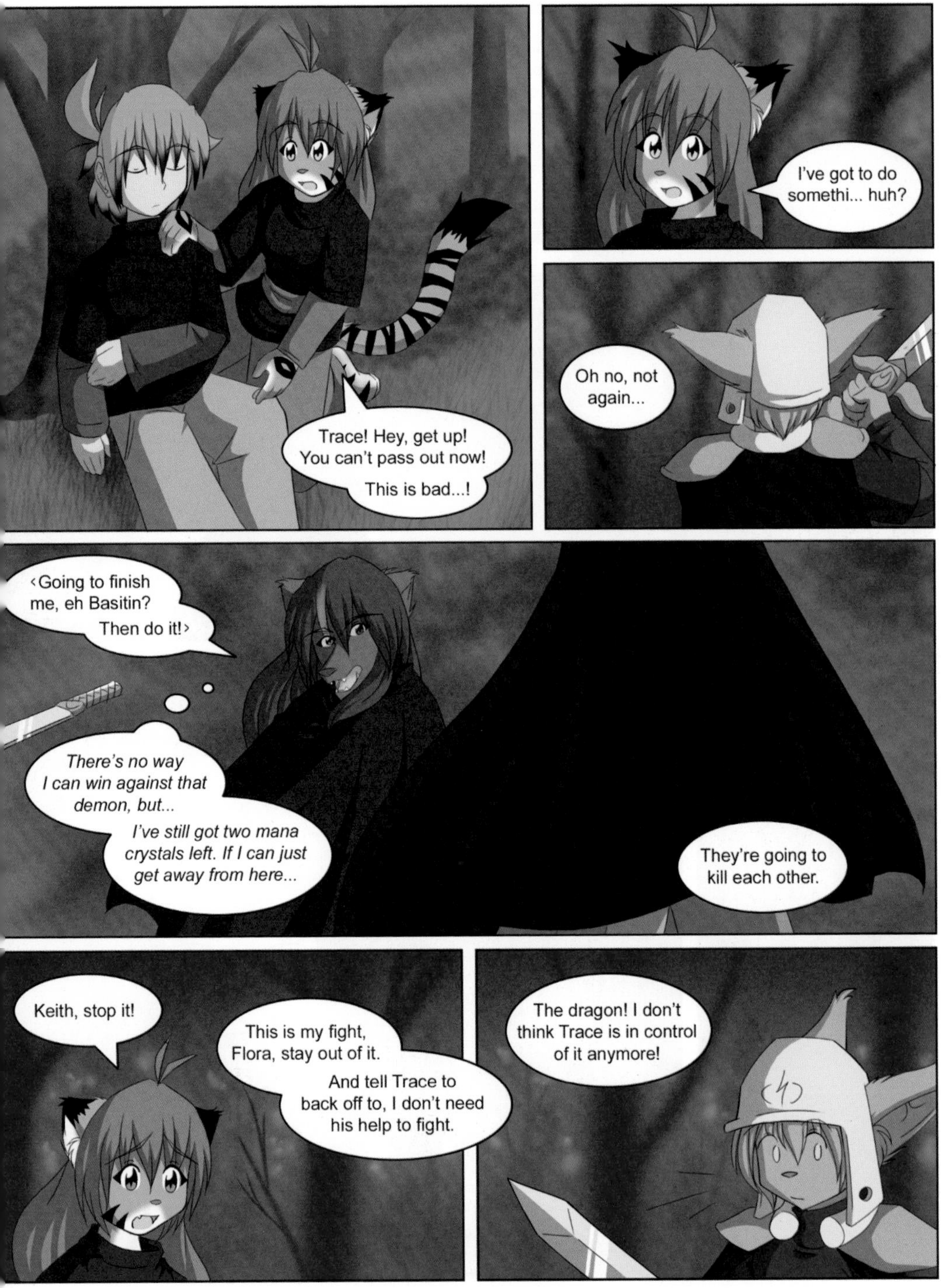
Trace! Hey, get up! You can't pass out now!
This is bad...!
I've got to do somethi... huh?
Oh no, not again...
‹Going to finish me, eh Basitin? Then do it!›
There's no way I can win against that demon, but...
I've still got two mana crystals left. If I can just get away from here...
They're going to kill each other.
Keith, stop it!
This is my fight, Flora, stay out of it.
And tell Trace to back off to, I don't need his help to fight.
The dragon! I don't think Trace is in control of it anymore!

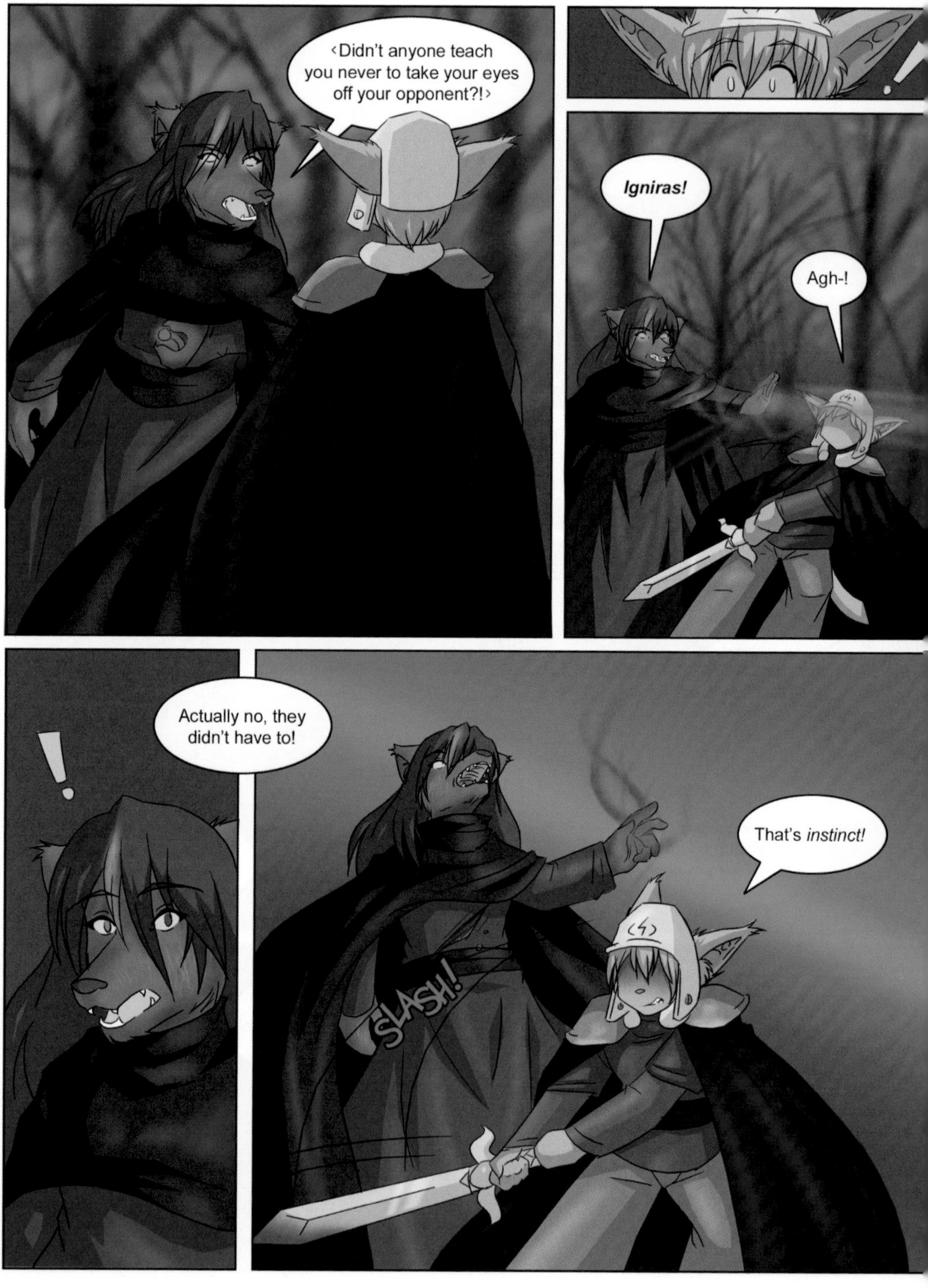
‹Didn't anyone teach you never to take your eyes off your opponent?!›
!
Igniras!
Agh-!
Actually no, they didn't have to!
!
That's *instinct!*
SLASH!

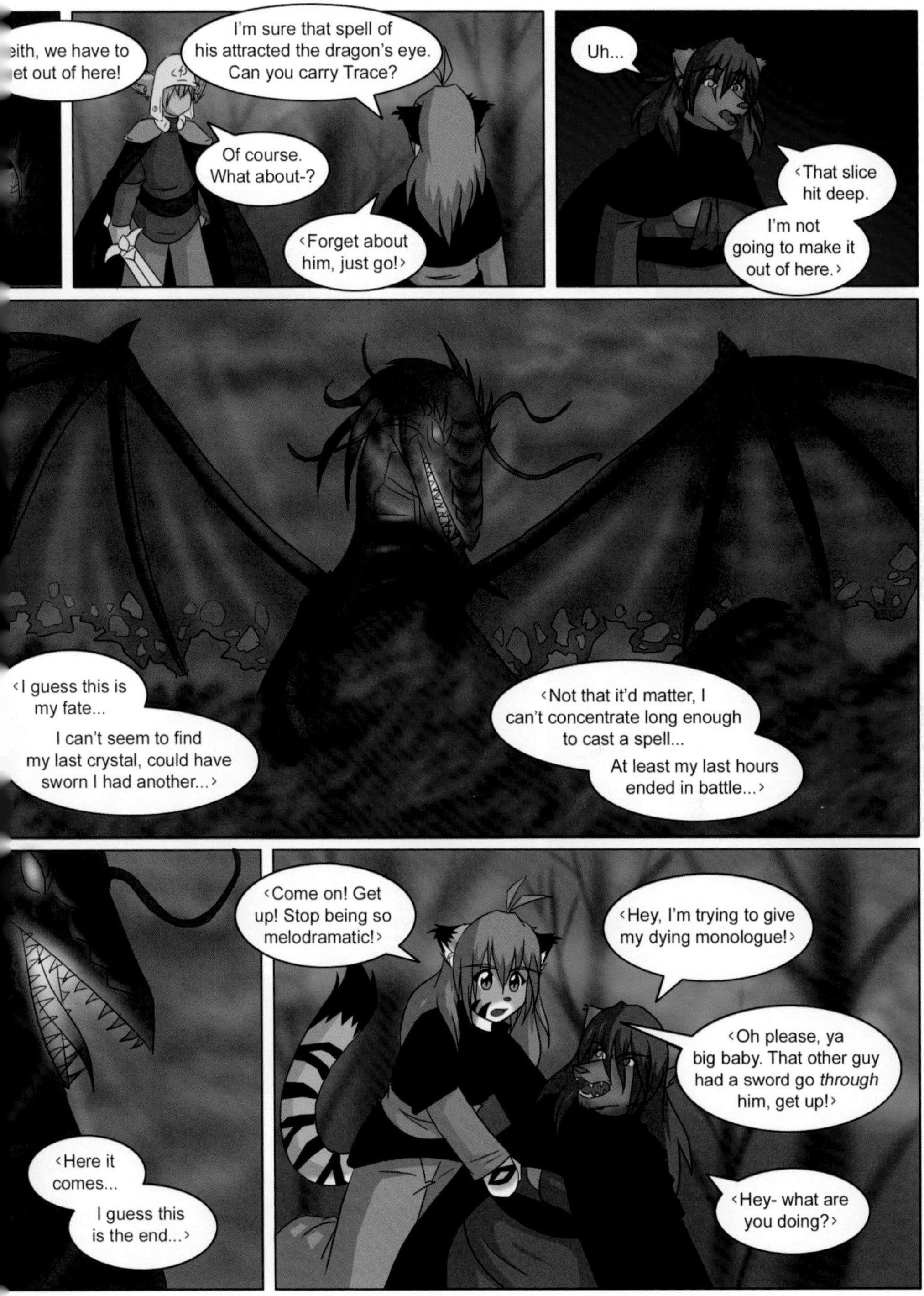
eith, we have to et out of here!
I'm sure that spell of his attracted the dragon's eye. Can you carry Trace?
Of course. What about-?
‹Forget about him, just go!›
Uh...
‹That slice hit deep.
I'm not going to make it out of here.›
‹I guess this is my fate...
I can't seem to find my last crystal, could have sworn I had another...›
‹Not that it'd matter, I can't concentrate long enough to cast a spell...
At least my last hours ended in battle...›
‹Here it comes...
I guess this is the end...›
‹Come on! Get up! Stop being so melodramatic!›
‹Hey, I'm trying to give my dying monologue!›
‹Oh please, ya big baby. That other guy had a sword go *through* him, get up!›
‹Hey- what are you doing?›

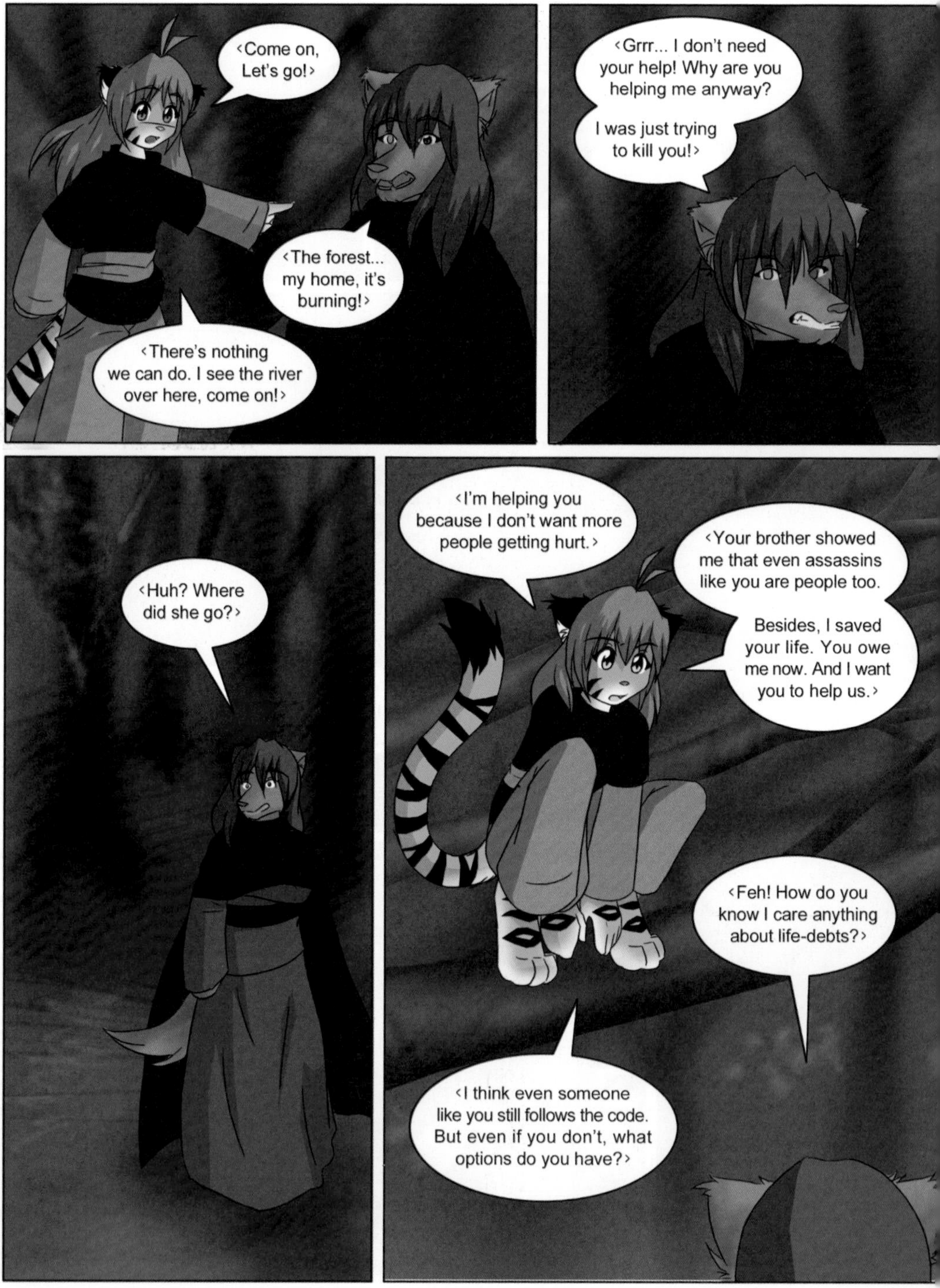
‹Come on, Let's go!›
‹The forest... my home, it's burning!›
‹There's nothing we can do. I see the river over here, come on!›
‹Grrr... I don't need your help! Why are you helping me anyway?
I was just trying to kill you!›
‹Huh? Where did she go?›
‹I'm helping you because I don't want more people getting hurt.›
‹Your brother showed me that even assassins like you are people too.
Besides, I saved your life. You owe me now. And I want you to help us.›
‹Feh! How do you know I care anything about life-debts?›
‹I think even someone like you still follows the code. But even if you don't, what options do you have?›

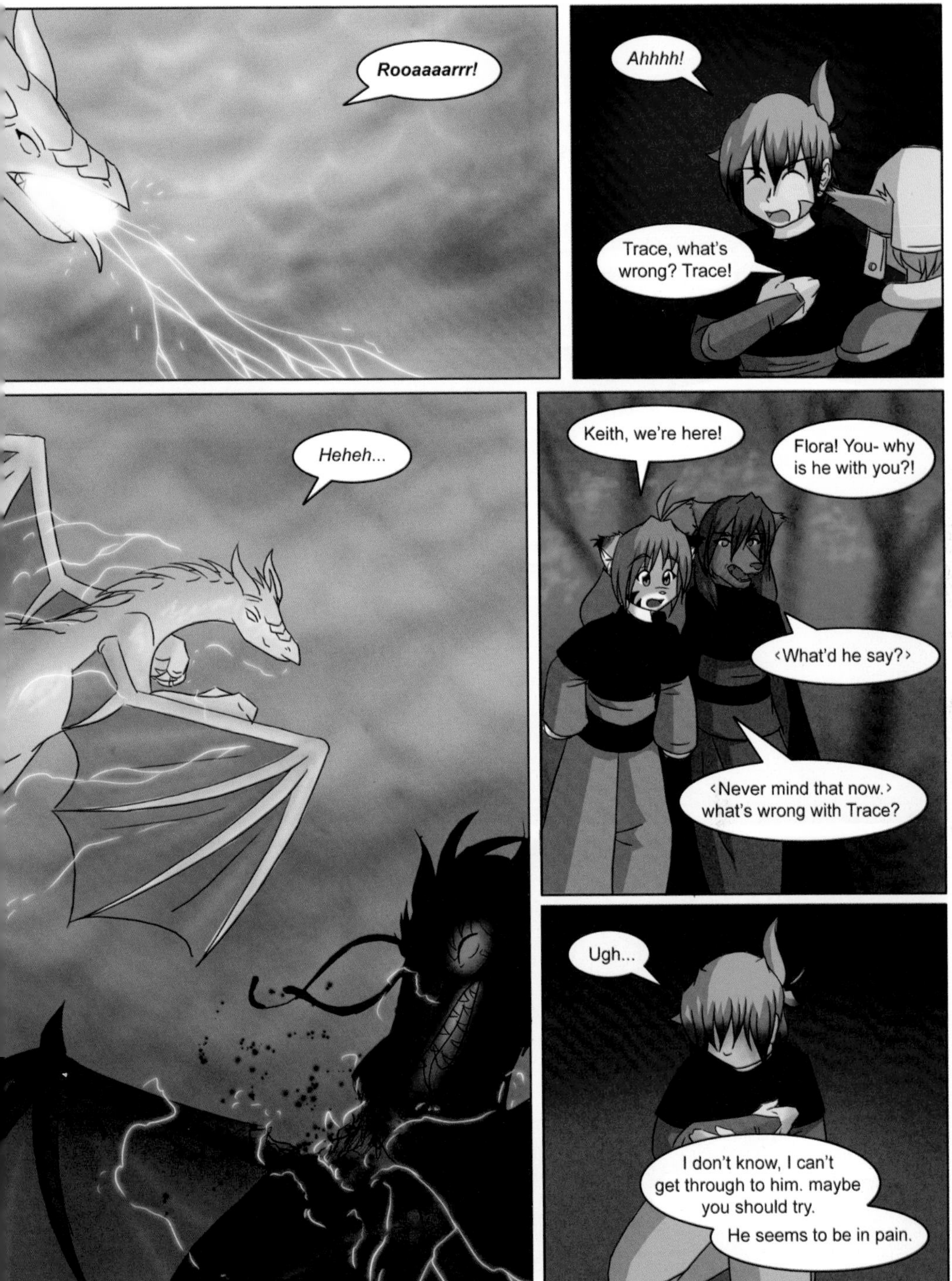

Rooaaaarrr!
Ahhhh!
Trace, what's wrong? Trace!
Heheh...
Keith, we're here!
Flora! You- why is he with you?!
‹What'd he say?›
‹Never mind that now.› what's wrong with Trace?
Ugh...
I don't know, I can't get through to him. maybe you should try.
He seems to be in pain.

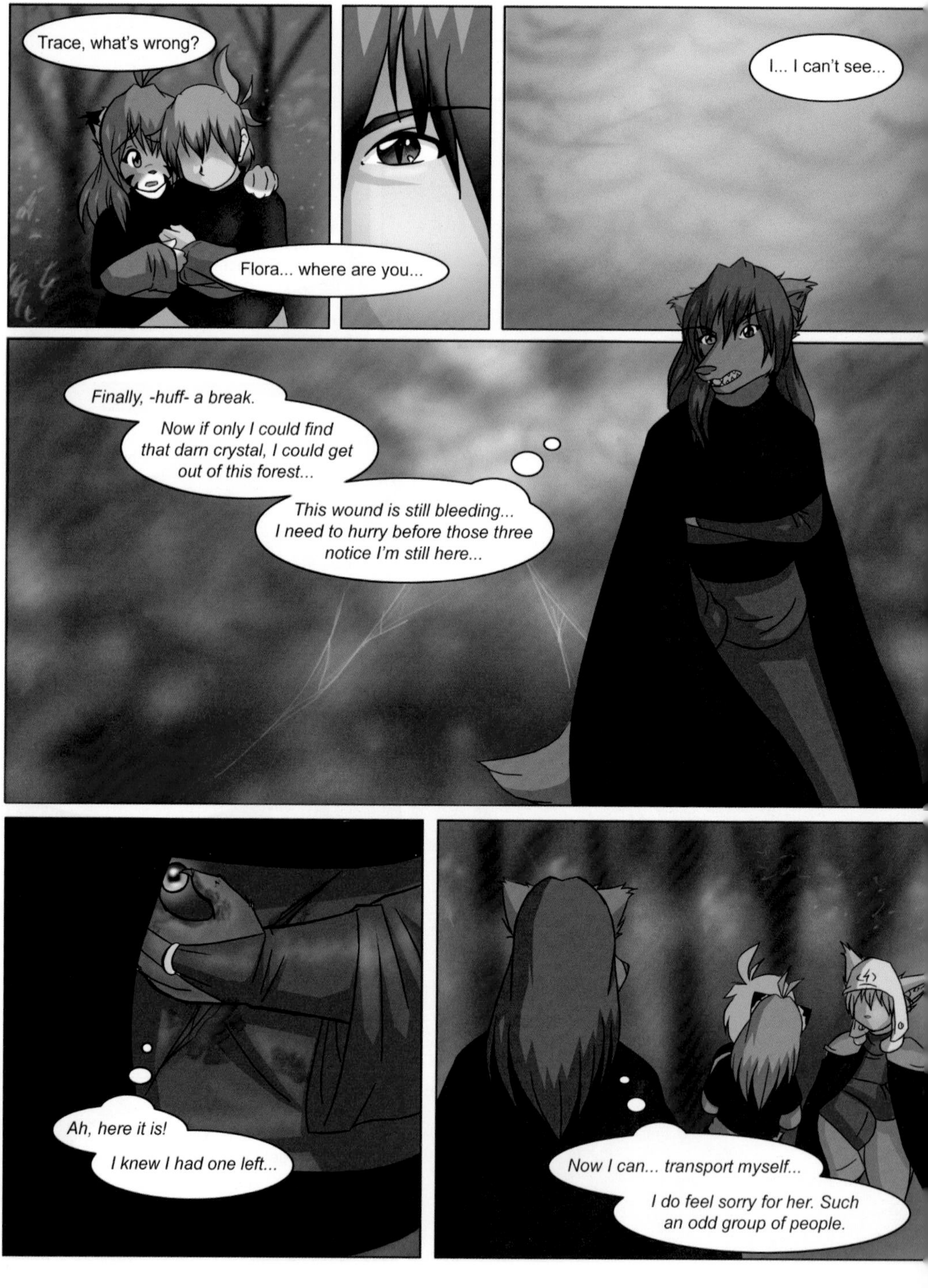
Trace, what's wrong?
Flora... where are you...
I... I can't see...
Finally, -huff- a break.
Now if only I could find that darn crystal, I could get out of this forest...
This wound is still bleeding... I need to hurry before those three notice I'm still here...
Ah, here it is!
I knew I had one left...
Now I can... transport myself...
I do feel sorry for her. Such an odd group of people.

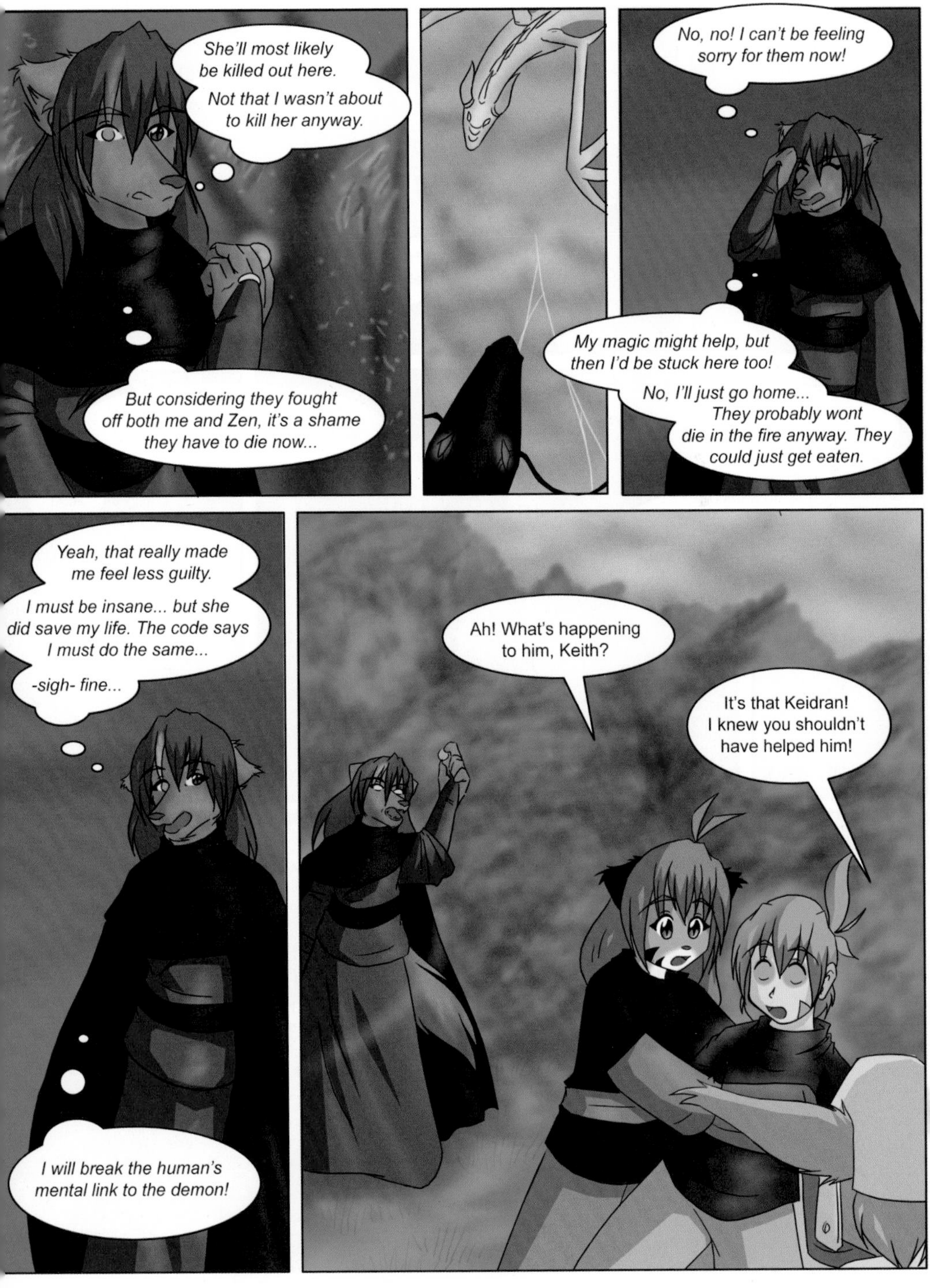
She'll most likely be killed out here.
Not that I wasn't about to kill her anyway.
But considering they fought off both me and Zen, it's a shame they have to die now...
No, no! I can't be feeling sorry for them now!
My magic might help, but then I'd be stuck here too!
No, I'll just go home... They probably wont die in the fire anyway. They could just get eaten.
Yeah, that really made me feel less guilty.
I must be insane... but she did save my life. The code says I must do the same...
-sigh- fine...
I will break the human's mental link to the demon!
Ah! What's happening to him, Keith?
It's that Keidran! I knew you shouldn't have helped him!

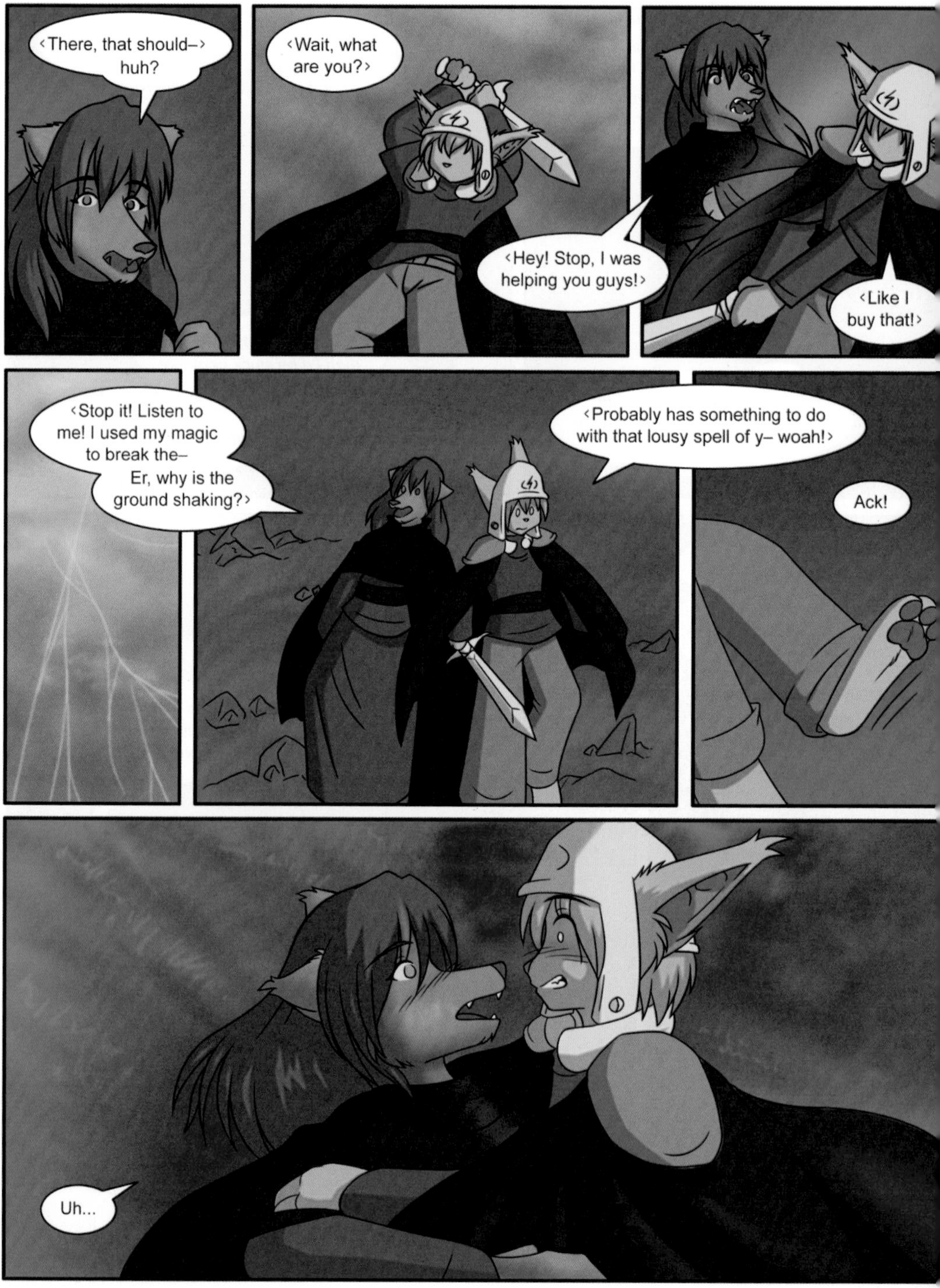
‹There, that should–› huh?
‹Wait, what are you?›
‹Hey! Stop, I was helping you guys!›
‹Like I buy that!›
‹Stop it! Listen to me! I used my magic to break the– Er, why is the ground shaking?›
‹Probably has something to do with that lousy spell of y– woah!›
Ack!
Uh...

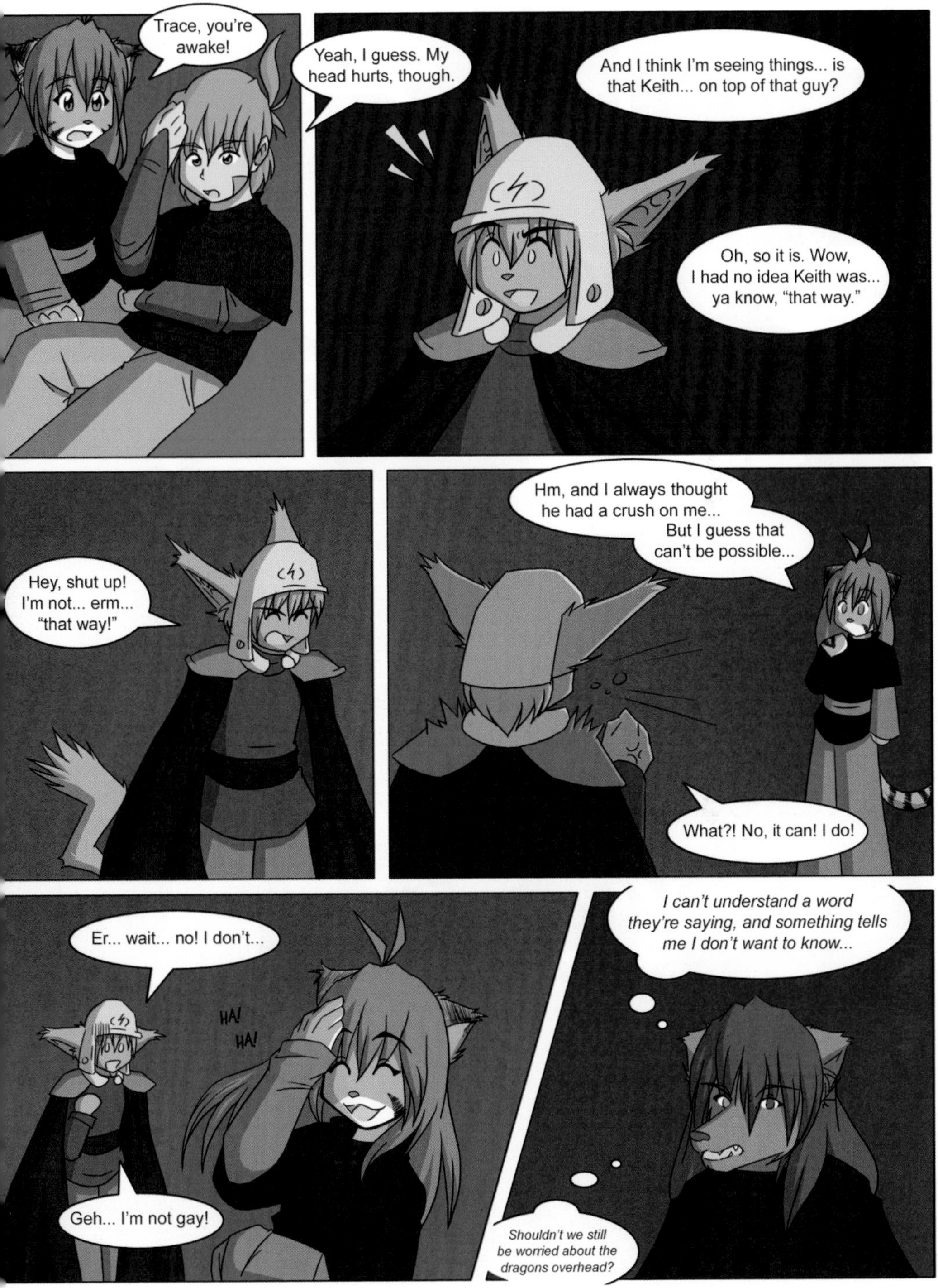

Trace, you're awake!
Yeah, I guess. My head hurts, though.
And I think I'm seeing things... is that Keith... on top of that guy?
Oh, so it is. Wow, I had no idea Keith was... ya know, "that way."
Hey, shut up! I'm not... erm... "that way!"
Hm, and I always thought he had a crush on me...
But I guess that can't be possible...
What?! No, it can! I do!
Er... wait... no! I don't...
HA! HA!
Geh... I'm not gay!
I can't understand a word they're saying, and something tells me I don't want to know...
Shouldn't we still be worried about the dragons overhead?

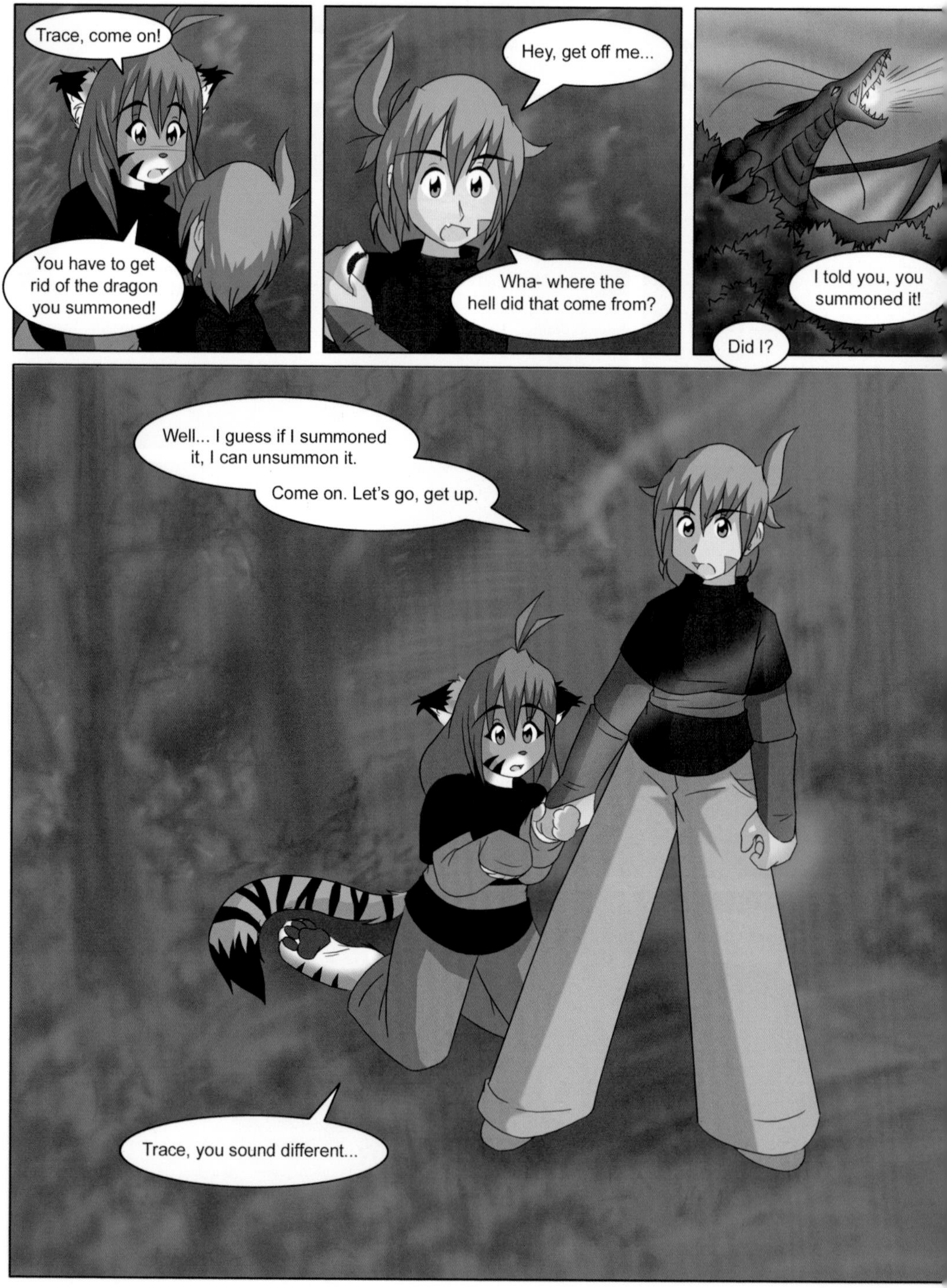

Trace, come on!
You have to get rid of the dragon you summoned!
Hey, get off me...
Wha- where the hell did that come from?
I told you, you summoned it!
Did I?
Well... I guess if I summoned it, I can unsummon it.
Come on. Let's go, get up.
Trace, you sound different...

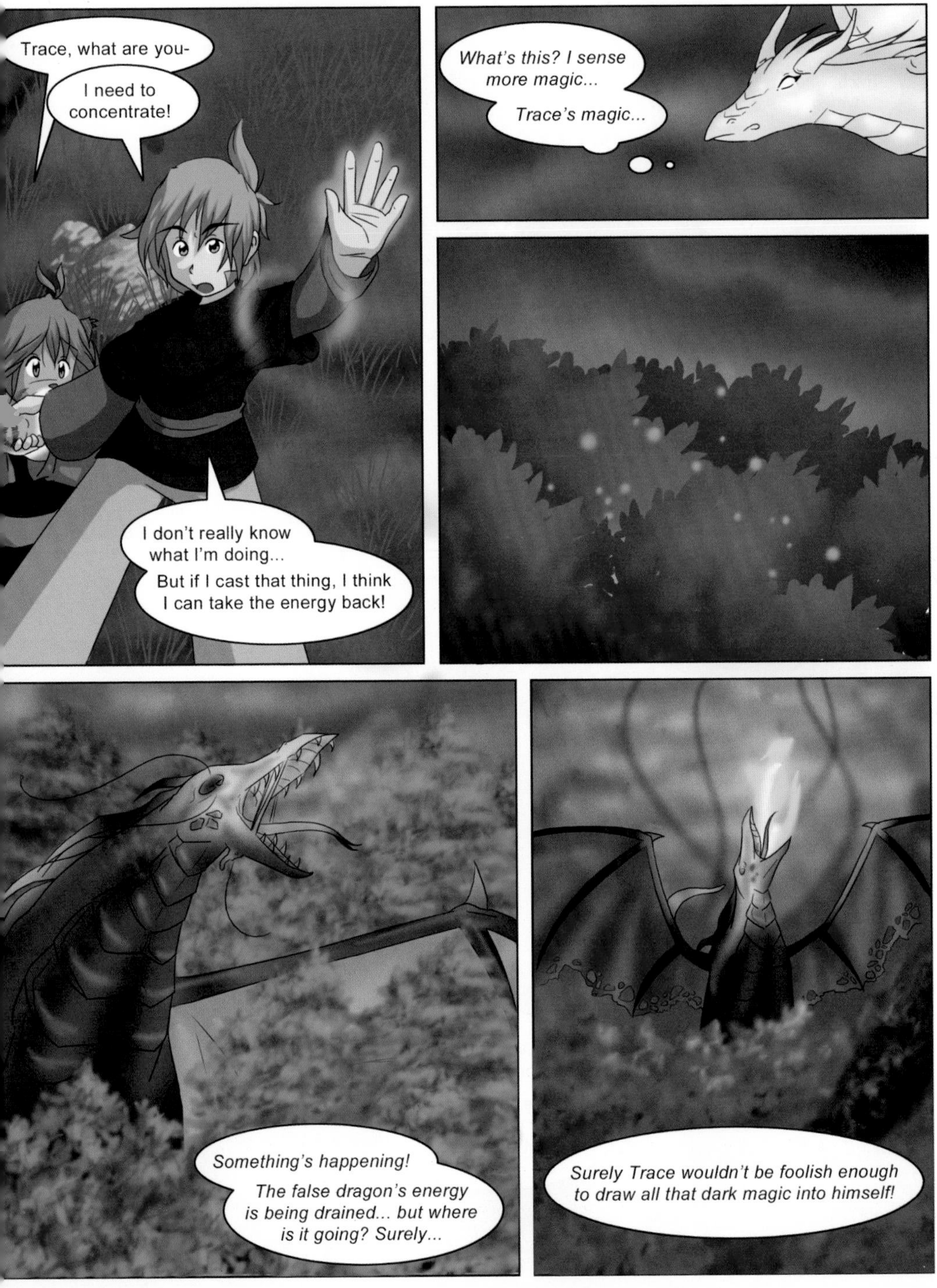
Trace, what are you-
I need to concentrate!
I don't really know what I'm doing...
But if I cast that thing, I think I can take the energy back!
What's this? I sense more magic...
Trace's magic...
Something's happening!
The false dragon's energy is being drained... but where is it going? Surely...
Surely Trace wouldn't be foolish enough to draw all that dark magic into himself!

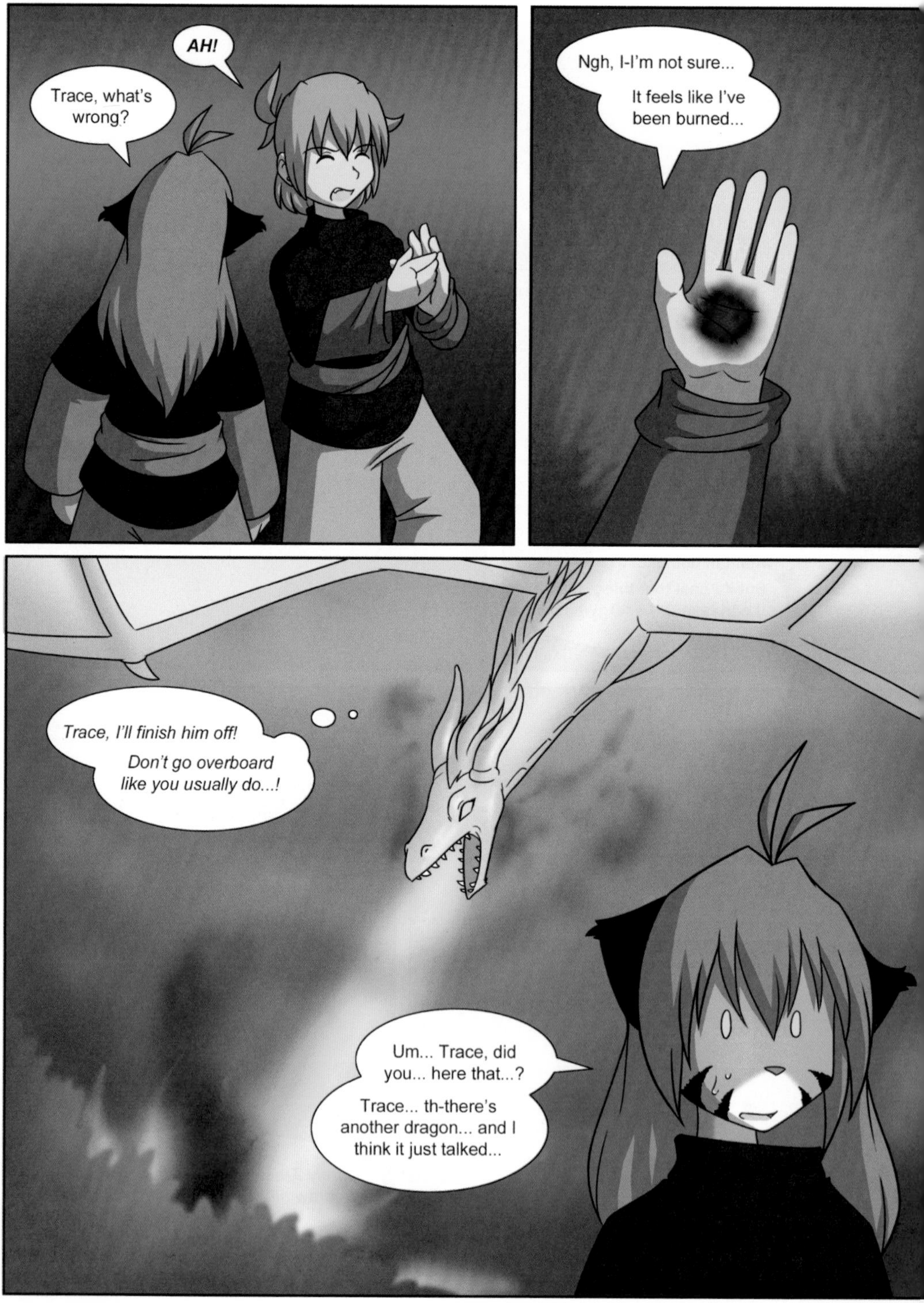

Trace, what's wrong?
AH!
Ngh, I-I'm not sure...
It feels like I've been burned...
Trace, I'll finish him off!
Don't go overboard like you usually do...!
Um... Trace, did you... here that...?
Trace... th-there's another dragon... and I think it just talked...

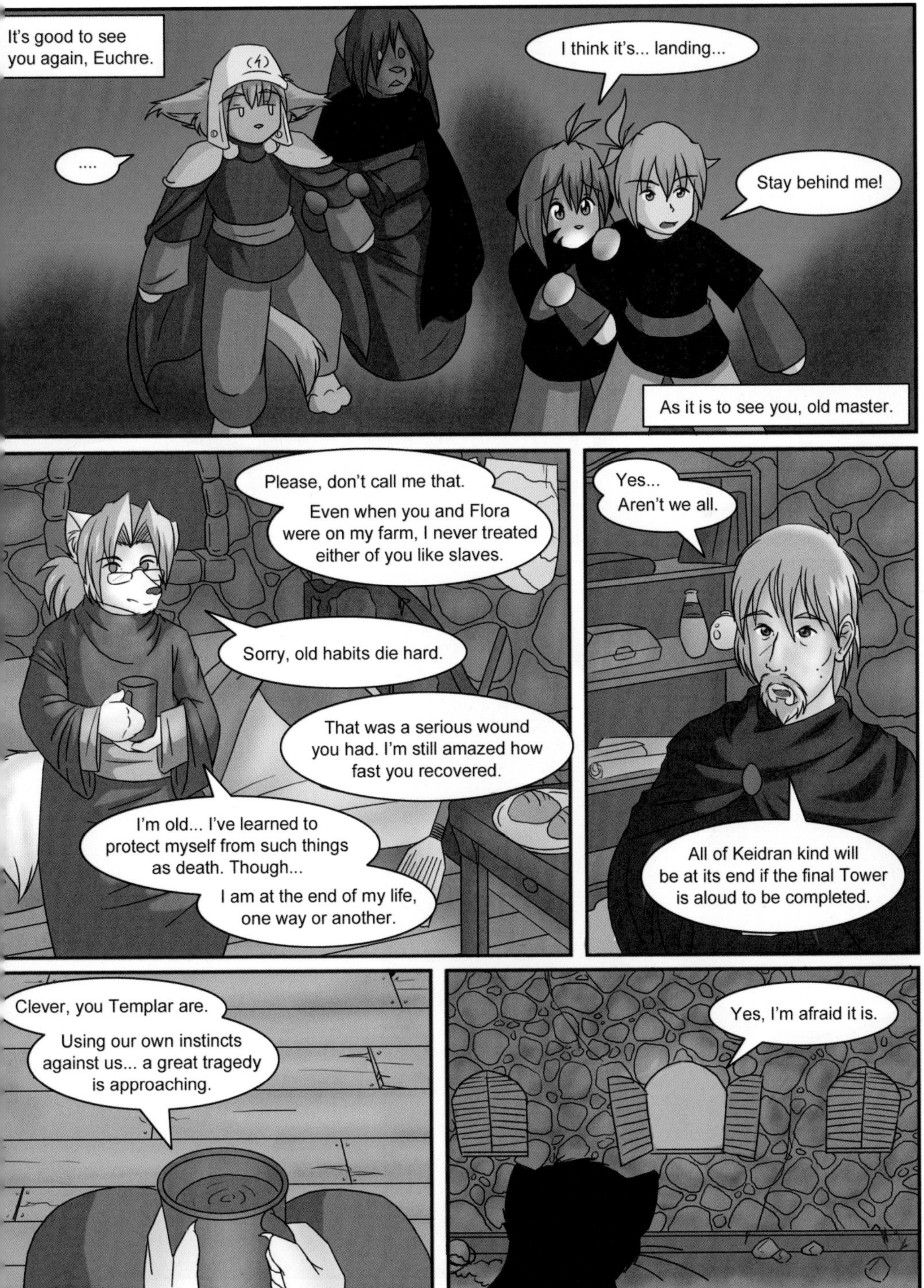

It's good to see you again, Euchre.
....
I think it's... landing...
Stay behind me!
As it is to see you, old master.
Please, don't call me that.
Even when you and Flora were on my farm, I never treated either of you like slaves.
Sorry, old habits die hard.
That was a serious wound you had. I'm still amazed how fast you recovered.
I'm old... I've learned to protect myself from such things as death. Though...
I am at the end of my life, one way or another.
Yes...
Aren't we all.
All of Keidran kind will be at its end if the final Tower is aloud to be completed.
Clever, you Templar are.
Using our own instincts against us... a great tragedy is approaching.
Yes, I'm afraid it is.

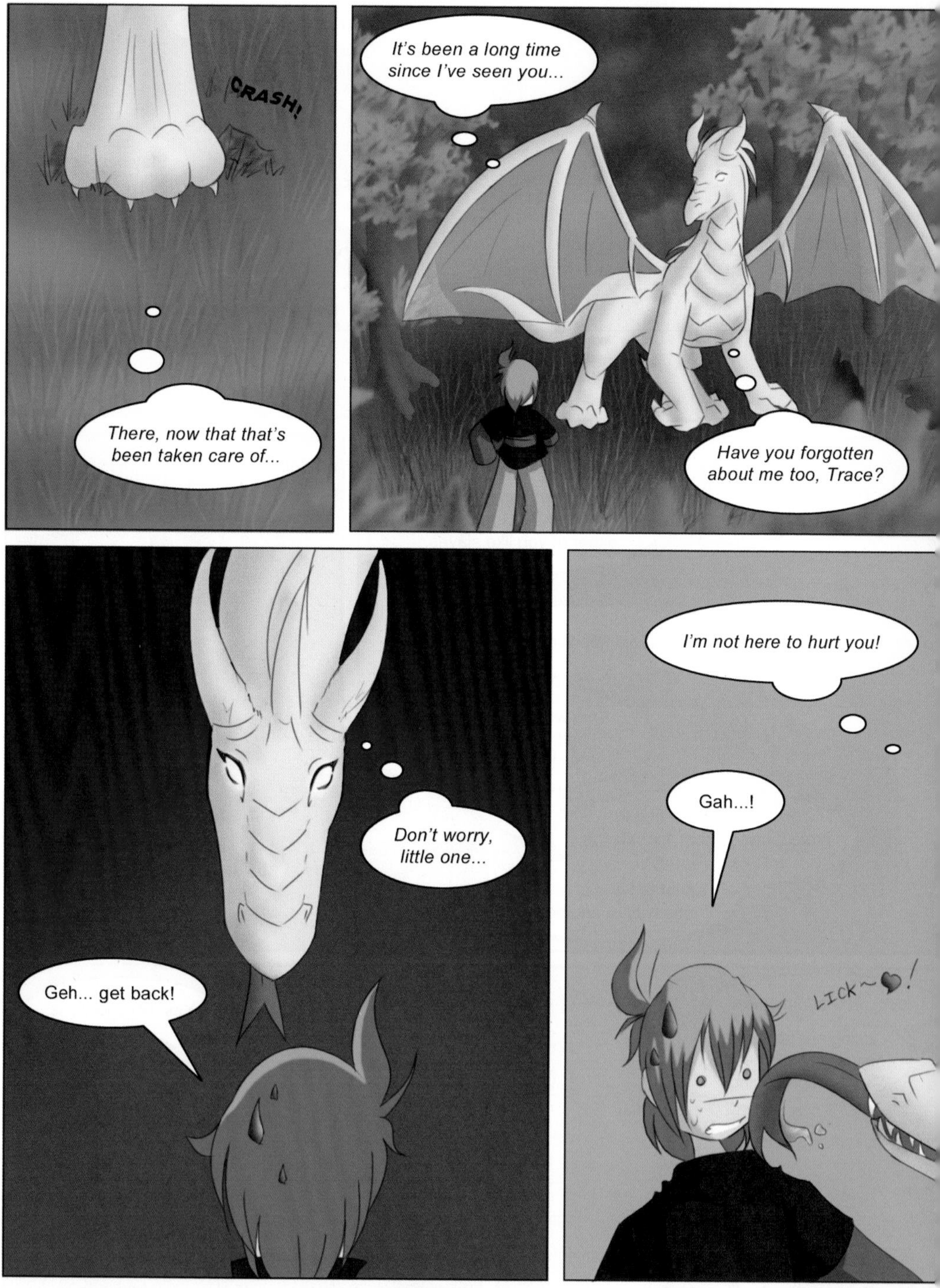
CRASH!
There, now that that's been taken care of...
It's been a long time since I've seen you...
Have you forgotten about me too, Trace?
Don't worry, little one...
Geh... get back!
I'm not here to hurt you!
Gah...!
LICK~

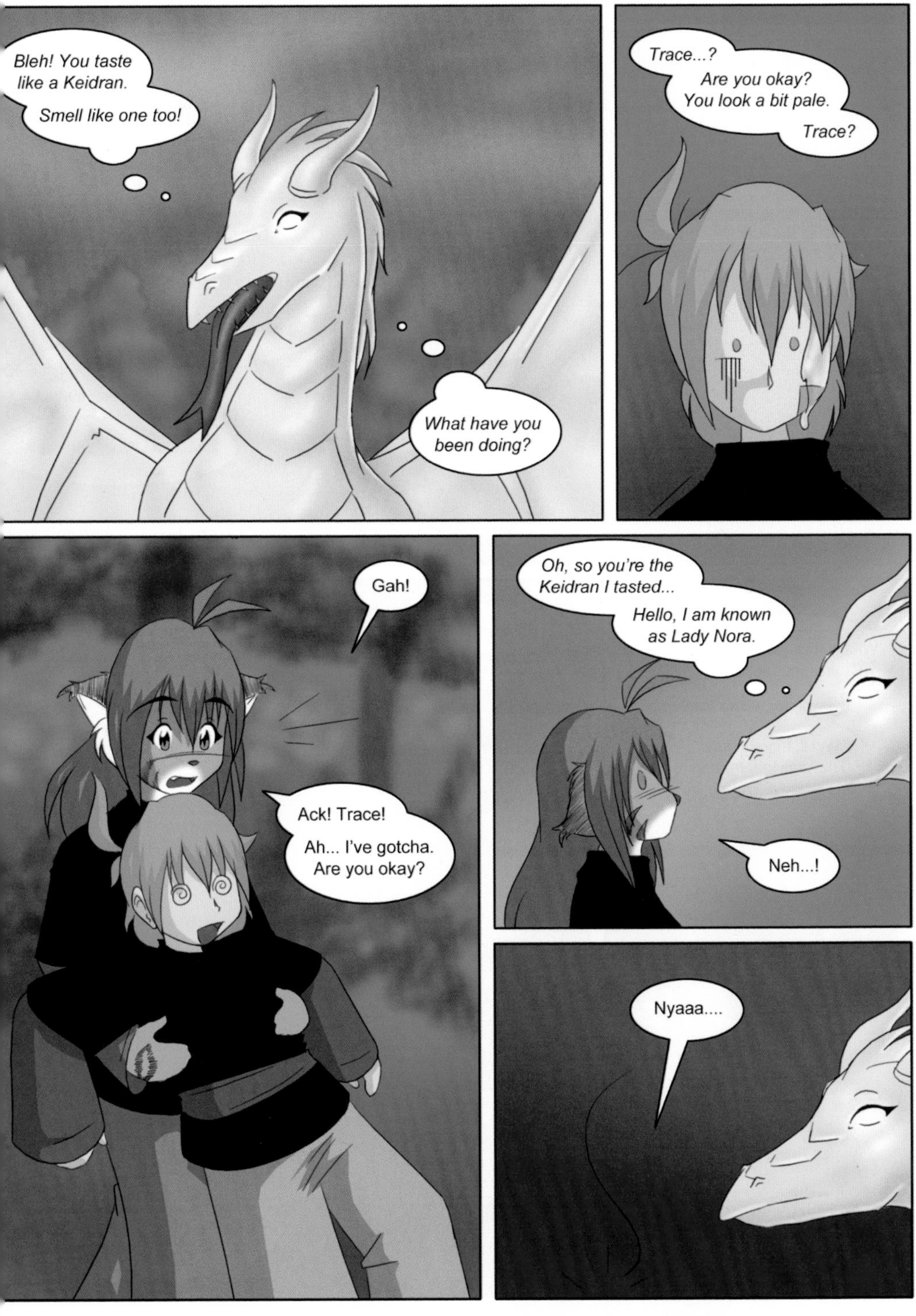
Bleh! You taste like a Keidran.
Smell like one too!
What have you been doing?
Trace...?
Are you okay? You look a bit pale.
Trace?
Gah!
Ack! Trace!
Ah... I've gotcha. Are you okay?
Oh, so you're the Keidran I tasted...
Hello, I am known as Lady Nora.
Neh...!
Nyaaa....

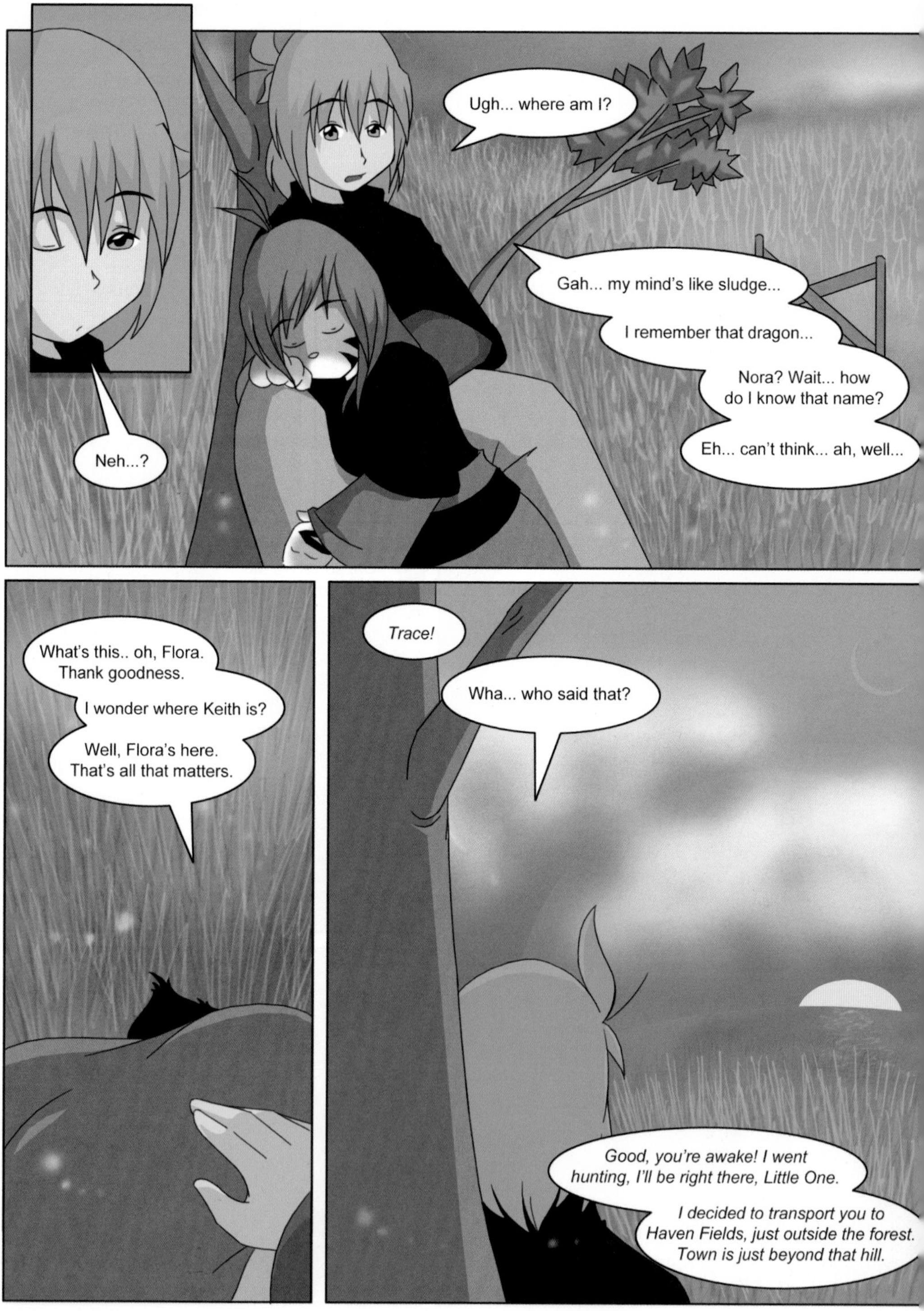
Ugh... where am I?
Neh...?
Gah... my mind's like sludge...
I remember that dragon...
Nora? Wait... how do I know that name?
Eh... can't think... ah, well...
What's this.. oh, Flora. Thank goodness.
I wonder where Keith is?
Well, Flora's here. That's all that matters.
Trace!
Wha... who said that?
Good, you're awake! I went hunting, I'll be right there, Little One.
I decided to transport you to Haven Fields, just outside the forest. Town is just beyond that hill.

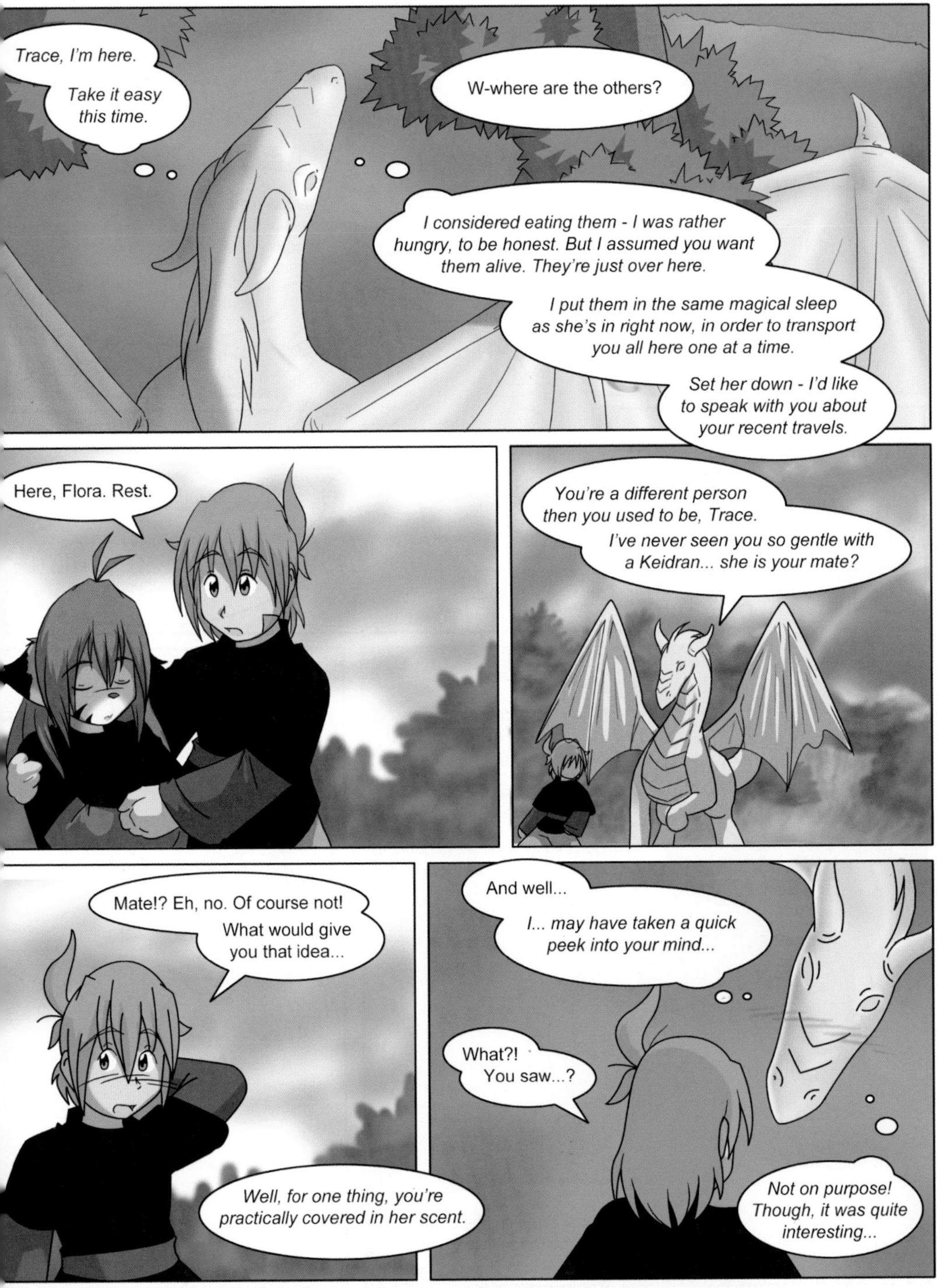
Trace, I'm here.
Take it easy this time.
W-where are the others?
I considered eating them - I was rather hungry, to be honest. But I assumed you want them alive. They're just over here.
I put them in the same magical sleep as she's in right now, in order to transport you all here one at a time.
Set her down - I'd like to speak with you about your recent travels.
Here, Flora. Rest.
You're a different person then you used to be, Trace.
I've never seen you so gentle with a Keidran... she is your mate?
Mate!? Eh, no. Of course not!
What would give you that idea...
Well, for one thing, you're practically covered in her scent.
And well...
I... may have taken a quick peek into your mind...
What?! You saw...?
Not on purpose! Though, it was quite interesting...

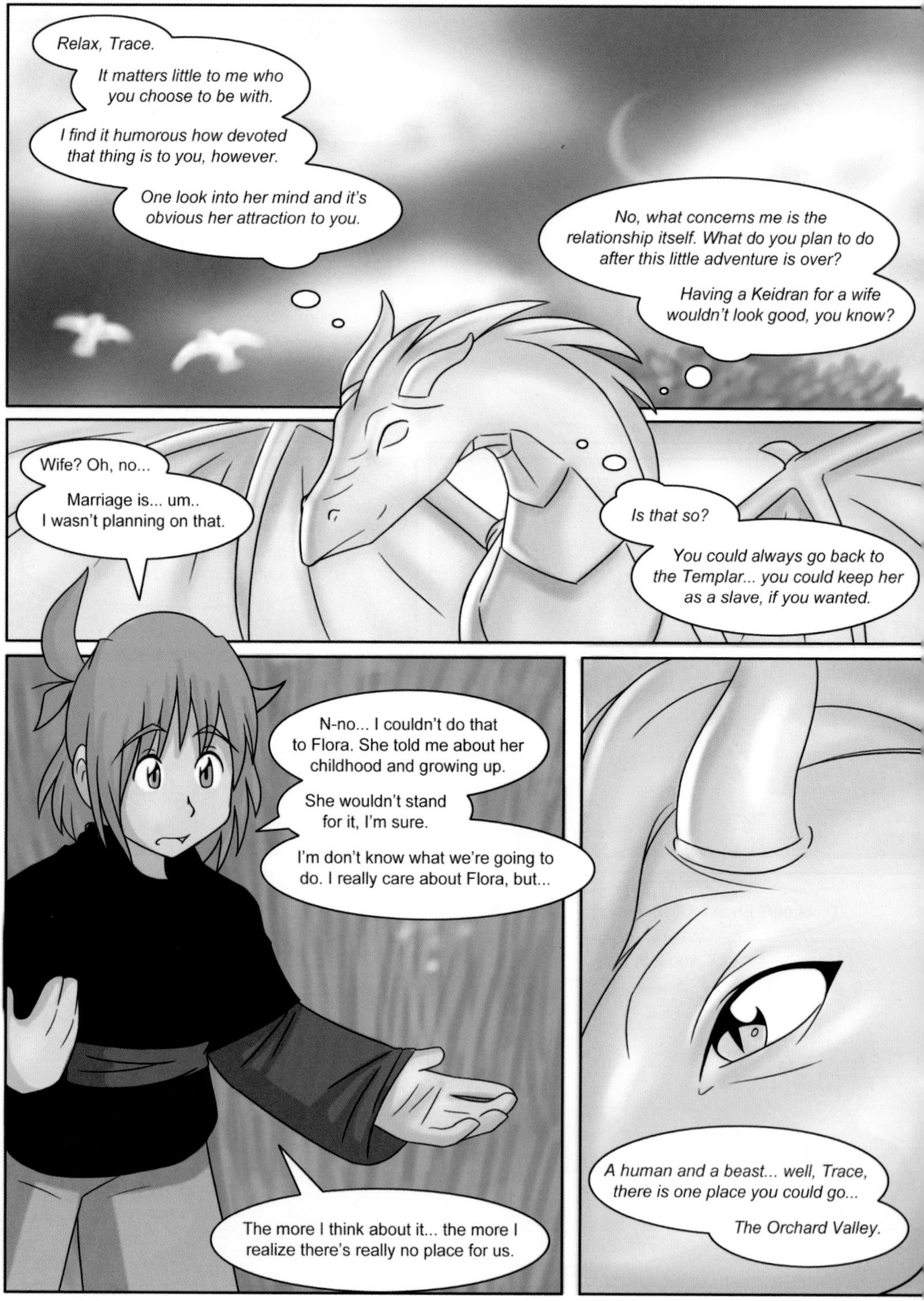

Relax, Trace.
It matters little to me who you choose to be with.
I find it humorous how devoted that thing is to you, however.
One look into her mind and it's obvious her attraction to you.
No, what concerns me is the relationship itself. What do you plan to do after this little adventure is over?
Having a Keidran for a wife wouldn't look good, you know?
Wife? Oh, no...
Marriage is... um.. I wasn't planning on that.
Is that so?
You could always go back to the Templar... you could keep her as a slave, if you wanted.
N-no... I couldn't do that to Flora. She told me about her childhood and growing up.
She wouldn't stand for it, I'm sure.
I'm don't know what we're going to do. I really care about Flora, but...
The more I think about it... the more I realize there's really no place for us.
A human and a beast... well, Trace, there is one place you could go...
The Orchard Valley.

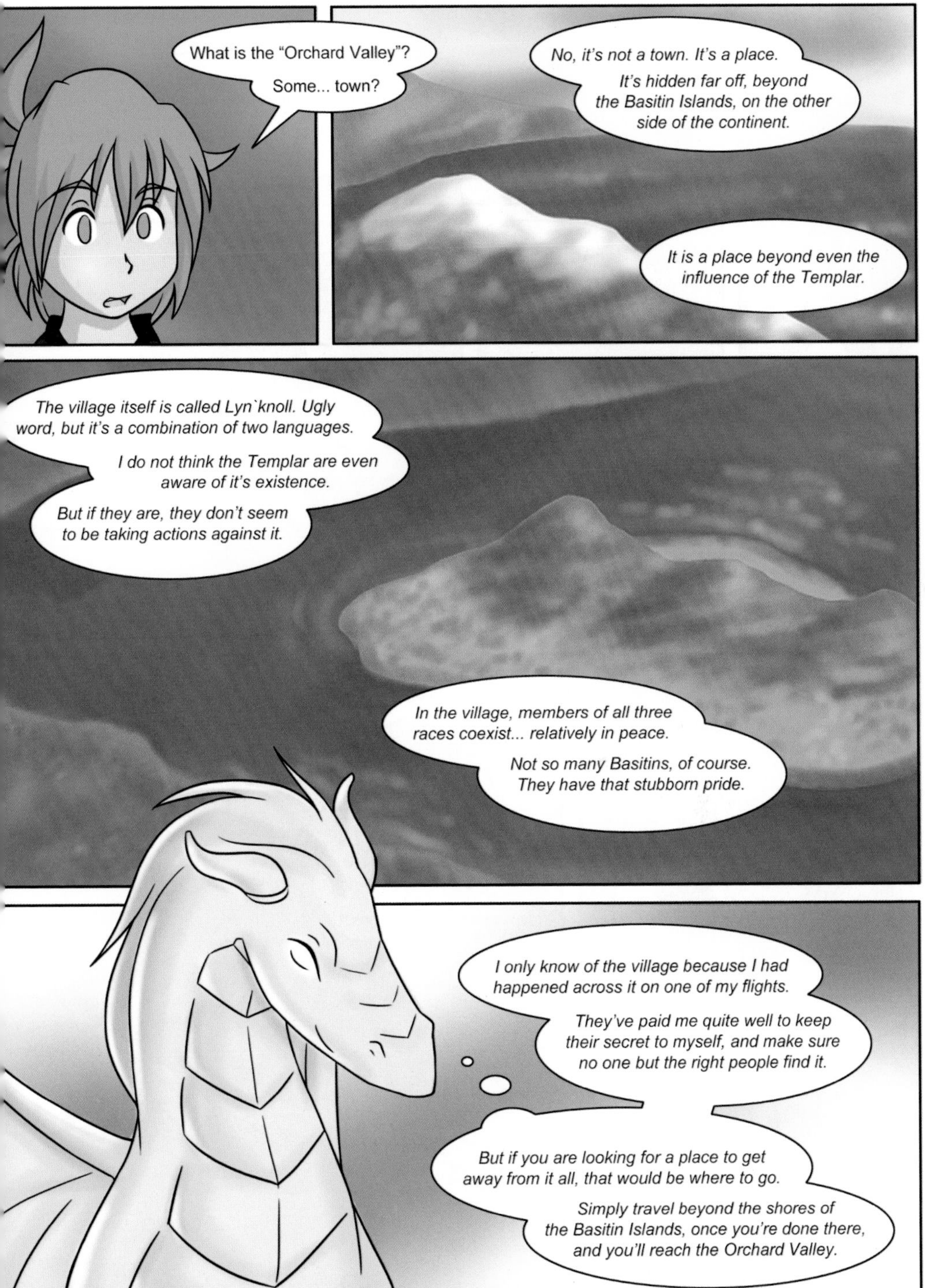
What is the "Orchard Valley"? Some... town?
No, it's not a town. It's a place.
It's hidden far off, beyond the Basitin Islands, on the other side of the continent.
It is a place beyond even the influence of the Templar.
The village itself is called Lyn`knoll. Ugly word, but it's a combination of two languages.
I do not think the Templar are even aware of it's existence.
But if they are, they don't seem to be taking actions against it.
In the village, members of all three races coexist... relatively in peace.
Not so many Basitins, of course. They have that stubborn pride.
I only know of the village because I had happened across it on one of my flights.
They've paid me quite well to keep their secret to myself, and make sure no one but the right people find it.
But if you are looking for a place to get away from it all, that would be where to go.
Simply travel beyond the shores of the Basitin Islands, once you're done there, and you'll reach the Orchard Valley.

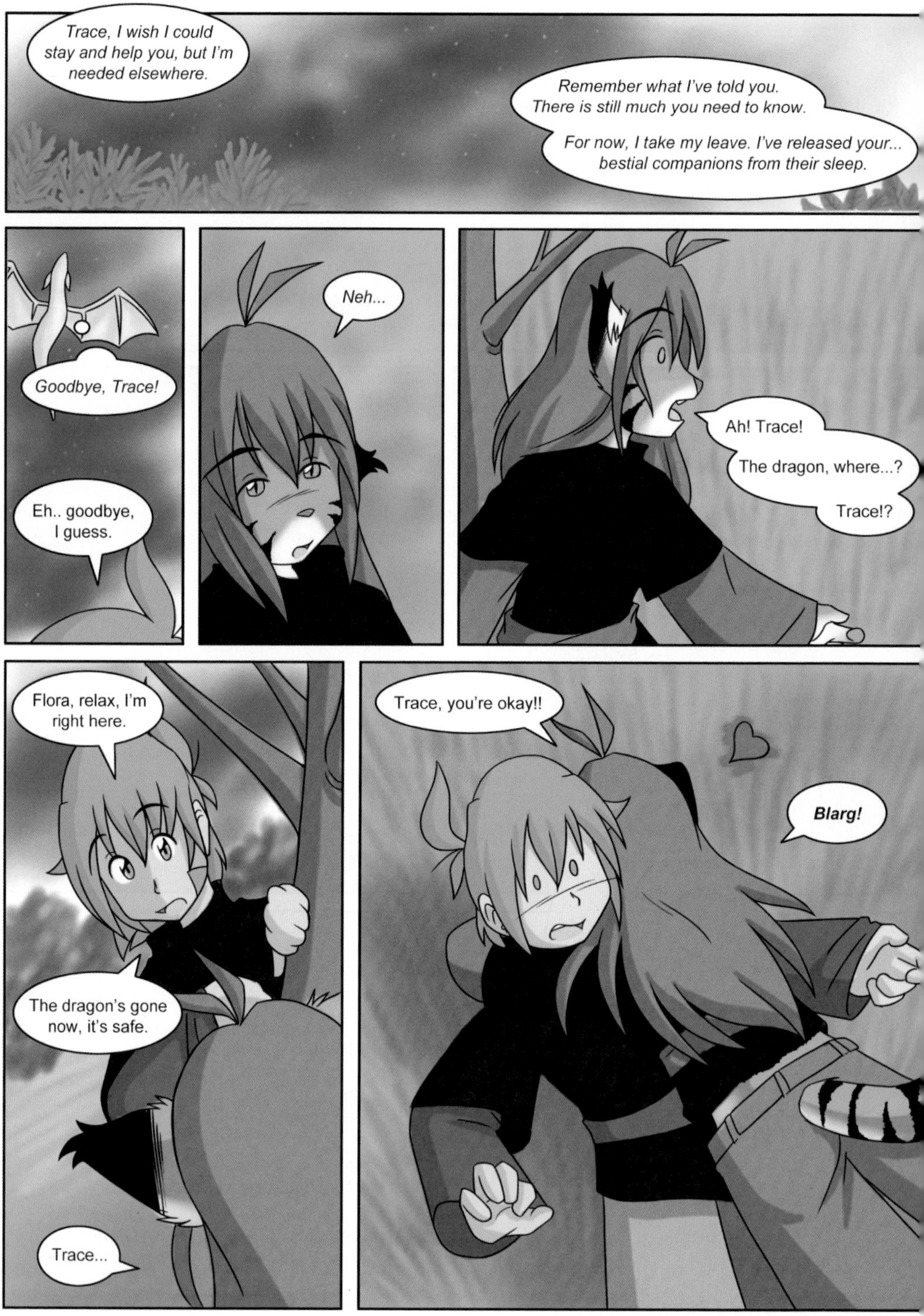
Trace, I wish I could stay and help you, but I'm needed elsewhere.
Remember what I've told you. There is still much you need to know.
For now, I take my leave. I've released your... bestial companions from their sleep.
Goodbye, Trace!
Eh.. goodbye, I guess.
Neh...
Ah! Trace!
The dragon, where...?
Trace!?
Flora, relax, I'm right here.
The dragon's gone now, it's safe.
Trace...
Trace, you're okay!!
Blarg!

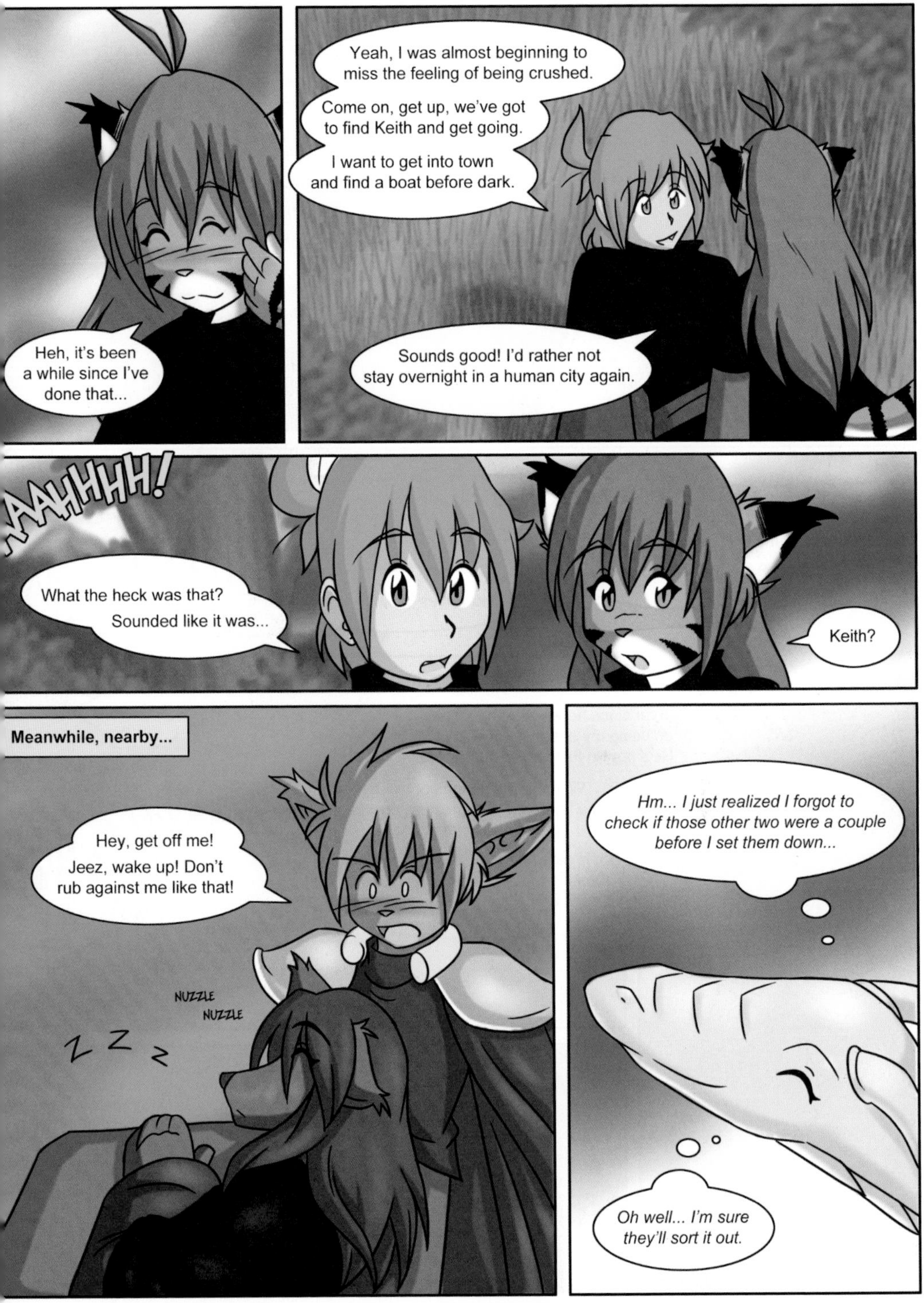
Heh, it's been a while since I've done that...
Yeah, I was almost beginning to miss the feeling of being crushed.
Come on, get up, we've got to find Keith and get going.
I want to get into town and find a boat before dark.
Sounds good! I'd rather not stay overnight in a human city again.
AAHHHH!
What the heck was that?
Sounded like it was...
Keith?
Meanwhile, nearby...
Hey, get off me!
Jeez, wake up! Don't rub against me like that!
NUZZLE NUZZLE
Z Z Z
Hm... I just realized I forgot to check if those other two were a couple before I set them down...
Oh well... I'm sure they'll sort it out.

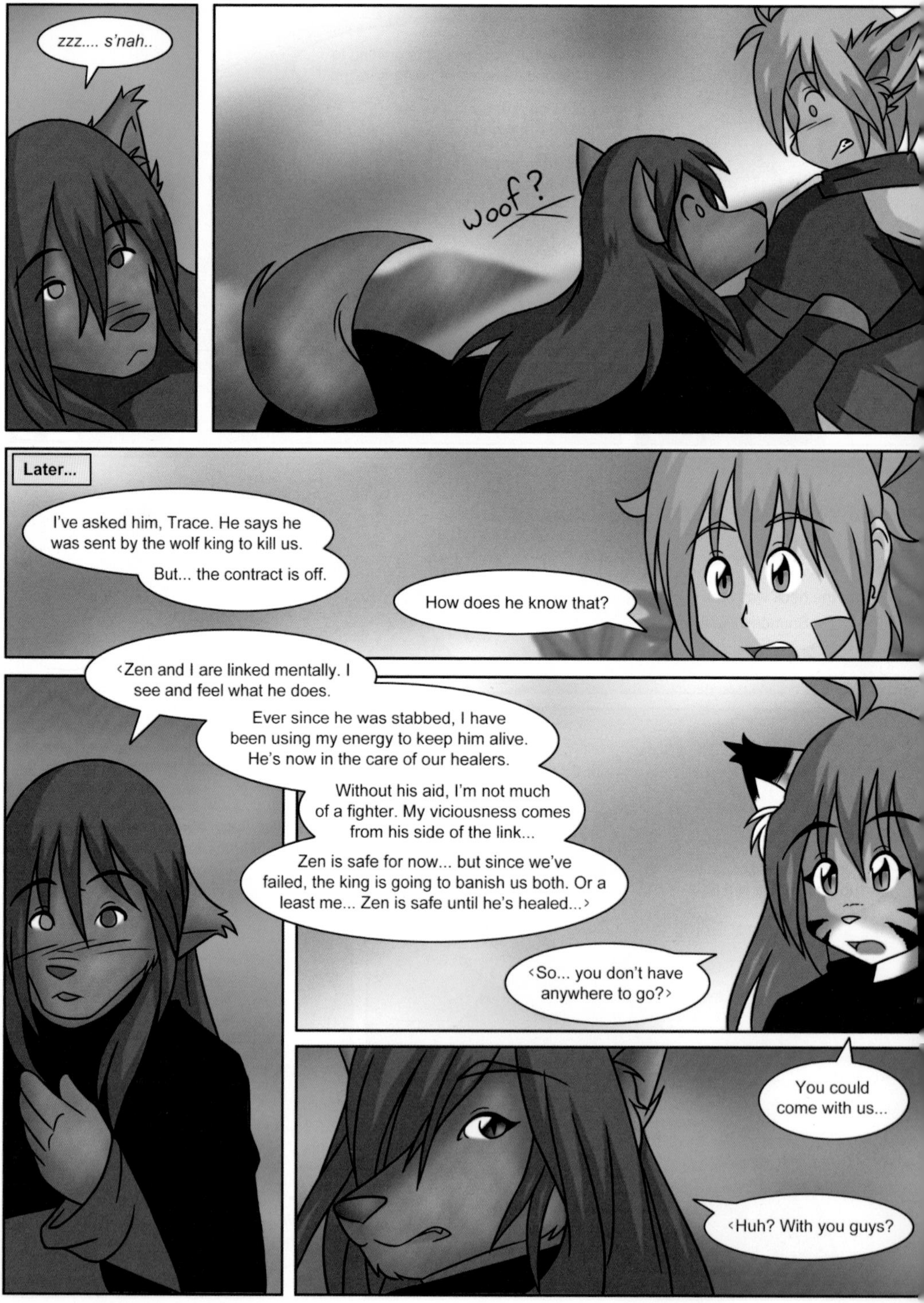

zzz.... s'nah..
woof?
Later...
I've asked him, Trace. He says he was sent by the wolf king to kill us.
But... the contract is off.
How does he know that?
‹Zen and I are linked mentally. I see and feel what he does.
Ever since he was stabbed, I have been using my energy to keep him alive. He's now in the care of our healers.
Without his aid, I'm not much of a fighter. My viciousness comes from his side of the link...
Zen is safe for now... but since we've failed, the king is going to banish us both. Or a least me... Zen is safe until he's healed...›
‹So... you don't have anywhere to go?›
You could come with us...
‹Huh? With you guys?

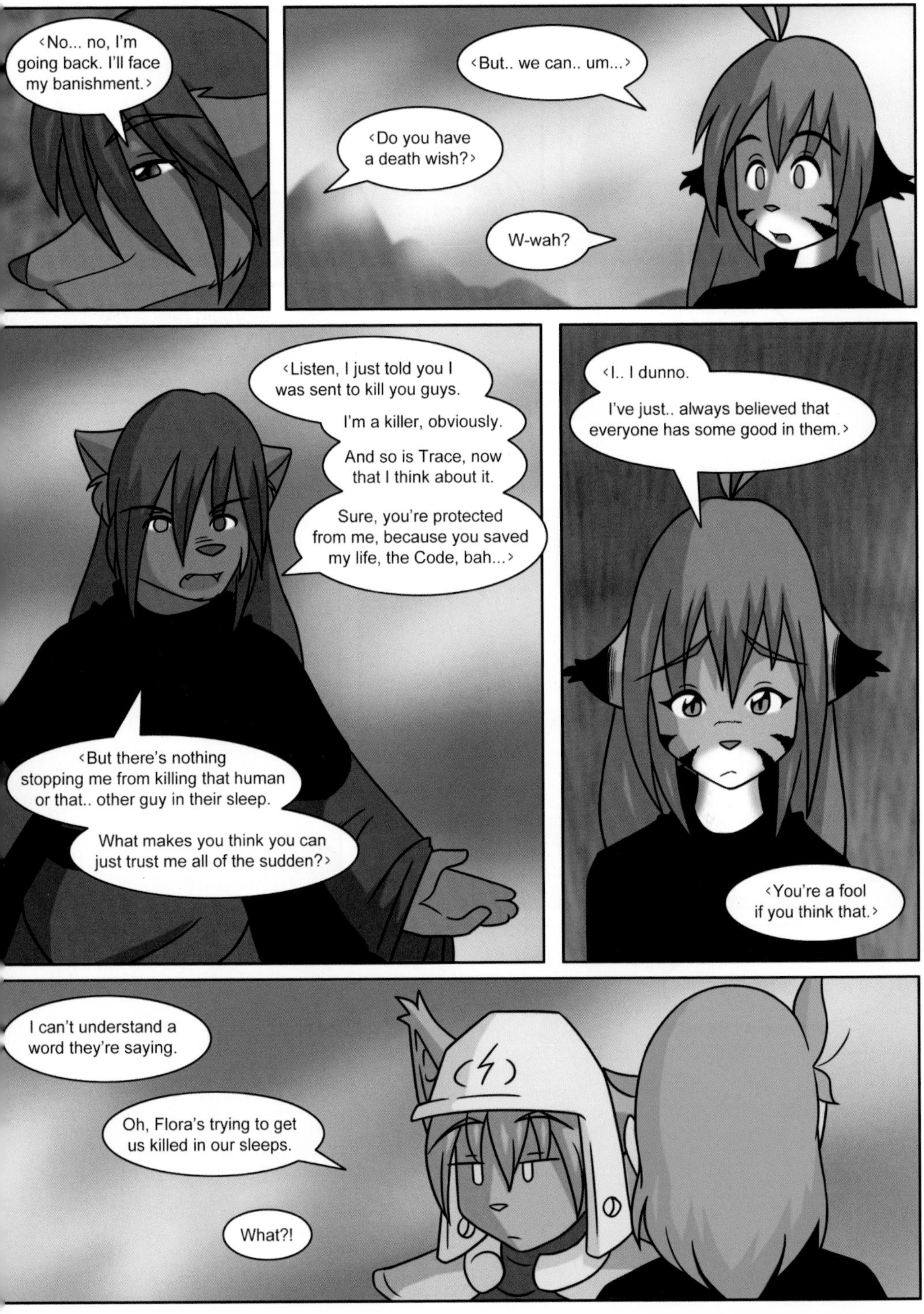
‹No... no, I'm going back. I'll face my banishment.›
‹But.. we can.. um...›
‹Do you have a death wish?›
W-wah?
‹Listen, I just told you I was sent to kill you guys.
I'm a killer, obviously.
And so is Trace, now that I think about it.
Sure, you're protected from me, because you saved my life, the Code, bah...›
‹But there's nothing stopping me from killing that human or that.. other guy in their sleep.
What makes you think you can just trust me all of the sudden?›
‹I.. I dunno.
I've just.. always believed that everyone has some good in them.›
‹You're a fool if you think that.›
I can't understand a word they're saying.
Oh, Flora's trying to get us killed in our sleeps.
What?!

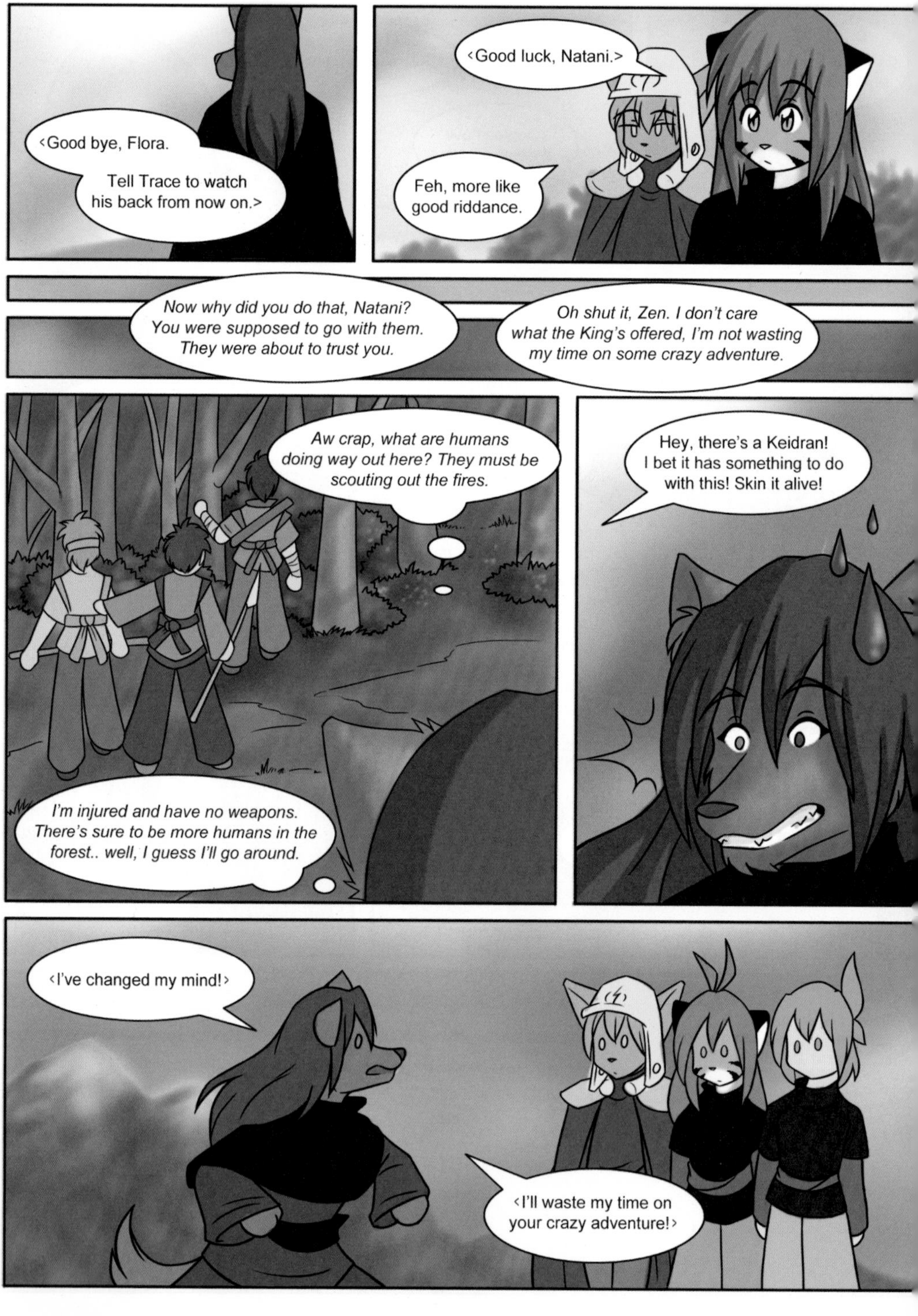

<Good bye, Flora.
Tell Trace to watch his back from now on.>
<Good luck, Natani.>
Feh, more like good riddance.
Now why did you do that, Natani? You were supposed to go with them. They were about to trust you.
Oh shut it, Zen. I don't care what the King's offered, I'm not wasting my time on some crazy adventure.
Aw crap, what are humans doing way out here? They must be scouting out the fires.
I'm injured and have no weapons. There's sure to be more humans in the forest.. well, I guess I'll go around.
Hey, there's a Keidran! I bet it has something to do with this! Skin it alive!
<I've changed my mind!>
<I'll waste my time on your crazy adventure!>

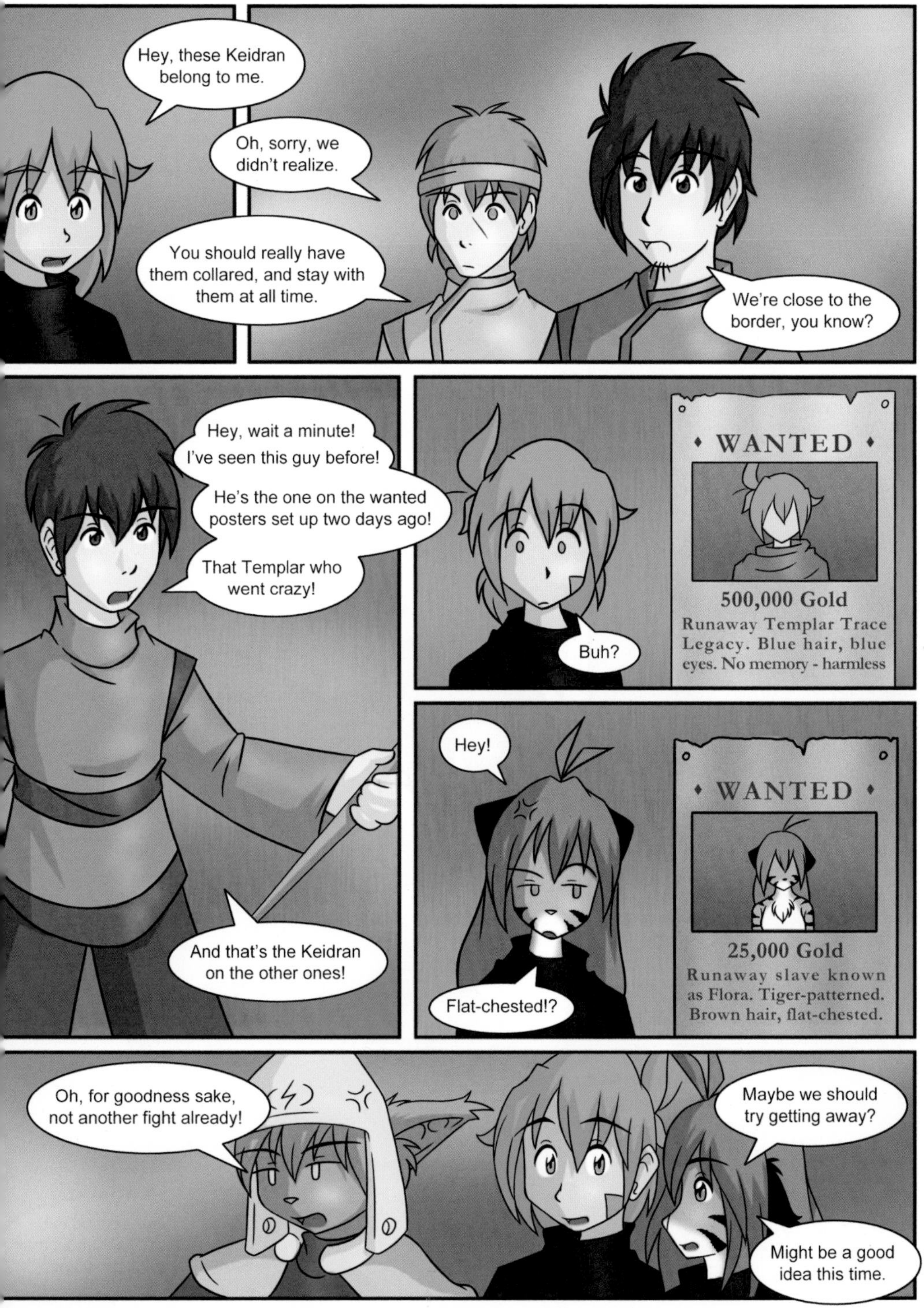
Hey, these Keidran belong to me.
Oh, sorry, we didn't realize.
You should really have them collared, and stay with them at all time.
We're close to the border, you know?
Hey, wait a minute! I've seen this guy before!
He's the one on the wanted posters set up two days ago!
That Templar who went crazy!
WANTED
500,000 Gold
Runaway Templar Trace Legacy. Blue hair, blue eyes. No memory - harmless
Buh?
And that's the Keidran on the other ones!
Hey!
WANTED
25,000 Gold
Runaway slave known as Flora. Tiger-patterned. Brown hair, flat-chested.
Flat-chested!?
Oh, for goodness sake, not another fight already!
Maybe we should try getting away?
Might be a good idea this time.

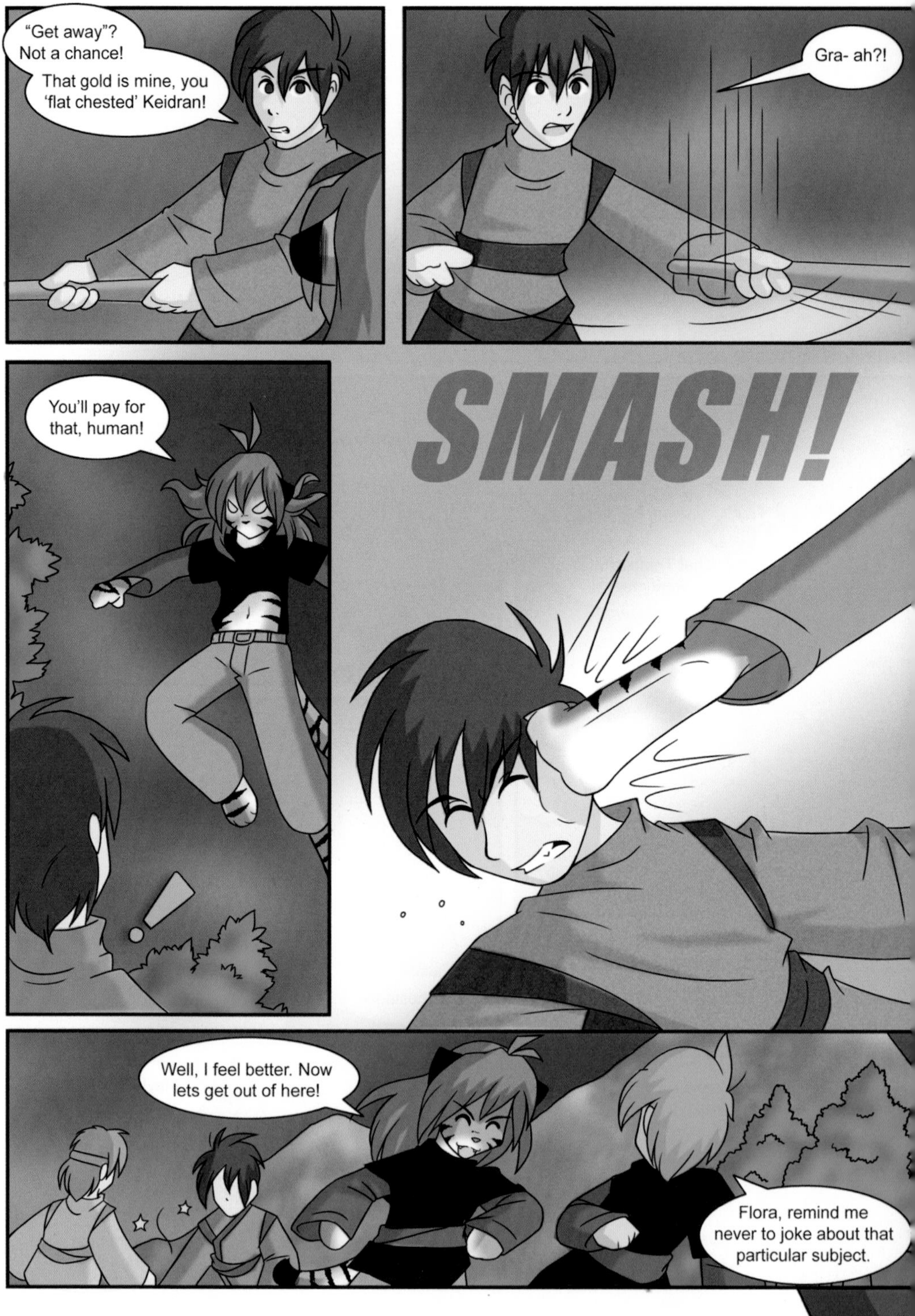

"Get away"? Not a chance!
That gold is mine, you 'flat chested' Keidran!
Gra- ah?!
You'll pay for that, human!
SMASH!
Well, I feel better. Now lets get out of here!
Flora, remind me never to joke about that particular subject.

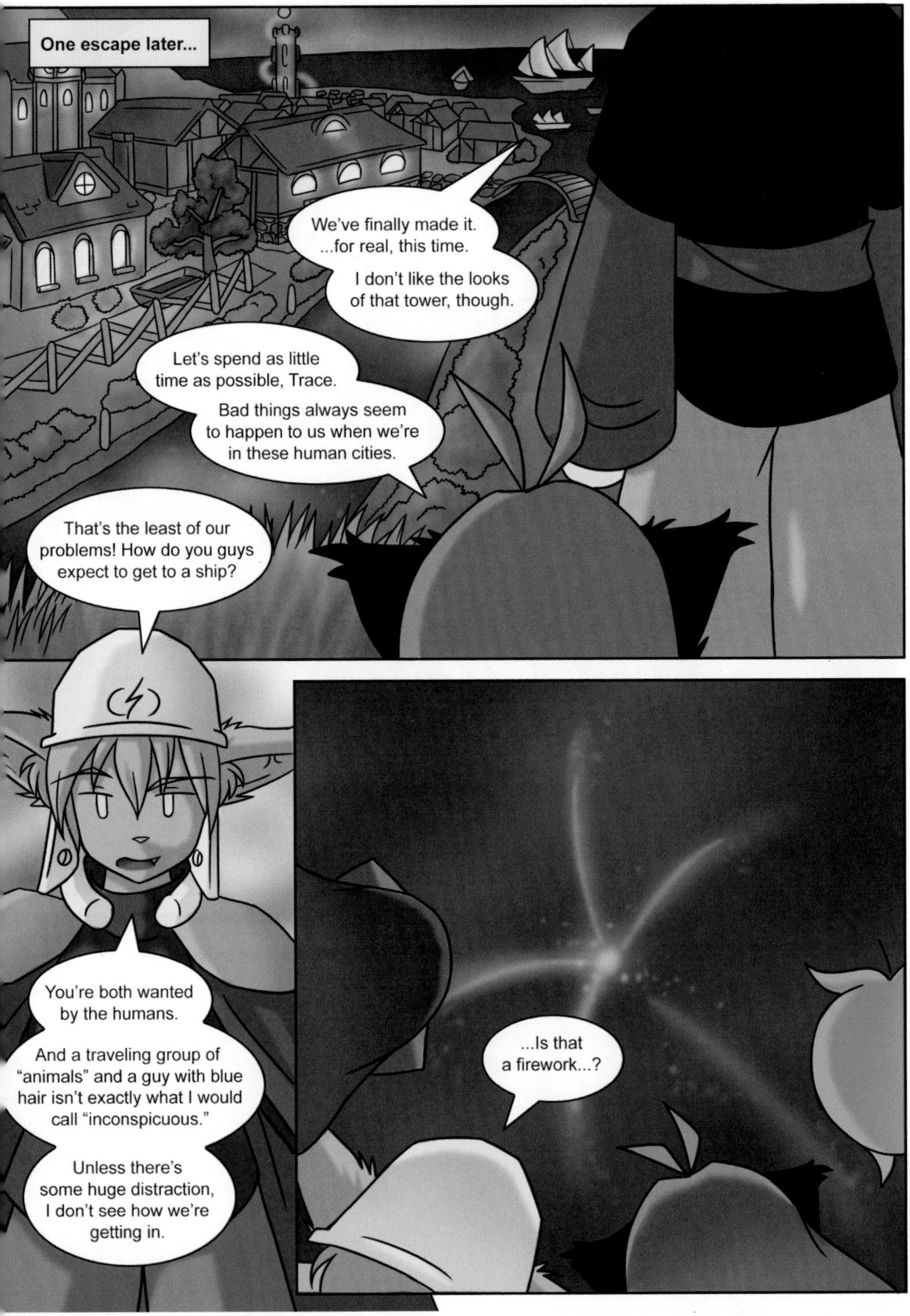
One escape later...
We've finally made it. ...for real, this time.
I don't like the looks of that tower, though.
Let's spend as little time as possible, Trace.
Bad things always seem to happen to us when we're in these human cities.
That's the least of our problems! How do you guys expect to get to a ship?
You're both wanted by the humans.
And a traveling group of "animals" and a guy with blue hair isn't exactly what I would call "inconspicuous."
Unless there's some huge distraction, I don't see how we're getting in.
...Is that a firework...?

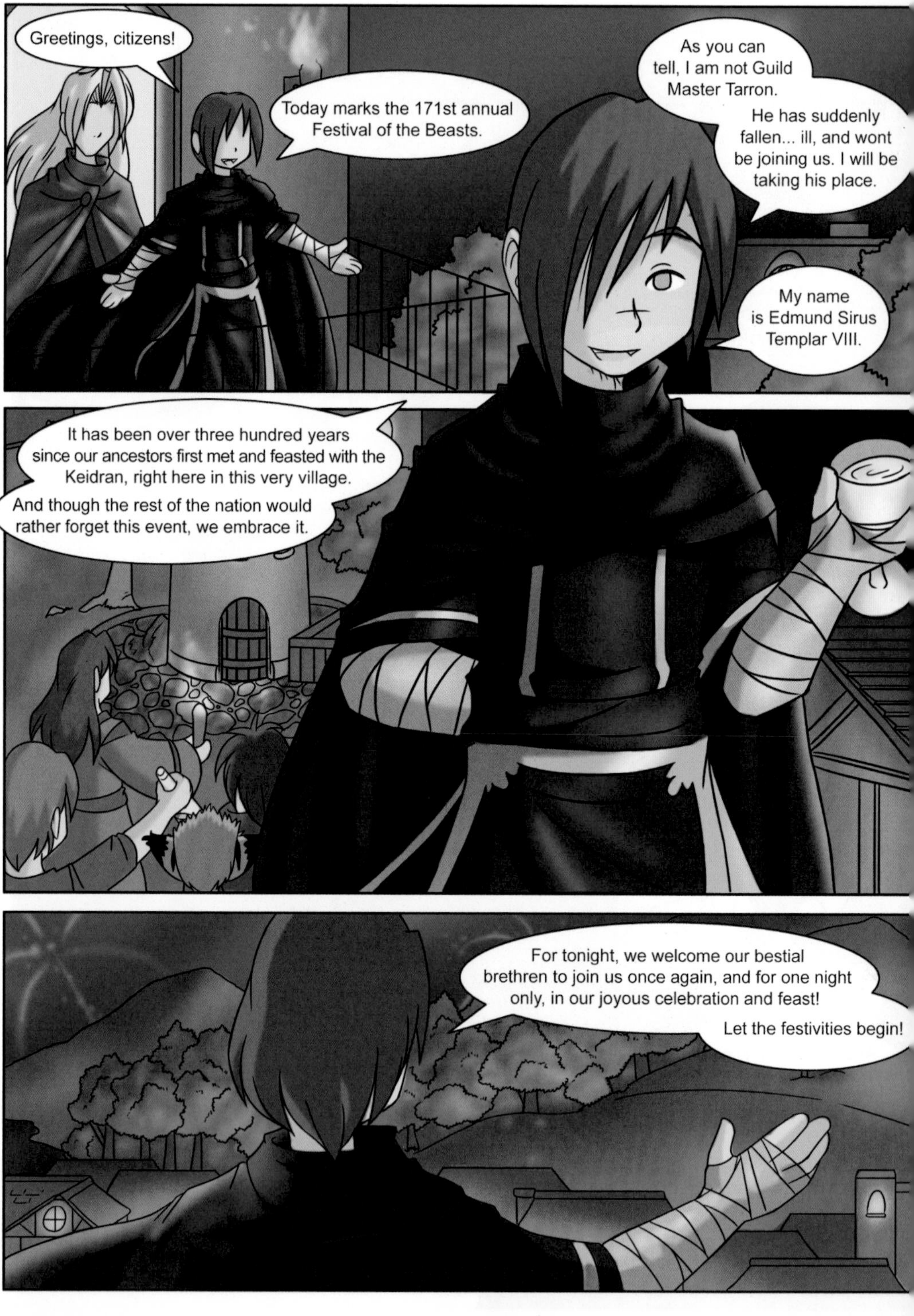
Greetings, citizens!
Today marks the 171st annual Festival of the Beasts.
As you can tell, I am not Guild Master Tarron.
He has suddenly fallen... ill, and wont be joining us. I will be taking his place.
My name is Edmund Sirus Templar VIII.
It has been over three hundred years since our ancestors first met and feasted with the Keidran, right here in this very village.
And though the rest of the nation would rather forget this event, we embrace it.
For tonight, we welcome our bestial brethren to join us once again, and for one night only, in our joyous celebration and feast!
Let the festivities begin!

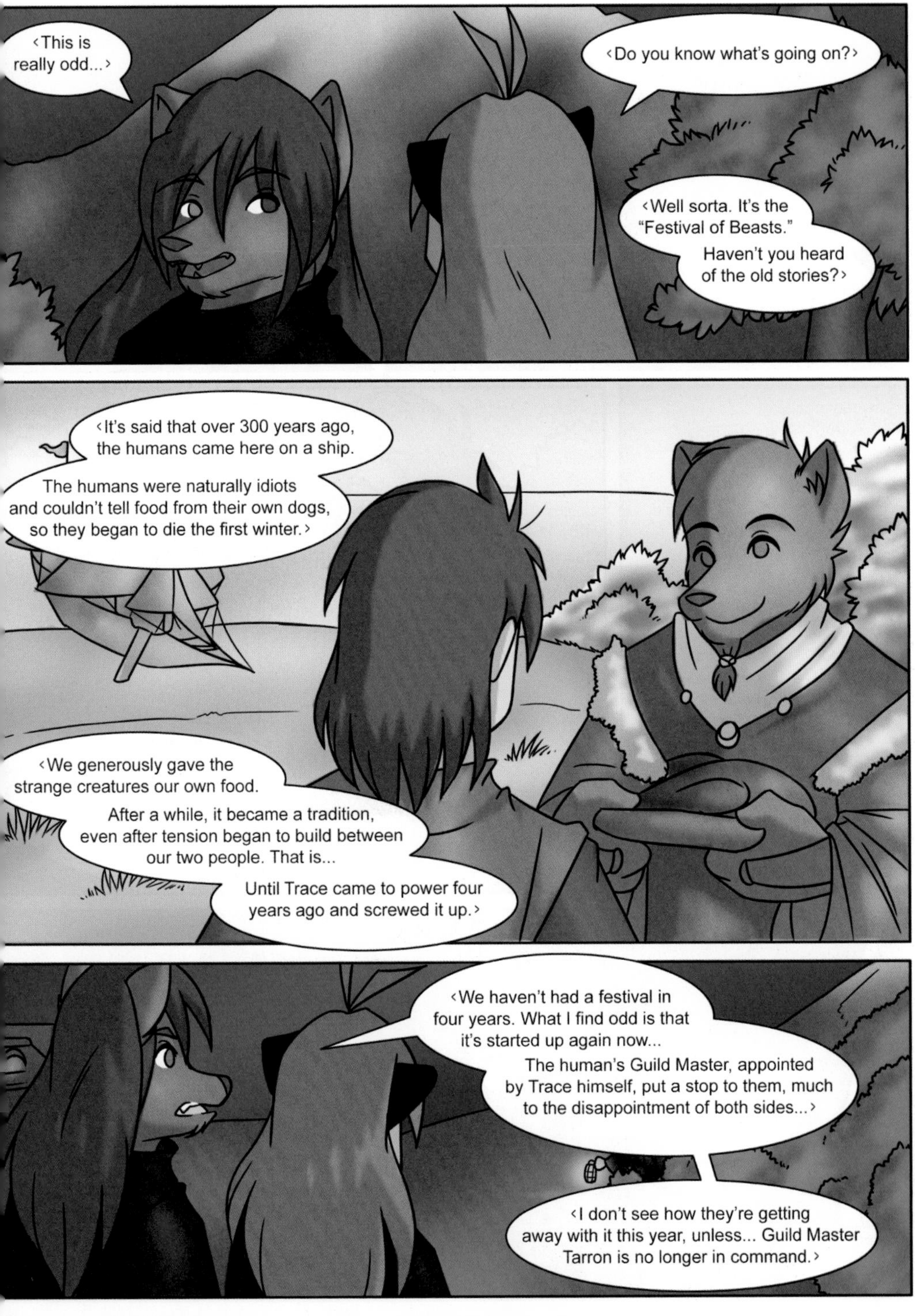

‹This is really odd...›
‹Do you know what's going on?›
‹Well sorta. It's the "Festival of Beasts." Haven't you heard of the old stories?›
‹It's said that over 300 years ago, the humans came here on a ship. The humans were naturally idiots and couldn't tell food from their own dogs, so they began to die the first winter.›
‹We generously gave the strange creatures our own food. After a while, it became a tradition, even after tension began to build between our two people. That is... Until Trace came to power four years ago and screwed it up.›
‹We haven't had a festival in four years. What I find odd is that it's started up again now... The human's Guild Master, appointed by Trace himself, put a stop to them, much to the disappointment of both sides...›
‹I don't see how they're getting away with it this year, unless... Guild Master Tarron is no longer in command.›

‹Uh, excuse me, Wolf.

I don't know where you learned your history, but that's not how it happened.›

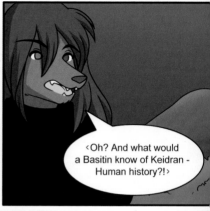

‹Oh? And what would a Basitin know of Keidran - Human history?!›

‹I've spent enough time around Humans to hear the real story.›

‹It was the Keidran who were hopelessly lost and starving that first year.›

‹Humans found these pitiful creatures and offered their food to help them survive the winter. The Keidran owed the Humans their lives.›

‹Oh, I see. So that's how it happened!›

‹That is not how it happened!›

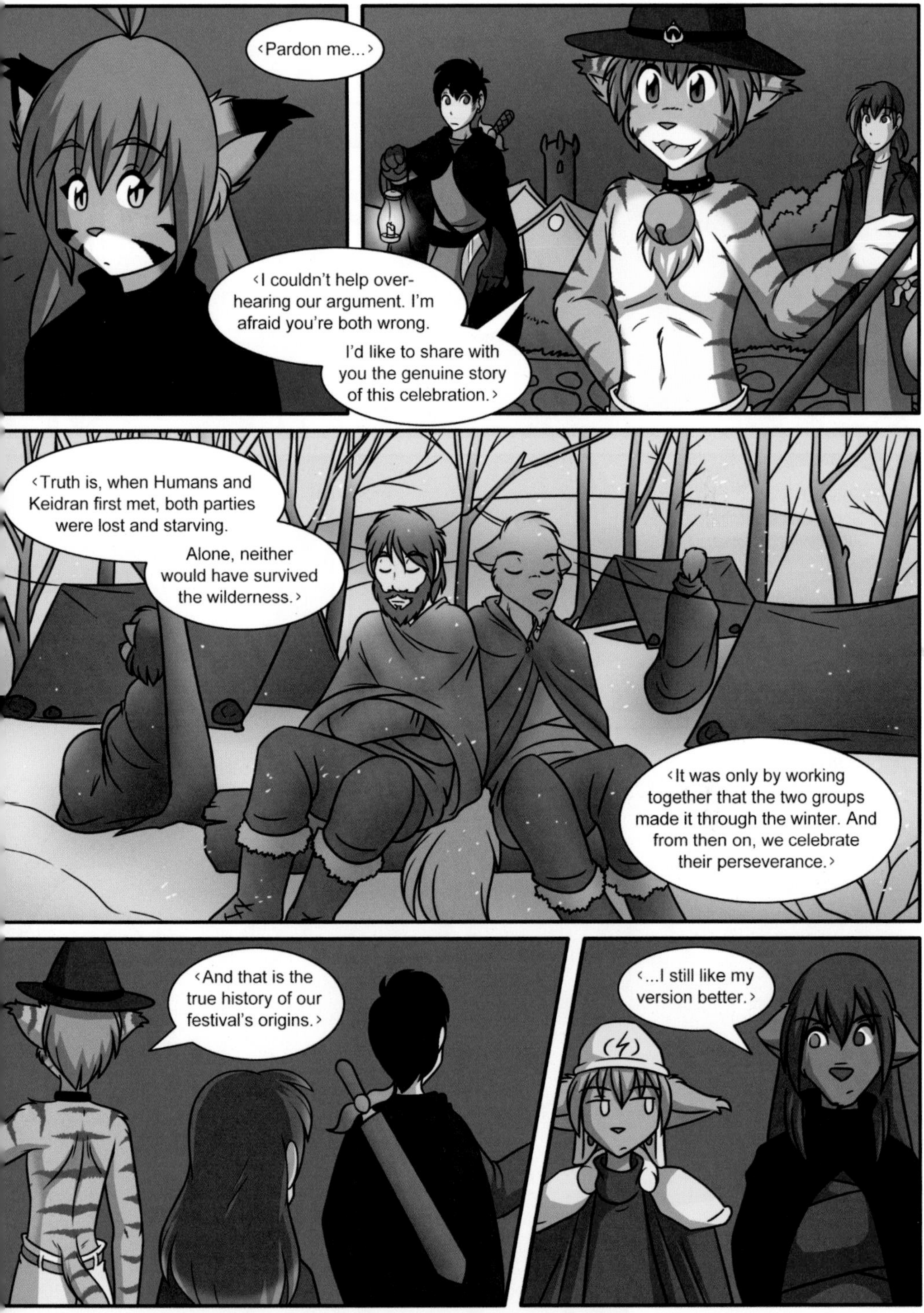
‹Pardon me...›
‹I couldn't help over-hearing our argument. I'm afraid you're both wrong.
I'd like to share with you the genuine story of this celebration.›
‹Truth is, when Humans and Keidran first met, both parties were lost and starving.
Alone, neither would have survived the wilderness.›
‹It was only by working together that the two groups made it through the winter. And from then on, we celebrate their perseverance.›
‹And that is the true history of our festival's origins.›
‹...I still like my version better.›

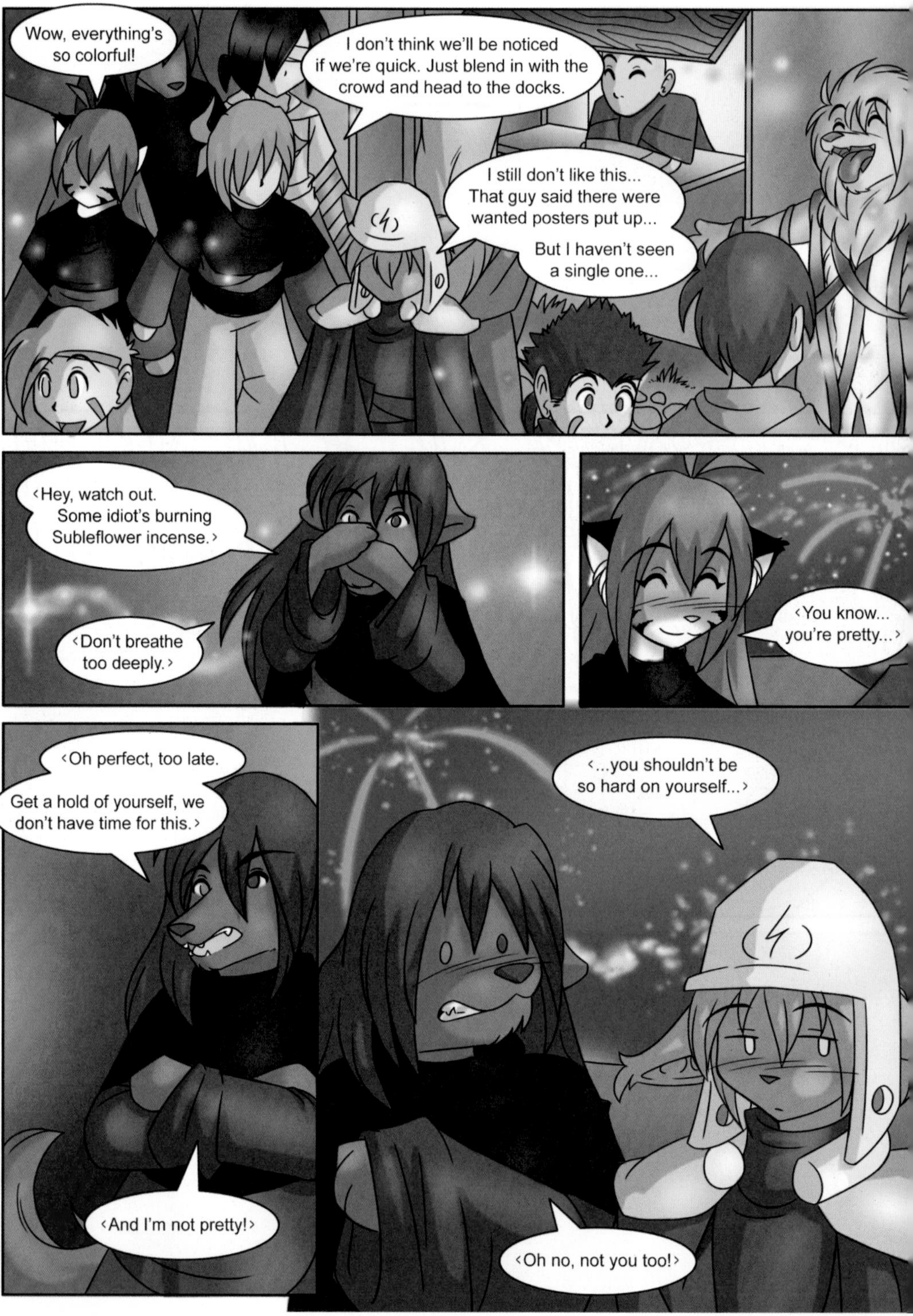
Wow, everything's so colorful!
I don't think we'll be noticed if we're quick. Just blend in with the crowd and head to the docks.
I still don't like this... That guy said there were wanted posters put up...
But I haven't seen a single one...
‹Hey, watch out. Some idiot's burning Subleflower incense.›
‹Don't breathe too deeply.›
‹You know... you're pretty...›
‹Oh perfect, too late.
Get a hold of yourself, we don't have time for this.›
‹...you shouldn't be so hard on yourself...›
‹And I'm not pretty!›
‹Oh no, not you too!›

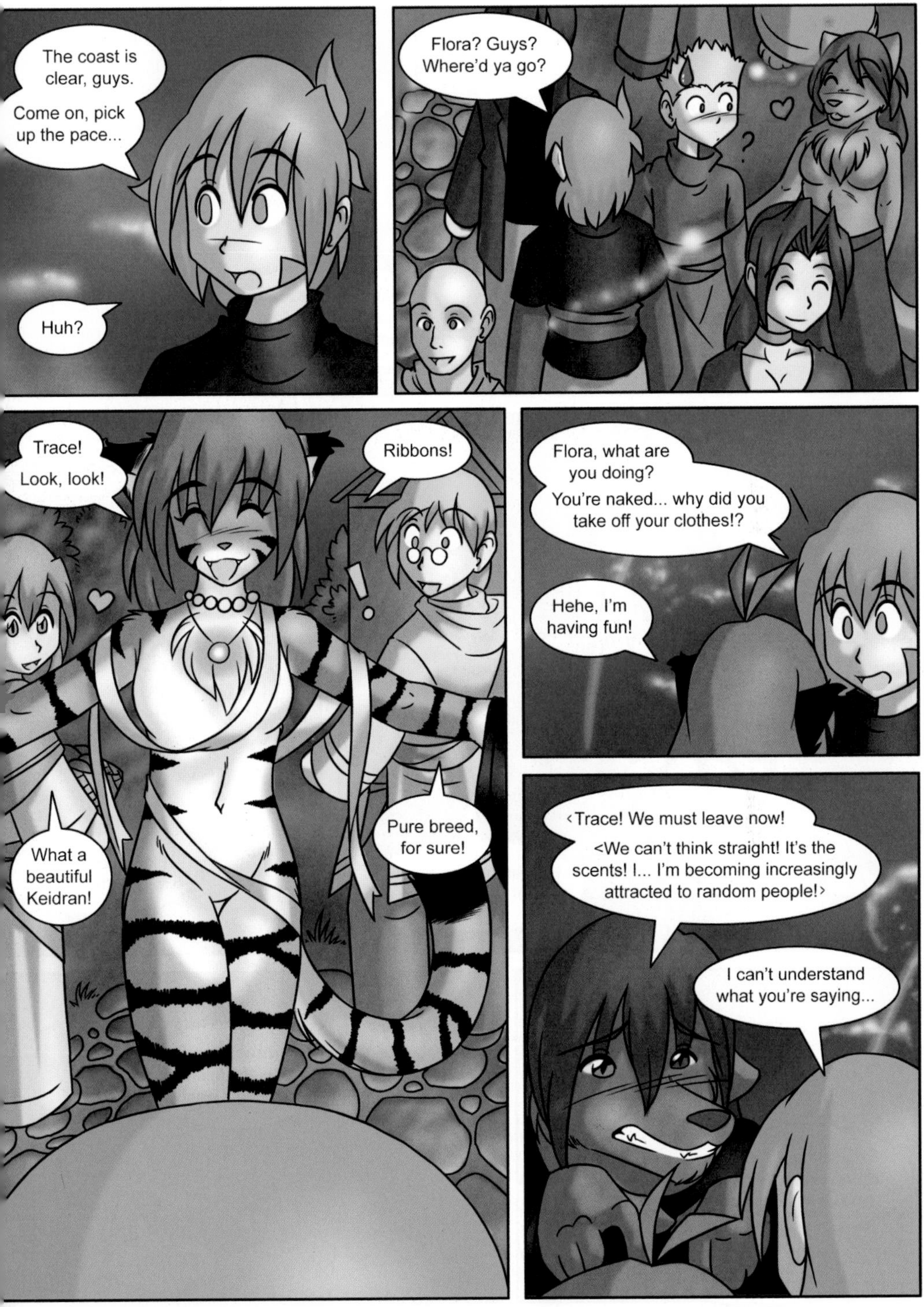
The coast is clear, guys.
Come on, pick up the pace...
Huh?
Flora? Guys? Where'd ya go?
Trace! Look, look!
Ribbons!
What a beautiful Keidran!
Pure breed, for sure!
Flora, what are you doing?
You're naked... why did you take off your clothes!?
Hehe, I'm having fun!
<Trace! We must leave now!
<We can't think straight! It's the scents! I... I'm becoming increasingly attracted to random people!>
I can't understand what you're saying...

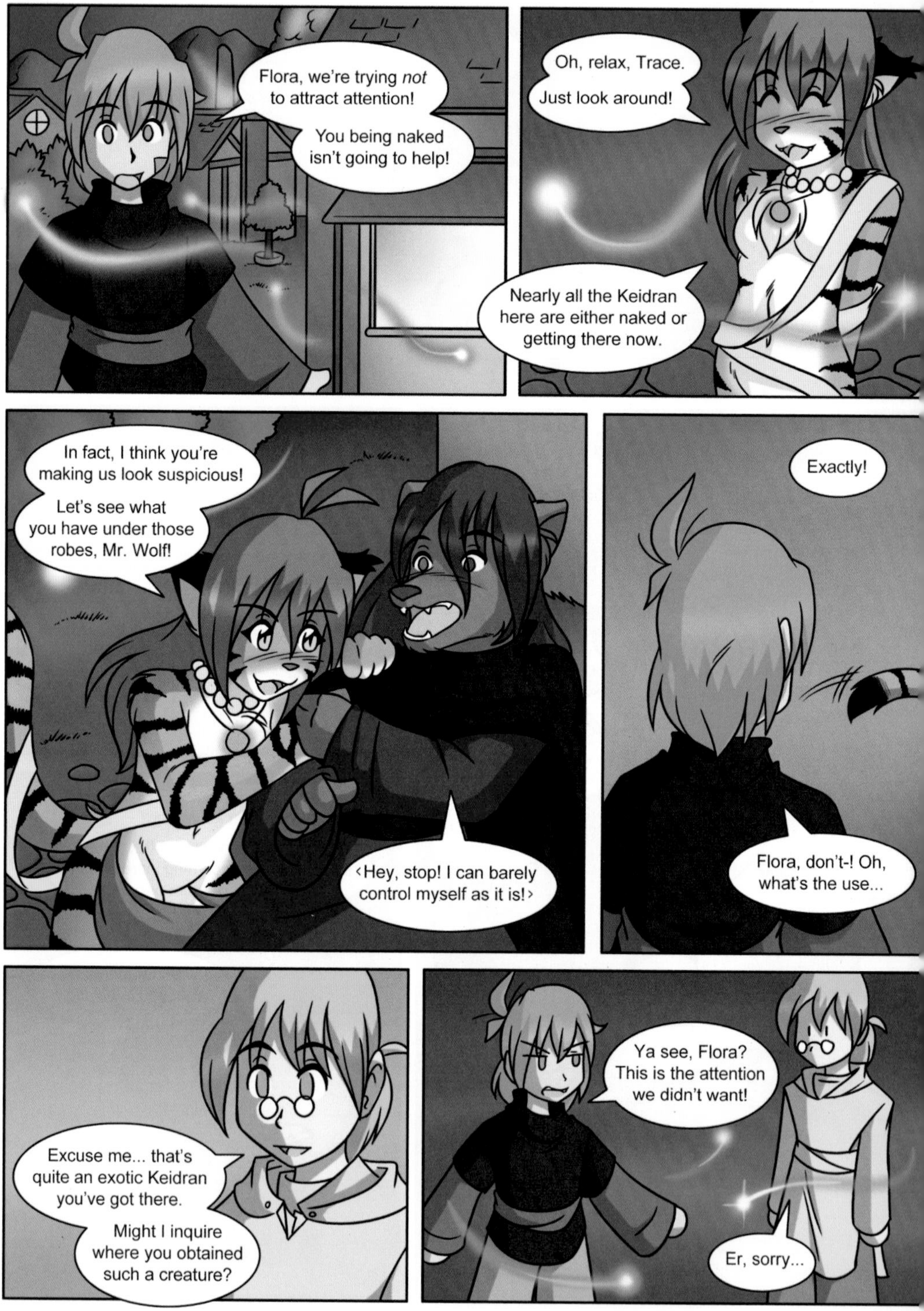
Flora, we're trying *not* to attract attention!
You being naked isn't going to help!
Oh, relax, Trace.
Just look around!
Nearly all the Keidran here are either naked or getting there now.
In fact, I think you're making us look suspicious!
Let's see what you have under those robes, Mr. Wolf!
‹Hey, stop! I can barely control myself as it is!›
Exactly!
Flora, don't-! Oh, what's the use...
Excuse me... that's quite an exotic Keidran you've got there.
Might I inquire where you obtained such a creature?
Ya see, Flora? This is the attention we didn't want!
Er, sorry...

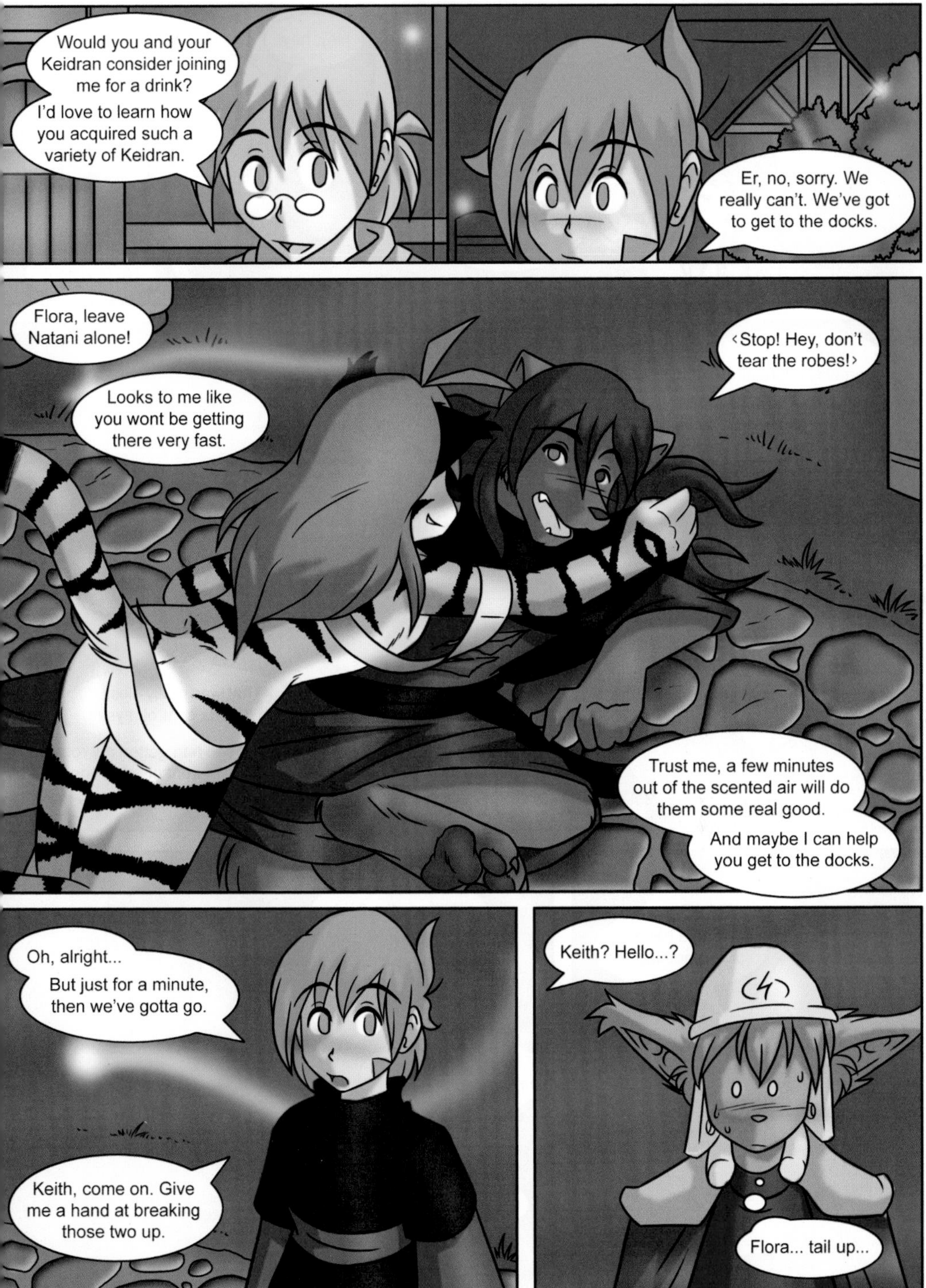

Would you and your Keidran consider joining me for a drink?
I'd love to learn how you acquired such a variety of Keidran.
Er, no, sorry. We really can't. We've got to get to the docks.
Flora, leave Natani alone!
Looks to me like you wont be getting there very fast.
‹Stop! Hey, don't tear the robes!›
Trust me, a few minutes out of the scented air will do them some real good.
And maybe I can help you get to the docks.
Oh, alright...
But just for a minute, then we've gotta go.
Keith, come on. Give me a hand at breaking those two up.
Keith? Hello...?
Flora... tail up...

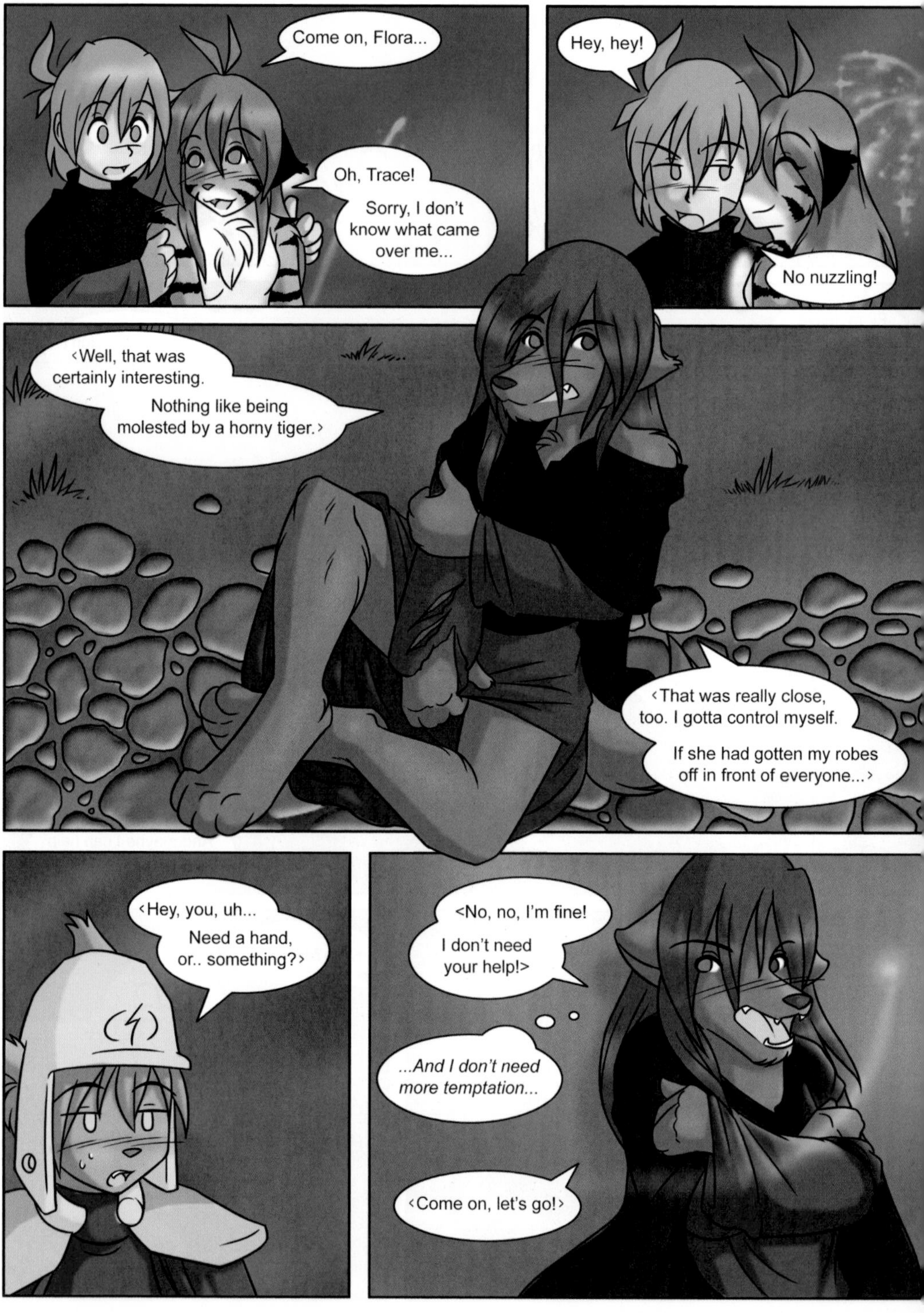

Come on, Flora...
Oh, Trace!
Sorry, I don't know what came over me...
Hey, hey!
No nuzzling!
<Well, that was certainly interesting.
Nothing like being molested by a horny tiger.>
<That was really close, too. I gotta control myself.
If she had gotten my robes off in front of everyone...>
<Hey, you, uh...
Need a hand, or.. something?>
<No, no, I'm fine!
I don't need your help!>
...And I don't need more temptation...
<Come on, let's go!>

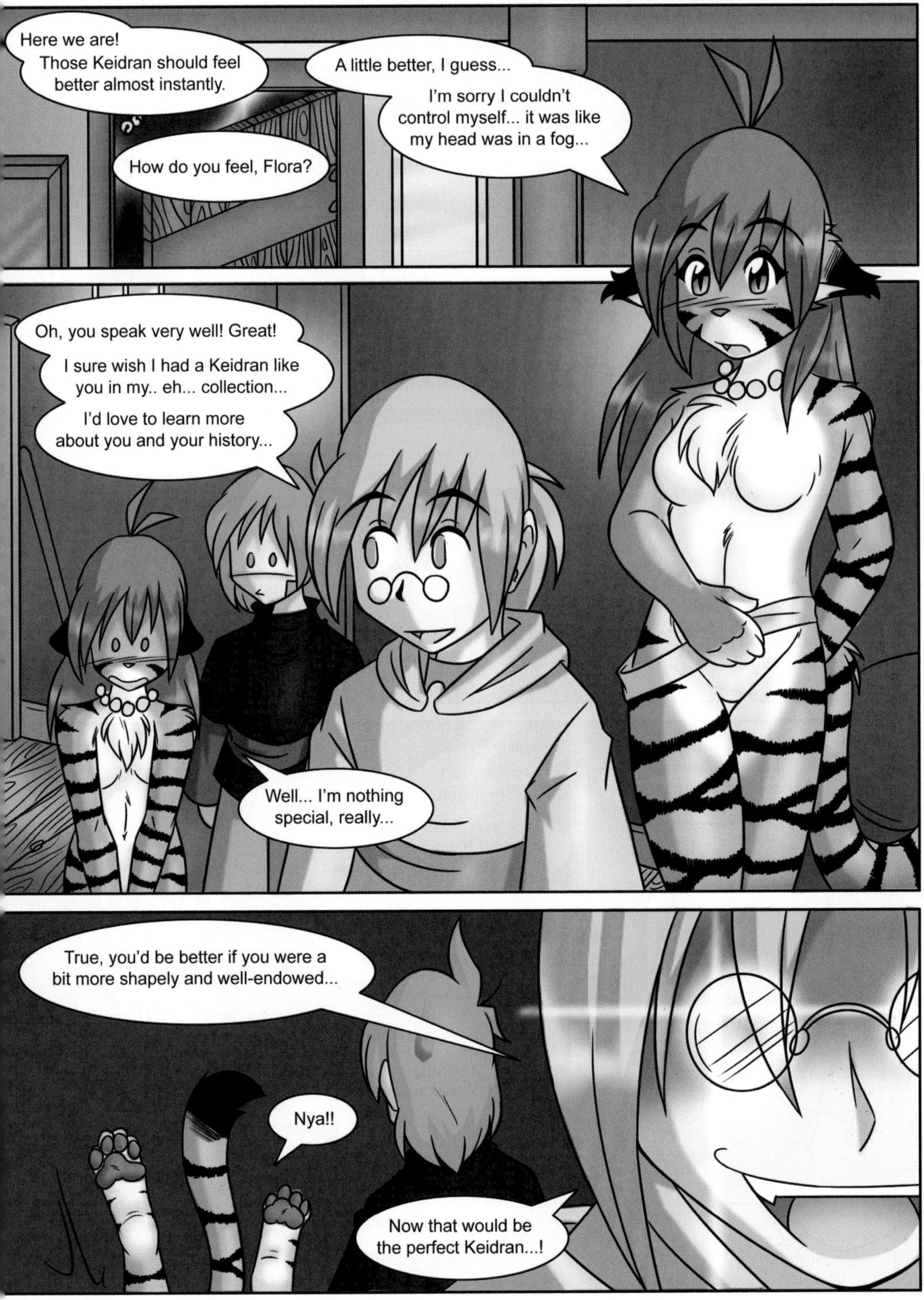
Here we are!
Those Keidran should feel better almost instantly.
How do you feel, Flora?
A little better, I guess...
I'm sorry I couldn't control myself... it was like my head was in a fog...
Oh, you speak very well! Great!
I sure wish I had a Keidran like you in my.. eh... collection...
I'd love to learn more about you and your history...
Well... I'm nothing special, really...
True, you'd be better if you were a bit more shapely and well-endowed...
Nya!!
Now that would be the perfect Keidran...!

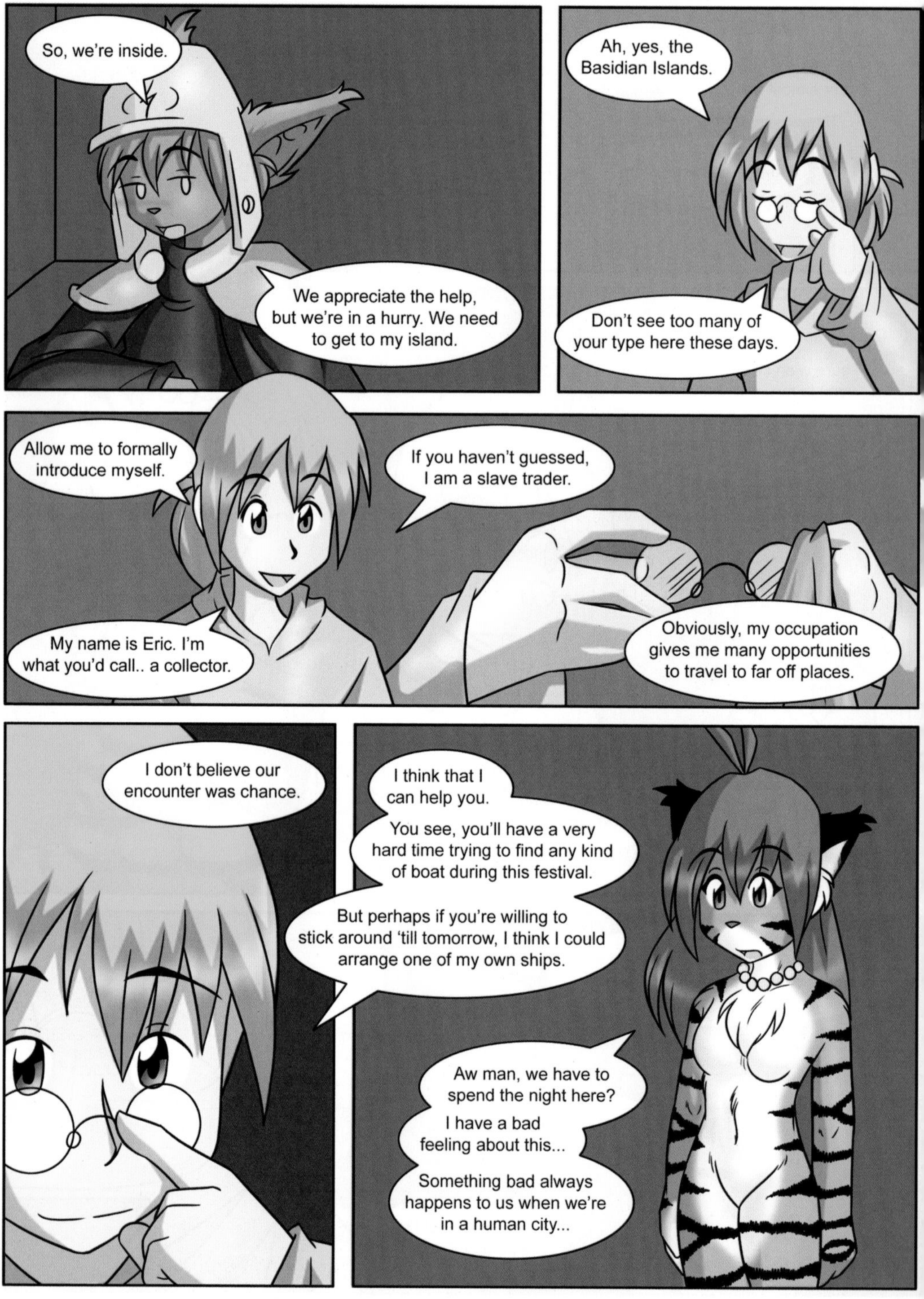
So, we're inside.
We appreciate the help, but we're in a hurry. We need to get to my island.
Ah, yes, the Basidian Islands.
Don't see too many of your type here these days.
Allow me to formally introduce myself.
My name is Eric. I'm what you'd call.. a collector.
If you haven't guessed, I am a slave trader.
Obviously, my occupation gives me many opportunities to travel to far off places.
I don't believe our encounter was chance.
I think that I can help you.
You see, you'll have a very hard time trying to find any kind of boat during this festival.
But perhaps if you're willing to stick around 'till tomorrow, I think I could arrange one of my own ships.
Aw man, we have to spend the night here?
I have a bad feeling about this...
Something bad always happens to us when we're in a human city...

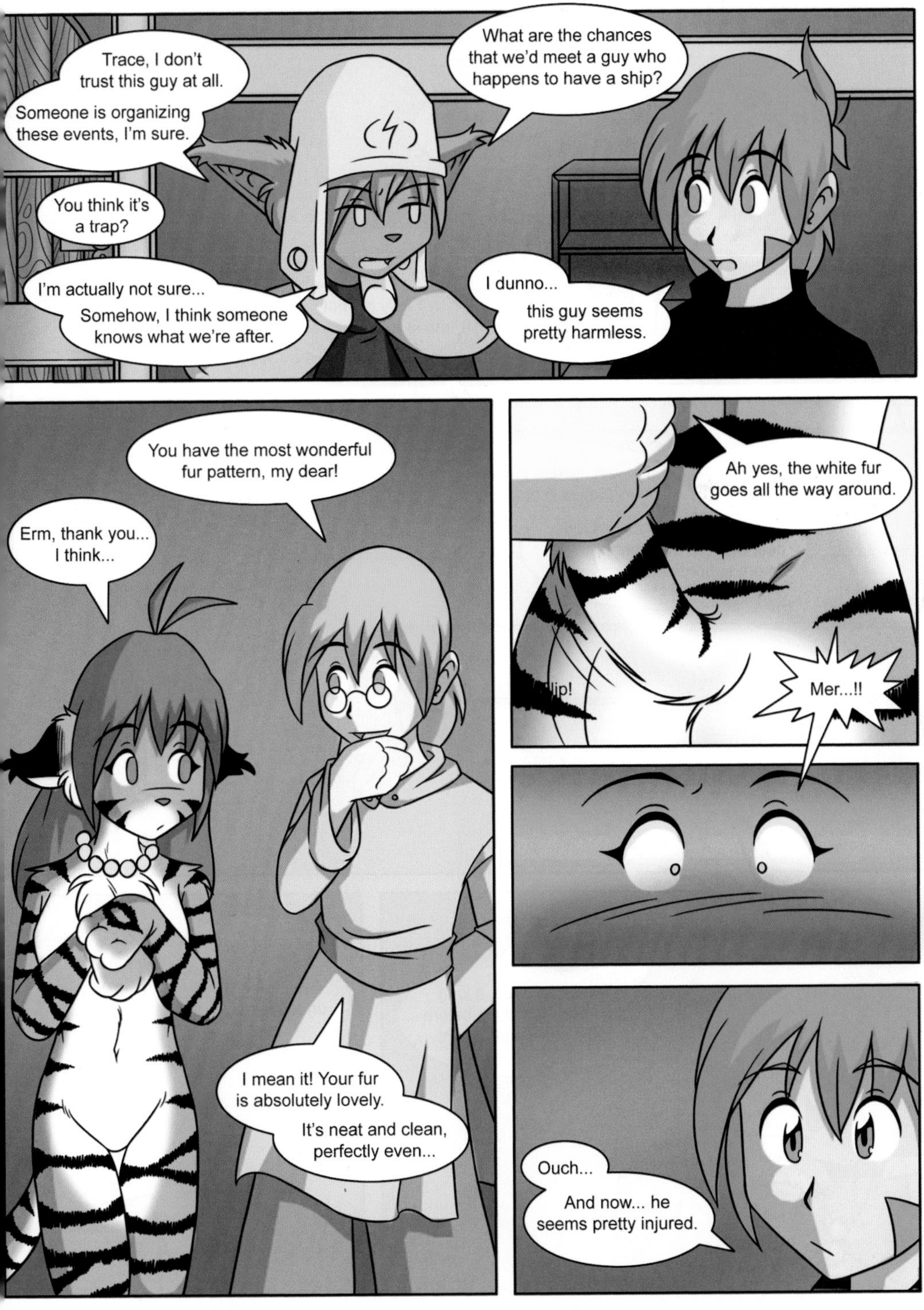
Trace, I don't trust this guy at all.
Someone is organizing these events, I'm sure.
What are the chances that we'd meet a guy who happens to have a ship?
You think it's a trap?
I'm actually not sure...
Somehow, I think someone knows what we're after.
I dunno...
this guy seems pretty harmless.
You have the most wonderful fur pattern, my dear!
Erm, thank you... I think...
I mean it! Your fur is absolutely lovely.
It's neat and clean, perfectly even...
Ah yes, the white fur goes all the way around.
Mer...!!
Ouch...
And now... he seems pretty injured.

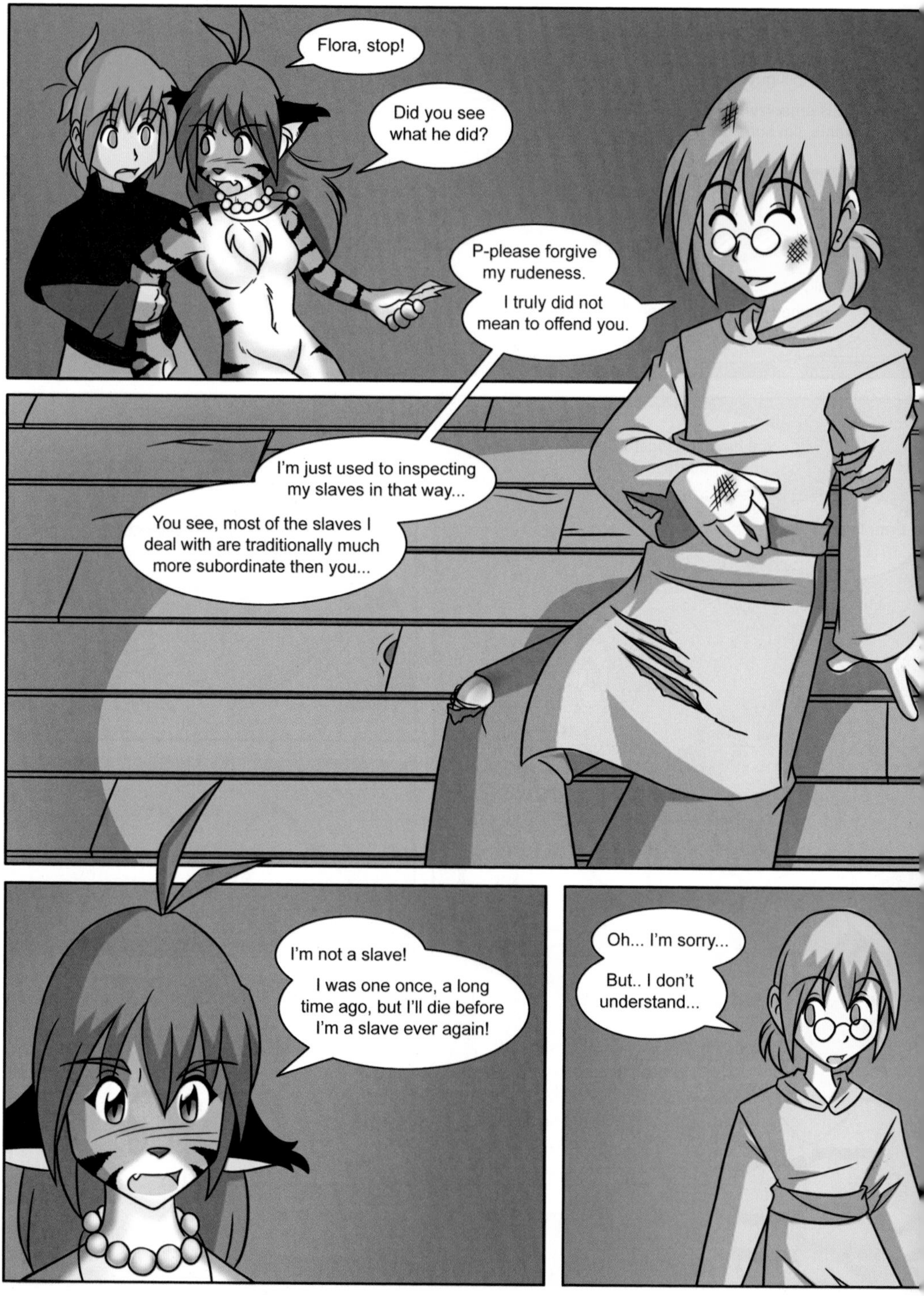
Flora, stop!
Did you see what he did?
P-please forgive my rudeness.
I truly did not mean to offend you.
I'm just used to inspecting my slaves in that way...
You see, most of the slaves I deal with are traditionally much more subordinate then you...
I'm not a slave!
I was one once, a long time ago, but I'll die before I'm a slave ever again!
Oh... I'm sorry...
But.. I don't understand...

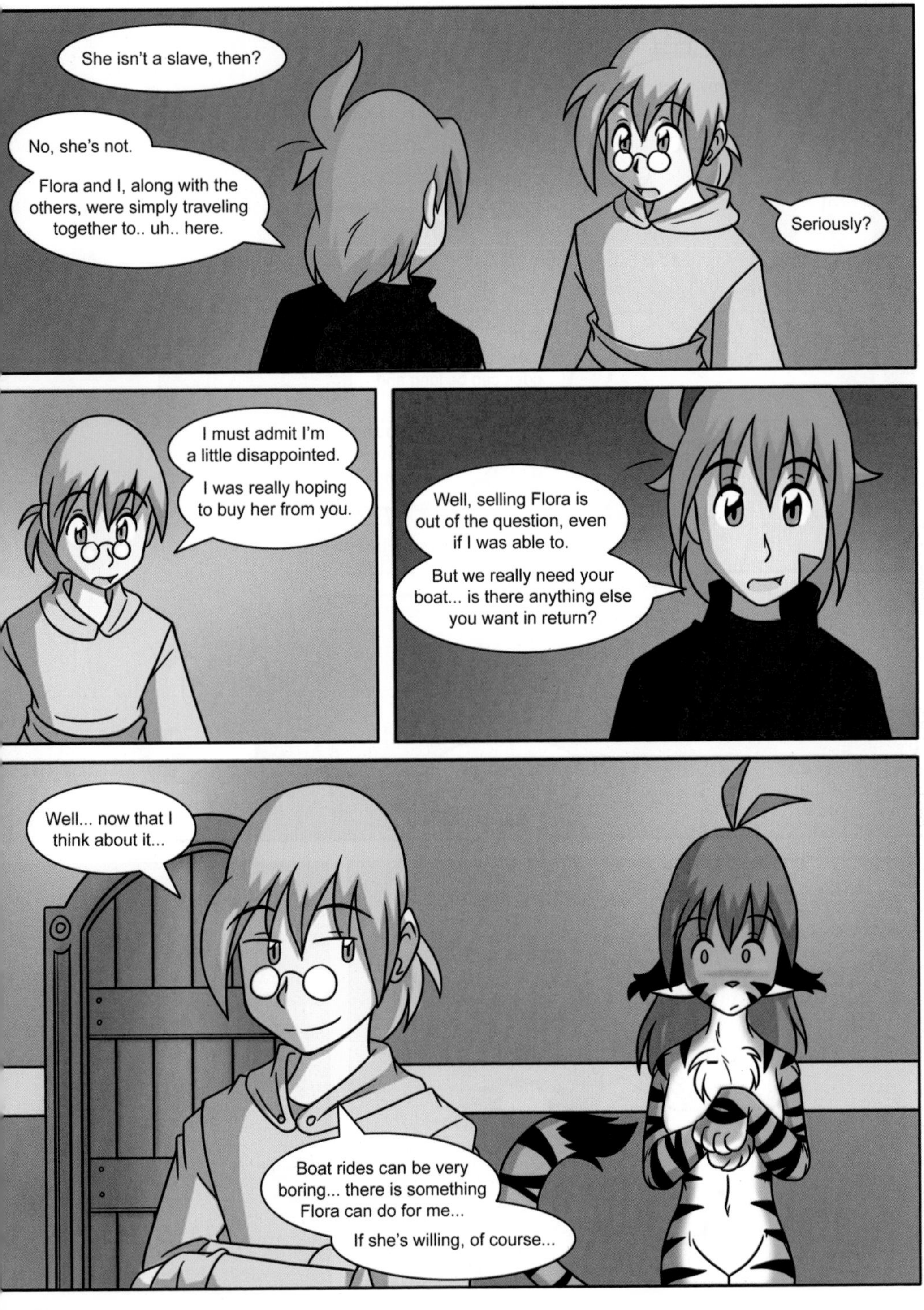
She isn't a slave, then?
No, she's not.
Flora and I, along with the others, were simply traveling together to.. uh.. here.
Seriously?
I must admit I'm a little disappointed.
I was really hoping to buy her from you.
Well, selling Flora is out of the question, even if I was able to.
But we really need your boat... is there anything else you want in return?
Well... now that I think about it...
Boat rides can be very boring... there is something Flora can do for me...
If she's willing, of course...

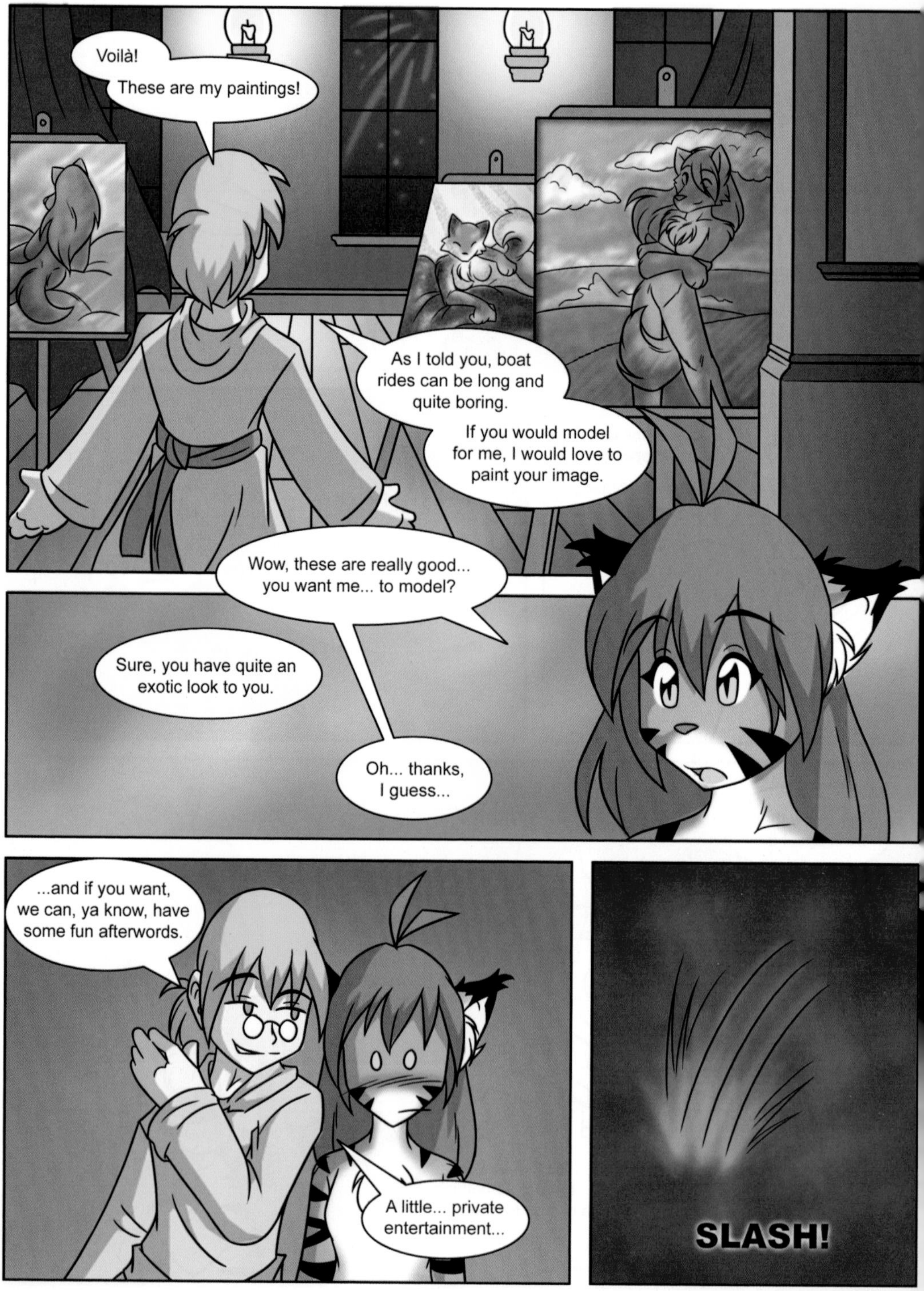
Voilà!
These are my paintings!
As I told you, boat rides can be long and quite boring.
If you would model for me, I would love to paint your image.
Wow, these are really good... you want me... to model?
Sure, you have quite an exotic look to you.
Oh... thanks, I guess...
...and if you want, we can, ya know, have some fun afterwords.
A little... private entertainment...
SLASH!

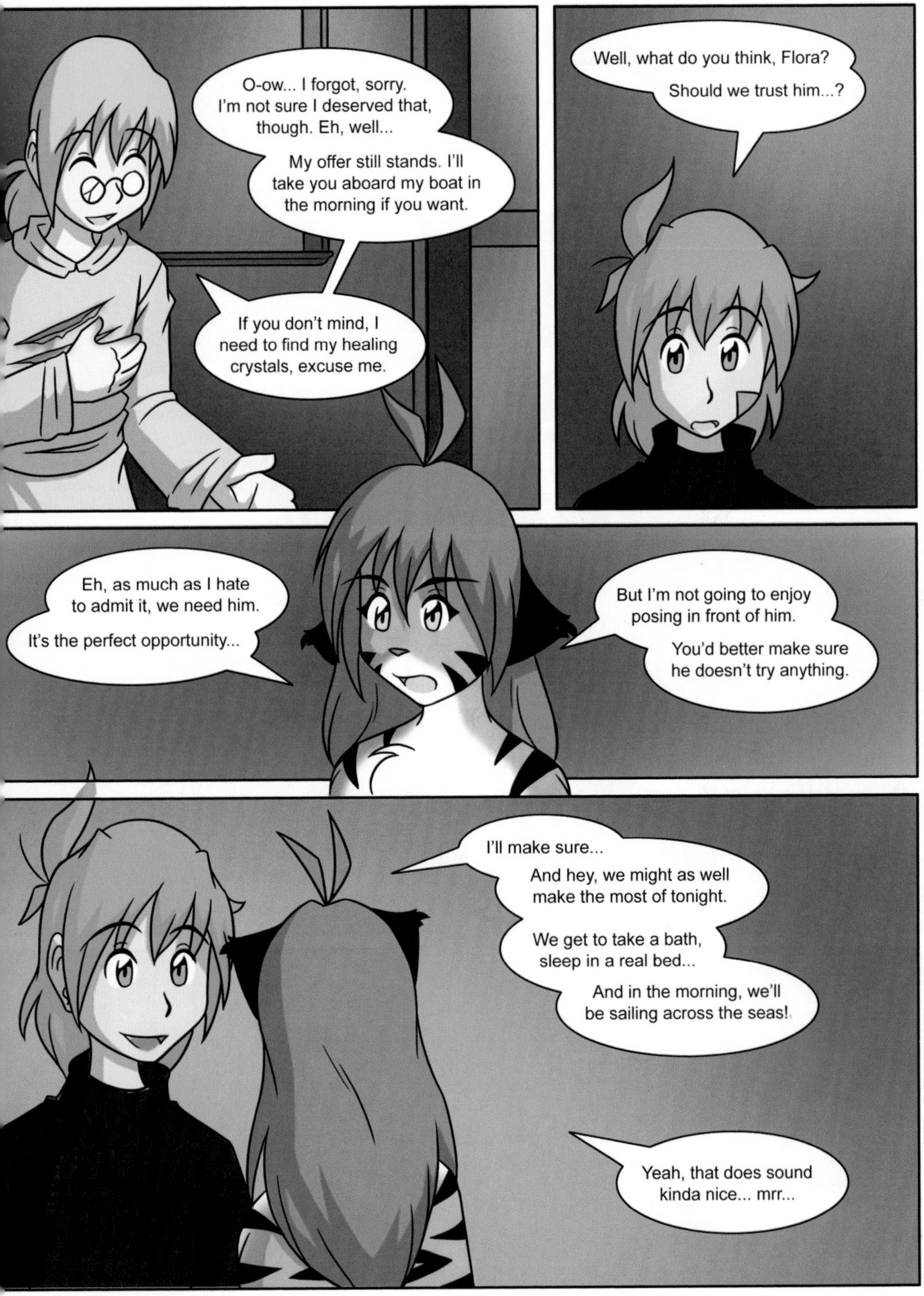
O-ow... I forgot, sorry. I'm not sure I deserved that, though. Eh, well...
My offer still stands. I'll take you aboard my boat in the morning if you want.
If you don't mind, I need to find my healing crystals, excuse me.
Well, what do you think, Flora?
Should we trust him...?
Eh, as much as I hate to admit it, we need him.
It's the perfect opportunity...
But I'm not going to enjoy posing in front of him.
You'd better make sure he doesn't try anything.
I'll make sure...
And hey, we might as well make the most of tonight.
We get to take a bath, sleep in a real bed...
And in the morning, we'll be sailing across the seas!
Yeah, that does sound kinda nice... mrr...

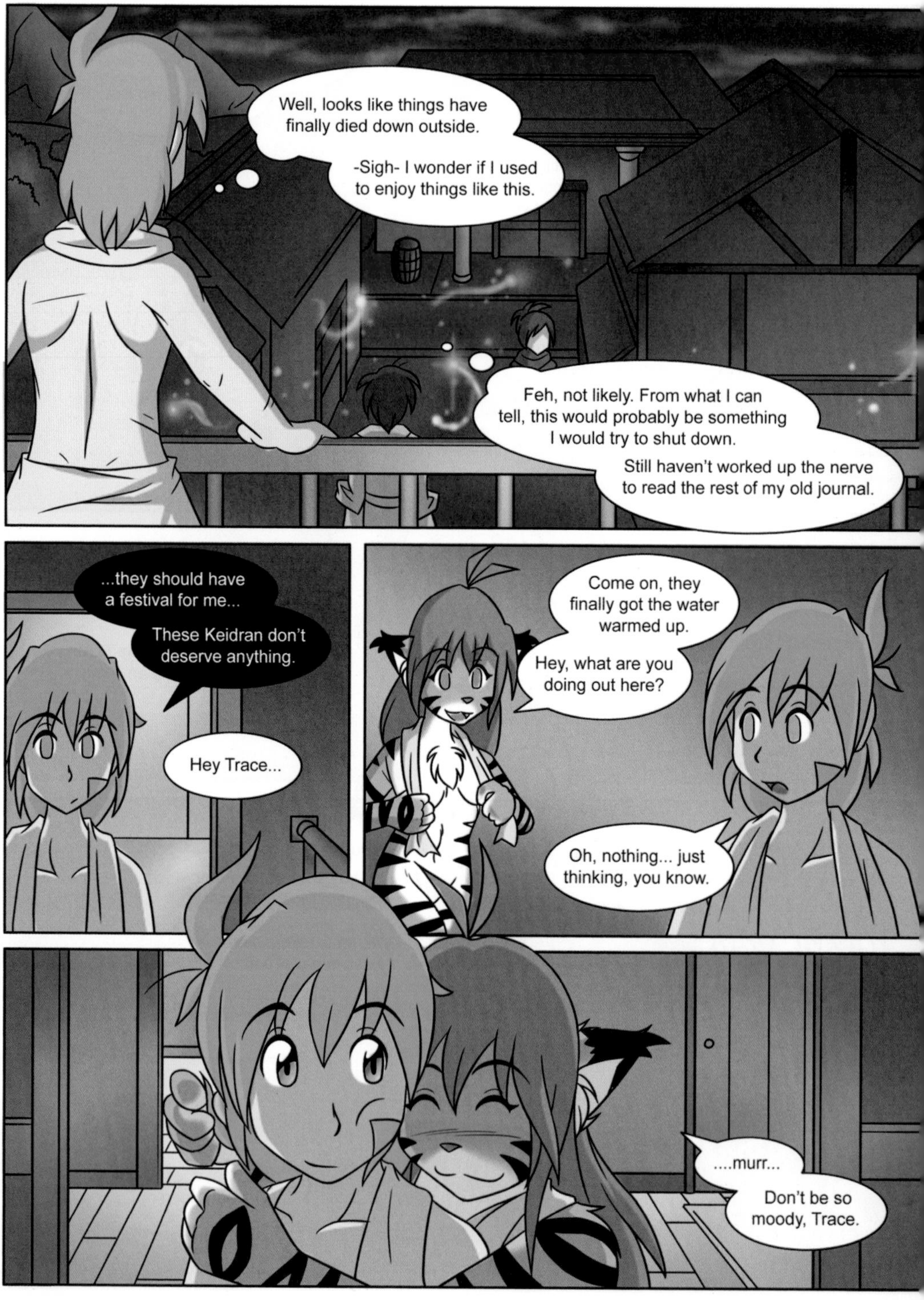

Well, looks like things have finally died down outside.
-Sigh- I wonder if I used to enjoy things like this.
Feh, not likely. From what I can tell, this would probably be something I would try to shut down.
Still haven't worked up the nerve to read the rest of my old journal.
...they should have a festival for me...
These Keidran don't deserve anything.
Hey Trace...
Come on, they finally got the water warmed up.
Hey, what are you doing out here?
Oh, nothing... just thinking, you know.
....murr...
Don't be so moody, Trace.

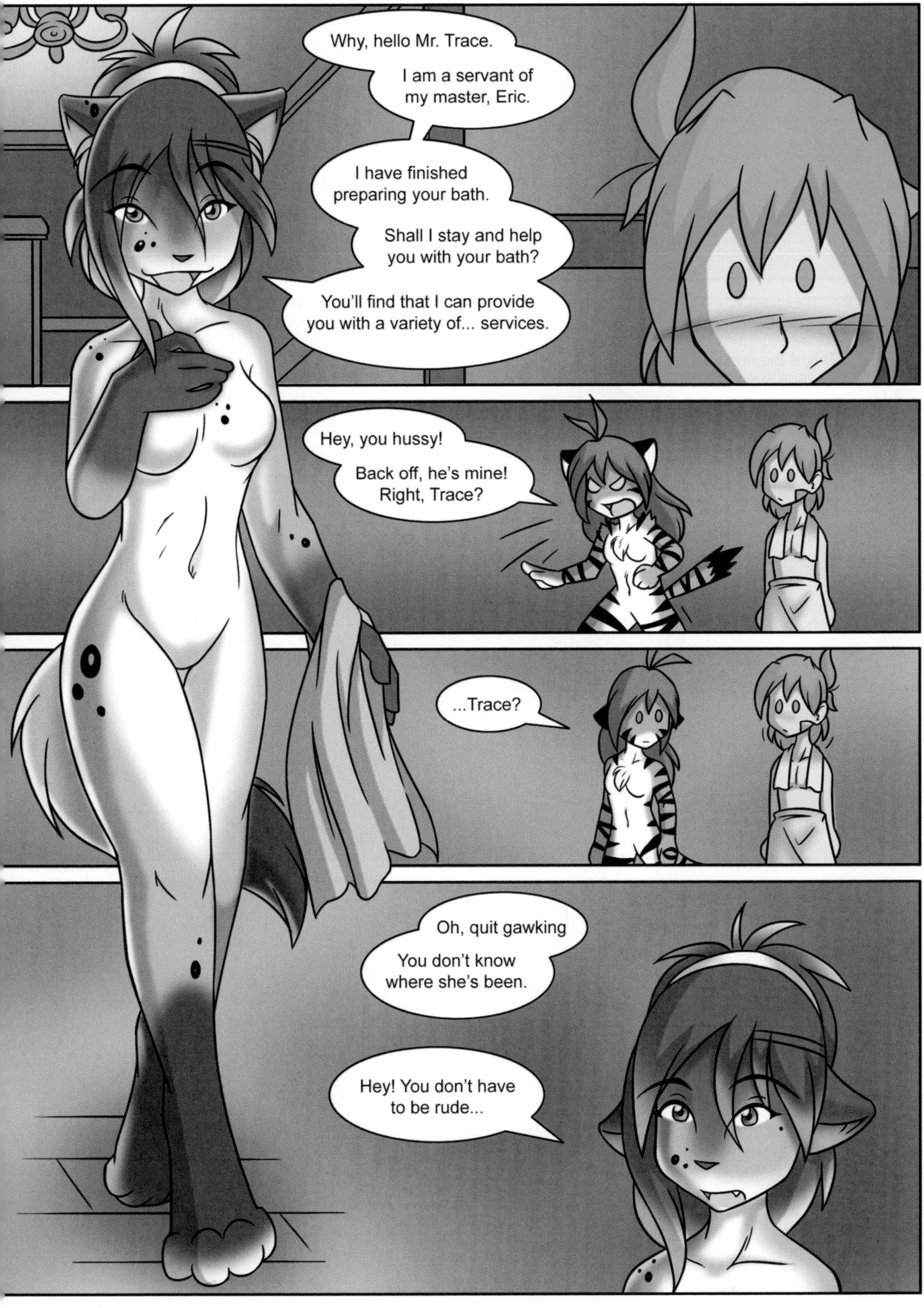
Why, hello Mr. Trace.
I am a servant of my master, Eric.
I have finished preparing your bath.
Shall I stay and help you with your bath?
You'll find that I can provide you with a variety of... services.
Hey, you hussy!
Back off, he's mine! Right, Trace?
...Trace?
Oh, quit gawking
You don't know where she's been.
Hey! You don't have to be rude...

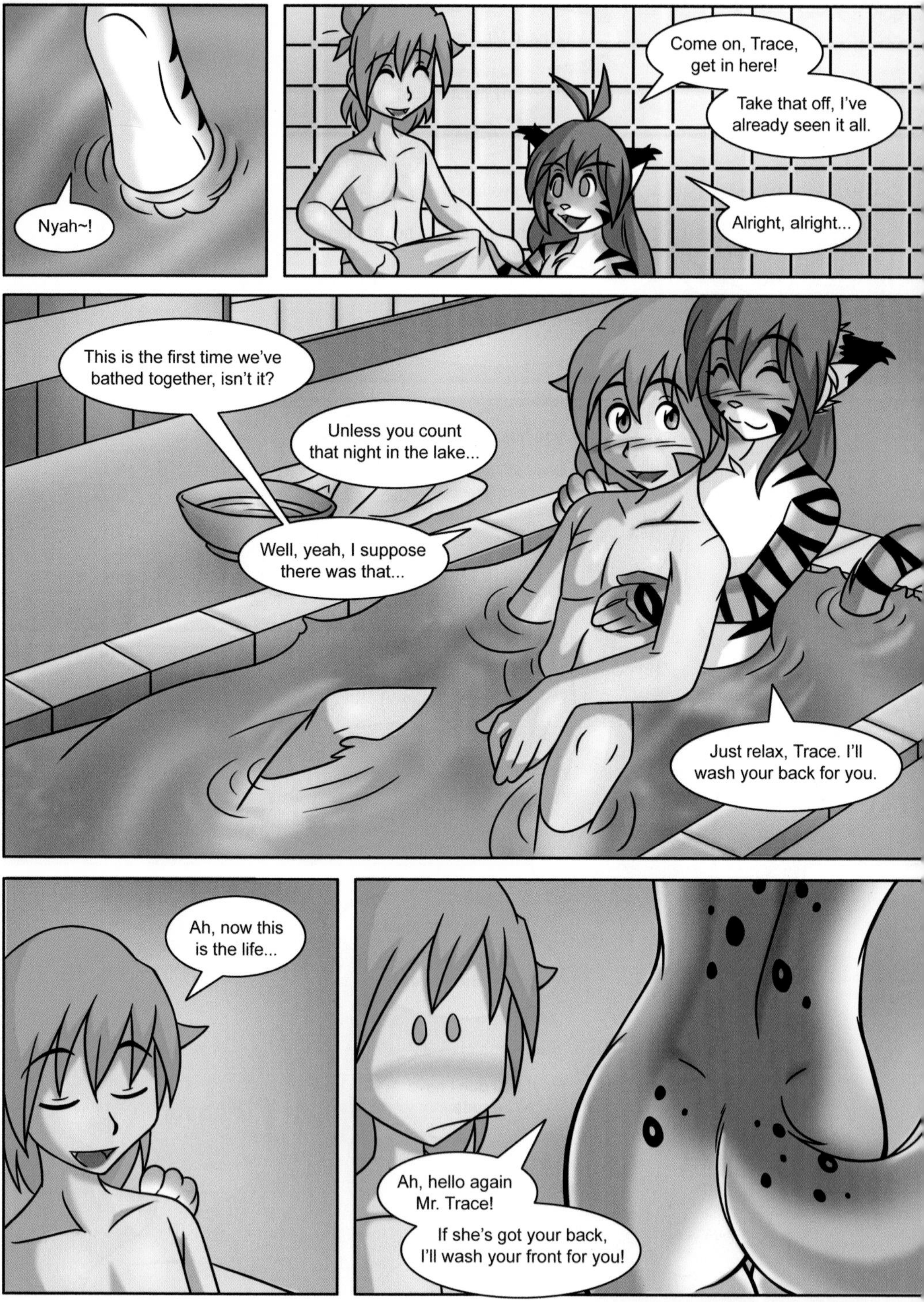
Nyah~!
Come on, Trace, get in here!
Take that off, I've already seen it all.
Alright, alright...
This is the first time we've bathed together, isn't it?
Unless you count that night in the lake...
Well, yeah, I suppose there was that...
Just relax, Trace. I'll wash your back for you.
Ah, now this is the life...
Ah, hello again Mr. Trace!
If she's got your back, I'll wash your front for you!

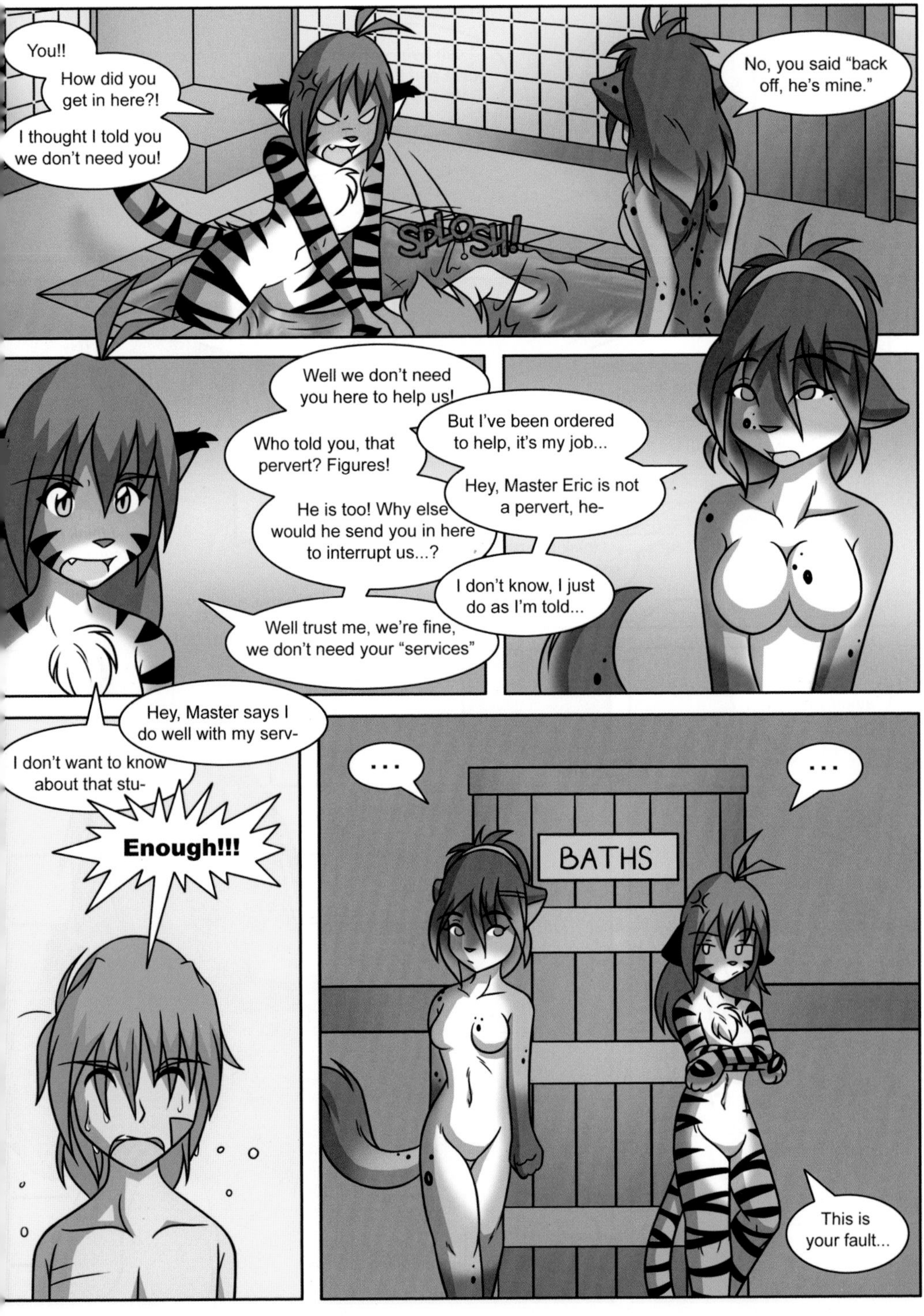

You!!
How did you get in here?!
I thought I told you we don't need you!
SPLOSH!
No, you said "back off, he's mine."
Well we don't need you here to help us!
But I've been ordered to help, it's my job...
Who told you, that pervert? Figures!
Hey, Master Eric is not a pervert, he-
He is too! Why else would he send you in here to interrupt us...?
I don't know, I just do as I'm told...
Well trust me, we're fine, we don't need your "services"
Hey, Master says I do well with my serv-
I don't want to know about that stu-
Enough!!!
...
BATHS
...
This is your fault...

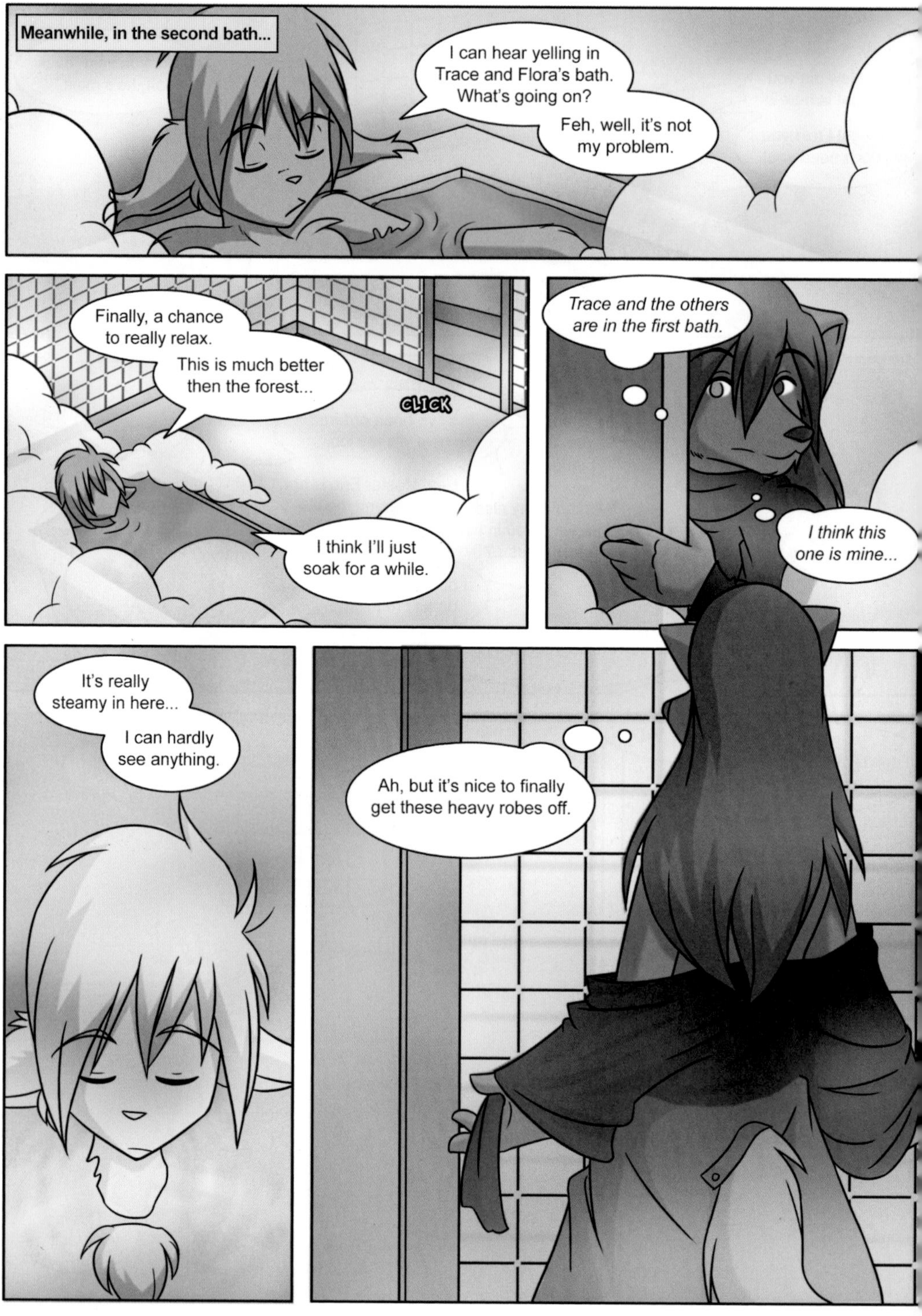
Meanwhile, in the second bath...
I can hear yelling in Trace and Flora's bath. What's going on?
Feh, well, it's not my problem.
Finally, a chance to really relax.
This is much better then the forest...
CLICK
I think I'll just soak for a while.
Trace and the others are in the first bath.
I think this one is mine...
It's really steamy in here...
I can hardly see anything.
Ah, but it's nice to finally get these heavy robes off.

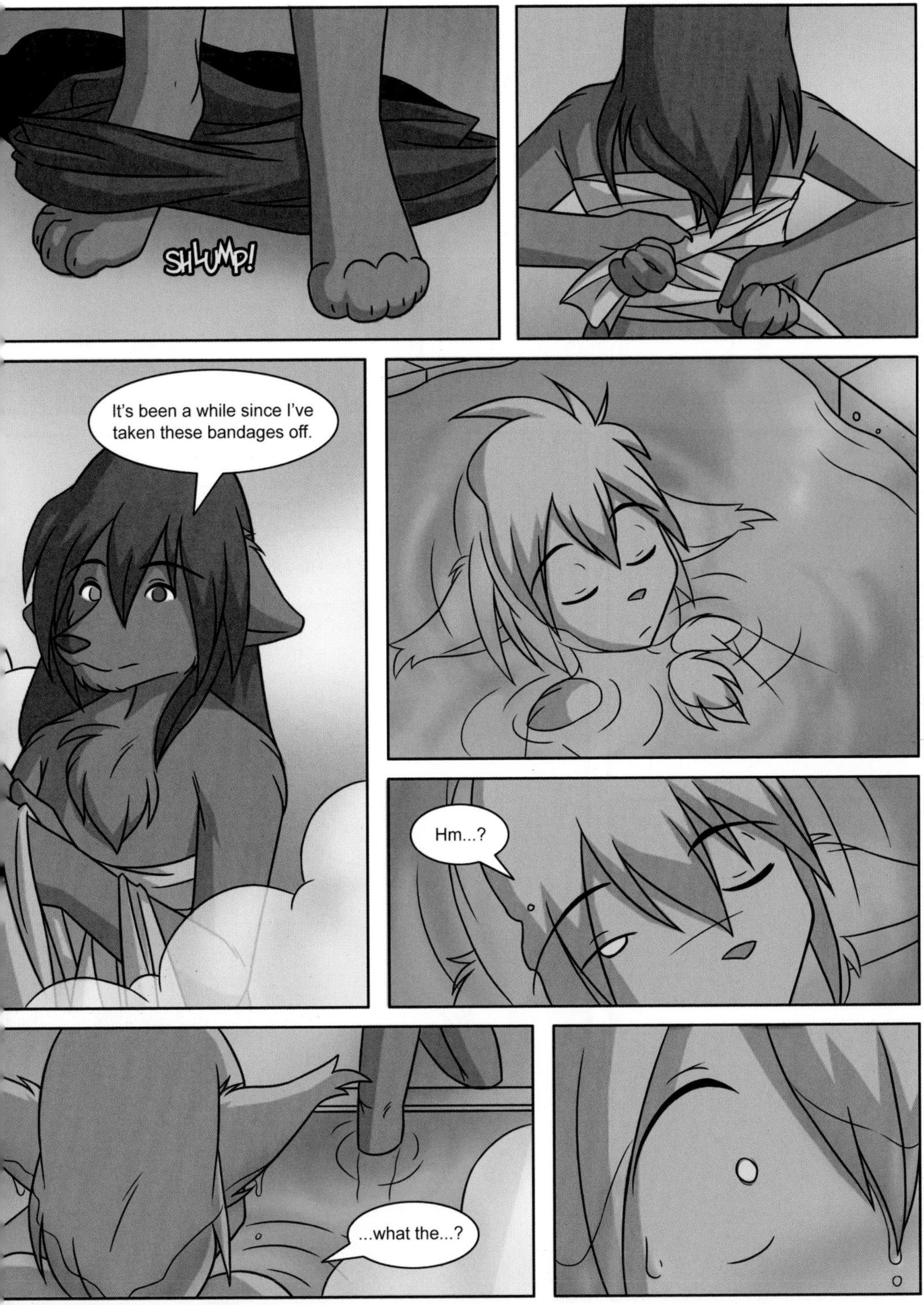
SHLUMP!
It's been a while since I've taken these bandages off.
Hm...?
...what the...?

G-geh...

Huh...?

‹Keith?›

You...

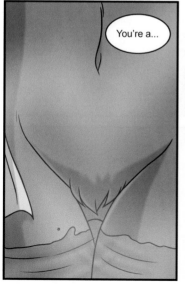

You're a...

‹You're a woman?!›

‹What? No I'm not!›

‹Then why do you have-?›

‹They're both lies! I'm a male! ...Shut up!›

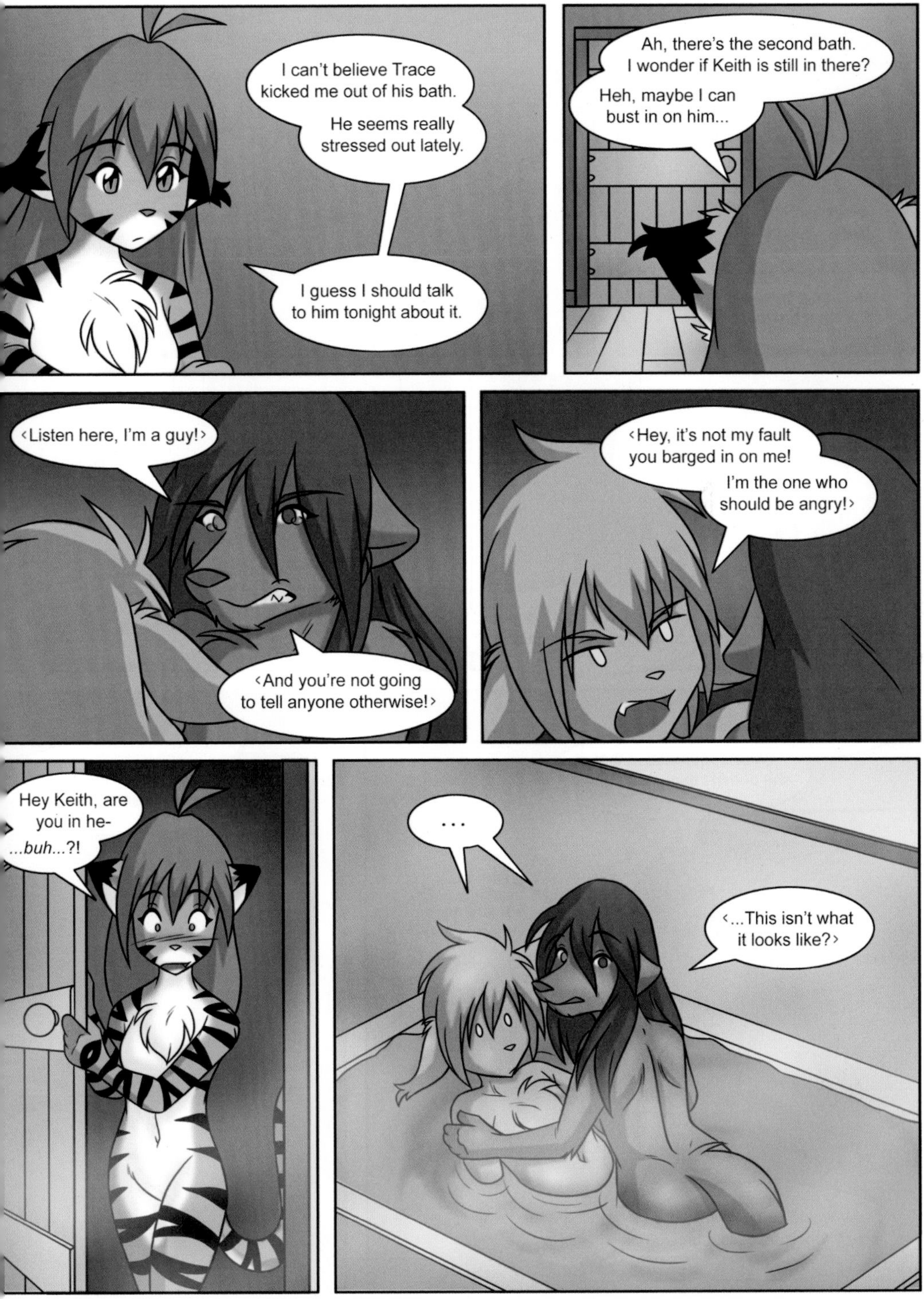
I can't believe Trace kicked me out of his bath.
He seems really stressed out lately.
I guess I should talk to him tonight about it.
Ah, there's the second bath. I wonder if Keith is still in there?
Heh, maybe I can bust in on him...
‹Listen here, I'm a guy!›
‹And you're not going to tell anyone otherwise!›
‹Hey, it's not my fault you barged in on me!
I'm the one who should be angry!›
Hey Keith, are you in he- ...*buh*...?!
. . .
‹...This isn't what it looks like?›

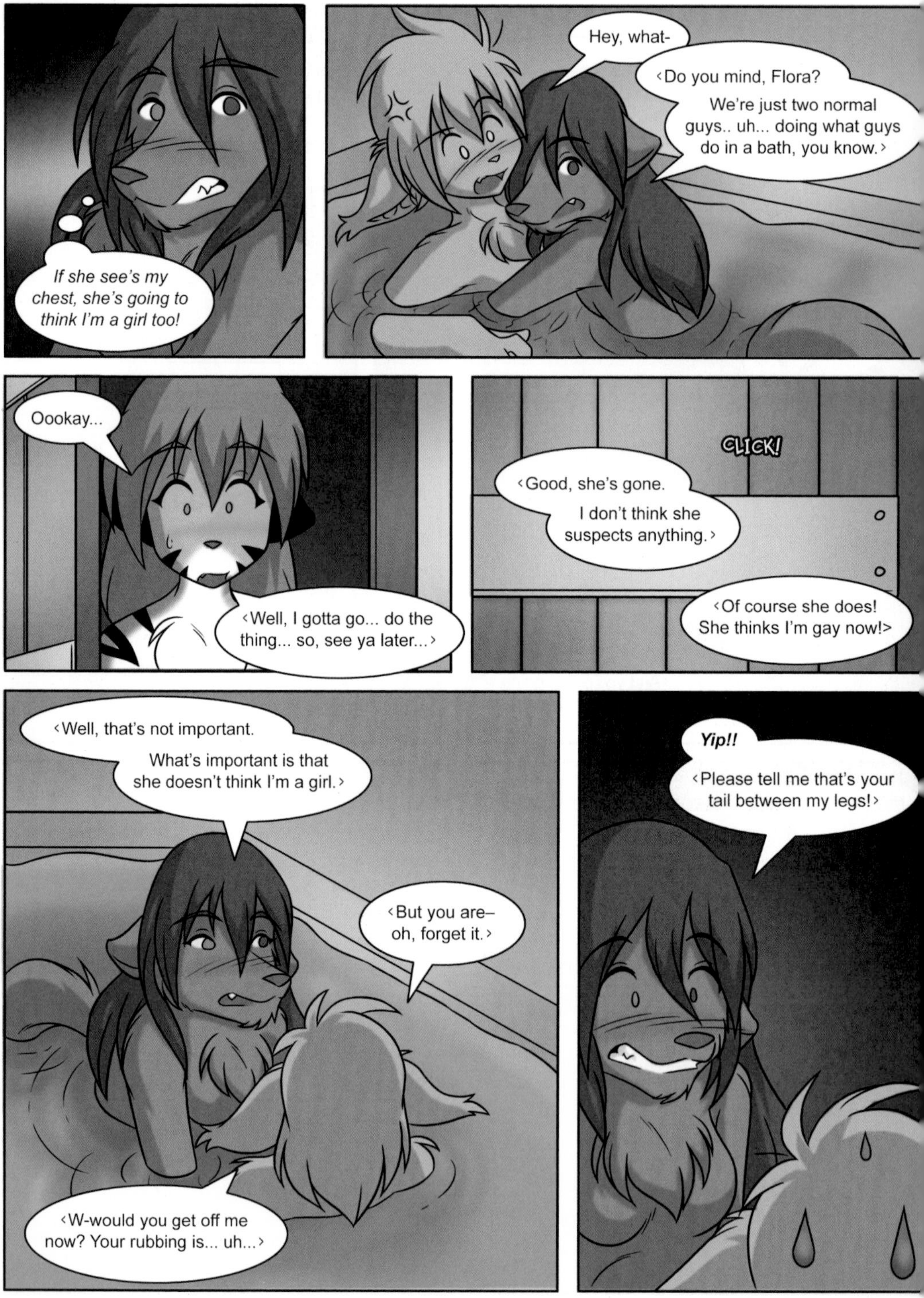
If she see's my chest, she's going to think I'm a girl too!
Hey, what-
‹Do you mind, Flora?
We're just two normal guys.. uh... doing what guys do in a bath, you know.›
Oookay...
‹Well, I gotta go... do the thing... so, see ya later...›
CLICK!
‹Good, she's gone.
I don't think she suspects anything.›
‹Of course she does! She thinks I'm gay now!›
‹Well, that's not important.
What's important is that she doesn't think I'm a girl.›
‹But you are– oh, forget it.›
‹W-would you get off me now? Your rubbing is... uh...›
Yip!!
‹Please tell me that's your tail between my legs!›

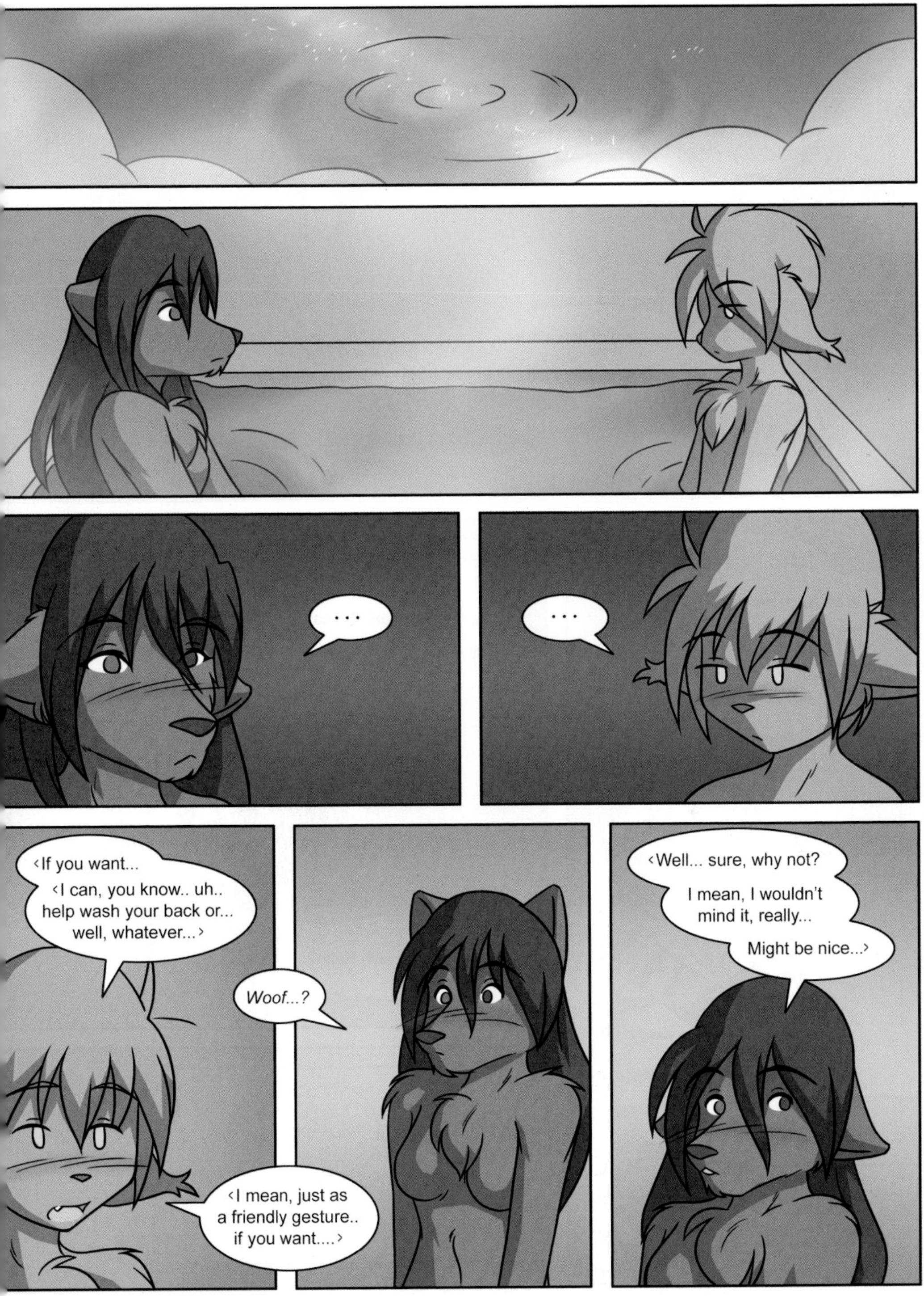
...
...
<If you want...
<I can, you know.. uh.. help wash your back or... well, whatever...>
Woof...?
<I mean, just as a friendly gesture.. if you want....>
<Well... sure, why not?
I mean, I wouldn't mind it, really...
Might be nice...>

Oh, Flora.

I wanted to say, I'm sorry about kicking you out of the bath.

I was out of line. I hope-

...uh, Flora...? Is everything alright?

Keith... the wolf guy...

In bath... together...

BATHS

Keith is... he's...

Flora, what are you saying?

You're not speaking clearly.

What's wrong with Keith?

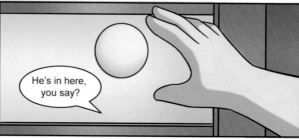

He's in here, you say?

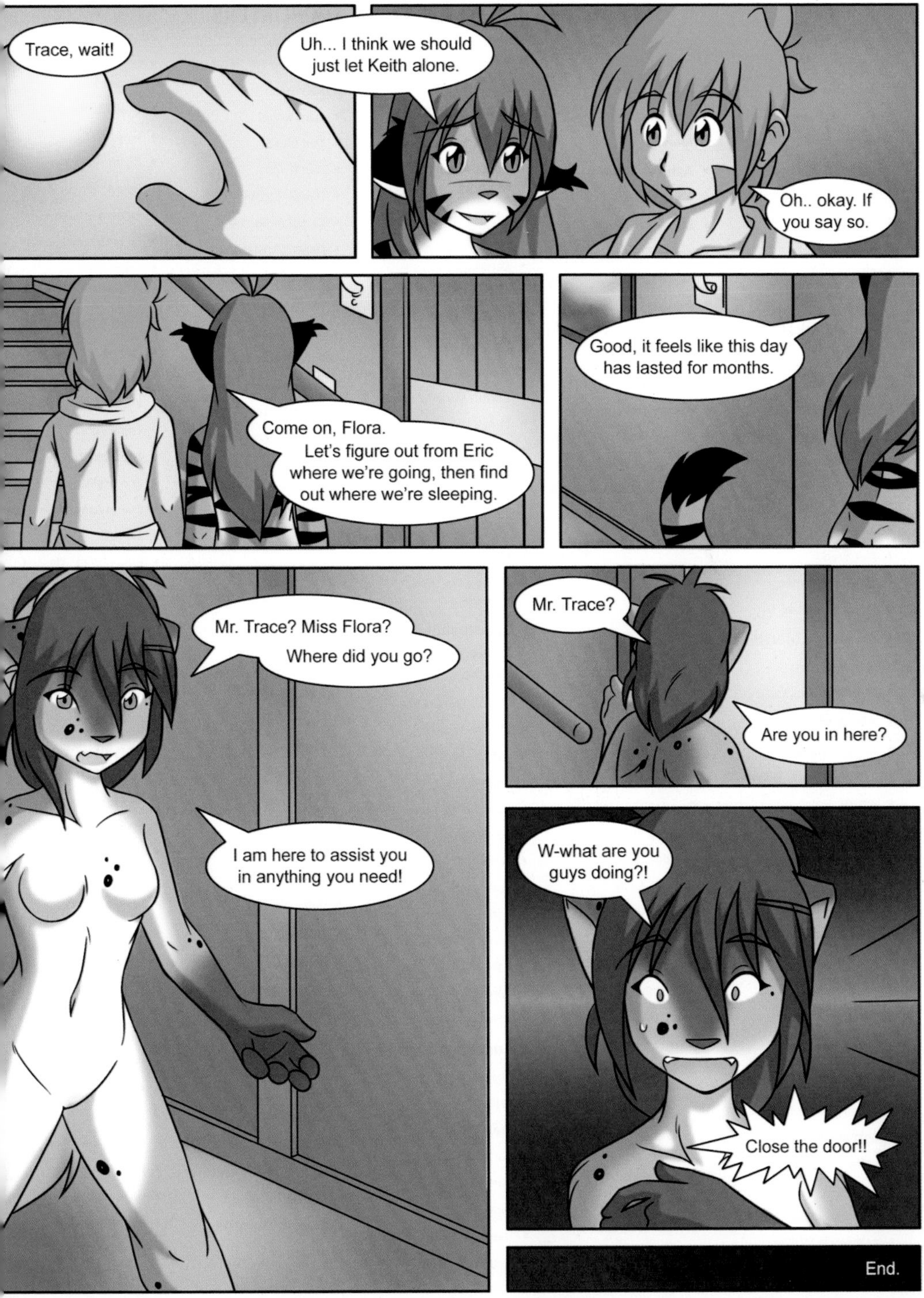

Trace, wait!
Uh... I think we should just let Keith alone.
Oh.. okay. If you say so.
Come on, Flora. Let's figure out from Eric where we're going, then find out where we're sleeping.
Good, it feels like this day has lasted for months.
Mr. Trace? Miss Flora? Where did you go?
I am here to assist you in anything you need!
Mr. Trace?
Are you in here?
W-what are you guys doing?!
Close the door!!
End.

SPECIAL THANKS TO ALL THESE SUPPORTERS

- AACMIV
- Aaron Dowhy
- Aaron Guzman
- Aaron Porte
- Aaron Stozicki
- Adam John Manns
- Adam King
- Adam Rauh
- Adowen
- Adrian Cepoi
- **Adrian Isak Lyngøy Kroken**
- Akura Davis
- Alex
- Alex "claymorre" Andrews
- Alex "Rocky Rockmaster" Marocchi
- Alex Lin
- Alex Napper
- Alex Webb
- Alexander Ferrier
- Alexander J Hoag
- **Alexander Marsteller**
- Alexander Sills
- Alexander 'Xan' Kashev
- **Alexandra Z.**
- Alexandre Bourdages
- Allan "Terabyte" Kelly-Watt
- Amaita
- Anders Wilson
- Andre' Rocha
- Andres "MaLAguA" Chion
- Andrew Allen
- Andrew 'Atrinal' Inches
- Andrew C. "Lionheart" Overton
- Andrew Ebert
- Andrew Neufeld
- Andrew Strong-Coleman
- Andy "Rednic" Deacon
- Andy Poelvoorde
- Animated Hero
- Anira
- Anthony
- Anthony Franca
- Anthony W Walker
- Antiman9

- Arbitrary Plaid
- Arne Teichmann
- Aron Lindberg
- Asaril
- **Ashielf Rydlen**
- Ashkan Paykar
- Ashley 'Koeru' Stewart
- Austin Blevins
- Avia Jiutai
- Aymasia
- Azkart
- Balázs Karajos
- Baldrek
- Baron Richard Butters
- Baxter "WolfsWinter" Heal
- Benjamin Ebert
- Benjamin James Christian
- Benjamin Juang
- Benjamin K. Sturgeon
- Benjamin Wallace
- Bernd Mayer
- Bernd Wieland
- **Bert "FrostBird" De Winter**
- Blake Raffaele
- Bradley Bates
- Braiden Kremnetz
- Brandon "Tehzull" Lewis
- Brandon "Turaiel" Dusseau
- Brandon Benard
- Brandon Levan
- Brandon Reilly
- Brandon Williams
- Brandylion Scott
- Brendon Piseczny
- Brett Wilson
- Brian Holme
- Brian Sookhoo
- Brian Wu
- Brittney and Peter
- Brôgon Ceannliath
- Bryan N.
- Bryan Surprenant
- Bryce Armstrong
- Bryson Pomaika'i Baqui
- CaduRyaq
- Caio A. D. Ribeiro

- Calde Marveen
- Caleb Frink
- Cameron Tindall
- Carlos "c-c foxclaw" Coto
- Carlos Antonio Richer Martinez
- Carlos Sandoval aka Zalcik
- Caspar
- Catprog
- Chakat Deirdre
- Charles Wilson
- Ch'Ih-Yu
- chompy
- Chris "Minccino" Mazie
- Chris Clarke
- Chris Ryan
- Chris Schoon
- Chris Sullivan
- Christian Sanders
- Christian Wenham
- Christopher "Howru" Valentin
- **Christopher "Silvercrystal" Taschuk**
- Christopher Corben
- Clayton Jaegers
- Cloudrunner
- Code Risen
- Cody Zimmerman (CodeZ)
- Cole Train
- Colin
- Colin Ryan
- Comrade Conrad
- Connell "Wolf" Gosling
- Connor McGroarty
- Corezy
- Cornelius Lehners
- **Corvis Shadowpaw**
- Cory Nichols
- Craig J. K.
- CrazyDelmar
- Curtis Andersson
- Curtis Carlson
- Daan Gunneman
- Daemon "D'Blitz" Blitzkrieg
- Damon Miller

- Dan "Comets_Revolver"
- Dan Guinn
- Dan Hooper
- Dan Meade
- Dan Nolan
- Daniel "Escobar" Willmette
- Daniel Armishaw
- Daniel Christensen
- Daniel Dobrowski
- **Daniel K. Nilsen**
- Daniel Kloed
- Daniel Luces aka Runecat
- Daniel Newman
- Daniel Porter
- Danielle Goodrich
- Danny Kriegbaum Laursen
- Dante Alexandre Caruso
- Daphne Pfister
- Dario Cimmino
- Dariusz Majkowski
- David "ShadyWolf" Murillo
- David Austin
- David de Lorenzo (PackMate)
- David Eggleton
- David Green
- David P. Kiehl
- David Rudin
- David Verigin
- David Wright
- DeHaven
- Deiwos
- Demeyuri
- **Demon**
- Denis P.
- Dennis Turner
- Denzil
- Devan Recalde
- Devin O'Reilly
- Dexter Falgout
- Disko Fox
- Dizit
- Dominic Dorian Ramondino
- Don Henderson
- Donovan 'Dawn' Kerry
- Douglas
- DragonEmotion

- Dustin E. Hill (The Infected Kitsune)
- Dusty Benjamin
- Dylan H.
- Dylan Woessner
- Dyxxander
- Edward Brough
- Einar B. Þorsteinsson
- Engel
- EniEx
- **Eoin Brown**
- Eponyx
- Eri "Sanchay" Dallmeyer
- Eric Carl Davis "Durasef"
- Eric Fortin
- Eric Steinbrenner
- Erin English
- Erlend Aadnøy
- Escobar
- Ethan "Blink" Hansen
- Ethan Kappelmann
- Evan
- Evan and Kat
- Execpower
- Fabian
- Feefers Lovecraft
- Feral & Charadan
- Firemane
- Folx
- Foulon Damien
- Fox "Simtra" Wolfe
- Fraggzy
- Francis Cournoyer
- Frank Chandler Henchy
- Fraser Gibbs
- Freddyz
- Frist & Zenobia
- Frode Wist
- Fruity Kitty
- Futeko Snowfeather
- Fzzr
- Gabe Schmidtlein
- Gabriel Svensson
- Gage Henry
- GambitSarcastic
- Gareth Smyth
- Gary D'Amico

SPECIAL THANKS TO ALL THESE SUPPORTERS

- Geoff Baccetti
- George Hulland
- Георги Бориславов Николов
- Geraint M G Williams
- Giacomo Mattioli
- Gitti Janwatanagool

Glassan

- Goatie
- Golddess
- Gordon Archibald
- Greg Ludwick
- Grievous544
- Guy Stewart
- Halbritter-Studer
- Hank
- Hannah Thibodaux
- Hans
- Hans-Jørgen
- Hayden Surman
- Heidi Vikki Munthe-Kaas
- Hilsbily
- HoboJoe
- Holden Wagner
- Idar Alexander Hasselvold
- Idward
- Iggy Koopa
- Iker Sanchez
- Imisnew2
- Insanepredator
- Isaac "coony" Hernandez
- Itachi Raven
- Ivan Jones
- Ivan Strife
- Ivan the Arctic Fox
- Ivor Doherty
- J "Jadedfox" Strom
- J. Patrick Walker

Jacob

- Jacob Stephen Bertrand
- Jake Felis
- James "Damian" Dahl
- James "MysticFox" Andrew Cole
- James Alexander Hettle

James C King

- James Cunningham

- James Keeney
- James Kolden
- James Matthew Black
- James Pond
- James Renner
- Jamin Carpenter
- Jan Buisman
- Jared "Yettie" Wall
- Jason Howson
- Jason Nettnin
- Jason Sperber
- Jasper (WeepingDragon)
- Jay H.
- Jean
- Jean-françois Masson
- Jean-Michel PETIT
- Jeff Fabian
- Jeremy Colelli
- Jeremy R. Hopkins
- Jeremy 'StormAngel88' Snowdon
- Jesse "Bakuryu" Schritter
- Jesse Y. McCausland
- Jim Buck
- Jinotad
- JintoLyn
- Joe Plotbunny
- John Bortolazzo
- John Idlor

John J. Chasse

John M Hopper

- John Tore Andrersen
- Jon Hekman
- Jon M.
- Jonas Hormann
- Jonas Maurer

Jonatan Gonte Kindh

- Jonathan M. Wester
- Jonathan Miller
- Jonathon W
- Joon Rian
- Jordan "Balmun" Cope
- Jordan Dean "Mystery" Ezekude
- Jordan Ford
- Jordan Kane
- Joseph Arzola

- Joseph Bell
- Joseph Fox
- Joseph Morrison
- Joseph Paul Pontacolone
- Josh "J.B." Blake
- Josh Campbell
- Josh Hadley
- Josh rader
- Joshua
- Joshua Chhuth (ConkerBirdy)
- Joshua Plair
- Joshua T Johnston
- Julian Bergmann
- Justin "Tharkis" Mercier
- Justin A. Beard
- Justin Adam Lee Bessinger
- Justin B. Fox
- Kadrasar
- Karsten Schustereit
- Katerater
- Katrina Swales
- Keaton S.
- Keith Stanley
- Ken Herner
- Kenneth Bluett
- Kenneth Iun
- Kevin "Silberwolf" Wegener
- Kevin L O'Brien
- Kevin Steedley
- Kevin Wehmeier
- Kevin Winter
- Kiewolf
- Kitsune
- Kitsune-Realm
- Kitthesoulless
- Kiwi Hedgehog
- K-J Kor
- Kolton Leasure
- Korin & Tom
- Kristopher kyle Sudduth
- Krystle Lisica
- Kuro919
- Kurt Jarmuz
- Kyle "Bass" Stinnett
- Kyle Lexmond

Kyle Ryan

- Kzin Silkencoat
- Landreth Boh
- Lars Kristian Løfall
- Laster
- Lemiah
- Lewis Riggs V
- libranfurrheart
- Lillykitti
- Linda Botne Svendsen

Loïck F. Legacy

- LoLsAlEd
- lostiger
- Lucas Galavics
- Lysia Rhianna Kotaren
- M. P. Gibbs

Maddison Bourke

- Magentawolf
- Magnus Hasselgård
- Magnus Nygren
- Marc-André Bousquet
- Marc-Andre St-Cyr

Mario Lee

Mark Stanley

- Mark Woolley
- Martine G.
- Marty "Ndoto" McGuire
- Matt Delano
- Matt Fonti
- Matt Poirier
- Matt Vossler
- Matteo "TeoWolf" Trivelin
- Matthew
- Matthew "Squato" Waddingham
- Matthew Czechowski
- Matthew Dawkins
- Matthew Heazlewood
- Matthew King
- Matthew Kuehl
- Matthew L. Murdock
- Matthew Phillips
- Matthew Unger

Matthew Walker

- Matthew Woodcook
- Matthias Vandenbussche
- Matti Rajahuhta

- Maxime Buffa
- Maxwel Eckes
- Meraxes
- Miacis

Micel

- Michael "B_Dog" Bettano
- Michael "Chaostraveler" Cencarik
- Michael "Sareen" Richardson
- Michael Chang :3
- Michael Ellis
- Michael Hofius (Fullmetal Ratchet)
- Michael Jenno
- Michael O. Arnold
- Michael Sweeney
- Michael Weskamp
- Michael. P. Ooms
- Michał "vlf" Wycisk
- Mika Ilmari Flinkman
- Mike Gulick
- Mike LeResche
- Mike Taylor
- Mikhail M.
- Mikko Uusitalo
- Miles Elskens
- Mirkon
- Mitchell D'Arcy
- Mitchell Frazer
- Mitchell Knowlton
- Mitchell"Vigil"May

Monoe Sparta

- Moonstar & Occam Aldanis
- Morak
- Morgan
- Morten Hellesø Johansen
- Mr Wibbles
- Mr. Tiddles, Esq.
- N✪ThiNG
- Naeshazel
- Nathan & Hailey

Nathaniel du Preez-Wilkinson

- Nathaniel Lindquist
- Neal Rideout
- Nicholas Bitwinski

SPECIAL THANKS TO ALL THESE SUPPORTERS

- Nicholas Grippo
- **Nicholas Marton**
- Nicholas McConaugha
- **Nick Richey**
- Nickifynbo
- Nicolas Tujetsch
- Nicole Nistler
- Nightwere
- **Nikolaj N Larsen**
- Nikolas Taylor
- **Nina Hansell**
- Niryx
- Noah Bratscher
- Nomine
- Noxanima
- Nyaliva
- Olivier "bluespart" Allard
- Otto Drangeid
- Øystein Andres Krogsæter
- Patrick Boyle
- **Patrick Chavigny, the Shadow of Derkential**
- Patrick Nelson
- Paul "Master_Scythe"
- Paul Clowes
- Paul Dutcher
- Paul Hachmann
- Paul Korade
- Paul Michel
- Paul Philbin
- Pavel Bacovsky
- Percilla Baltazar Weskamp
- Perkey
- Phenrir
- **Phieipi**
- Phil Cowan
- Phil Elpers
- **Phil Trubey**
- pic
- Pieter Leon
- Pseudostein
- Puma "Pink Pummy" Namanari
- Q-dk
- Quentin D. Altemose
- Rahirrah

- rakiru
- Ralf Paaschen
- Ramsey Hasala
- Randy Tran
- **Rapier Kamigawa**
- Ratino
- Rax
- Ray Powell
- Razmoudah
- Rebecca Woolford
- RedWolf
- Reece
- Rémy COSTA
- Rene S Svendsen
- Renee Brown
- Ricardo Gomez
- Richard "Miles" Musgrave (Decatsmeow)
- Richard DeCremer
- Richard Little
- Richard Meyer
- RMC
- RobbieThe1st
- Robert Cartwright
- Robert Johnson
- Roberto Gonzalez
- Robin Kennedy
- Rocktoberfest
- Ross Hunter Cassan Hagen
- Russell "Lucky" Zweers
- Ryan Bonavia
- Ryan Cosgrove
- Ryan F
- **Ryan Hennerbichler**
- Ryan Mitchell
- Ryan W. Anderson
- Ryuijirou
- S Leedell
- S. KELLER
- Sabrina and Brandon
- Saiori
- Sam Bailey
- Samuel Firekeeper Towb
- **Samuel Rau**
- Sarah J. Johns
- Sayonaki Tatsu
- Scott Oberlag

- Sean
- Sean Ellis
- Sean Fleming
- Sean Kelley
- Sean Treese
- Sebastian C.
- **Sebastian D. DuHolm**
- Sebastian.M.V.Petersen
- Sergey "Lazy Dragon" Zolin
- Shark5060
- Shawn M. Dawson
- Shawn the Platypus Shinobi
- Shawn, Hayden
- shifter
- ShineyFighter
- Simcha-Yitzchak "TGIF" Lerner
- Simmml
- Sir Reginald Lee IV
- Skull-Kid
- Smithers
- Snowfallgamer
- Snowodin
- Sophia Tedman
- Sora Hjort
- Spencer G
- Squival
- **Stephen Babcock**
- Stephen J. Moore
- **Stephen Kuiack**
- Stephen Powell
- Sterling Rodd
- Steven A Murray
- Steven Beltran
- Steven Coldbeck
- **Steven King**
- Stormdragonblue
- Stovetop General
- Stuart
- SuburbanFox
- Superpet2
- Sven Fischer
- Sven Knudsen
- Symphona
- T.Kleinsteuber
- TacticalSheep
- Taji

- Taki
- Tamer
- Teckly
- Teddy Wells
- Tenshi
- That One Roadie
- **The Bear Jew**
- The Cake is a Lie
- The Freudian Slip
- The Painiac
- **The Shepherd**
- Thedrass
- Thedrun
- Theo
- Theo Luiggi-Gørrissen
- Theodore Maslanka
- Thomas "Calva" Sting
- Thomas LeBlanc
- Thorsten Just
- Thorsten Lucht
- Tim Kirk
- Tim Persson
- Timothy Lyon
- **Timothy Ort**
- Tinker
- Tirominos
- Tom Ascione
- Tom Lonsdale
- Tom Wood
- Tomi Luotonen
- Tommy Henry
- Tony Rouse
- TotemCoyote
- Travis A Metzger
- Trevor
- Troy
- Troy Anderson
- Tuna
- Two PawPad
- Twocats
- Tyler "Tychas" Goppert
- Ultimatekaiser
- Varg Silvermane
- Venorik Barra
- Venron
- Viethra

- Villeus
- Vincent P.
- Vincent Verheyen
- Vindum
- Vito Fuoco
- Wade Gossage
- Warren G. Holley
- Wei-Hwa Huang
- Wesley Jackson
- Wilddingo
- William J. Helmer
- **William Kenny**
- **William Pattison**
- William Temeraire
- Wolfgang
- Yageira
- Yroark
- Zacchaeus I. Warrington
- Zachary C. L.
- Zachary Lucas
- Zachary Neuschuler
- Zachary Sowers
- Zachery De Palma
- Zech Ross
- Zeta Syanthis
- Zoe Kihira Lee
- *****kitsune

THANK YOU!